Praise for James H. Cobb

TARGET LOCK

"Cobb's hallmark lovingly detailed settings and high-tech naval hardware, irresistible nonstop action, and slightly larger-than-life characters are as effective as ever."

—*Booklist*

SEA FIGHTER

"Amanda Lee Garrett is an original." —*USA Today*

"Cobb knows his modern weapons of war. But he also knows people who operate them." —*Houston Chronicle*

SEA STRIKE

"A vividly imagined future war scenario, populated by quirky characters and steeped in the techno-poetry of modern weapons systems." —*Kirkus Reviews*

CHOOSERS OF THE SLAIN

"Breathtaking . . . This is the rare military thriller whose message is gender-bending and leading-edge."

—*Publishers Weekly* (starred review)

"Brain candy for gadget lovers . . . packed with complex battles and encounters." —*The Orlando Sentinel*

"A taut military thriller that grabs the reader's attention and holds it to the last word. This page-turner is as hot as a Sea SLAM missile with target lock. Buy this book: that's an order." —*Library Journal* (starred review)

P9-EMQ-005

Target Lock

James H. Cobb

JOVE BOOKS, NEW YORK

This is a work of fiction. Names, characters, places, and incidents either are the product of the author's imagination or are used fictitiously, and any resemblance to actual persons, living or dead, business establishments, events, or locales is entirely coincidental.

TARGET LOCK

A Jove Book / published by arrangement with
G. P. Putnam's Sons

PRINTING HISTORY
G. P. Putnam's Sons hardcover edition / February 2002
Jove edition / December 2002

Copyright © 2002 by James H. Cobb
Cover art and design by oyster pond

Visit our website at
www.penguinputnam.com

ISBN: 0-515-13413-9

A JOVE BOOK®
Jove Books are published by The Berkley Publishing Group,
a division of Penguin Putnam Inc.,
375 Hudson Street, New York, New York 10014.
JOVE and the "J" design
are trademarks belonging to Penguin Putnam Inc.

PRINTED IN THE UNITED STATES OF AMERICA

10 9 8 7 6 5 4 3 2 1

There ain't no such thing as a totally original plot or character. Any author who claims to have produced one is fooling either you or himself. The best a writer can ever hope to do is to use some of the threads spun by those storytellers who came before him to weave a different and interesting pattern for his reader.

Having confessed this, I would like to dedicate this book to the diverse group of authors, artists, and creations that have both given me great pleasure over the years and lent inspiration to the world of Amanda Garrett:

Ian Fleming and James Bond
Peter O'Donnel and Modesty Blaise
James H. Schmitz and Trigger Argee
Norman Reilly Raine and Tugboat Annie Brennan
Shoji Kawamori, Haruhiko Mikimoto, and Misa Hayase

Ladies and gentlemen, thank you.

The Earth glowed frost-white and sapphire-blue, its vibrant colors separated from the infinite velvet black of space by the haze line along the planet's curving horizon. And arcing silently toward that horizon was a great silvery lozenge shape, its winglike solar-cell arrays trimmed to catch the piercing light of the distant sun.

Six weeks earlier, a Russian-built Proton VI heavy-lift booster fired from the Boeing Aerospace sealaunch platform south of Hawaii had hurled the bus-sized unmanned spacecraft into orbit. Since that time, it had silently and efficiently proceeded about its cybernetic affairs, the seeds of a new mode of existence germinating in its commodious belly.

Powered by the flow of free energy from the sun, experiment packages clicked and whirred in the payload bays. Robotic microfactories and computer-guided autolabs tinkered tirelessly with the gravity-free environment, seeking to produce new and unique compounds and materials impossible to create at the bottom of the earth's gravity well.

Perfect ball bearings were formed out of glass, metal, and nylon. Undistorted by a gee field, they promised to lengthen the service life and improve the energy efficiency of any mechanical device utilizing them. Unwarped by weight, perfect crystalline fibers were grown. Matted properly with the right carbon-based bonding compound and a Fiberglas with ten times the tensile strength of the finest high-grade steel, it loomed on the horizon. Foamed metal castings were made, utilizing one-third the material at one-third of the weight yet losing none of their durability. New alloys were blended, not merely of metal and metal, but of radical combinations of metal and ceramic and glass and plastic. Materials with qualities that engineers and technologists had only dreamed of before.

With each new creation, a door opened and a thousand possibilities crowded through. On the earth below, the various project teams salivated over the rain of data pouring down from their creation and visualized the day they would perform their orbital experiments hands-on instead of via remote telepresence.

Given the full potential of the new technologies they were creating, that day might not be far distant. The INDASAT (Industrial Applications Satellite) project was the most ambitious and far-reaching private space project in history. Created by a consortium of U.S. and Western European corporations, the INDASATs were laying the foundation for the commercial development and industrial utilization of Near Earth Space.

But for now, however, the dreaming had to stop. The experiment bays were powering down, their stocks of raw materials exhausted and their exotic payloads secured. For INDASAT 06, it was time to go home.

Slowly, the great solar cell wings reefed back into the vehicle body, thermal-proof doors closing over them. Thrusters fired. The INDASAT reoriented, its nose-mounted heat shield and retrorocket pack aiming ahead along its flight path. Over the data links, the onboard computers conversed with their ground-based counterparts at INDASAT mission control, an avalanche of systems checks and rechecks taking place.

All boards read green. The computers staged a final consultation with their human masters and received their clearance to proceed. Above Pretoria, South Africa, retrorockets blazed and INDASAT 06 began its long fall.

Its fuel expended, explosive bolts kicked the retropack free, leaving the thermoceramic heat shield bare and ready to meet the holocaust to come. Like some titanic rifle slug, the huge satellite slammed into the atmosphere over the Indian Ocean, pushing an incandescent shock wave of ionized air ahead of it as it continued its deceleration. Far below, off the Seychelle islands, native fishermen looked up in awe and wonderment at the great silvery fireball that illuminated the night sky as it streaked away toward the northeast.

The thermal flare faded and died as the descending satellite's speed bled away. At 150,000 feet, the first small drogue chute was streamed, stabilizing the fall.

At 90,000 feet, a second, larger drogue blossomed, pitching the satellite over into its vertical descent to the recovery target, a set of coordinates in the Arafura Sea north of Australia.

The four main parachutes deployed at 30,000 feet, a football field's worth of nylon fabric that lowered the spacecraft on the final leg of its journey to the dark waters below.

Onboard the INDASAT, the computers conducted a last-minute housecleaning. Blinking marker strobes and radio beacons were switched on for the convenience of the recovery team. The remainder of the thruster fuel was vented overboard for safety's sake, and flotation bags were inflated in preparation for the water landing. With these final tasks completed, the computers powered down and an inert mass of metal and composites settled into the warm tropical seas.

Arafura Sea   **2147 Hours, Zone Time:**
97 Miles North-Northwest of Cape Wessel   **July 8, 2008**

"We have visual! Strobes bearing thirty-seven degrees off the port bow."

"Very good, Mr. Carstairs. Helm, come left to three-three-zero. All engines ahead standard." Captain Phillip Moss, the master of the *INDASAT Starcatcher,* was ex–Australian navy and, as such, he preferred to maintain the formalities on his bridge. "Have the boat teams stand by to launch, and inform docking-well control that they may commence flood-down."

Stepping out onto the wheelhouse, the spare, hawk-faced mariner lifted his binoculars to his eyes, focusing in on the pulsing flare of light settling from the night sky. Beneath his feet, the decks of the 270-foot converted cannery ship began to tremble, her blunt bow coming about to bear on the splashdown point.

The chunky shadow of Dr. Alan Del Rio joined Moss out on the bridge wing. "A very pretty splashdown, Captain," the INDASAT recovery director commented.

"So far, so good," Moss grunted. "Better than the first one, at any rate. We had to chase across two hundred miles of ocean and barely made acquisition before she sank."

"It's all part of the learning curve, Captain," the recovery director replied philosophically. As an ex–NASA mission controller, Del Rio was a veteran of numerous battles with sulky space hardware. "Every time out we get better. God willing, this will all be routine before too long."

"My policy is, Doctor, that it will never be all that routine."

Floating horizontally between its double row of flotation bags, INDASAT 06 rode low in the easy ocean swells. Sea-anchored by its sodden parachutes, the satellite marked its location with streamers of luminescent sea dye and by the pulsing strobes atop extended telescoping masts. Early on in the program, it had been discovered that spotting and recovery were actually easier in darkness than in daylight, and thus, night recoveries had become standard operating procedure.

The *Starcatcher* churned up to within fifty meters of the drifting spacecraft before ringing down on her main engines and heaving to. Her arc light banks blazed on, illuminating a square mile of sea. Maneuvering gingerly on her steering thrusters, she pivoted in place and brought her aft end to bear on the satellite.

During the *Starcatcher*'s conversion into a recovery vessel, a floodable well deck large enough to accept the industrial satellites had been built into her stern. Now the tailgate of this well deck dropped, releasing a swarm of Zodiac workboats.

For the next hour, the rubber-sided inflatables nuzzled around the drifting mass of INDASAT 06. Their wet suit-clad crews worked through the first postmission checkout, inspecting the spacecraft for damage, detaching and retrieving the parachute array for reuse, and connecting the recovery tether.

With the tasking lists completed, air horns brayed from the *Starcatcher*'s upper works and the workboats scurried back into the sheltering belly of the mother ship. Winches howled as the recovery tether came taut, and slowly the *Starcatcher* began to back down onto her cargo.

Once the INDASAT had been walked into the water-filled well deck, gantries would deploy from the bay sides, locking the satellite in place for transport. With that done, the deck could be pumped dry and the voyage to Port Darwin could begin. There, at the Australian INDASAT service facility, the spacecraft's payload of precious material and data could be downloaded and the satellite refurbished and reconfigured for its next mission. Within a month, 06 would be ready to fly once more.

On the *Starcatcher*'s bridge, Captain Moss and Mission Director Del Rio immersed themselves in the details of the loading operation, overseeing each phase from the bridge wings or via the bank of closed-circuit television monitors on the rear bulkhead of the wheelhouse. The remainder of the bridge watch was deeply involved in the recovery operation as well—so much so that the realization that they were not alone on the sea and in the night came quite late.

"Captain, we have traffic crossing the bow at three hundred yards. Range closing."

Moss looked up sharply at the watch stander's call. "Identify?"

"Fishing boats, I'd guess, sir. Looks to be three of them. Speed about six knots. Now bearing off the port bow."

Moss crossed swiftly to the port side bridge wing and brought up his night glasses. Yes, there was something out there. Three tall, shadowy shapes running bow to stern and trailing a wisp of wake luminescence behind them.

"What is it, Captain?" Del Rio inquired from the wheelhouse door.

"I'm not quite sure," Moss replied. "Small craft of some kind. They aren't showing any running lights, but the locals, both ours and Indonesia's, can get sloppy about that sort of thing."

The moon had started to rise, casting a shimmering light path across the surface of the tropical sea. The first of the newcomers now glided through this glow, silhouetting itself, and the breath caught in the throats of both Moss and Del Rio.

She was an image of beauty from another age. A low and sleek twin-masted schooner, gaff-rigged and rakish and outlined in the pearlescent moonlight, her dark hull sweeping up and back from a sharp cutwater to a high-set and angular sterncastle, the latter enhancing the touch of exotic alienness to her design.

"Well, I'll be damned," Moss murmured appreciatively.

"What the hell is that, Captain?" Del Rio asked, awed.

"She's a *pinisi*," Moss replied. "An island trading schooner belonging to one of the Indonesian mariner tribes. The Bugis, the people some folk call the sea gypsies."

"Sea gypsies? You're kidding." Del Rio said, stepping up to the rail.

"Not a bit of it. They're one of the great seafaring cultures of the world. For over a thousand years, they've ranged these waters from the Malay coast to the Philippines. I doubt there's an occupied island in Indonesia that doesn't have a Bugis colony on it somewhere."

Del Rio chuckled. "The Bugis, huh? You mean the bogeymen really are going to get us?"

"That wouldn't have been so funny a few hundred years ago," Moss grunted. "Where do you think the term came from? Back in the days of the old East Indies trade, having the Bugis man come over the rail with his kris between his teeth was about the biggest nightmare one could have. Not only were these lads master seamen, but they were also the most notorious, most savage pirates in the Pacific."

Del Rio shrugged. "I've never even heard of them before. I certainly didn't expect anyone out here to be using sailing ships at this late date."

"Oh, quite so. These craft are a unique Bugis design. The sea gypsies crossbred the schooners of the Dutch and Portuguese colonialists with the Chinese junk and produced a vessel that was handier and more seaworthy than either. They're still quite common up in the archipelago. You don't usually see them this far south, though."

Moss frowned in the darkness. "And I don't like to see anybody working in this close while we're recovering. Mr. Albright"—the captain turned back toward the wheelhouse door—"get on the loud hailer. Warn those schooners off."

It was the last order Captain Phillip Moss would ever give. Nor would it ever be carried out.

A cluster of dazzling red points of light blipped into existence on the side of the wheelhouse—the death dots of long-range laser sights. A concentrated barrage from three heavy machine guns and a dozen automatic rifles sleeted through the *Starcatcher*'s bridge structure an instant later, ripping the life out of every man and woman on watch there.

The laser-targeted machine guns swung aft then, focusing on the antenna arrays on the main mast and upper works, chewing them away, stifling the recovery ship's scream for aid before it could be issued.

Powerful auxiliary engines roared to life. Two of the Bugis schooners darted in toward the *Starcatcher*'s flanks while the third sailing craft, the gunship, held off and mercilessly raked the recovery vessel's decks, lifting fire only as its cohorts slid alongside their prey.

Stripped to the waist and shrieking, brown-skinned men swarmed over the rail, panther-lean and panther-deadly. Some were armed with modern submachine guns and automatic pistols. Others carried only the razor-edged kris daggers and panga cutlasses wielded by their corsair ancestors.

For the remaining crewmembers of the *Starcatcher* crew, the exact mode of death would be irrelevant. The decision had been made early on in the planning of this operation. No prisoners. No witnesses. No survivors.

There was no means of meaningful resistance. There was no place to hide that couldn't be hunted out. There was no offer of mercy. After only a few minutes the screams and gunfire trailed off.

The *Starcatcher*'s work and running lights were extinguished and full darkness returned to the Arafura Sea. Under the cover of that darkness, a meticulously drilled plan of action replaced the blood-sodden chaos of the boarding.

A Bugis work detail swept the decks of the recovery ship, dragging all bodies into the superstructure. Life-jacket lockers were emptied. Life rafts were dragged out of their storage pods and slashed, and the hulls and the flotation chambers of the ship's launch and whaleboat were chopped open. Life rings, wooden deckchairs, wet suits, anything at all that could be found topside that could float, was stricken below and secured.

A second work party went about another task. Hoses snaked down into the *Starcatcher*'s bunkerage tanks and powerful pumps purred to life, drawing the diesel out of the recovery vessel and into the swelling fuel blivets in the holds of the boarding ships.

Yet a third detail worked within the recovery ship, this one not made up of Bugis alone. A group of outsiders, a small mixed bag of Asian and Caucasian technicians, labored with the pirates. Pale-featured and nauseated at the sight of the sprawled bodies and scarlet-streaked bulkheads, yet decisive in their actions as they selected and re-

JAMES H. COBB

moved hard-copy manuals, computer files, and key components from the *Starcatcher*'s systems bays.

Astern, the third of the schooners drew alongside of INDASAT 06 itself. Loincloth-clad swimmers went over the rail and set to work around the satellite, deactivating its marker strobes and hacking away the antenna of its radio transponders, working to the diagrams shown to them by their foreign advisers.

The flotation bladders were carefully vented until the spacecraft floated just awash beneath the waves. Then a camouflage shroud was wrestled up and out of the schooner's hold and lowered over the side. A huge bag of lightweight parachute-grade nylon, colored in mottled seatone blues and greens, it slipped smoothly over the INDASAT, concealing its stark white thermal shell.

The recovery tether to the *Starcatcher* was cast off and a short towing harness rigged to the stern of the Bugis schooner. The swimmers came back aboard, and diesel engines far more powerful than would be needed for a craft of the schooner's displacement rumbled to life. The heavy wake streaming back from the hard-driving propellers would wash back over the towed satellite, helping to conceal its shadowy outline from all but the closest aerial observation pass.

All tasks were done. It was time to depart.

Casting off from the lifeless *Starcatcher*, the two boarding ships pulled away, following the craft towing the satellite. All deck hatches on the recovery vessel were tightly dogged down. Belowdecks, however, all watertight doors and hatches gaped wide. Sledgehammer blows had smashed open the intakes and outlets of the power-plant cooling system and half a dozen six-inch streams of water geysered into the rapidly filling engine room.

Half an hour after the departure of the pirate force, the first broken porthole dipped beneath the ocean's surface. Seven minutes later, the *INDASAT Starcatcher* capsized and sank, disappearing from the ken of man.

A classic Indonesian rijsttafel had been held at House Harconan for the new U.S. ambassador to Indonesia, honoring his first visit to Bali. Ambassador Randolph Goodyard and his wife had been introduced to the savory and exotic pleasures of the Indonesian "rice table" and to a select cadre of Indonesian movers and shakers, both courtesy of Makara Harconan.

Several hours of good conversation and excellent brandy had followed on the broad beachfront lanai of the sprawling single-story mansion. Eventually, however, group by small group, the guests had departed, borne back through the night to the Bali mainland. The majority was transported by a small flotilla of expensive motor yachts standing by at the estate pier, a select handful by the helicopters spotted on the commodious private helipad. Finally only the guests of honor and the host lingered.

Ambassador Goodyard lifted his glass in a final salute. "Mr. Harconan, my wife and I would like to thank you for a most entertaining evening. If this is the kind of hospitality I can look forward to, my tour here in the Far East will be most pleasantly memorable."

Harconan tilted his head in mild self-effacement. "It was my pleasure having you honor my home, Mr. Ambassador. I hope your time with us will be both enjoyable for you and productive for your nation and mine."

Although an Indonesian citizen, Makara Harconan was a man of many worlds. The multimillionaire trader and commodities broker was tall, with the tapering broad-shouldered solidity of his Dutch father. Yet, his dark and angular handsome features held the exotic kiss of his Asian mother's blood as well. Born in Jakarta, he had chosen the island of Bali as a suitable base of operations for the growing business empire of a twenty-first–century taipan.

Harconan was a formidable individual and potentially both a valuable ally and a resource worth cultivating. Goodyard, a canny yet internationally inexperienced former governor from Nebraska, recognized this fact full well and had taken the opportunity to pump the trader on the local political and economic environment. Harconan in turn had been both forthcoming and helpful with his replies.

Now, at the tag end of the evening, there was one final question.

"Mr. Harconan, in your opinion, if one word could be used to sum up what I could expect from this part of the world, what would it be?"

Harconan frowned and lightly stroked his pencil-line moustache, a long-standing habit when he was in thought. For a long moment he considered the answer.

"Contrasts, Mr. Ambassador," he replied finally. "In dealing with Indonesia, one must expect remarkable contrasts at all times."

Rising from his rattan chair, he gestured westward toward the looming mountains and scattered coastal lights beyond the Bali strait. "There you have Java, the island with the highest population density on the planet. Yet, a comparatively few sea or air miles from here, you will find other islands where not a soul dwells and where one can still find ground that no other human foot has ever rested upon.

"Jakarta, the city where you have your embassy, is one of the most modern and sophisticated cosmopolitan areas in the world. Yet at the other end of the archipelago, you have Irian Jaya—New Guinea, as you would know it— where the Stone Age is still very much a going concern.

"To the northeast you have the oil sultanate of Brunei, possibly the richest nation on the face of the earth. Yet crushing poverty is also common. There are more followers of Islam in Indonesia than there are in all of the Mideast. Yet here also dwells the largest body of Hindus outside of India, while other islands have almost entirely been converted to the Christian faith. And over all, ancient tribal sorcery and animist beliefs linger on.

"Indonesia has the world's fourth-largest population. Yet it is a population broken down into over three hundred separate and distinct cultures, speaking over two hundred and fifty different languages, rendering any kind of true single national identity a dream held only in Jakarta.

"You will find piercing beauty everywhere, yet also great ugliness. Kindness and joy abound, as do anger and hatred. Here is diversity beyond anything you have ever imagined, Mr. Ambassador, and always in vivid contrasts."

Goodyard frowned, his expression indicating his sudden surge of homesickness for the simplicity of Lincoln. "It's going to be a challenge," he said, setting down his glass.

Harconan gave a minute nod to the Nung Chinese security man standing unobtrusively back in the shadows of the lanai. In turn, the guard whispered a few words into the lip mike of his radiolink. The cranking wail of a turbine engine came from the direction of the seaplane ramp as the pilots of Harconan's corporate aircraft readied it for departure.

Harconan bowed over the hand of the ambassador's wife, then extended his own to the ambassador. "Mr. Goodyard, I am at your disposal at any time. If I may be of assistance to you or your government, you need but call."

"I'll remember that, Mr. Harconan. And I thank you again. In a world where anti-Americanism sometimes seems rampant, your offer of friendship is a comfort."

From the lanai, Harconan watched as his Canadair CL215 Turbo drew a silvery streak of spray across the waveless surface of the strait before lifting into the sky. Angling away to the northwest, it bore the ambassador and his wife back to Jakarta. The running lights of the big twin-engine amphibian were soon lost amid the star-blaze of the tropic midnight.

Settling his dinner jacket, the taipan turned and passed through the set of sliding glass doors that led to his commodious den/office.

Stepping forward from the shadows, the Chinese security man silently took up his station in the center of the lanai, facing outward to the sea and standing at a relaxed parade rest. A whisper of a breeze tugged the tail of his light linen sports coat aside, momentarily revealing the butt of a military-caliber Beretta automatic pistol.

He was not alone. Beyond the muted circle of illumination cast by the house lights, the outer perimeter guards prowled quietly through the shadows, Steyr assault rifles slung over camouflage-clad shoulders.

Within the office, the airy batik wall hangings and expensive golden rattan furnishings effectively set off the polished teak of the massive centralized desk. Mr. Lan Lo, Makara Limited's senior business manager and Makara Harconan's personal aide-de-camp, stood respectfully beside the desk, hands clasped behind his back at a near parade rest, awaiting his employer. The stark white hair of the spare and venerable Chinese contrasted with the dark, well-tailored fabric of his conservatively cut suit.

"The dinner went very well indeed, *Bapak,*" Harconan replied, using the Bahasa Indonesian "father" honorific. "Ambassador Goodyard is a pleasant enough sort. Intelligent, albeit inexperienced. I think we will be able to do good work with him."

Harconan crossed the office, giving the bow tie of his evening wear a loosening tug. "How do the openings look on the London and Paris exchanges?"

"Favorable, sir. Nickel, tin, and petroleum are stable. Mild upward trends continue for vanilla and pepper."

"Excellent. And the Von Falken contract?"

"I have been in communication with our agents in Hamburg and the situation appears to be developing positively. The vote by the board of directors will not be taken until Friday; however, our preliminary polling indicates that the Harconan Lines bid will be accepted over that of PELNI for their regional container service between Singapore and Bali."

The faintest ghost of a disapproving expression crossed Lo's face. "Unfortunately, our agents also indicated it required an additional eighty-four thousand Euros in gifting beyond our projected budget to ensure the acquisition of the contract."

Harconan laughed and tugged the tie from around his neck. "German businessmen are like their automobiles: expensive to buy, but the performance is worth it. Don't worry, Bapak, we'll get our money back and more. And now, the satellite operation?"

"Proceeding nominally, sir. The acquisition is complete and the spacecraft is under tow. Intelligence Division indicates no distress calls or alert notifications on the international distress frequencies and no unusual activity by Australian naval forces. Our operations group is proceeding on course to the holding site."

"Very good indeed. It seems to be a successful night on all fronts."

"So it would appear, sir."

Arafura Sea   **0540 Hours, Zone Time:**
97 Miles North-Northwest of Cape Wessel   **July 9, 2008**

When their recovery ship failed to meet its third scheduled radio call, the INDASAT agency in Darwin notified the Australian coast guard that a potential emergency existed. The response was rapid. An RAAF Orion maritime patrol plane was scrambled from its base at Cooktown, arriving over the last known location of the *INDASAT Starcatcher* just at first light. To the consternation of all involved, no trace of the vessel was found. The *Starcatcher* had vanished completely, without even a trace of wreckage or an oil slick left behind.

As the confusion grew and the search widened, a trio of Bugis *pinisi* reached the tangled straits of the Indonesian archipelago. There they, too, disappeared from the ken of man.

Operations Center, United States Navy   **0455 Hours, Zone Time:**
Special Forces Command   **July 24, 2008**
Pearl Harbor Fleet Base, Oahu, Hawaii

Lieutenant Commander Christine Rendino wheeled the yellow Chevrolet Electrostar cabriolet into her reserved slot in the Intelligence Section parking lot. Squinting blearily into the sunrise that flamed over Diamond Head, she switched the solar-cell array of the little electric commuter car to "recharge" before dismounting from the vehicle. Slinging the strap of her uniform handbag over one shoulder and lugging the burden of her laptop case, she trudged across to the operations-center entrance.

A battered silver Porsche Targa sat parked in the lot's first rank. A tall, square-set man in razor-creased tropic whites stood beside it, the stars of a Navy flag officer glinting on his shoulder boards. An amused smile cut across his leathery, tanned features as the blond intel approached.

"Good morning, Commander," he said, returning the younger officer's salute. "It looks like the beginning of a beautiful day."

"I can neither confirm nor deny that rumor at this time, sir. I'll require additional input for verification."

Admiral Elliot "Eddie Mac" MacIntyre, Commander in Chief, U.S. Naval Special Forces, laughed and collected his briefcase from the Porsche's passenger seat. "I believe Captain Garrett did mention something about you not being a morning person."

Christine gave another hitch to her purse strap. "Try me at about eleven-thirty, Admiral. That's still morning and I'm usually pretty good by then."

"Today, we're keeping Washington time. Stand on, Commander. Our lords and masters await within."

"Isn't it traditional for us to get a tumbrel, sir?"

The intel and the admiral cleared the multiple layers of security at the opcenter entrance. Proceeding through the white cinderblock corridors to the communications center at the core of the sprawling, single-level complex, Christine, as usual, found herself half-trotting to keep pace with MacIntyre's decisive, rangy stride.

At communications, a small, stark conference room awaited them. After tossing their uniform hats atop the gray metal government-standard coatrack, they settled in behind the central table. MacIntyre flipped open his briefcase while Christine deployed her laptop, jacking into the table's access and power points.

Set into the conference room wall across from them was

the two-meter-wide flatscreen of a videoconferencing system, its camera lens staring down glassily from over the top of the frame.

"Set, Chris?" MacIntyre inquired.

"Anytime, sir." She flipped open her pair of close-work glasses and settled them over her nose.

MacIntyre nodded and lifted the receiver from the table's phone deck. "Communications, this is the C in C. Authenticator, Ironfist-November-zero-two-one. We're ready for that conference link with the State Department."

The red "active" light over the video receptor winked on. The wall display filled for an instant with a State Department screen logo and then broke to the image of a conference room far plusher than the utilitarian Navy facility.

Two men faced out from the monitor. One—tall, spare, and instinctively dignified—wore a gray suit cut with a Savile Row flair. The other individual, shorter, broader, and scowling, was clad in a conservative banker's pinstripe.

MacIntyre took the lead. "Good morning, Harry," he said, nodding to the man in gray. "It's good to see you again. How's Elaine doing?"

Given the nature of the coming confrontation, it would be good to remind certain individuals that both he and NAVSPECFORCE as a whole had friends in high places.

Secretary of State Harrison Van Lynden returned a smile at the gambit. "Good morning, Eddie Mac. She's doing fine and she'll be expecting you to come by for spaghetti next time you're in town. Good morning to you as well, Commander Rendino. I'd like you both to meet Senator Walter Donovan. Senator, this is Admiral Elliot MacIntyre, the commanding officer of U.S. Naval Special Forces, and one of his intelligence officers, Lieutenant Commander Christine Rendino."

The senator responded with the briefest of nods. Intel and admiral alike could read the leashed truculence in his demeanor.

Van Lynden continued smoothly. "It seems that interests within the senator's constituency have a strong involvement in the INDASAT program. They have requested that he approach the State Department concerning the incident that occurred off Australia earlier this month. As NAVSPECFORCE has become the lead agency involved in the investigation, I thought that a direct conference would be the best way to respond to these inquiries."

"Understood, Mr. Secretary," MacIntyre replied. "Commander Rendino has been in charge of the intelligence task force we've created to work the problem, and they've completed their preliminary investigation. We're ready to respond to any question for which we have an answer."

Senator Donovan cut in abruptly. "I hope you have plenty of them, Admiral. There were a dozen American citizens on that ship. And not just your average men off the street, either, but some of our best scientists and technicians. This above and beyond the billions invested in this project by both the government and American industry. All I've gotten from the State Department and the Pentagon up to this point is a lot of runaround! Now I want some straight talk on how, why, and who!"

The secretary of state lifted a hand. "You'll get it, Senator, you have my word on that. But for now I suggest we allow the admiral and Commander Rendino to bring us up to speed on this matter in their own way. Proceed, Eddie Mac."

MacIntyre nodded his acknowledgment. "Here's the situation, Senator. As has been released to the press, the wreck of the *INDASAT Starcatcher* has been located on the ocean floor, not far from the designated recovery point in the Arafura Sea. The satellite is not aboard, but we fear that the entire crew is. The Australian navy has a salvage vessel on site at this time, and they are endeavoring to recover the bodies. Given that the wreck is resting in almost a thousand feet of water, this will likely be a protracted and difficult process.

"A survey of the wreck by Remotely Operated Vehicle indicates that there is no chance of this being an accidental sinking. The *INDASAT Starcatcher* was attacked, fired upon, and deliberately scuttled. We may presume the intent was to steal the Industrial Applications Satellite it had just recovered and the payload the satellite carried."

"I think that many of us concluded that a long time ago, Admiral," Donovan replied caustically. "What took the Navy so long to be convinced? And why did it take more than a week to find this ship? There had to have been an oil slick, wreckage. Who was asleep at the switch? The Australians? Us? Who?"

"No one, sir," Christine Rendino interjected. "The ship wasn't found sooner because someone went to a great deal of trouble to make sure it wouldn't be found."

"How's that?" Donovan lifted a bushy eyebrow.

"We're dealing with an exceptionally sophisticated and capable group of people here, Senator. The sinking of the *Starcatcher* was deliberately concealed. The Australian navy's ROV survey indicates that the ship was neither blown up nor burned but underwent a controlled scuttling via the opening of its sea cocks. Buoyant materials topside on the recovery vessel were also stricken and secured belowdecks so there would be no floating debris field from the sinking. The fuel must have even been emptied from the ship's bunkerage tanks into another vessel so there would be no large oil slick.

"Accordingly, the Australian navy's search problem was vastly complicated. They couldn't tell if the *Starcatcher* had been sunk, hijacked, or had just sailed away. They had to cover all of the possibilities. When an extensive air and sea sweep by their assets failed to turn up anything, they requested our assistance."

"How did we find the wreck?" Van Lynden inquired, leaning back in his chair.

"An Oceansat, sir, a Navy Ocean Surveillance Satellite. We conducted a scan of the Arafura Sea from orbit, using varying filtered light spectra, and we picked up a reflectivity shift on the ocean's surface. There was an oil slick after all, but only a faint residual, so thin and dispersed it was invisible to the naked eye.

"We backtracked the oil plume upcurrent to its source,

JAMES H. COBB

and the Aussie salvage vessel started working the area with a side-scan sonar. After a brief search, they acquired the *Starcatcher*."

Christine turned to her laptop, opening a pair of insert windows in the videophone display. "In the right corner of your screen, gentlemen, you will see a chart of the Arafura Sea with the sinking site indicated. In the left I'll be showing an imaging series taken by the Remotely Operated Vehicle sent down from the salvage ship."

Christine executed the call-ups, narrating as each flashed before its small audience. "Okay, here you can see the distinctive bullet-hole patterns of heavy machine-gun fire on the *Starcatcher*'s upper works.... Here's a view of the empty well-deck bay. Obviously no INDASAT.... Here's a very indicative picture of one of the ship's Boston Whaler power launches. It's been lashed down in its deck cradle and you can't mistake the ax blows that caved in its flotation tanks.... And here is a view through one of the portholes into the crew's quarters.... By this time the body had been worked over pretty badly by the local sea life but the wound in the skull is still quite distinctive. Pathology confirms that she was shot in the head, execution-style, at point-blank range, with a military-caliber weapon."

Even Senator Donovan was momentarily suppressed.

Christine closed out the windows. "All evidence confirms that the *INDASAT Starcatcher* was attacked and boarded and the satellite she was carrying was stolen. Her crew was massacred, right down to the last man and woman, and the recovery ship was scuttled deliberately in a way to conceal its location and fate."

"Do we have any clue as to the identity of the terrorist group or nation responsible for this act of barbarism?" Van Lynden asked quietly.

MacIntyre fielded the question. "In our opinion, Mr. Secretary, it was neither a nation nor a terrorist group as you may mean the term."

"Then who, Eddie Mac?"

"Pirates, Mr. Secretary," MacIntyre replied levelly. "By

our best estimation, the INDASAT recovery ship was attacked and its satellite seized by pirates."

Senator Donovan's scowl deepened. "You are aware, Admiral, that this is the twenty-first century? Captain Kidd has been out of business for a long time."

MacIntyre raised his brows. "And are you aware, Senator, that you are living in the new golden age of high-seas piracy? That today, piracy is a major international criminal concern, with shipping and cargo losses that run into the hundreds of millions of dollars each year? Or that more than five hundred incidents of piracy are reported annually and that those numbers have been growing steadily for the past decade?"

"And the operative word here is *reported* incidents, Senator," Christine Rendino added. "The ones with survivors left alive to file a report."

The senator was taken aback. "Well, I suppose I've read things in the papers. But I've always thought those were comparatively minor incidents—native fishermen pillaging yachts, that kind of thing. With the theft of this satellite, we're talking about a completely different scale of events."

"That once might have been the case, Senator, fifteen or twenty years ago, but not any longer." Christine's fingertips did another swift dance on her laptop keyboard. "Here's another incident report from Indonesian waters near where the *INDASAT Starcatcher* was taken. It concerns a comparatively new eleven-thousand-ton tanker of Philippines registry with a crew of twenty-four."

The file had long been committed to her eidetic memory, but she read from the screen for form's sake. "After taking on a full load of mixed petroleum products at a Brunei refinery, the vessel sailed on its return voyage to Manila. Shortly afterwards, all communications with the tanker were lost and the ship and crew vanished.

"The only result of the immediate search following the disappearance was the discovery of several members of the tanker's crew washed up dead on an island beach. Their hands were wired behind their backs and their throats had been cut. Of the ship itself and its cargo, no trace was found for over two years.

"Eventually," she continued, "insurance investigators found the tanker operating off South America. It was sailing under the Ecuadoran flag with a new name, a new owner, and a masterfully falsified set of ship's documentation. The ship's new owners testified that they had purchased it in good faith a year and a half before from a ship's brokerage in Goa, India, and that they had no clue that they had been operating a pirated vessel. Further investigation revealed that the involved ship brokerage was a 'one-of' operation set up specifically to dispose of the tanker and that the broker and his staff had long since closed shop and disappeared."

Christine turned back to the wall screen. "Over the past decade there have been numerous other instances on this same scale."

Donovan shook his head slowly. "I had no idea."

"Not many people do, sir. In most instances, piracy is an 'invisible' crime. The events usually take place in isolated corners of the world: the Indonesian archipelago, the South China Sea, the coasts of Africa and South America. Also, it's mostly been a Third World problem. Much of the world's shipping operates under various flags of convenience and sails using Third World crews. The U.S. media generally would consider the disappearance of a Greek-owned, Panamanian-flagged freighter with a Malay crew a non-story. No flash for the news bites.

"You'll see articles about it in the dedicated trade journals now and again," she concluded, "but the shipping lines don't like to talk piracy up too much, even while they're the ones being victimized. They're scared of spooking their crews and clients and of seeing their insurance rates skyrocket."

"What's triggered this explosive growth in piracy?" Van Lynden inquired.

"I can name any number of general reasons, Mr. Secretary," Christine replied with a shrug. "The draw-down of the world's navies following the end of the Cold War. The international turbulence caused by the collapse of Communist China and by the various Third World splinter conflicts. A failure of the First World powers to recognize the renewal of high-seas piracy as a critical point of concern. But in the Indonesian archipelago, we may be facing another, much bigger, problem."

"Which is, Commander?"

"In my opinion, we may very well have a new pirate king out there."

"A pirate king! Now, that is preposterous!" Donovan exploded. "This is the real world, Commander, not a...Gilbert and Sullivan opera!"

An edge came to Christine's voice. "Excuse me, Senator, fa' sure this is far, far too real. Maybe I picked an inappropriate word for it, but there is a growing body of evidence that we have someone who is attempting to weld the Indonesian pirate clans into a single unified naval combat force capable of dominating the Indonesian littoral and the sea-lanes that pass through it."

The intel continued. "The Indonesian pirate clans are primarily factions of the Bugis tribal grouping. These people have a long, long history as shipwrights, master mariners, and sea warriors. Until broken by the coming of the British and Dutch colonial navies, the Bugis fleets ruled the archipelago.

"However, during the twentieth century, their buccaneering operations had mostly been small-scale, disorganized, and primitive—as you said, Senator, primarily targeting yachts, small craft, and local coastal traffic. A few years ago, however, that started to change dramatically.

"Suddenly, someone began providing them with large-scale logistical and organizational support. They're receiving better boats and equipment, including electronics and military heavy weapons. They're also receiving training on how to effectively maintain and use this new higher-tech gear. Someone is also providing the pirates with a secure multi-currency money-laundering link and is serving as a fence for high-value ships and cargoes on the international market. This individual or group of individuals is also procuring advanced cargo-targeting data from within the shipping industry and, I suspect, is systematically buying off senior government and security officials within the region."

She spun back to her personal computer and executed another call-up. The image of a sleek merchant ship with a stern deckhouse rezzed into the corner of the video screen.

"Consider this case, Senator. This is the Dutch containership *Olav Meer*. Two months ago, she sailed from Amsterdam eastbound to Kobe, Japan, with full tier loads of mixed cargo. Off the coast of Surabaya, she was intercepted by a flotilla of Boghammer gunboats, fast outboard motor launches mounted with automatic weapons and light antitank rocket launchers. The *Meer* was ordered to heave to and then was boarded by a well-organized band of Indonesian natives, believed to be Bugis, all armed with modern assault rifles, submachine guns, and hand grenades.

"As the *Meer* was being boarded, the captain got off distress calls to both his company home office and to the International Maritime Bureau's Regional Piracy Center in Kuala Lumpur, Malaysia. Both immediately notified the Indonesian authorities of the event. However, for reasons explained only as 'communications difficulties,' the nearest Indonesian naval patrol craft was not informed of the situation.

"While the *Meer* crew was held at gunpoint, pirate demolition teams proceeded to blow open a series of outer-tier cargo containers with the expert use of shaped plastique charges. Two million dollars' worth of high-value cargo was stolen, including pharmaceuticals, bricks of ultra-high-purity silicon used for the manufacturing of computer chips, and industrial lens-grinding compounds—stuff that your average Bugis raider would not recognize as treasure trove."

Christine looked up from the laptop's screen. "Here is where it really gets interesting, Senator. Not only did the pirates have the specific bill of lading numbers for these specific cargo containers, but high-value loads of this kind are routinely stored in the core tiers of a containership's cargo stacks, where they are impossible to get at while the ship is at sea. According to the ship's load manifests and those of the Amsterdam container port that had stacked the *Meer*'s cargo, that's where these items had been stored."

Christine tapped the tabletop with a fingernail to emphasize each word. "But they hadn't been. The books had been cooked and the high-value cargo containers had been loaded into the outer tiers of the stacks, right at weather-deck level—easily accessed by the pirates. Someone within the Amsterdam stevedoring crew had been bribed to misload this cargo specifically so it could be intercepted and stolen in Indonesian waters ten thousand miles and three weeks later."

Christine leaned back in her chair. "I'd call that some kind of an organization."

"I would as well, Miss Rendino," the secretary of state replied. "Do we have any direct links between this piracy cartel and the INDASAT incident?"

"Only in the form of probabilities, Harry," Admiral MacIntyre said. "In our best estimation the cartel is the only force in the region that has the assets in place to do the job and to effectively move the merchandise. Either they have the satellite up for sale to the highest bidder within the industrial espionage networks or they're already working on consignment for one of the corporate multinationals. The zero-gee industrial systems aboard the IN-DASAT and the materials they've produced would be worth tens of millions on the covert international tech market. The National Security Agency and the FBI are already working that end of the problem."

Christine nodded in agreement. "Either way, we aren't going to have much time before the INDASAT is completely disassembled and shipped out to ... wherever."

"Fine. You know who stole our satellite and why," Donovan said. "Now, what are you doing about getting it back?"

MacIntyre lifted his hands from the table. "At this moment, Senator, there's very little we can do...directly. In theory, this is a matter for the Indonesian authorities, as the satellite is probably within their territorial waters. Unfortunately, as Commander Rendino has pointed out, the fix is likely in and we can expect little joy from that line of attack."

"What about our reconnaissance satellites?" Donovan demanded. "The ones that you used to spot the wrecked recovery ship. Why can't you use them to spot where they've taken the INDASAT? I've been told that you can practically read a newspaper from orbit with one of them."

"We can," Christine replied, "literally. But first we have to know exactly where that newspaper is. The Indonesian archipelago is three thousand miles long, Senator. That's the width of the Atlantic Ocean. There are seventeen hundred islands within that stretch of sea miles. Many of them have rugged, broken coastlines and many are blanketed with dense tropical rain forests and jungle. We'd be looking for a single cylindrical object roughly ten feet wide by forty in length in all of that. It'd be like trying to use a microscope to spot one particular germ on the surface of a basketball court.

"Beyond that, these guys know about satellite recon. The whole reason behind their attempt to conceal the sinking of the *Starcatcher* was to buy themselves enough time to get the satellite somewhere where it could be camouflaged or concealed. I'm not saying we couldn't spot it with enough reconsat passes and enough Black Manta and Aurora overflights, but I am saying the analysis would take time. They could knock that satellite down to its nuts and bolts and mail it out by Federal Express before we could even make a decent start."

Donovan muttered a curse under his breath.

"If we can't do this by recon alone, and we can't rely on the Indonesian authorities, what other options do we have, Eddie Mac?" the secretary of state asked quietly.

"There's only one that we can see, Mr. Secretary. We

work the problem from the top down. We don't go after the INDASAT, we go after the cartel that stole it. I propose we bypass the Indonesians and go direct action. We move a covert intervention and intelligence-gathering force into the archipelago and we start targeting the piracy cartel operations. If we can shake their tree hard enough, the INDASAT may fall out of the branches and back into our hands."

"You're talking about an intrusion into the affairs of another sovereign nation, Admiral," Donovan cut in. "That satellite is your problem. The criminal activities of this pirate cartel are a matter for the Indonesians to sort out."

"If you recall, Senator," MacIntyre's voice hardened as he leaned forward over the conference table, "there is considerably more involved here than just stolen property. As you pointed out earlier, there were twelve American citizens murdered aboard the *Starcatcher*. I'd call that a matter for the United States government and the United States Navy to 'sort out.'

"Above and beyond that, in my professional opinion, the United States has allowed this piracy problem to go unchecked for far too long. If something is not done soon, we could see this piracy cartel not just operating within but controlling the Indonesian littoral. That will include the strategically critical international shipping lanes that pass through those waters and the forty percent of the global maritime trade that regularly utilize them.

"The freedom of the seas has always been a paramount concern of the United States," MacIntyre concluded, winding down, "and this is definitely a freedom-of-the-seas issue. I'll say that to you now, Mr. Secretary, and to you, Senator, as I intend to say it in the situation reports I'm preparing for both the Joint Chiefs and for the President on this matter. It's time we clean out this viper's nest before we have real problems in that theater."

"It's still an unwarranted and unnecessary involvement in foreign affairs!" Donovan rejoined hotly.

Christine Rendino peered over the top of her glasses at Donovan. "Senator, excuse me, but do you want your damn satellite back or not?"

Donovan subsided.

"If the word from the JCS and the Old Man is go, who would you propose committing to the operation?" Van Lynden inquired.

"The most suitable outfit available would be our littoral warfare test-bed unit, the Sea Fighter Task Force," MacIntyre replied. "They aren't completely up to speed yet, but they are partially operational and are on a working-up deployment in the Med at this time. They have the tools and expertise, and I believe they're our best bet at getting the job done."

Van Lynden grinned. "That's Mandy Garrett's command, isn't it?"

"That's right, Harry. That's why I said it's our best bet to get the job done."

Donovan scowled. "Amanda Garrett? She's that... officer who got us tangled up in that UN mess in Africa."

MacIntyre smiled behind his poker face. The West African operation had been a major foreign-policy victory for the administration of President Benton Childress, and a humiliating defeat for the isolationist faction in Congress that Donovan supported.

"That's correct, Senator. Captain Garrett is the officer responsible for the success of the UNAFIN blockade. I'm sure you recall her being invited to speak before the General Assembly at the conclusion of the operation... and the special medal of commendation the Security Council awarded her for leading the raid on Port Monrovia."

Donovan's scowl deepened. "To many of us, Admiral MacIntyre, Amanda Garrett is a loose cannon."

MacIntyre's eyes narrowed slightly, iron-frosted brows lowering. "I prefer to look upon her as a top gun, Senator."

It was a scene out of the Bible.

The sheep, spread across the moonlit hillside, grazing drowsily or asleep on the sun-crisped grass. And watching over them, the shepherd boy.

In ages gone by, he would have been guarding the flocks from wolves or from a prowling Sinai lion or a Bedouin raiding party.

Now, though, the wolf and the lion were extinct in these lands. Likewise, the time of the Bedaoui raider was past. Still, the watch must be kept by day and by night.

Sakim Tuhami shared the experience of those youthful guardians of long ago.

And, as frequently they must have been on such still and silent evenings, he was bored out of his mind and thoroughly pissed off at the entire universe.

Huddled down behind the low, dry stone walls of the shepherd's shelter, the Syrian teenager drew his rough woolen cloak closer about him and reviled sheep, his parents, and kismet in general.

He loathed spending his summer vacation in his grandfather's backcountry village. However his mother, a professor of history at Damascus University, had insisted, saying that it would "put him in touch with his Arabic heritage."

Sakim scratched and swore again. To date, all it had done was to put him in touch with a thriving population of fleas. At the moment, all he wanted was a hot bath, his personal computer, and the cordiality of his well-endowed, blonde, Swedish exchange-student girlfriend. Heritage be damned.

Suddenly, stock bells clanked and rattled from the direction of the bed ground, accompanied by a chorus of perturbed bleating. Something was stirring the flock. Sakim rose to his feet and peered out into the darkness.

The sheep were all on their feet uneasily, as if they sensed a threat. Sakim's hands tightened around his shepherd's staff, the black shadows suddenly more tangible around him. Nervously he reminded himself that there were no wolves or lions left in his world to be afraid of.

And then he heard the sound, a strange hissing whine like nothing he had ever heard before, a metallic whisper that seemed to crawl over the ground, growing rapidly in intensity.

And then it was upon him and the future crashed in upon the past.

It was overhead, just for an instant! The moonlight gleamed on a flattened dishlike shape in the sky, so low that it seemed as if Sakim could reach up and touch it. He felt a brush of hot wind on his face as the disk blasted past, and then, as swiftly as it had come, it was gone.

The flock exploded, panicking sheep scattering in all directions. The shepherd ran as well, back for the village, frantic to tell someone that he, Sakim Tuhami, had seen a flying saucer.

Upon hearing his grandson's breathless report of the phenomenon, Sakim's grandfather first beat the boy thoroughly for abandoning his flock and then sought out the village imam for advice. That worthy suggested that Sakim be beaten again for disrespect, the telling of a falsehood, and a generalized godlessness.

Miles away and unaware of the havoc it had wreaked in the life of a Damascus high school student, the flying saucer proceeded about its mission: to seek out a particular set of Global Positioning System coordinates locked into its guidance package and to perform a certain series of actions upon its arrival there.

The coordinates designated a point along a narrow two-lane highway that served as the solitary access to a well-guarded industrial complex in an exceptionally isolated corner of the Syrian desert some sixty miles from the coast.

Inbound, the saucer had been painted repeatedly by defense radars. However, its small size, ground-hugging flight path, and stealth composite structure gave it immunity to the probing beams.

Approaching its target, the flying saucer (or the discoid aeroform reconnaissance drone, if one preferred) went to hover a quarter mile off the roadway. Balancing on its lift fans, its sensors scanned the highway for movement or activity.

There was none. At this moment, as had been projected in the mission planning, the armored-car patrols that routinely prowled the road were out at the far ends of their sweeps.

Guiding in via the invisible infrared impulses of a ground-scan laser radar, the four-foot-wide disk crept closer to the highway. Precisely twenty feet off the pavement, the drone went to hover again, sinking to within a few feet of the ground. The door of a small internal payload bay cycled.

A stone plopped onto the parched and dusty soil.

Roughly the size of a man's fist, it was literally identical to a thousand other desert-varnished stones within a quarter-mile radius. This stone, however, cost not quite one million dollars.

A layer of thermocouples lined the stone's artificial shell. By day, they would use the heat of the desert sun to recharge a long-duration battery. This battery in turn would power an instrument originally designed for use aboard a NASA space probe, specifically an area scintillator capable of detecting minute changes in the radiation background count of the local environment. The battery would also power the tiny burst-transmission radio that would beam the recorded data from the instruments up to a National Security Agency ferret satellite in orbit high above the earth.

The drone zigzagged back and forth over the highway, dropping a pattern of other hypertech "rocks." *Plop,* a gravimeter that would register the variances in the local gravitational field produced by the passage of traffic on the roadway. *Plop,* a micro-seismometer sensitive to vehicle-generated ground vibration. *Plop,* an omni-directional microphone pickup capable of registering the sounds of engines and running gear.

The data from this sensor net would permit NSA analysts to identify the type of every vehicle entering or leaving Syria's largest special-weapons research and development facility, its ambient radiation emission, and its approximate payload mass.

Combined with the other data accrued from the NSA's fleet of orbital intelligence-gathering platforms, it would give the United States a fair notion of just where Syria stood with its covert atomic weapons program.

Its mission accomplished, the drone reversed its course, racing back for the sea.

Off the Syrian Coast   **0145 Hours, Zone Time:**
13.7 Miles South of Jablah   **July 27, 2008**

Lieutenant Commander Mahmud Shalakar paced the narrow patch of deck available within the wheelhouse of the Syrian navy's fast-missile corvette *Raqqah*. Tonight's operation should have been routine, a standard offshore security sweep such as he must have performed a hundred times in his career. Yet, this had not turned out to be the case.

This night was . . . haunted. He could not produce a better term for it than that. Intermittently since nightfall, ghosts had stalked his radar screens. Faint, transitory contacts appeared at varying ranges, only to fade before a plot could be established. At seemingly random intervals, blotches of mysterious interference materialized and then dissolved, looking suspiciously like some form of jamming. Likewise, his electronic-warfare receivers recorded mysterious blips and chuckles in the radio spectrum, but never anything that could provide a definite bearing for a direction finder.

The *Raqqah*'s systems operators were sweating blood from their captain's repeated and raging demands for more data. So far, they had not been able to produce anything solid enough to act upon.

The Syrian officer fished a buckled cigarette out of his uniform shirt pocket and kindled it with a quick snap of his lighter. All Shalakar had to work with was the sensation that the events were thickest along this particular stretch of coast. Something was going on out there, right under his nose. He could feel it.

But what? And maybe more importantly, who?

Syria's strategic naval position in the eastern Mediterranean was far from enviable. They were wedged in tightly between Israel and Turkey, both of whom were regional maritime superpowers. What was worse, Shalakar brooded, the damn Jews and the damn Turks had become thick as thieves over the past decade. They were always up to something.

Beyond that, Syrian fleet intelligence reported that a small American task force was lurking offshore, and Allah alone knew what the Americans were going to do next.

Be that as it may. There was nothing for Shalakar to do but to keep all hands at their battle stations and stand ready to act.

"Helm," he snapped, "reverse course! Bring us about one hundred and eighty degrees and take us half a kilometer closer inshore."

"As you command, Captain."

The brass spokes of the *Raqqah*'s wheel glinted in the CRT glow as they spun to the new heading and the corvette's sharp-edged prow raked the wave crests as she made her turn.

Three miles closer shoreward, from a position atop a semi-submerged sandbar that paralleled the Syrian coastline, two watchful pairs of eyes caught the flash of reflected moonlight as the bow of the Tarantul IV–class corvette came around.

"He's repeating his sweep," Lieutenant Commander Jeffrey "Steamer" Lane commented from the *Queen of the West*'s pilot's station. "That guy knows something's up."

"Um-hum," Amanda Garrett agreed from the copilot's seat. "We can live with 'something,' Steamer. Just as long as he isn't sure about us."

Amanda twisted around, looking back at the third occupant of the PGAC (Patrol Gunboat Air Cushion) 02's cockpit. "How about it, Mr. Selkirk? Anything new to report on our Syrian friend out there?"

Seated at the navigator's console, the intel glanced up at Amanda's words, the screen glow glinting off the upraised night-vision visor of his helmet. "There are no situational changes, Captain," he replied with the scholarly sobriety that was his usual operating mode. "Signal intelligence indicates a series of rapid frequency and power shifts on his radars but no scan-rate changes. He's hunting, but he isn't finding anything."

Amanda nodded thoughtfully. Lieutenant Gerald Selkirk was one of Christine Rendino's pups, hand-raised in the raven's roost of the *Cunningham*, Amanda's old command. If she couldn't have Chris at her side this night, Selkirk was a strong second best.

"Anything on his communications bands?"

"Nothing detected beyond his standard half-hour radio checks."

Amanda nodded once more, her eyes narrowing. The Syrian was uneasy, but not yet so uneasy that he was calling for help. They still had time, she judged, at least a little.

"How long do we have until recovery?"

Selkirk checked the time line display hack on his panels. "Seven minutes and forty-five seconds until unit recovery, three minutes and forty-five seconds until we get the boundary warning and approach call."

Lane chuckled in the semidark of the cockpit. "You have a great deal of confidence in that glorified Frisbee, Ger."

"There's no reason not to, Commander," Selkirk replied stiffly. "We received the deployment verification prompt, right on the dot, and the NSA reports they have good signals from the ground sensors. The Cipher *will* recover as per the ops plan."

The intel made it sound as if he would see to the errant machine personally if it failed to measure up.

Lane chuckled again. "We'll see.... Yo, Scrounge!"

"Yes, sir?" Chief Petty Officer Sandra "Scrounger" Caitlin stuck her attractive brown-haired head up through the ladderway access into the main hull.

"Pass the word to button up and look alive. We're blowing this pop stand. Initiate main engine-start sequence! Stand by to answer bells!"

"Aye, aye, sir." The *Queen*'s chief of the boat dropped out of sight.

"Loud and straight up the middle, Steamer?" Amanda inquired, calling up the copilot's checklist on her console screens.

"That's how I'd suggest doing it, ma'am. Sure as hell, we're going to attract attention when we take Ger's dingbat back aboard, either from the beach or from that spooky Syrian missile boat. I'd rather have us moving than sitting when we break stealth. Besides, that thing recovers better when we have some wind over the deck."

"I concur on all points, Mr. Lane. Light us up and get us under way."

One of the most critical secrets Amanda Garrett had learned during her career was to know when to pass the baton of command to a subordinate. She might be the TAC-BOSS of the Sea Fighter Task Force as a whole, but Steamer Lane was master of both the USS *Queen of the West* and of Patrol Gunboat Air Cushion Squadron 1. No officer in the Navy knew more about the capabilities and limitations of the deadly Sea Fighter hovercraft than did the sandy-haired California surfer who sat to her left.

The light patterns shifted on the power panels, yellow to green, as the turbine techs brought the *Queen*'s four massive Avco Lycoming TF 40C fanjet power plants to the edge of life. They'd crept in to ground on this sandbar, running on the *Queen*'s silent electric auxiliary propulsors. They would blast out to sea again on the eleven-foot ducted airscrews of the primary drive.

Amanda called up the tactical command channel on her helmet lip mike. "Frenchman, Rebel, Possum One, this is the Lady. Royalty is preparing to execute recovery and departure. We are on the time line. Report status?"

"Rebel to Lady. On station. Boards green. Ready to cover."

Lieutenant Tony Marlin's hard-edged voice replied from

over the horizon. There, the PGAC 04 USS *Manassas* drifted, standing by to act in support of her squadron leader.

"Frenchman to Lady. Same here. We're good too."

The response was milder, easier going, the voice of Lieutenant Sigmund Clark of the PGAC 03 USS *Carondelet,* the third hull of the Sea Fighter squadron.

"Possum One is standing by. ECM aerostat streamed. All drones on station. Ready to initiate coverage jamming."

Amanda could not put a face to this voice. It was one of the watch standers in the Combat Information Center of their mother ship, the USS *Evans F. Carlson*. This was the task force's first deployment aboard the San Antonio–class LPD and she was still learning this mammoth new addition to her command.

"Lady acknowledges. All elements stand by."

At the navigator's station, Selkirk leaned into his screens. "We have the boundary acquisition signal," he announced.

"Good 'nuff," Lane responded.

"And right on the mark, too, sir," Selkirk concluded, aiming his comment at the back of Steamer's head.

"I'll buy the dingbat a beer next time we hit Haifa, Ger. Crank 'em up, Captain!"

"Engine start sequence." Amanda keyed the row of engine initiators with a single press of her fingertips. Blue flame danced behind the blurring blades of the gas turbines, and the still Mediterranean night was cut by the rising kerosene-fired scream of the compressors.

"Cranking...cranking...cranking..." Amanda chanted, watching the tachometer and pyrometer bars. "Ignition! Four green lights. Clean starts. We have power!"

"Put her on the pad!" Lane acknowledged with a new command.

Amanda came forward on the lift throttles. Moan segued in with scream as the lift fans pressurized the plenum chamber beneath the *Queen*'s flattened, boatlike hull. The Kevlar chamber skirts inflated and, with a flurry of spray and sand, the ninety-foot length of the Sea Fighter lifted off the semisubmerged coastal bank, riding on a thin friction-free surface of compressed air. An armed derivative of the Navy's LCAC air-cushion landing craft, she had been built to take advantage of waters like these.

"On the pad, Steamer."

"Acknowledged. We're movin' out." Lane rolled the propeller controls and drive throttles ahead. Twin penta-bladed airscrews dug in and the *Queen* was under way, slipping off her grounding point and accelerating into the night.

The shadowed smear of the Syrian coast with its scattering of shore light began to fall away at the end of the *Queen*'s scant wake.

"Steer three-double-oh, Steamer. Let's get a little range from that Tarantul. Mr. Selkirk, bring our little friend home."

"Aye, aye, Captain. Initiating recovery," Selkirk reported, excitement growing in his voice as the automated sequences checked off on his display. "Recall and docking transponder now active. . . . Drone is responding. . . . We have good data links!"

Lane's eyes shifted from his console instrumentation to the night beyond the windscreen and back again in an instinctively repetitive cycle. "Verify the docking speed you want, Ger."

"Twenty-five knots, sir."

"Right. Captain, what's our wind out there?"

Amanda glanced at the meteorology display. "Four knots. Quartering out of the northwest. Holding steady. We are inside the gates for auto-recovery."

She returned her focus to the threat board and the tactical display. Up until this moment on the mission time line, they had been able to rely on unobtrusiveness for survival. All of the *Queen*'s weapons systems had been retracted inside the stealth envelope of her RAM-jacketed hull, reducing her radar cross section to that of a floating log. She had also been running EMCON with only passive sensors in use and with communications limited to the briefest of transmissions on low-probability-of-intercept jitter-frequency channels.

Now, however, the *Queen* must radiate a beacon signal

to toll her recon drone home, a signal that could be detected by Syrian ELINT monitors as well as by the Navy robot aeroform. It was a systems limitation that must be worked around, as with the limited range of the Cipher drone that mandated the tight inshore launch and recovery.

"There she is!" Selkirk called. "Coming right up the slot!"

The laser lock warning on Amanda's threat board started to flicker intermittently, reacting to the pulse of the drone's navigation Ladar. She activated a secondary screen on her console, accessing the imaging from the mast-mounted sighting system.

Selkirk had the low-light television cameras atop the sea fighter's snub mast trained aft, looking out over the stern antenna bar and the airscrew ducts. The Cipher drone materialized out of the horizon shadow, creeping in, its onboard artificial intelligence matching the speed and bearing of its mother ship.

The *Queen*'s quadruple air rudders flexed as Steamer Lane held her steady against the intermittent brush of a wave crest. A trio of docking probes deployed downward from the rim of the drone, ready to mate with the three sockets set into the hovercraft's upper deck.

"Easy..." Selkirk murmured. "A little more... you're lining up... lining up..."

Amanda held her breath as the little robot edged into position over the Sea Fighter's weatherdeck. It wasn't alive, but damn it, it was still part of her command.

The Cipher dropped abruptly. There was a thud from back aft and a series of sharp clicking bangs.

"Hard dock!" Selkirk exclaimed jubilantly. "Three probes, three locks, and three green lights! Recovery completed. Drone systems are powering down."

"All right!" Lane lifted his hands off the air rudder yoke for an instant, fists clenched in victory.

A red light flickered near Amanda's right knee and an audial warning from the threat board demanded her attention. "I'm very pleased to hear that, Mr. Selkirk, because we've just been painted by a Plank Shave search radar. The bearing is from the south, and it has to be our friend the

Syrian Tarantul . . . and he has just gone to tracking sweep interval. He's getting a return off of us!"

Selkirk wiped his telescreens clear of the drone recovery displays, calling up the *Queen*'s ECM systems. "He's got more than that, ma'am. Bass Tilt fire-control radars coming up now. He's trying for a firing lock!"

The decks of the *Raqqah* shuddered as her CODAG propulsion system rammed its maximum output through her three racing propellers.

"All engines answering ahead flank, Captain," the helmsman yelled over the combined diesel roar and turbine howl. The glowing numerals of the iron log on the helm console registered thirty-five knots. The little Russian-built warship was giving her all to close the range with the intruder.

"Where in damnation did he come from, Taluk?" Shalakar gripped the bridge grab rail, holding himself in place beside the radar operator.

"From inshore, sir. From inside our patrol line. A single, very small, fast surface contact. I thought for a moment that there were two . . . an airborne as well . . . but now there is only the one."

"How did he get inside of us? Identify!"

The SO shook his head. "Impossible to say. It is a very faint return. Possibly a Zodiac-type small craft. . . . Speed holding steady at twenty-five knots. Range closing. . . . He's cutting across our bow at five kilometers."

"Acknowledged. Lookout! Do you have a visual sighting?"

"No visual at this range, Captain!"

Shalakar's fist slammed against the side of the radar cabinet. "Zodiac or not, I want target locks! Lieutenant Sadrati! Arm the SSN 22s and the bow 76 turret both! Prepare to engage on my command!"

"We've got missile-seeker heads activating." The tension level in Selkirk's voice rose a notch. "SSN 22 Sunburns, arming for launch. He's getting serious about this, ma'am."

"Understood, Mr. Selkirk. Stand by on your chaff launchers and decoys. Mr. Lane, I think it's time we get out of here."

"I'm good with that, ma'am. Jumping to light speed!"

Steamer's lips peeled back in a fierce, tight grin. His palm shoved the propulsion power levers forward to their check stops. The roar of the airscrews grew into a frame-shaking thunder, and acceleration shoved all hands back into their seat padding.

"This is the Lady to all elements," Amanda called over her command circuit. "Initiate broad-spectrum counter-measures. Commence! Commence! Commence!"

"Captain"—the radar operator's shout was half strangled with surprise—"the target is greatly increasing its speed. Forty-five knots . . . fifty . . . fifty-five and still accelerating! It is now opening the range, sir!"

Shalakar glared down into the screen. The bogey wasn't just opening the range, it was pulling away effort-lessly, turning almost twice the *Raqqah*'s best rate of knots.

"That's no Zodiac!" he growled. "Missile Officer! Clear master safeties on all cells! Stand by to fire!"

"Captain," the SO cried out again, "look at the screen."

From a broad arc all along the western edge of the radarscope, flickering cartwheels of light strobed and inter-meshed, blanketing the screen image. A myriad of smaller sparks and blobs of illumination crawled and danced be-tween the pulsing spokes. The faint, spectral image they had been pursuing began to melt into the electronic chaos.

"Captain," another urgent voice cut in from the overhead squawk box, "this is communications. All voice channels and datalinks have just gone down. High-intensity cascade jamming all across the range. Multiple sources!"

Shalakar's dry throat resisted his swallow. *What is out there? Blessed Allah, what is out there?*

"Captain!" His missile officer wouldn't give him time to pray or to think. "Targeting systems no longer have acqui-sition! Missile-tracking locks broken! Switching missiles to independent proximity homing...! Captain, we can still fire on the bearing...! Captain, what are your orders?"

In the *Queen of the West*'s cockpit, Amanda accessed a data link from one of the *Carlson*'s Eagle Eye Remotely Piloted Vehicles. A distant cousin of the Cipher reconnaissance drone the *Queen* had just recovered, a trio of these little robotic tilt-rotors had popped up over the horizon a few moments before. The jamming modules they carried, combined with the integral electronic countermeasures (ECM) of the Sea Fighters, wreaked havoc with the local ether.

The onboard radars of the Eagle Eyes themselves, however, were unaffected. Tuned to peer through a narrow crack in the scrambled electromagnetic spectrum, they could be used to develop a tactical display of the developing engagement. Amanda did so now.

"Bass Tilt and Plank Shave locks broken, Captain," Selkirk reported. "We're below his return strengths."

"Very good, Mr. Selkirk. Stay on the ECM. Steamer, bring us left to two-seven-zero. Let's get off his last bearing."

"Steering two-seven-zero, aye." Lane eased the wheel over, slipping the hovercraft onto its new course. "Think he might try a blind shot anyhow? Should we elevate the weapons pedestals?"

Amanda stared into the cool glow of the tactical screen, considering the target hack of the Syrian corvette and the man who commanded it. She'd been watching him all evening as he had trudged up and down the coast on his patrol line. Doing everything the book said should be done, but never anything more.

Would he have it in him to go for broke, attempting a literal shot in the dark against an unidentified and inassessable foe? Slowly she shook her head. "No. He's past it. I think we're clear."

All hands in the *Queen*'s cockpit held themselves alert for another two minutes. Then, as the range continued to open and the threat boards remained clean, there came the mutual release of held breath and tautened muscles. Amanda settled back into the copilot's seat and spoke into her lip mike. "This is the Lady to all Little Pig Elements. Form up on Little Pig Lead and proceed to Point Item for recovery. Possum One, Little Pigs are inbound. Maintain coverage jamming for another five minutes, then stand down and secure the operational time line. You may inform NAVSPECFORCE the mission is accomplished. All elements, well done."

"Rebel, raja."

"Frenchman, aye."

"Possum acknowledges."

Out in the night, two sleek, finned shadows converged on the *Queen of the West*. Riding on hazy streaks of starlit mist, the *Queen*'s two sisters pulled into echelon formation with their leader. Reunited once more, the squadron ran free for the open sea.

Amanda slid her seat back on its rails. Unbuckling her safety harness, she popped the latches on her combination life jacket/flak vest. Lifting off her helmet, she shook her sweat-matted hair out over her shoulders. Scrounger Caitlin, with the instincts of a good chief of the boat, leaned in between the pilots' stations, passing her captains a couple of cans of Orange Crush, fresh from the galley refrigerator.

Amanda took a long pull at the soft drink, relishing the cleansing chill in her tension-soured throat. Glancing at the tactical display once more, she noted that the Syrian corvette had broken off its pursuit and had turned away. Humiliated, it crept back toward the coast.

I suspect I may have destroyed your career out here tonight, she thought, beaming her words through the darkness to the nameless Syrian commander. *I'm sorry it had to be done, but such are the fortunes of not-war.*

An hour later and fifty miles farther offshore, the Sea Fighters reached "Point Item."

Ever since their departure from the Syrian coast, the

threat boards of the Sea Fighter group had been reacting to the vigilant radiating of a powerful SPY–2A Aegis radar array. Now a pale slash of phosphorescent wake could be made out along the median between the black velvet sea and midnight satin sky. Fast ships moving through the darkness, their running lights extinguished.

Amanda smiled and lowered the nite-brite visor of her helmet to watch the closing with the two-vessel task group. For her, this was more than just a return to base. In a way, she was coming home, and she still savored the experience.

The lead ship, the escort, ran closer inshore, poised ready to interpose itself between its charge and the hostile coast.

Amanda knew this ship the way she might know the body of a long-favored lover. So much was the same, the great angular shark fin of the freestanding mast array, the low, slope-sided deckhouse, and the uncluttered sleekness of the silhouette against the sky glow, the great radically raked bow slashing open the sea.

The only readily visible difference were the deck guns, below the bridge amidships and on the well deck aft of the helipad. Replacing the smooth, hemispherical bumps of the old OTO Melara 76mm Super Rapids were the larger "ax blade" stealth turrets of her new and vastly more potent 5-inch .62-caliber ERGM systems.

The changes within that rakish hull were too numerous to catalog however.

Once upon a time designated as a guided-missile destroyer, the USS *Cunningham* had served as the Navy's advanced test-bed hull for navalized stealth technology. Now, with that mission accomplished, she carried a new designation at her bow, CLA (Cruiser Littoral Attack)-79, and a new tasking, the proving of the evolving technologies of the fleet's "Force from the Sea" battle doctrine.

But still, she was the Duke. In Amanda's heart, she was still "her" ship.

When she had started to assemble this new littoral-warfare unit, Eddie Mac MacIntyre had given her a free hand at drawing from the available NAVSPECFORCE resource pool. When it had come to selecting a heavy-firepower escort for the Sea Fighters, Amanda hadn't hesitated for a second.

High up on the *Cunningham*'s signals deck, an Aldis lamp blinked a brief signal: *All's well, Captain.*

Commander Ken Hiro, her old exec, held sway on the Duke's bridge now. But he remembered the old days too.

Holding in their echelon formation, the Sea Fighters cut around the stern of the cruiser sequentially ski-jumping her wake. Ahead, the faintly glowing sea track of a second, even larger vessel cut across the Mediterranean.

The USS *Evans F. Carlson* was both one of a kind and one of many, for LPD (Landing Platform Dock) 26 was the bastard child of the San Antonio class.

Originally the Navy had wanted only an even dozen of this new-model amphibious assault ship, one for each of the fleet's twelve Marine-hauling amphibious warfare groups. But somewhere in the pitch and toss of congressional monetary and political wrangling, an undesired thirteenth of the design had become wedged immovably into the Defense Department budget, a slab out of the pork barrel with no home and no mission.

However, Elliot MacIntyre had a saying: "When confronted with pork, make gravy." Under his astute machinations, this thirteenth orphan found a home within Naval Special Forces, undergoing conversion into the Navy's largest and most potent seaborne Special Operations platform.

In honor of this distinction, the Navy had "broken class" with her naming. Instead of an American city, she bore the name of an American hero, Brigadier General Evans F. Carlson, the bold and radical creator and commander of the legendary 2nd Marine Raider Battalion of the Second World War.

Given her mission, it was an honor suitable for ship and man alike.

As the *Queen of the West* swept in behind the *Carlson,* Amanda scanned the chunky lines of her new flagship through the night-vision visor, comparing them for the hundredth time with her beloved Duke.

It was rather like matching a massive, stocky Percheron with a lean and long-lined Thoroughbred. Yet, much was similar as well. Although built for entirely different missions, the *Carlson* and the *Cunningham* were sisters, or at least cousins, under the skin.

At 684 feet in length, the *Carlson* was not as long as the *Cunningham*. However, at 25,000 tons, the LPD displaced almost three times as much. While she had a far greater beam and a more massive superstructure than the Duke, the *Carlson* had a similar geometric, art deco simplicity to her design that denoted a ship with an integrally low radar signature.

Both vessels carried their sensors in clean-lined free-standing mast arrays or built into their angled superstructures as "smart skin" segments. Both were cutting-edge military technology and neither could be taken for granted in any kind of a fight.

Unlike their predecessors, the San Antonio–class LPDs were not mere helpless naval auxiliaries. Their mission would take them close inshore, into "Indian country," where a fight was something to be expected. Accordingly, these "auxiliaries" mounted more firepower than three quarters of the world's dedicated surface combatants.

Beyond that, the *Carlson* possessed a few special surprises unique unto herself.

Steamer Lane eased the *Queen of the West* in astern of the LPD. Decelerating to twenty knots, he bumped the hovercraft into the trough of the larger vessel's wake.

"Little Pig Lead to Little Pigs," he murmured into his lip mike, "prepare for recovery. Formation change. Echelon to line astern . . . go."

Two matter-of-fact "Rogers" came back out of the dark as *Carondelet* and *Manassas* smoothly folded in to trail behind their squadron leader.

"Permission to recover, Captain?" Lane inquired with a glance in Amanda's direction.

Amanda nodded. "Proceed, Mr. Lane. Take us in."

She flipped up her nite-brite visor to watch the procedure with conventional vision. This was by now a routine evolution for the squadron, but she still found it impressive.

"Okay ma'am. Doin' it. . . . Possum One bay control, this is Little Pig Lead. On station for recovery and ready to come back in the pouch."

"Acknowledged, Little Pig Lead," the radio-filtered voice of the BAYBOSS replied. "Initiating recovery. Little Pigs, welcome home."

A streak of dull scarlet light cut across the top of the *Carlson*'s broad, square stern. Widening rapidly, the streak grew into a ruddy glowing rectangle in the night as the LPD's huge boarding ramp swung down, its trailing edge touching and flattening the ship's boiling wake.

Revealed was a huge double-leveled internal bay that ran far forward within the hull of the amphibious ship. Under the blood-colored illumination of the battle lights, the docking crew and the Sea Fighter service teams could be seen jogging to their stations along the gantryways that lined either side of the bay. For her current tasking, the *Evans F. Carlson* had been optimized for "dry deck" hovercraft operations. There was no need for ballasting down at the stern to flood her internal well, as would be mandated by the use of conventional landing craft. Thus, she was something new, not an aircraft carrier, but a *sea*craft carrier.

With a masterful jockeying of air rudder and throttle, Steamer Lane eased the *Queen*'s foreskirt over the edge of the stern ramp. A surge of power to the airscrews then kicked the Sea Fighter upslope and into the bay, her wailing turbine song folding in around her, reverberating within the steel-walled cavern.

Steamer came back on the airscrew throttles and killed the main propulsion turbines, shifting his right hand to the T-stick "puff port" controller on the central console. A deck guide stepped out in front of the idling hovercraft, beckoning forward with his glowing wands. With bursts of the puff port thrusters, Lane taxied the *Queen* deeper into the bay, clearing the boarding ramp for the *Carondelet*.

As they trundled forward, Amanda glanced up at the bold artwork mounted above the gantries on the bay bulkheads. In pride, the different elements that made up the Sea Fighter task force had mounted man-tall copies of their unit shields there.

She checked them off in her mind as each badge crept past. Portside...the bamboo-lettered GUNG HO! crest of the *Carlson*....Starboard...the ghost-ship silhouette and STRIKE IN STEALTH battle cry of the *Cunningham*....Port...the ferociously Disneyesque trio of African warthogs of PGAC 01, THE THREE LITTLE PIGS....Starboard...the rampant sea dragon of the 1st Marine Raider Company (Provisional)....Port...a raider-boat silhouette butted into a dagger hilt for Bravo detachment, Special Boat Squadron 1....Starboard...the all-seeing eye and crossed lightning bolts of Tactical Intelligence Group Alpha....Port and lastly, the twinned gold and blue Oceanhawk helicopters of Heloron 24.

Each of these elements had been drawn from the NAVSPECFORCE unit pool or, in some instances, created specifically at Amanda's request to fill out her visualization of the task force. Eddie Mac MacIntyre had given her a blank check to create a "best of the best," a balanced and self-supporting Navy, Army, and Air Force in miniature that could deploy rapidly to any littoral hotspot in the world and deal with any low- to mid-grade threat.

One empty shield space remained to starboard, one unit left to merge into the whole. Then it would be time to see how correct her vision had been.

For Amanda Lee Garrett, ex–destroyer driver, it was a new way of war. But then, there had been a great deal of newness in her life of late. New technologies, new doctrines, new relationships, and new ways of thinking as a task group TACBOSS instead of a single-ship captain. Much had changed over the past year.

At least that sense of frustration and lack of purpose that had once plagued her as the dockside captain of a crippled ship had dissipated. Amanda had come to like this current command and the revised place she had carved for herself in her trade.

But with the gaining of the new, there is frequently a loss of the old. There were lingering thoughts of a youthful, dark-haired lover, a last perfect golden day off Cape Hatteras, and a conversation that had never been finished.

Still, if certain lonely holes remained in her personal life, she could live with them for the time being. Maybe with her career back on track and the task force coming together, she could start to think about patching them up.

"Anything wrong, ma'am?" Lane asked, glancing across from the pilot's station.

"Nothing, Steamer," she smiled. "Not a thing in the world. Stand on."

Captain Stonewall Quillain stood six foot three in his custom Danner Fort Lewis combat boots and was shouldered and muscled to look mountainous instead of merely tall. He considered Valdosta, Georgia, to be the best place in the world to be from, just as he considered the United States Marine Corps the best profession a man could have.

His features were an accumulation of blunt wedges assembled in a way that could never be called handsome, a scowl settling onto them far more readily than a smile. In fact, it was said among his Sea Dragons that "the skipper never actually looks happy, just less pissed off."

Still, though no one would dare accuse him of it to his face, Captain Stone Quillain had a broad streak of sentimentality in his makeup. Neither he, nor the unit he commanded, had any direct role in this night's operation, but he had people he called friends who did. Accordingly, he would see them home.

The guts of the *Carlson* rang with concentrated sound, like the interior of some gigantic brass horn. Quillain had to press the earphones of his command headset closer to his skull to make out the words being passed through it.

"Hangar bay, level two. Prepare to receive and spot hovercraft."

Below him, at the foot of the interior vehicle ramp, the *Queen of the West* reached the head of the boarding bay. Voluminous though it was, there was spotting room for only two of the three hovercraft gunboats on the lower entry level. Accordingly a deft piece of deck-ape choreography was required.

As Stone looked on, two seamen dropped down from the overhead gantries onto the *Queen*'s broad back. Safety-lined against the tug of the lift fan intakes, they pulled the locking pins at the base of the swept-back snub mast just aft of the cockpit bulge, folding it flush with the Sea Fighter's deck.

Simultaneously, another handling team dared the air blast boiling from beneath the plenum skirts to hook a heavy steel cable into a pad eye in the *Queen*'s stubby bow. Hauling clear, they gave the high sign to the winch operator in the bay overhead.

With the whir of its electric drives buried in the turbine howl, the cab of the traveling winch drew back along its tracks. Still riding on her air cushion, the *Queen* was cranked up the vehicle ramp into the midships hangar bay, a grade too steep for the hovercraft to climb under her own power.

In a Baseline San Antonio, a pair of garage decks would have occupied this space, storage for the trucks and AFVs of a Marine expeditionary unit. Aboard the *Carlson,* however, bulkheads and overheads had been removed and restructured to stretch the parking "foot" for the Sea Fighter squadron.

Stone pressed back against the bulkhead, holding his headset in place against the warm tornado blast of the Sea Fighter's lift fans. Moving with ponderous deliberation, she squeezed past between the deck guide curbs, her bulging plenum chamber skirts and outwardly sloping underhull looming above the Marine and squadron service hands.

The Sea Fighter was painted in a mottled camouflage pattern that would show as a dusty low-rez gray in normal light. All, that is, except for the phantom-outline lettering of her name and hull numbers and for the black snarling shark's jaws painted across the full face of the bow and the two leering eyes just below the stubby forepeak.

The pressurized skirts sagged as the *Queen*'s nose lifted above the curve of the ramp lip, the air pad partially collapsing as she "burped the cushion." The top of the cockpit almost brushed the overhead winch tracks, then the Sea Fighter flumped level again, bobbling slightly as she eased onto her parking slot behind the single, standard Landing Craft Air Cushion assigned to the task force.

A few moments later her lift throttles were closed, and the *Queen* sank down with a whining metallic sigh, her deflating skirts making a crumpled nest of black rubberized Kevlar.

Quillain nodded approvingly. The Sea Fighters weren't his particular area of expertise or authority, but he could appreciate any kind of military evolution well and smartly done.

Below, in the main landing bay, the *Manassas* and *Carondelet* completed recovery. Creeping to their tie down spots, they, too, powered down in sequence. The sudden silence seemed perturbingly empty—so much so that the voice that thundered over the MC-l circuit was almost startling.

"Hovercraft recovery completed and stern gate secured. All hands, stand down from recovery stations. Be advised, ear protection is no longer required in the hangar or recovery bays."

The bay lighting snapped from night red to standard white and the service hands moved in.

Like an aircraft, each sea fighter had two crews responsible for her: the onboard conning crew, who actively handled the hovercraft at sea, and an equally vital team of base service personnel who looked after her technical well-being.

Tie-down hands belayed the *Queen* to deck hard points, while access gangways swung out from the bayside gantries to her weather decks. Grounding wires were connected, auxiliary power cables were plugged in, and refueling hoses were hauled across the deck to filler points. Not an instant was wasted in readying the big war machine for its next call to arms.

Stone could appreciate that as well.

Keeping close to the bulkhead and out of the way of the bustling service hands, the Marine walked forward along the flank of the hovercraft to the midship side hatch.

It swung open just as he reached it.

"Good morning, Stone," Amanda called down from the open hatchway.

"How did it go tonight, Skipper?"

"As per the mission profile," she replied. "We had a brush with a coastal patrol, but things never went beyond swapping electrons."

Without waiting for the portable ladderway to be hooked in place, Stone's redheaded (well, pretty much redheaded; there was some brown and blond in there that made an exact color hard to call) CO made the five-foot jump down to the antiskid decking. Sinking almost to her knees on landing, she accepted Stone's extended hand to help lift her to her feet again.

Once, to Stone's chagrin, there had been a time when he'd been extremely dubious about accepting this lady as a commander and a comrade. That had been in West Africa. He'd wised up considerably since then.

Steamer Lane thumped to the deck a moment later, another veteran of Africa and another proven friend.

"And how'd the flying saucer do?" Quillain asked.

Amanda glanced up toward the *Queen*'s weather deck. Lieutenant Selkirk was already out of the cockpit hatch and hard at work examining the docked Cipher drone.

"The sensor pods are on the ground and Mr. Selkirk indicates that they seem to be working as advertised. From here on out, it's in the hands of our friends in the NSA."

Quillain's perpetual frown deepened. "I guess remotes are all well and good, but I still think I should have taken some of my boys in there for a real look around."

Amanda arched her eyebrows. "Be careful of what you wish for, Stone. It may come to that one of these days. If the Syrians get serious about their plutonium play-pretties, we might have to do a covert plug-pulling on that operation. Neither the Israelis nor the Turks would take a Syrian bomb attempt casually, and the last thing this corner of the world needs is another excuse for a war."

At that, a corner of Quillain's mouth quirked up, just slightly. Stone could appreciate many things, but none more than a challenge. "Now, that," he said, "could be a real interesting job of work. There are things this old boy could do with an atomic reactor . . . or to it."

Lane chuckled and aimed a thumb at Quillain. "You know, ma'am, this guy scares me sometimes."

Quillain did smile then, a grin that could only be described as wolfish. "Only sometimes?"

Amanda Garrett laughed and stretched luxuriantly, working the mission tension out of her muscles. "I'm sure our Mr. Quillain will try harder, Steamer. Now, would you gentlemen care to join me in the wardroom for a cup of coffee before—"

The MC-l speakers cut her off.

"Now hear this. The TACBOSS is requested to contact the bridge immediately. I say again, the TACBOSS is requested to contact the bridge immediately."

Before the amplified voice of the quartermaster faded, Quillain had snatched off his command headset, passing it to Amanda. Holding one of the earphones to the side of her head, she adjusted and keyed the lip mike.

"Bridge, this is Garrett. Go."

Lane and Quillain looked on as Amanda's features underwent the subtle transformation from relaxed comrade to alert and wary commander.

"Understood. You may inform the captain I'll be joining him immediately on the bridge. In the meantime, bring the task group to general quarters."

As the overhead Klaxons began to squall out the call to battle stations, she passed the headset back to the Marine. "Gentlemen, we may have underestimated the Syrian's level of irritation. We're being sharked by an unidentified aircraft. Steamer, get your crews back aboard the Little

Pigs. Stand by for a combat launch. Stone, set your point defense procedures. Let's move!"

"TACBOSS on the bridge!"

Amanda brushed past the light curtain, entering the star- and telescreen-lit dimness of the LPD's bridge. As with everything else aboard the *Carlson*, this, too, was of cutting-edge sophistication.

The helmsperson, lee helm engine controller, and duty quartermaster sat at computerized workstations in comfortable airliner-style seats. A score of additional repeater monitors glowed in a double row above and below the broad bridge windscreen. Continuously updating, they kept the officer of the watch apprised of ship's operations, the status of the surrounding environment, and the developing tactical situation.

Lack of information was no longer a problem. With a single sweep of her eyes, Amanda could access more information than she could ever dream of gaining from a ship's phone talker. The new naval officer's challenge was not in accessing, but in assessing and using this wealth to build a true situational awareness.

The input flowed in not only from the *Carlson*'s sensors, but from the *Cunningham*'s as well. The two warships were symbiotically connected via the multiple data links of their onboard Cooperative Engagement Battle Management Systems.

Cybernetically speaking, the task group was a composite fighting entity, capable of reacting to any perceived threat as a single focused force. Should it be necessary to launch Sea Fighters, LAMPS helicopters, or RPVs, they, too, could be merged into the Cooperative Engagement net, magnifying their fighting capacity.

Commander Lucas Carberry, the *Carlson*'s commanding officer, looked up from the central tactical display, his pink-jowled face underlit in the graphics glow.

"Captain," he stated formally, "the task force has been brought to general quarters."

Over the prior month of deployment, Amanda had come

to find Carberry a bit too formal for the likely propagation of a real friendship. Likewise, she found his personal command style a touch too autocratic for her tastes. However, she did acknowledge the chunky, dapper little officer to be a master of the unique and highly specialized field of amphibious warfare.

Effectively driving a "gator freighter" is not a task for just anyone. In addition to requiring both a capable naval officer and a superb ship handler, the position demands an individual who has the nerve and the cold-blooded steadiness required to take his vessel and crew into a high-risk situation and keep it there until the task at hand is accomplished.

Amanda had ascertained Carberry to be such a man, and she could forgive him a great deal because of it.

"Very good, Commander," she replied, joining him at the tac table. "What's our situation."

"The *Cunningham* is currently our actively radiating vessel and is defense coordinator. Commander Hiro reports we have a single aircraft coming in from the southeast." Carberry's blunt fingertip indicated a yellow graphics track crawling up the display toward the blue task-force hack in the center. "He is requesting instructions, Captain."

Amanda nodded. The Duke, with her more potent radars and weapons systems, usually served as the task force's stalking horse, permitting the more vulnerable *Carlson* to run emission-silenced and fully stealthed, the link between their Cooperative Engagement systems maintained via intercept-proof laser com.

"Put me through to Commander Hiro."

Carberry glanced at the battle-management specialist standing by silently at the far end of the tac table. Snapping his fingers softly, he pointed to one of the overhead screens. The enlisted woman's fingers danced briefly over her keypad, calling up the hot talk-between-ships channel.

The flatscreen filled with the image of Amanda's former executive officer, lounging back in what had been her captain's chair in the center of the *Cunningham*'s Combat Information Center.

The seat suited the stocky Japanese-American, as

Amanda had known it would. It was very much non-reg for an officer to directly move into the command slot of a ship he had served aboard as an exec. However, when Amanda had been called to serve with the Sea Fighters, she had pulled the strings required to ensure her ship would be left in hands she approved of.

"Good morning, Ken. What do you have for us?"

"Morning, ma'am," he replied, nodding back. "We have an Aegis contact. A slow mover. Speed one hundred and forty knots. Altitude fifty feet. The Bogey is running under full EMCON. No IFF transponder. No radio. No radar. We have no absolute target ID at this time but we're getting a rotor flicker off him. I'd call it a big ASW helicopter, maybe a Syrian Super-Hip."

"Um-hum." Amanda glanced down to the tactical display, studying the bogey's track. Sub-hunter helos could be a threat to more than submarines. They could also carry antishipping missiles—big ones. "Any chance this fellow could just be passing through?"

"I would doubt it, Captain. He knows we're out here and he's coming for us. Shortly after he popped over the horizon, he turned onto a direct bearing with the task force. As he's not radiating himself, he must be homing in on our radar emissions."

Amanda looked up again, this time at the low-light television monitor covering the *Carlson*'s foredeck. One level below the LPD's bridge, the hexagonal box launcher of bow RAM (Rolling Airframe Missile) system was autotracking on the approaching aircraft, guided by the targeting relay being received from the escorting cruiser. Farther forward, in the sixteen-cell Vertical Launch System inset into the main deck, a silo door had swung open, revealing the dark plastic water seal over a quad pack of Enhanced Sea Sparrow Missiles. Farther forward still, at the peak of the *Carlson*'s forecastle, a Marine missileer team crouched, the gunner holding the tube of a Stinger shoulder-launched SAM at the ready.

Beyond that, the nonreflective shadow of the *Cunningham* could be made out occulting the stars along the horizon. A look at yet a third screen verified that the cruiser's bristling Standard IV batteries and five-inch mounts were also on line and armed to fire. All told, her task force could throw up a five-layered defense against any air-launched attack.

Still, trusting implicitly in a line of defense, no matter how formidable, was an act of military imprudence Amanda Garrett had long ago grown beyond.

The unknown was crossing the twenty-mile line on the tactical-display-range scale. Who or whatever he was, there was no time left for dithering.

"Gentlemen, if our friend out there is listening to us, let's give him something impressive to listen to. Commander Carberry, bring up your fire-control radars. Ken, have the task force designate the bogey. All effective systems."

A yellow targeting box blinked into existence around the bat-shaped air target hack.

The threat boards on the approaching helo must have screamed in agony as the interlocking guidance beams of multiple gun and missile radars fixed onto the aircraft. In the international military lexicon, it was a demand, succinct and unmistakable.

"Account for yourself! Now!"

A few seconds later, a double line of transponder coding blinked into existence beside the outlined target hack. The tactical systems operator tilted her head, listening to the voice within her headphones. "CIC reports Contact Able is now emitting both Israeli Air Force and NAVSPECFORCE IFF codes."

"NAVSPECFORCE," Carberry murmured in puzzlement. "Captain, are we expecting a rendezvous with anyone out here?"

Amanda shook her head, frowning. "*I* certainly wasn't."

The SO tilted her head again. "CIC reports Contact Able has established voice radio communications. The pilot identifies his aircraft as an Israeli Air Force CH-53 operating under their special operations executive. He states he has a VIP passenger aboard for us and he's requesting approach and landing clearance."

"That would explain the wave hugging and the EM-

CON," Hiro commented from the overhead screen. "An Israeli special-ops helicopter operating alone off the Syrian coast wouldn't want to be obvious."

Carberry stared balefully down at the target hack on the table display. "But what would one of our people be doing trying to come aboard like this?"

Amanda shook her head. "Gentlemen. I haven't got an answer for you, but I intend to get some. Commander Carberry, notify your AIRBOSS that the Israeli is cleared for landing. Put your ship across the wind and stand by to recover aircraft."

"Very good, ma'am." Carberry lifted his voice: "Watch officer! Aviation stations! Clear the helipads and lay to all aircraft-handling details. Inform the tactical air control center they are to bring that helo aboard on the double!"

"Shall we secure the task force from general quarters as well, ma'am?" Hiro's screen-filtered voice inquired.

"No...not yet, Ken. Cease targeting designation but keep the group at battle stations. I want to find out a little more before we stand down."

The LPD's commodious flight deck, capable of handling half a dozen VTOL aircraft simultaneously, took up the full rear third of the *Carlson*'s topside length. Turning ponderously, the big amphib put the prevailing wind across deck at the prescribed forty-five-degree angle for a helicopter approach. Night vision-filtered strobe lights began to pulse at the corners of the helipad, beckoning the newcomer aboard.

On the bridge, they waited out the last minutes of the approach.

"Visual contact," one of the lookouts called out from his low-light monitor. "Bearing two-nine-oh relative. Range two thousand meters and closing. Target is confirmed as a CH-53."

The big Sea Stallion swept in literally at wave top height, the downblast of its five-bladed main rotor flattening a path through the whitecaps. Avenging himself for the radar painting he had received, the Israeli pilot aimed dead on for the *Carlson*'s bow. Pulling up at the last second, the thunder of his passage made the windscreen panes buzz in their frames.

With the mast cameras tracking it, the Stallion circled the LPD, lining up on the helipad, the extended-range drop tanks readily apparent on its sponsons.

Extending its landing gear, the Stallion flowed down onto the deck with an amazing delicacy for a flying machine its size. As Amanda and Carberry looked on, a side hatch on the helicopter popped open and a single passenger dropped to the flight deck. Clad in khakis and a dark navy Windcheater, the individual exchanged a cranial flight helmet for the computer bag and single suitcase handed down by the Israeli crew chief.

With a farewell wave, the small form ducked clear of the rotor blast. Within seconds of its touchdown, the Sea Stallion was ramping back up to flight power.

"Passenger transfer complete, Captain," the bridge systems operator reported as the helo lifted off into the night again. "Israeli aircraft now taking departure."

Amanda frowned up at the deck monitor. There had been something about that passenger . . .

"Commander Carberry," Amanda murmured, "resume prior speed and heading and inform Commander Hiro that we're standing down from general quarters. I'm going down to the flight deck."

The personage in question was waiting for her in one of the hangar bay passageways, and no, it had not been Amanda's imagination.

"Request permission to come aboard, ma'am?" Christine Rendino said solemnly, firing off a picture-perfect salute.

"Permission granted," Amanda replied by rote, her hand starting to lift in response. Before she could complete the gesture, however, the smaller woman was on her, locking her up in a fierce hug.

"Hi, Boss Ma'am. You miss me?"

Amanda returned the embrace of her old shipmate and dearest of friends with an equal fierceness. "Chris, my God! What are you doing out here?"

"I flew out with Eddie Mac." The Intel took a step back, grinning up into Amanda's face. "The Old Man's in Saudi

Arabia right now, handshaking with assorted sheiks and potentates to borrow an air base."

Amanda struggled to catch up. "An air base? For what?"

"It's a long story, and I'm here to tell it to you. Personal briefings for you and for all senior task force officers. First things first, though. Get us headed for Port Said four bells and a jingle. The Egyptian navy will refuel us, then we head through the Suez Canal tomorrow night on a priority passage. We rendezvous with Admiral MacIntyre somewhere in the Red Sea day after tomorrow."

"The Red Sea? Chris, slow down. Where are we headed, and why?"

"Indonesia, Boss Ma'am. It seems that some bad boys over there are sailing 'on the account' again and we have the job of closing it."

Palau Piri Island, Indonesia　　　**0614 Hours, Zone Time:**
Off the Northwestern Tip of Bali　　　**July 29, 2008**

Makara Harconan began his morning ritualistically with a double circumnavigation of his island. Clad in swim trunks, he alternated between a run along its lava sand beaches and a fast swim parallel to its shore, hardening his well-muscled body and clearing his mind for the work ahead.

It also provided him the opportunity to personally check on the security posts covering the far side approaches and to verify that his roving patrols were on the move and alert. Only a single mistake could be made in covering one's back, the first that is also the last. Harconan did not intend to make that one error.

A cold and stinging shower followed his run and swim, then a session with his personal masseuse. Finally, after donning slacks, sandals, and a safari shirt, he retired to the central garden patio of the mansion for a simple meal of rice, fresh fruit, and strong Javanese coffee.

As he ate, Mr. Lo sat across the table from him, a cup of green tea centered untouched before him. The latter was an insistence of Harconan's, a symbol of a battle of wills with his aide-de-camp over the subject of Lo's joining him for breakfast. Lan Lo, a staunch traditionalist, considered such familiarity in the presence of his employer decidedly improper.

In accordance with the morning ritual, following the withdrawal of the serving maid, none of the staff would approach the breakfast table unless summoned. Even the interior security man held well back out of earshot, monitoring the operation of the integral bug scanners and ultrasonic white-noise jammers that rendered the inner garden secure.

"And what is our first point of consideration today, Lo?" Harconan inquired.

"There are a series of developments in the satellite project, sir. Primarily positive, but including one point of possible concern."

"Proceed."

"We have received favorable responses from the Falaud Group, from Yan Song International, and from the Marutt-Goa Combine. Each has put forward the necessary commitment money, shifting five million U.S. dollars or a pound sterling equivalency into our secured accounts in Zurich and Bahrain. Each client also has an R&D team standing by for deployment to the holding site.

"The Mittel Europa Group has declined direct involvement but has placed an initial bid of one million sterling for certain castings and alloy samples from the satellite payload. The Japanese Genom zaibatsu also declines direct involvement but has offered a bid of two million dollars for the satellite's full run of orbital-grade ball bearings. Moskva-Grevitch continues to declare an interest but demands we present further specifications on the involved systems before making a monetary commitment."

Lo made no reference to notes or other documentation during his quiet-voiced recital. Not only did he not require such props, but none of Harconan's "special consideration" business was ever committed to hard copy.

Harconan was not displeased with the report. He'd had his doubts about the Poles and Czechs making a full commitment. Too many strong economic ties with the U.S., and they were trying for their full membership in the European Union this year. The Japanese weren't risk-takers either, and the Russian corporates still lacked the monetary muscle to play out in the deep waters. Still, three out of the six was sufficient.

Harconan freshened the coffee in his cup. "You may tell Falaud, Yan Song, and Marutt to dispatch their teams. Inquire about any special equipment they may desire and arrange for their reception and transportation to the holding site. For Mittel Europa, hold out for at least another half million. They're good for it. Accept the Genom offer as it stands.

"As for the Russians, as usual, they're trying to get something for nothing. Tell them we have shown them adequate bona fides; we have a property of value equal to what we are asking. They have our terms. They remain fixed. They can either accept them or not."

Lo inclined his head. "Very good, sir. I concur on all points. This now brings us to our point of concern."

"Which is?"

"A possible...radical reaction by the United States to our acquisition of their industrial satellite."

"Radical, Lo?"

Lan Lo's old ivory features assumed the total neutrality he reserved for what he felt were truly critical matters "Our business agent in Port Said reports a U.S. naval task force passed through the Suez Canal last night on a priority scheduling. Although only two vessels were involved, both were powerful special operations units and both were proceeding eastbound into the Indian Ocean. No eventual port of destination was listed with either the canal authorities or the Egyptian government.

"By accessing various naval affairs sites on the global Internet, we have learned this was not a planned redeployment. These vessels were scheduled to remain in the Mediterranean for at least another two months. An examination of affairs within the Indian Ocean basin and Pacific Rim indicates no other difficulty involving U.S. interests that would warrant such a sudden shifting of military power at this time. My presumption would be that this is a reactive event targeted against our operations."

Harconan nodded slowly, taking a sip from the potent black brew in his cup. "What about our contacts in Singapore and Jakarta, Lo? What do they have on U.S. naval intentions?"

"They have nothing, sir," the Chinese executive replied. "Which leads me to two other possible presumptions. Firstly, that my presumption is wrong and that the Americans are bound elsewhere for other duties, or..."

Harconan's dark eyes narrowed. "...or they have grown frustrated with the applied ineffectualism of the Indonesian government over their lost satellite and they intend to take matters into their own hands."

"Quite so, sir. A definite point of concern."

"That depends, Lo. That depends greatly on who they've sent out to hunt us."

"Yet another point of concern, sir. The involved units constitute what is called the Sea Fighter Task Force by the American navy. They are specialists in small craft and coastal operations and are held responsible for the successful United Nations resolution of the Guinea–West African Union conflict of last year. I have briefly discussed this task force with our people knowledgeable in military affairs. They assure me it is most formidable in its capabilities. Likewise in its leadership."

Harconan slowly lifted his cup to his lips again, his eyes set in the middle distance but his internal vision focused elsewhere. Things read: articles in popular magazines and international military journals. Things heard: whispered stories told by government officials in Taipei and Singapore. Things seen: a global-net television broadcast from the UN General Assembly and a striking amber-haired woman in a naval officer's uniform, speaking with a quiet and level-eyed conviction.

"Captain Amanda Lee Garrett," he said softly.

"Indeed, sir. A very definite point of concern."

The desert and the sea held their breath.

In moments the cruel sun would lift above the horizon to brand the earth for another day. The winds would rise with it, staining the sky with the restless migration of the sands between the Arabian Peninsula and the Horn of Africa.

For this moment, though, a cool and perfect stillness held sway. The dark sapphire bowl of the heavens gleamed with the last few fading stars. The dark velvet hills of Saud defined the eastern horizon and the sea had the glossy smoothness of poured oil.

The stems of the two great gray warships slit open the waters like sword blades cutting silk, their bow waves radiating outward and back in foamless geometric perfection. In the stillness the breathy whine of gas turbines and the humming rumble of maritime diesels could be heard for a distance of ten miles. Closer, a faint whisper of music could be heard.

No class of ship built for the United States Navy had ever been designed with as much integral living space for the individual crewperson as the San Antonio–class LPD. Yet, privacy remained at a premium. One of the few places where it might be found was the short stretch of weatherdeck at the rear of the superstructure.

Located between the two aft RAM launchers and shielded from the signals bridge by the mast arrays and a small systems shack, an individual might find a degree of solitude here for a time. Amanda had discovered this shortly after coming aboard the *Carlson,* and she had made it clear that this space was hers alone during the dawn hour of all fair-weather mornings. When she danced, she generally preferred not to have an audience.

This day, there was an exception.

The theme issuing from the portable CD player lifted from broken despair to a somber but rising end movement that called for rebuilding and revenge. Amanda pursued the music with her body, flowing from *pirouette* to *pirouette passé* to *relevé,* her mind free for a few precious moments from the responsibilities of command.

The piece swelled and lifted to its conclusion and Amanda followed it, a fist stabbing into the sky. Then the player spun into silence and she sank to one knee on the dojo pad, the music and the movement lingering for a few moments more in her mind. Then, with deliberation, she snapped the spell, opening her eyes and taking a deep deliberate breath.

"That was beautiful," Christine commented from where she sat at the edge of the mat. "What was that music anyway? I didn't recognize it."

"It's something I've been experimenting with." Amanda rose to her feet and took another deep breath. " 'The Pacific Boils Over' by Richard Rodgers. It's the Pearl Harbor theme from *Victory at Sea.*"

"I should have known." Christine held out a chilled bottle of Evian water. "Just anybody could do *Swan Lake.*"

"Well, nobody has done anything with it, and it's a pity." Amanda took a long sip from the bottle, then sluiced the remainder of the cool fluid over her limbs and maroon leotard, relishing the refreshing chill as evaporation explosively leached the moisture away. "The *Victory* soundtrack is the world's longest and most complex symphony. There are some terrific dance movements in there if someone would use them."

She sank down beside Christine, putting her back to the systems shack bulkhead. "Pass me that brush, would you?" she asked, unpinning her hair.

Christine collected the brush from the gym bag at her side. "You're letting it grow out a little more," she commented, reaching up to touch Amanda's tousled amber mane.

"Mmm, just too lazy to do anything with it."

"Want me to do it?"

"Be my guest."

Sitting cross-legged, Amanda turned half away to accept the grooming, and the two sat in the silence that is so different between old and comfortable friends from the silence between uneasy strangers, watching the *Carlson*'s wake boil white in the growing dawn.

"Hear anything from Arkady lately?" Christine inquired after a time.

"Now and again. He's up in Japan at the moment, working with the Maritime Self-Defense Force on their aviation ship program. I gather he's taken enthusiastically to being a fighter pilot and he's having more fun than kittens."

Chris glanced away, keeping her voice casual. "That's what I'd heard. I was just wondering if he'd been saying anything...special to you."

Amanda tilted her head to let Christine work out a snarl. "We exchange a letter now and again, Chris. Friends' letters."

"Oh."

Amanda poked an elbow back into the intel's ribs. "And there is no reason to go 'Oh' on me, Christine Maude. Arkady and I have no regrets and a lot of very happy memories. It was just time to set it aside for a while."

"Cool, then. Who's the replacement?"

"Replacement? Good Lord, Chris. I haven't replaced him with anyone."

"Well, why not?"

"Because I haven't had the time...or the particular inclination."

Christine thumped the palm of her hand into the center of her forehead. "I can see it all now. After office hours, your staff turns off your main power switch and throws a dust cover over you. I knew it was a mistake to accept that tour with NAVSPEC. You need a keeper."

"I'm doing just fine, thank you kindly." Amanda gave her brush-glossed hair a final setting shake into place.

Christine snorted. "Sure. And what are you going to carve on your tombstone? 'Here lies Amanda Lee Garrett, who got too busy to have a life.'"

"I intend to be buried at sea, Chris."

The intel sighed and tossed the brush back into the gym bag. Leaning back against the bulkhead again, she closed her eyes. "That was a bad line, Boss Ma'am....Amanda, I'm sorry. It's just that you drive me just a little bit crazy sometimes. You have got to be the most...generous person with yourself I've ever met. You give it all away, to the Navy, to the mission, to your crew, to your friends and lovers. Hey, I just wish you'd learn to keep a little bit of it for yourself. It *is* okay to do that, you know?"

Amanda gave a brief wry chuckle and reached back to lightly slap her friend on the thigh. "I've heard rumors to that effect, yes. And to tell the truth, I've been giving the subject some thought. I missed something very good with Vince Arkady because the time simply wasn't right. I don't want the time to be wrong again, whether I pick up with Vince or whether I move on with someone else."

An odd speculative tone came into Christine's voice. "Have you talked with Eddie Mac lately?"

Amanda looked over her shoulder. "To Admiral MacIntyre? Of course. I brief him a couple of times a week on how the task force is shaking down. Why?"

Chris only shrugged and looked out to sea. "No reason. Just wondering."

Amanda's command headset had been hooked over one end of her open gym bag; now its exterior alarm chirped, demanding attention. Christine passed it across as Amanda came up onto her knees. "Garrett here," she said, fitting the earphone to the side of her head. Intently she listened for a moment.

"Very good. Carry on."

Lithely getting to her feet, Amanda reached for the set of wash khakis she had draped over the topside railing. "Speak of the devil, Chris. That was the task group AIR-BOSS. Admiral MacIntyre's inbound."

Admiral Elliot MacIntyre had served for three years as CINCLANT (commander in chief, Atlantic Fleet) operating from FLEETLANTCOM's bunkerlike headquarters complex in Norfolk, Virginia. Upon leaving that assignment for NAVSPECFORCE, he had sworn he would never again, as he phrased it, "fly his flag from a brick shithouse."

These days he spent fully half of his time in the field with his combat elements. Accompanied by a minimal tactical staff, he utilized the advances made in military telecommunications to the maximum, remaining electronically linked with his headquarters responsibilities while working face-to-face with his unit commanders.

Within NAVSPECFORCE, it had been learned that the phrase "Eddie Mac will be on the ground in half an hour" could be spoken at any time, day or night. Depending upon the situation, this could be cause for relief or trepidation.

MacIntyre would agree that perhaps it was an unconventional way to run a major military command. However, peering down at the frost and jade wakes of his ships cutting across the Red Sea, he would also state it was a hell of a personal improvement over staring at a briefing-room flatscreen.

The desert-camouflaged Sikorsky S-70 gingerly eased in over the *Carlson*'s flight deck, its Saudi air force pilots demonstrating an understandable lack of familiarity with a shipboard landing platform. Eventually the landing gear of the export variant Blackhawk bounced down onto the deck, and the Saudi airmen throttled back to idling power. As the aircraft's side doors slid open, MacIntyre led a mixed dozen of U.S. Navy enlisted hands, CPOs, and junior officers out of the helicopter's cargo bay and onto the LPD's deck.

In his own personal operating style, the admiral carried his own luggage off the aircraft; as per his standing orders within NAVSPECFORCE, no ceremony heralded his arrival beyond the small group of officers clustered at the head of the helipad.

Keeping the bill of his uniform cap tugged down against the rotor wash, he ducked across to his waiting officers. Straightening, he turned and saluted the colors aft, then turned to reply to the crisp volley of salutes offered to him.

"Request permission to come aboard, Captain," he yelled to Commander Carberry over the rotor thunder.

"Permission granted, sir!"

Deckside communications then became temporarily impossible as the Saudi helicopter lifted off behind them. As the aircraft hauled away toward the Saudi coast and the sound level dropped, MacIntyre gave his [ ] tling tug. "Well, that's an improvement. C[ ] berry, it's a pleasure to see you again[ ] Commander Rendino . . . and you, Captain Garr[ ]

As always, MacIntyre found himself stricken [ ] poise and natural regality of Amanda's bearin[ ] dammit, by the striking and unself-conscious beauty o[ ] woman, the rich reddish brown of her hair and the golden glow of her skin contrasting with her tropic whites and rakish black Sea Fighter beret.

"It's a pleasure to have you aboard, sir," she replied in her purring alto. "Chris says that you have an interesting job for us."

"Among other things. But first be advised you can expect about a dozen more Saudi helos in this morning. Beyond my staff people, we have personnel transfers for both the *Carlson* and the *Cunningham,* and some sling loads of parts and munitions. You've got company coming aboard."

Even as the noise of the departing Saudi aircraft faded in the distance, a new droning, differently toned, grew in intensity. Four dark specks in an echelon could be seen against the intensely blue sky, crossing the coast outbound for the task group.

Amanda Garrett's golden hazel eyes widened. "You've got them for me!" she exclaimed, taking a step forward.

The admiral was pleased at her pleasure. It was a rather unusual gift to bring to a lady, but then, Amanda Garrett was a most unusual lady.

"When I talked to Cobra a couple of days ago, he claimed they'd need at least another month of work-up before they'd be ready to come aboard," MacIntyre said. "But when I mentioned that we had a potentially fangs-out job going out here, he said, 'Hell, if you're talking about *operating,* we're set to go now.'"

"That's Commander Richardson for you, Admiral." She shot an amused glance back at MacIntyre. "So that's what you were doing in Riyadh?"

Eddie Mac nodded. "I had to dicker for the loan of the SAAF air base outside of Mecca. Military Airlift Com-

ought Cobra's lead detachment in yesterday. They
d all night assembling their aircraft so they could
e aboard the task group this morning."

Amanda shook her head slowly, studying the approaching helo formation. "Ladies and gentlemen, this is a great day. The Seawolves fly again."

And it was, MacIntyre mused. The return of a legend is a rare thing.

The Seawolves, or, more formally, Helicopter Attack (light) Squadron 3, had been born during the desperate, savage days of the U.S. involvement in the Indochina war. Driven by the necessity of providing immediate on-call air cover for its riverine patrol forces and SEAL detachments, the Navy had created its first and only dedicated helicopter gunship formation.

Flying their first-generation UH-1B Hueys out of isolated swamp-country bases and from the decks of anchored LST "aircraft carriers," the Seawolves accumulated a list of combat honors second to none in that grim, twilit conflict, along with a reputation for fearlessness, dedication, and bold battlefield ferocity.

Seawolf was a name to conjure with. MacIntyre suspected that was why Amanda had called for this proud old unit's reactivation. Battles are sometimes won by factors beyond mere numbers and firepower.

Drawing closer, the readily recognizable pollywog silhouette of the UH-1 Iroquois became apparent. However, instead of the distinctive twin blade *whup, whup, whup* of the Vietnam-vintage Huey, these machines produced the vibrant, humming roar of modern flex-rotor flight systems.

As they swept past astern of the *Carlson*, a meager hundred feet off the deck, other differences could be noted. A twin-turbine power pack rode atop each squat gray fuselage, augmented with Black Hole and Flicker Flash anti-infrared systems. Hardpoint studded snub wings were set low at the aft end of the cabin, and the ominous, stumpy barrel of an OCSW projected from a chin-mounted gun and sensor turret.

The breed had improved over the intervening four decades.

Turning around sharply, Amanda caught the eye of a flight-deck talker standing by with a command headset. "Hey, sailor," she called, lifting her voice. "Relay this to the task group AIRBOSS. I want one Seawolf section positioned on each ship. Two aircraft here. Two aboard the *Cunningham*. Got that?"

"Aye, aye, ma'am. Two and two."

"As you asked for, Amanda," MacIntyre commented. "UH-1Y gunship conversions. I'm still not quite sure why you wanted the Super Huey rebuilds instead of Whiskey Cobras or armed Oceanhawks. Hell, I could have gotten you Sea Comanches if you'd yelled for them loudly enough."

"I had my reasons, Admiral," Amanda replied. "Cockpit-style gunships might offer more firepower, but they aren't as flexible for special-operations work. A Y-bird can transport and deliver a four-man Marine fire team as well as a weapons payload. They're also smaller than Oceanhawks, so we can shoehorn more of them aboard our available platforms. These will do me."

With her arms crossed and the *Carlson*'s way breeze tugging lightly at her hair, she turned with the circling Seawolves, following them intently with her eyes. Already MacIntyre could see her projecting possibilities and considering options, weaving his gift into her plans. "Yes," she said, nodding, "these grand old ladies will do me just fine."

The *Carlson*'s wardroom was large, with a triple row of dark oak mess tables in its center and comfortably outfitted with matching brown leather couches and lounge chairs spaced around its perimeter. Yet, a new ship's starkness still lingered about it. The accumulation of awards, mementos, and cruise memorabilia that would personalize this living space of the task force's officers had barely begun.

Still, some progress had been made. Commander Carberry had a framed set of Treaty-era battleship and cruiser lithographs mounted on the bulkheads. Coming from his personal art collection, they underlined his decided fondness for the days and ways of "The Old Black Shoe Navy."

Junior officers had learned to sidle for the door whenever Carberry started to wax eloquent about some detail or anecdote concerning a Texas-class dreadnought or Milwaukee light cruiser. The next installment of his continuing "What-all's wrong with the fleet today" lecture loomed.

And then, of course, there was the palm tree.

Bearing an ominous resemblance to an interior decoration of the Pearl Harbor officers' club, it had materialized mysteriously in the corner of the wardroom during the night prior to the *Carlson*'s sailing, complete with a hand-lettered CAPTAIN GARRETT'S PROPERTY sign spiked into the soil of its redwood planter.

The officer of the deck, the gangway watch, and the interior security patrols all stoutly denied knowledge of the miniature palm's arrival. While Amanda thought that the handwriting on the sign bore a significant similarity to that of a certain female intel of her acquaintance, there wasn't enough definitive evidence to warrant action.

There was only one possible dignified counter to the Ensign Pulverish prank. Amanda took the little palm under her personal care. Setting a grow light up over the leafy intruder, she bid that it stay.

The funny part was that she was actually growing rather fond of the ridiculous thing.

Stone Quillain was waiting for them at the center table. As the task force's senior Marine officer and Amanda's personal ground-warfare advisor, she wanted the rawboned leatherneck in on this ad hoc planning session.

Quillain came swiftly to his feet as Amanda, Christine, and MacIntyre entered.

"Good to see you again, Stone." MacIntyre exchanged a handshake with the Marine. "How are your Sea Dragons working up?"

"Tolerable, sir, tolerable. Of course, so far it's just been drill work and exercises." A speculative glint came to the

Marine's dark and rather narrow eyes. "We're going to have to take some real fire before we can say for sure."

Quillain's 1st Provisional Raider Company, more commonly referred to as the Sea Dragons, was yet another of the "great experiments" Amanda found herself dealing with. A unique five-platoon company, three of its elements, the heavy-weapons platoon and two of the rifle platoons, were standard Marine SOC (Special Operations Capable) line units. The remaining two platoons were fourteen-man Marine Force Reconnaissance units, specialists in deep battlefield infiltration and covert intelligence gathering.

"I warned you about being careful of what you ask for, Stone," Amanda murmured. "Wishes can sometimes get granted at the most awkward of times."

Coffee mugs were filled from the big stainless steel urn, more by reflex than from any real desire, and the four officers clumped at the center table.

"All right, ladies and gentlemen," MacIntyre began, "let's use the short form. The National Command Authority has handed off this Indonesian piracy problem to NAVSPECFORCE. In turn I've passed the baby on to the Sea Fighters. You've been given the word on what we're facing and you've had a couple of days to work the problem. What are your intentions and what else are you going to need get the job done?"

Amanda exchanged glances with her two junior officers. "Well, there's one thing we're certain of already: Absolutely nothing conventional is going to work."

MacIntyre grimaced and took a sip of coffee. "I was afraid of that."

"That's just how it cuts, Admiral," Quillain added. "The Indonesian archipelago's the goddamnedest littoral combat environment on the planet. Even if we had the whole combined 7th Fleet and 1st Marine Expeditionary Force committed to this job, we could be working it for the next ten years."

MacIntyre nodded. "I'm quite willing to cede the point. What I want to know is what we can accomplish with the time and the assets we have available."

"We do have some ideas," Amanda resumed. "For a starter, we're going to have to get clearance to work from inside of Indonesian territorial waters. How are our diplomatic relations with them currently?"

MacIntyre scowled. "Sore. State's been pushing them hard over this INDASAT matter, and Jakarta's getting muley on the whole subject. They're not doing much about this entire piracy matter and they don't like having it pointed out to them."

"It's not PC to say it," Christine commented, "but face still matters a great deal out there."

"And that can work very much in our favor," Amanda added. "Admiral, you still have influence with the secretary of state, don't you?"

"Harry Van Lynden and I still swap fishing lies and lures, if that's what you mean."

"Could you get him to do us a favor?"

MacIntyre shrugged. "It depends on what it is."

"Get him to back off. Overtly get him to drop the *INDASAT Starcatcher* question and Indonesian piracy as a whole. In fact, he could even slip an under-the-table apology to the Indonesian ambassador for our overreaction to the matter."

The admiral cocked a gray-frosted eyebrow. "State's catching hell from certain factions in Congress over this. I'd have to give the secretary an awfully good justification."

Amanda smiled. "Because it would give the United States a reason to conduct a goodwill visit to an Indonesian port as a fence-mending gesture of friendship and solidarity with the Jakarta government."

MacIntyre's grin grew to match Amanda's. "And this will give us our excuse to move into their waters."

"Exactly, sir. We'll lollygag around on our way in and out, collecting intelligence on pirate operations as we go. As Christine has pointed out, the piracy cartel has likely infiltrated both the Indonesian government and their defense forces—or at least they have contacts on the inside. Anything we hope to accomplish must be done independently and covertly. When we zero the location of the INDASAT and the pirate leadership, we make our move and take them out."

MacIntyre dubiously scratched the back of his neck. "And what does the Indonesian government do when we declare a private war on some of their own citizens on their own territory?"

"We give them a choice, Admiral, sir," Christine answered. "They can either be exposed as a bunch of corrupt and ineffectual bumblers who had to have their mess cleaned up by somebody from the outside. Or they can be our heroic allies in defeating a major threat to the world maritime community." She propped her chin up on a slim hand. "As Captain Garrett said, face has its uses."

MacIntyre stared down into his cup, considering. "This all hinges, of course, on our recovering enough hard intel to find where the INDASAT is hidden."

"Very true," Amanda acknowledged. "Intelligence gathering is going to be the keystone for this operation. Because of that, I'm going to need more collection assets placed directly under my command."

"Say the word and you'll have them."

"I am. I want a half-squadron of Global Hawks for the duration of this operation and an advanced base for them in Australia."

MacIntyre winced. "It couldn't be something simple like a few H-bombs or an aircraft carrier, could it? I could pick those up in-house. For Global Hawks, I'll have to go to the Air Force."

"I'm sorry, sir, but that's an asset I'm going to need if I'm going to pull this off, real-time regional recon, on call, twenty-four hours a day. That means G-Hawks directly attached to the task force. We have a functional control node setup here aboard the *Carlson,* and we can fly the systems operators out from Diego Garcia while we're in transit."

"I'll get them for you somehow," MacIntyre growled. "I just have to worry about what the bandits in blue are going to want in return one of these days."

Amanda smiled over her coffee cup. "I'm pleased to say

that's your problem, sir. I just have to deal with the day-to-day of tracking our pirate king to his lair."

MacIntyre chuckled deep in his chest. "I rather like the sound of that. There's damn little swashbuckling left in This Man's Navy. If you don't mind the company on your flag bridge, Amanda, I think I'll ride along on this one. It's still your show all the way, but I want to get the feel of how this new Sea Fighter task structure is going to work."

"All I can say is: Excellent and welcome aboard, sir. I suspect that there's going to be some politicking and diplomacy required on this run, and a vice admiral's stars pack a lot more weight than a captain's birds. Beyond that, we'll be operating in an Islamic cultural environment where having a male senior officer aboard could make things a little less complicated."

MacIntyre nodded. "Just leave the assorted pooh-bahs, potentates, and powers that be to me. It can't be any worse than dealing with Congress. Anything else you're going to need?"

"Some additional air logistics. The covert kind. We might have to support a microforce at any point within the archipelago. Can you get me a Combat Talon while you're picking up those Global Hawks?"

"Done. What else do we need to consider?"

"Tactical security," Stone Quillain said. "Operating inside of an Indonesian port and in their coastal waters can work good for us, but it can work for the bad guys too. They can get at us with their available assets. We're going to have a lot of ship and personnel vulnerability to sabotage and terrorist action."

"Very true, Stone," Amanda agreed. "And not just from the piracy cartel. This whole operational area is volatile. The Jakarta government is bucking a number of rebellious factions within the islands, and the usual knee-jerk anti-Americanism can also be expected. We're going to push our shipboard security and anti-boarding drills all the way across the Indian Ocean. How are your boys doing with our crew combat training."

"Pretty fair. All hands should have completed the advanced cycle by the time we hit the operating theater. We could do with some spare crew-served weapons and a bigger ship's ammo reserve, though."

Amanda nodded. "I'll see they'll be on the beach waiting for us in Singapore." She glanced back at MacIntyre. "One of the programs we've instituted within the task force is augmented weapons training. We're carrying enough small arms, body armor, and units of fire in our arsenals to load out all hands. Stone's Marines have also been giving us an advanced indoctrination in shipboard and ground combat. If we're pushed, not only can we protect our ships but we can back up the Raiders with shore assault parties."

"Not that my boys are all that likely to need any help," Quillain murmured.

Amanda lifted an eyebrow at the big Marine. "Be that as it may, I've got a hunch we're going to be needing those assault parties before this show is over."

"I'm not taking bets on any aspect of this operation," MacIntyre grunted. "Not until we know a lot more about what we may be facing out there. Until then, Captain, what do you propose as your first move? It'll take a while for State to get you a clearance for your Indonesian port call. By the way, where do you intend to put in, Jakarta?"

She shook her head. "No, Benoa, on Bali. It's centralized within the archipelago; it's quieter and some distance away from the military and governmental centers in western Java. It's also a resort area, it's laid-back, good for shore leave and more in line for the image of a friendly port call."

"How do you want to work the approach?" MacIntyre inquired.

"I've been thinking about that." Setting down her cup, Amanda crossed her arms on the tabletop. "If Chris is correct about this piracy cartel, they have a terrific maritime intelligence-gathering network in place in the major ports of the world. As it's the gateway to the Suez Canal, that likely includes Port Said. So probably they know we're en route to Indonesian waters. Shortly after our State Department contacts the Indonesian government about our port call, the cartel will know where we're going and, theoretically, when we're going to arrive."

She leaned forward slightly, golden-hazel eyes intent. "What I intend to do is to use their own intelligence-gathering capacity against them. We're going to let them know exactly where we are, but then, we're going to also be somewhere else at the same time."

"Keep talking," MacIntyre said slowly.

"To begin, we set an arrival date for Bali as well as a routine replenishment stop at our fleet base in Singapore, both timed to match the time frame for a leisurely routine transit across the Indian Ocean for an LPD. The pirates will know a task force can never move faster than its slowest ship. Both of the task-force ships will be scheduled for the replenishment in Singapore, but only the *Carlson* will show up.

"Once we clear the mouth of the Red Sea, I intend to cross deck aboard the *Cunningham* with a Marine boarding platoon and half of the Seawolf gunships. From there, the Duke will detach from the *Carlson,* go full stealth and EMCON, and conduct a flank-speed sprint across to the East Indies. An at-sea replenishment from the Australian navy would be helpful when we arrive in their waters. After that, we start hunting pirates several days ahead of our listed port call in Singapore."

Another grin cut across MacIntyre's craggy features. "Damn, I like it! The cartel will likely be circumspect when they know we're in their waters, but they might try to squeeze in a last operation or two before we arrive on station."

"Exactly. The *Carlson* arriving alone may catch them by surprise with some of their raiders still at sea conducting operations. With a little luck we may be able to grab some prisoners for interrogation, along with some hard intelligence and documentation. It may produce a crack we can slip a crowbar into."

Stone Quillain growled approvingly. "With the Skipper's permission, I'd like a piece of that action. My company exec can cover the action here aboard the amphib. It'll do him good."

"Welcome aboard, Stone. I'll be glad to have you running point. This first move's going to be critical."

"And also with the Boss Ma'am's permission," Christine Rendino added, "I'd like to go on ahead, too, but in a different kind of way."

"How do you mean, Chris?"

"I want to go ashore with the last Saudi helo this afternoon. From Riyadh, I'd like to fly on to Singapore, but under the table, as a civilian tourist."

"What's up?" Amanda inquired.

"I think I may have a lead on what you might call a native guide."

Details of the outfitting had changed, but the feel was the same. The ride of the low-set hull through the waves. The whirring whisper of the air through the ventilation ducts. The neutral warm paint and kerosene scent in the passageways....

Amanda made her way slowly forward through the *Cunningham*'s superstructure from the helipad, taking the time to savor it all. She had no complaints about her current command, but as any former captain can tell you, there is something very special about that one unique vessel you always remember as "your" ship. At night, her bridge is the one you always return to in your dreams.

Before heading up to officers' country, she took a moment to stick her head into the wardroom. Here, beyond the freshened outfitting, nothing had changed at all. Her father's commissioning portrait of the *Cunningham* still graced the starboard bulkhead beside the entry, while the naval aviator's wings presented to the ship by her namesake, Admiral Randy "Duke" Cunningham, rested in their glass case to port. No, Ken wouldn't let that change.

One level up in the superstructure, she dropped her

seabag and briefcase off in the ship's minute guest cabin. The Duke's accommodations didn't run to flag quarters, and she'd flatly refused to have any of the cruiser's officers shift living spaces for her.

With that done, she made the familiar climb up the ladder to the bridge level.

"Commodore on the bridge!"

"Stand easy," she replied by rote; then for a long minute she just stood in the entryway, looking over the shoulders of the helm team seated at the central console and down the long, open stretch of foredeck to where that sharp-tipped bow cut the waves.

She'd briefly been back aboard on other occasions since the shift of command, for planning sessions and tours of inspection. But this was different: This was at sea and not bound to a dock somewhere. Here, she and the ship were both fully alive.

"Welcome aboard, ma'am." Ken Hiro stood at her shoulder, a *Cunningham* baseball cap tugged low over his dark eyes. The Japanese-American's usual reserve was totally shattered by the wide grin on his face.

Amanda quirked an eyebrow at him. "You two make a lovely couple, Ken. I knew it would be a good marriage."

"The best, ma'am."

"I'm pleased for you both. Ready to take departure?"

"Give the word."

"Then make it so, Captain Hiro. Make signal to the *Carlson* that we are proceeding independently."

"Very good, ma'am." Hiro lifted his voice slightly. "Helm, engage Navicom. Select departure heading Easting one on your course presets. Lee helm, all power rooms to fast cruise. All engines ahead two-thirds. Make turns for thirty knots."

Skilled eyes and hands played across the master console and power pedestal, calling up systems, rolling throttles and propeller controls forward, and verifying responses.

"Sir, Navicom engaged and the ship is tracking on course plot Easting one."

"Sir, main engines and power rooms are indicating fast cruise. Ship is coming to thirty knots."

The Duke trembled from her keel up, gaining way with each beat of her twin sets of contra-rotating propellers, and Amanda found herself reaching for a seat-back grab bar to steady herself against the surge of acceleration.

The cruiser's bow wavered briefly as her autopilots and navigational systems hunted and found the great circle course that would take her across the Indian Ocean. Smoothly she swung to the new heading, the foam V streaming back from her cutwater deepening as she impatiently brushed the waves out of her way.

Hiro fired his net volley of orders into the command headset he wore. "Combat Information Center, this is the captain. Disengage Cooperative Engagement links and reconfigure for independent operations. Signals, you may inform the *Carlson* we are executing breakaway."

Amanda drifted over to the port bridge wing door and peered aft. The Duke was pulling rapidly away from the *Carlson,* cutting across the LPD's course line and leaving her to make her own more leisurely way east to the Indies. A dazzling point of light danced at the larger ship's signal bridge, outshining even the glare of the Indian Ocean sun. No doubt the reply to Ken's departure notice. To her surprise Amanda found she was going to miss the looming presence of the big amphib. Coming back aboard the *Cunningham* was like returning to visit the hometown where you grew up. The *Carlson* was where her tomorrows rested.

"What's the word, ma'am?" Ken inquired, coming up behind her as she lounged in the hatchway. "I never had the eye for blinker code."

"Let's see: 'Godspeed and good...hunting....Break.... See...you...in...Singapore....Break....Leave...some... for...us.'"

Hiro chuckled. "I didn't think Carberry would loosen up that much."

"He's not so bad, just different. And I seem to recall a certain exec of mine who tended to be a little bit stiff at times as well."

"Well, that was before a tough lady captain knocked the starch out of me."

They withdrew into the cool of the wheelhouse. "Any further orders, ma'am?" Hiro inquired.

"Not for the moment, Ken. Carry on. I'll just lean back in a corner and watch some water for a while if I may."

"Would you care to take the captain's chair, ma'am?" Ken nodded toward the elevated seat on the right-hand side of the bridge, traditionally sacrosanct for the ship's commanding officer. Amanda had lounged there for many a watch and sea mile.

She shook her head. "No, Ken, that chair belongs to the skipper of the Duke, and that's you. I'm just a high-ranking hitchhiker at the moment."

"Acknowledged and understood, ma'am. In that case, may the captain of the *Cunningham* respectfully request that the task force commander grace his personal chair with her presence for the remainder of the watch...just once, for old times' sake?"

Amanda chuckled. "Request granted."

She crossed to the captain's chair and lifted herself into it. There was new padding and a revised bank of chair arm controls; yet the flick of her heel on the base ring still rotated it that forty-five degrees relative to the bow that permitted her to brace her feet comfortably on the bridge grab rail. Crossing her arms, she tilted the seat back and lounged. It still felt just right.

Maybe they were wrong. Maybe you could come home again, if only for a little while.

Flag Quarters, USS *Carlson*   **0944 Hours, Zone Time:**
180 Miles Southeast of the Yemeni Headlands   **July 30, 2008**

It had been some time since Elliot MacIntyre had shared quarters with a woman, even when the lady herself wasn't present.

Amanda had insisted that MacIntyre take over her flag cabin while she was away aboard the *Cunningham,* pointing out that it made no sense whatsoever to leave accommodations empty aboard a living-space-starved man-of-war. Having refused her proposal that she turn her cabin over to him altogether during his stay aboard, he had to allow her to win on this point.

Still, it felt damn peculiar, and Eddie Mac couldn't define exactly why.

There was nothing overtly feminine about the two-room suite with its connecting private head. Nor was there anything especially extravagant about them beyond the fitted navy-blue carpeting on the deck and the artificial pine paneling on the bulkheads. The overhead was still raked with the naked conduits and cable clusters of a warship.

The little office/living space had room enough for a large gray steel desk and computer terminal, along with a small leather-and-steel-tube couch and a rather battered and mismatched leather recliner chair that MacIntyre remembered as Amanda's favorite from the wardroom set of the *Cunningham.*

The paintings mounted on the bulkheads were definitely worth a look. Amanda had several thousand dollars' worth of original maritime art here, all of it done by Wilson Garrett, Rear Admiral, USN, retired—Amanda's father.

MacIntyre grinned reminiscently. Back in the Persian Gulf aboard the old *Callahan,* they'd always thought the Old Man was just a little eccentric with his sketchpads and easels.

Two of the paintings were also transfers from the Duke, the one of Amanda's first command, the fleet ocean tug *Paigan,* and the other of her Cape Cod sloop, the *Zeeadler.* But there was a third he had never seen before, a painting of a young girl looking out to sea from the top of a rocky beachside bluff. Clad in blue jeans and cradling a toy sailboat in her arms, the child gazed at the distant horizon, a yearning dream in her eyes.

"Damnation," MacIntyre murmured. There was no mistaking who the girl might be. A lot of father's love had gone into that picture.

MacIntyre crossed to the door that led into the sleeping cabin. The blue carpet and pine panel motif held over here as well, a blue blanket drum-taut on the bunk inset in the bulkhead. Again, not a trace of overt femininity, and yet, there was something. . . .

The scent! That was it! The soft sweetness of cologne and talc overrode the usual warm metal neutrality of a ship's atmosphere. He remembered now how it would strike him when he entered his bedroom back home after a long stint at sea. The scent of his late wife and the promise it held. The ways they would make up for their time apart.

Eddie Mac gave an impatient shake of his head, stuffing those memories back in their box and slamming the lid down. That was past now, and not returning.

Brusquely he turned to the lockers and drawers built into the bulkhead across from the bunk, checking to see how the steward's mate had his gear secured. However, the third drawer he pulled open revealed an explosion of filmy femininity. MacIntyre slammed the drawer hastily shut.

A totally inappropriate set of images involving Amanda Garrett and a small handful of black lace raged behind his eyes. Eddie Mac lifted a hand to his forehead and massaged his temples. This . . . was going to be difficult.

Seeking to refocus his attention, MacIntyre turned back toward the bunk. An inset shelf railed against wave action ran above it for its full length. Here MacIntyre found his diversion. An expensive portable CD player had been racked at its center along with a long row of music disks.

And there were books.

The admiral noted that a disk was already loaded in the player. He reached over and tapped the Start key. After a few moments the haunting strains of a familiar movement of music issued from the speaker. "The Song of the High Seas"; he should have expected that.

Intently he studied the row of book titles over the head of the bed. One of the surest ways of learning what was in an individual's heart and mind was in having a look at what they read. Amanda had another bookcase full of professional reading out in the office space, but these were old friends, comfort books, battered and worn from many rereadings.

Not surprisingly there was a strong maritime orientation. There were a few Foresters, *The Ship, The Good Shepherd, Gold from Crete*. No Hornblower, though: MacIntyre recalled Amanda once saying that she found the character's incessant mullygutsing over his own inadequacies annoying. There was also a Jack London, *The Adventures of Captain Grief,* and Jan de Hartog's *Call of the Sea* anthology.

There was humor as well, a couple of Admiral Dan Gallery's "Cap'n Fatso" books and a massive reprint volume of the "Tugboat Annie" stories from the old *Saturday Evening Post*. On a hunch, MacIntyre took down the latter volume and flipped it open to the title page. Sure enough.

> To THE SKIPPER:
>   MERRY CHRISTMAS
>   WITH REGARDS, RESPECT, AND AFFECTION,
>   THE OFFICERS AND CREW OF THE USS *PAIGAN*

MacIntyre returned the book to its place. Finally, there were two real old-timers that must have come from Amanda's father's collection, Lowell Thomas's *Count Luckner, the Sea Devil* and *The Sea Devil's Fo'c'sle*.

The former had a bookmark tucked in it. Amanda must have been rereading it just over the last couple of days. MacIntyre smiled and took down the venerable hardcover. Propping the pillows up to a good reading angle, he stretched out on the bunk and turned to the first page.

**Curtin Royal Australian Air Force Base   0723 Hours, Zone Time:
The Kimberley, Northwestern Australia   August 2, 2008**

In the lexicon of the Australian military, it was called a "bare base." That is, it had no assigned squadrons, no garrison, no base section, no guards. It was only a naked, sun-scalded strip of concrete and a scattering of empty buildings between the shimmering waters of King Sound and the distant rusty-gold peaks of the King Leopold range. Its sole advantage over the surrounding thorn scrub pans being that airplanes, large and fast ones, could take off and land and be staged from it.

Curtin's mission was simply to be there on this, Australia's loneliest coast. Just in case. Just so there might be a place to stand should a threat again arise from beyond the seas.

This morning began much as many others had, with the parching winds swirling across the empty parking aprons and taxiways and the heat shimmer starting its day's dance over the runway. A small herd of kangaroos clustered around one of the capped wellheads near the main compound, jostling with one another to lick at the precious drops of water leaking from a defective seal.

Abruptly, the 'roos looked up as a thudding drone rolled across the desert. Seconds later they broke into a mad scramble for the brush as Curtin received its first incoming flight.

An Australian army CH-47D Chinook helicopter lumbered slowly down the flight line, its big twin rotors kicking up a small tornado of sand as it settled onto its undercarriage trucks beside the empty control tower.

Men and women disembarked, almost two score of them, clad in the field fatigues of both the Australian and United States air forces. Lugging a heavy burden of personal gear, toolboxes, and equipment cases, they trudged down the tail ramp of the grounded helicopter.

Emptied, the Chinook lifted into the sky again, leaving its former passengers to their tasks.

Some of the Australians produced massive key rings and scattered toward the sealed and deserted buildings along the flightline. U.S. communications personnel established a satellite phone link to the outside world and climbed the control tower carrying backpack SINCGARS radios with them. Other airmen began the long walk in the beating sun along the runways, searching for and clearing away foreign objects from the concrete. There was no time to waste. More traffic was inbound, a lot of it.

The first USAF C-130J entered the pattern an hour later. After circling once to survey the approaches to the semi-controlled field, it gingerly settled out of the sky to land.

Braking hard and with its quadruple turboprops reversing, the transport came to a halt at the airfield centerline. Its tailgate opened and swiftly it gave birth to a mobile airfield radar truck, a dozen more ground personnel and a humvee towing a power unit.

With its payload disembarked, the C-130 taxied back to the end of the runway for takeoff. One of its sisters was already circling impatiently, demanding a clear field.

All through the day a steady stream of C-130s and C-17s flowed in, and with each aircraft, Curtin Field came a little more alive. Generator sets snored, pumping electricity into the reactivated power grid. Water lines spat rust and hissed before gushing clean. Windows and doors were slammed open, allowing the wind off the sound to blow the hot staleness from the living quarters.

Portable landing lights were deployed along the runways, even as aircraft touched down. Sitting in their air-conditioned vans, GCA controllers worked traffic as casually as might have been done at LAX. A growing fleet of ground vehicles trundled along the base roadways: humvees, pickups, tankers, fire and rescue trucks.

A field kitchen served hot A rations. Field desks were carried into empty offices. Sleeping bags were unrolled on barracks floors.

Not all of the aircraft that arrived departed again. An iron-ball–black MC-130J Combat Talon transport from the U.S. Air Force's First Special Operations Wing taxied over to its reserved slot on the parking apron and shut down, disgorging its own ground crew and the support equipment and parts inventory it would need for a protracted stay.

The Air Commando Combat Talon was a relation to the standard C-130 Hercules transports flying into Curtin, but at best a cousin. Stealthed and equipped with an extensive, cutting-edge array of sensors and countermeasures systems, the Talon was intended to go into places where conventional cargo aircraft couldn't survive, and to get out again.

On another stretch of apron, preparations were made to receive a very different class of airplane. The small fleet of white vans and trailers belonging to the mission control and the launch-and-recovery elements deployed with practiced speed. Multiple radio masts extended hydraulically, and satellite dishes elevated and tracked across the sky, sensing for their incoming charges.

The justification for it all arrived just as the sun touched the western horizon, the red light flaming off of its composite skin. In silhouette, it was rather like an exceptionally futuristic sailplane, with the span of its narrow straight wings being twice the length of the stumpy fuselage. A sharply angled V tail was set aft and a pronounced hump atop the fuselage contained its Rolls-Royce/Allison turbofan engine, now throttled back to a bare whisper of power.

Smoothly it ghosted in over the main runway, landing gear extending from its belly. There was a puff of smoke as tires touched tarmac and it was down, completing its eleven-thousand-mile deployment flight from its base on the West Coast of the United States.

As it taxied toward its parking stand, an observer might also note a strong similarity with the legendary U-2/TR-1 family of reconnaissance aircraft.

There was one decided difference: The Global Hawk UAV (Unmanned Aerial Vehicle) didn't have a cockpit. One was not required. The "pilot" who had landed it sat in a virtual-reality cockpit within one of the mission control vans.

With the first bird safe on the ground and powered down, the UAV systems operator flipped up the heavy display visor of his VR helmet and paused to take a gulp from a can of lukewarm Diet Pepsi balanced on his console top. Keying the intercom that linked him with the gang over in the cruise monitoring trailer, he advised them he was ready to assume link with the second of the four inbound UAVs, and could they please hurry it up before the lasagna was gone over at the chow line?

As night fell over Curtin, the transformation was complete. Bustling activity had replaced abandonment. Lights blazed within its hangars and buildings. Come the next dawn the first Global Hawk would sortie northward into the skies over Indonesia. The base had a mission and meaning again.

In the thorn scrub beyond the base perimeters, the 'roos thirstily watched the activity and dimly wondered how they would reach the wellhead.

Sentosa Island was the Disney World of the Orient.

Lying just off the mouth of Keppel Harbor, it could be reached from mainland by cable car, causeway, and ferry. Gardens, museums, theme parks, and the finest beaches in Singapore were spaced around the perimeter of the three-kilometer island like the beads of a necklace. An ultramodern monorail system served as the string linking them, shuttling Sentosa's visitors, international and Singaporean alike, from amusement to amusement with swift and silent efficiency.

Sentosa was a place of beauty, education, and pleasure. However, Inspector Nguyen Tran of the Singapore National Police had come here for none of those things.

Stepping back into a deeply shaded nook near the monorail entrance, Tran checked his wristwatch and then the Glock Model 19 that rode in the shoulder holster beneath the coat of his tan linen suit.

Singapore was by far the safest city in Southeast Asia when it came to overt street crime. Tran knew this to be true because his job was to help keep it so. He also knew full well that taking chances was a fool's game. Especially when one was responding to an anonymously E-mailed request for a covert rendezvous. A request that specified he come alone.

From his shadowed point of concealment, he scanned his back trail, seeking a suspicious face, a suspicious act, a look or an expression out of place. He found none in the scant early-morning flow of tourists and pleasure seekers.

With computer-controlled precision, the eight-thirty run of the sleek monorail sighed into Orchid Fantasy Station.

Tran let the departing passengers disembark before crossing to the boarding platform. Stepping through the doors of the near-empty car at the back of the train, he retired to the rearmost bench, a position that would give him a full commanding view of anyone who came aboard during the upcoming circuit of the island.

The doors thumped shut. With a smooth surge of acceleration, the train flowed on its way, riding its single, pylon-mounted rail above the lush greenery of the forested parkland.

His instructions were simple and succinct: Cross to Sentosa from the mainland on the Causeway Bridge. Board the monorail at Orchid Fantasy station at eight-thirty. Wait for contact. Tran had obeyed and now he waited, his hawkish, darkly handsome features impassive.

Nothing occurred at the "Night Market" or "Lost Civilization" stops. However, at the "Underwater World" seaquarium, a young Caucasian woman boarded the car. A tourist, no doubt, given the sheaf of travel fliers stuffed into the side pocket of her shoulder bag and the theme-park balloon bouncing saucily on the string looped around her wrist.

On his own time, Tran might have shot an appreciative glance at the sleek, golden-tanned legs below the brief skirt of the blonde's summer shift. As it was, he was here on business. He added a little more stone to his expression, seeking to scare her off a few seat rows. He was somewhat nonplussed when, instead, the girl dropped into the seat beside him.

"Inspector Tran, I presume," she murmured as the train gained way.

Trans' brows shot up in surprise and he had to catch himself before replying. "Yes, I am Nguyen Tran," he replied in English, keeping his voice low. "And you are . . . ?"

"The person you're supposed to meet," the girl—woman—replied. Close up, Tran could catch the carefully camouflaged maturity of the newcomer. "The person who contacted you."

"You can prove this?" Tran inquired warily.

The blonde smiled. "In the message you received, there was an odd word included as an authenticator: *Winnowill.* Am I correct?"

Tran gave a nod. "Correct. There was. I accept that you are the person who sent me a most mysterious message. But I still do not know who you are or why you contacted me. I trust I will be enlightened before this goes much further?"

"My name is Christine Rendino, Lieutenant Commander Christine Rendino, United States Naval Special Forces."

"United States Naval Special Forces?"

"That's right," she replied, presenting an identification card she'd been palming, "and I'm here to talk with you about matters of mutual concern."

"What matters of mutual concern would I have with the United States Navy, Commander Rendino?"

"Pirates, Inspector Tran," the young woman replied, crossing her legs. "We're all just crazy-mad about pirates."

Shaded by rustling palms and backdropped by the velvet greenness of its world-class golf courses, the lanai café of the Hotel Beaufort seemed an unusual locale to discuss piracy with a naval officer. But then this Christine Rendino seemed a most unusual naval officer.

"Might I ask why you've sought me out in this manner, Commander?"

"Of course." She kicked off her sandals and leaned back comfortably in her rattan chair. "It's in relation to a series of articles you wrote last year for the *International Journal of Maritime Affairs,* the ones on the changing face of modern-day piracy in Asia. I and a number of other people found them very impressive. I hope your superiors gave you the recognition you deserve for your investigation."

"Those articles were purely a private project on my part," Tran replied stiffly. "They had no relationship with my duties as a member of the Singapore National Police."

The American woman chuckled and took a sip of her

French-vanilla latte. "I know. I also know that your superiors and your government attempted to distance themselves from both you and your articles in the face of the furor they kicked up. What was some of the phraseology used in the rebuttal issued by the Indonesian Foreign Ministry? 'Speculative, unproven, the promotion of needless hysteria' and other such buzzwords as are used by a nervous bureaucracy confronted with a dangerous reality leakage."

In spite of himself, Tran smiled. Mysterious or not, this young lady was easy to like. "It was suggested to me that truth is sometimes too dangerous a commodity to simply leave lying about. But which truth in particular are we talking about?"

She continued. "In your articles, you suggested that the piracy operations within the Indonesian archipelago are coming under a single centralized command. Instead of a hundred individual raider groups, we're seeing the organization of a united pirate fleet, something that has not happened in these waters since the sixteenth century. You indicated that this fleet is developing a sophisticated support and logistics network as well as a money and cargo operation. You also broadly hinted that it had corrupted officials within both the international business world and the regional governments."

Tran scowled. "As was stated in the Indonesian Foreign Ministry's rebuttal, Commander Rendino, this was all speculation on my part."

"Really." She leaned forward, her gray-blue eyes intent. "And what if I say that I know your 'speculations' are all dead-on? There is a piracy cartel. It is real. It is growing, and if somebody doesn't do something about it soon, it's going to control a block of ocean the size of the North Atlantic as well as the destiny of every living soul between Port Moresby and the Malay Peninsula."

Tran sensed the opening of a door, whether to a trap or to an opportunity he was not yet sure. "And who is proposing to do something about it, Commander Rendino?"

"Have you heard of the *INDASAT Starcatcher*?"

Tran nodded. "I have been tracking the case for my files, yes."

"That's the one that got our attention. We've been ordered to clean out the cartel."

Tran openly chuckled. "I'm sure the navy of the United States has some very formidable assets at its disposal. But if you expect to wipe out East Indian piracy in a single blow, I fear you will be sadly disappointed. Piracy is not a crime in these waters, it's a culture."

Tran raised his glass of ice water. "Western and regional governments have been trying to eliminate the trade for over six centuries and have failed. Your nation should not expect to do better."

Christine Rendino continued to study him with that cat-like fixation. "No, we shouldn't, not in the sense of eliminating every Bugis marauder hiding out in every backwater cove in the archipelago. But maybe we can return East Indian piracy to what it once was, a scattering of disorganized criminal gangs operating independently with limited resources. Just maybe we can take out this new pirate king and the infrastructure he's building. Oh, and on the side, we can grab our satellite back. Does that hit you as doable?"

Tran scowled. He wasn't certain yet, but if this could somehow be real... "Answer me this, Commander: How serious is your government about this affair? Is this only someone's politically expedient stunt, or are they willing to go to the extremes that may be necessary?"

"I personally know the two individuals who'll be running this operation," Christine replied soberly. "You have my word that they will do whatever has to be done. And they aren't the kind to worry overmuch about the rulebook."

"And you have contacted my government concerning this operation?"

"No, we have not contacted the governments of either Singapore or Indonesia concerning our intentions. Nor do we plan to until we have located and identified the cartel leadership beyond all questions. We'll be working covertly within Indonesian territorial waters. We've elected to operate in this fashion because, like you, we suspect that the cartel has infiltrated the security and foreign affairs ministries of certain of the regional governments. We're no longer sure whom we can trust."

"Commander Rendino," Tran replied, "I can assure you that Singapore has the most honest, secure, and corruption-free government in all of Asia."

The inspector paused and took a sip of his ice water. "And having said that," he continued with an arch smile, "I may also assure you that any communication you might have with my government concerning anti-piracy operations in these waters would be in the hands of the cartel leadership within...I would say, twenty-four hours at the outside."

The intel's eyes widened. "That bad? Even here in Singapore?"

"That bad, Commander. And it's worse in Kuala Lumpur, Bangkok, Bandar Seri Begawan, Manila, and Jakarta—especially Jakarta. You might even want to be circumspect to a degree in your dealings with Canberra. But to continue, how might I be of help? I am only one man."

"A man who has spent his entire life studying the problems of piracy in Southeast Asia. My people at NAVSPEC-FORCE intelligence have been looking at your career very intently for the past couple of weeks. We have the articles and papers you have written as well as copies of the memos and reports you've filed on the subject with various government ministries here in Singapore."

She shook her head, cutting off his puzzled query. "Don't ask, we just have them. At any rate, we think you may very well be the most knowledgeable 'hands-on' expert alive concerning East Asian piracy. Also, by reading between the lines of those reports, we suspect you know a hell of a lot more about certain things than you've written up."

"I do," Tran replied frankly. "But as you say, I'm the most knowledgeable expert *alive.* To speak...imprudently in these matters could bring about an abrupt change in that status."

The American woman's eyes narrowed and she smiled humorlessly. "But you'd risk it if it would mean hitting them hard, just once, wouldn't you?"

Tran studied the glass in his hand. It was like something from the old Muslim seamen's myths, the Sinbad stories that had been born here in the East Indies. One day, when you least expect it, a pretty genie pops out of a bottle and offers you your most heartfelt desire. But at what price?

"What would you want me to do?" Tran inquired slowly.

"We'd like you to come with us. We want you to serve as an adviser on the region and on the cartel's operations. Tell us what we don't know. Show us what doors we have to kick in. Help us take down the king. It will all be unofficial. We can offer you nothing in return except for maybe a little satisfaction."

"And maybe peace." Tran barely heard his own murmur. He looked up at the intelligence officer. "A final question. If you can't trust my government, how can you trust me? How do you know I might not be in the pay of the cartel as well—a professional red herring, as it were?"

Christine Rendino smiled again, her eyes softer and the smile sympathetic and knowing. "I've been studying more than your reports, Inspector. I've been studying you as well.

"For example," she continued, "you're Vietnamese, a boat person. You were born in Saigon and, in 1986, when you were eight years old, your family attempted an escape from Communist Vietnam. You, your father and mother, and your fourteen-year-old sister attempted a crossing to the Malay Peninsula with twenty-four other Vietnamese aboard a small fishing boat.

"You didn't make it. You were intercepted in the South China Sea by pirates. After shooting or knifing all of the men, including your father, and raping the women, including your mother, they stripped everything of value from the boat, including your older sister. Afterwards, they emptied an automatic rifle through the bottom and left a dozen women and children aboard a sinking wreck without food or water.

"You clung to the semisubmerged hulk for four days before being rescued by the USS *Sacramento*. There were three of you left alive; your mother was not one of them."

Images wheeled behind Tran's eyes as the American officer continued to speak in that soft, even voice. "You ended up in an orphanage here in Singapore. You proved to be an exceptional student and school athlete. After volunteering for a tour in the Naval Defense Forces, you went on to college, and then to the national police.

"For all of this time, you had two driving motivations. One was an abiding hatred for piracy and all pirates everywhere. The other was the search to find your sister."

"You are indeed a skilled investigator," Tran commented ruefully.

Christine gave her head an acknowledging tilt. "I have my moments. Eventually, you did succeed in finding your sister, but not in the way you hoped. In the summer of 2002, you learned she'd died of a combination of AIDS and syphilis two years before in a Bangkok brothel."

How clear those storm-toned eyes were. How they held his own. "Oddly enough," she went on, "the brothel owner who had purchased and managed your sister died shortly thereafter. He was found shot in his apartment, execution-style, with a single 9mm bullet behind the ear. The usual suspects were rounded up but the killer was never found. Not that anyone bothered to look all that hard.

"Interestingly, there was a second unsolved murder a short time later, this one in a coastal village on the Malay Peninsula. A wealthy but rather notorious retired fishing-boat captain with a suspected history of South China Sea piracy was also found dead, execution-style, a single 9mm round behind the ear."

Christine Rendino set aside her cup and reached across the table. With a single fingertip, she lifted the side of Tran's jacket, revealing the butt of the 9mm Glock automatic.

"I prefer a SIG Sauer P226 myself," she said, settling back into her chair. "No, Inspector. I believe that if there is any person in Southeast Asia we can trust in this matter, it's you. Throw in with us, Tran. Help us take these guys down. There are a lot of other girls out there like your sister."

He realized that the glass in his hand was about to shatter, and he carefully set it on the rattan tabletop. "I have been working very hard of late, Commander Rendino. I think that a vacation would be beneficial." The corner of his mouth quirked up. "Perhaps a long sea voyage."

"Yes!" Christine Rendino gave a happy squirm that instantly transmuted her from a military officer back into the tourist girl he had watched board the monorail. "Do you think you can give us a lead on who is behind the cartel? The real leadership."

"I can do better than that," Tran replied decisively. "I can tell you his name and where you can find him. I can also list his assets, his allies, his goals, and a partial list of his contacts inside the business and international community. I can *tell* you a great deal. Unfortunately, I can prove almost none of it."

East Indies   **Early August 2008**

For a week, a sleek and deadly predator stalked the sea-lanes of the Indonesian archipelago. From Great Channel in the Andaman group, south along Kepulauan Mentawai and east past Christmas Island to the mouth of the Timor Sea, the huntress hunted in the night, using the merchant shipping of the world as her stalking goat.

Electronically silent and stealthed against radar detection, she trailed the lumbering container ships into the Straits of Malacca and invisibly intercepted the break-bulks as they came through the Selat Sunda. She lurked to seaward of the interisland ferries as they shuttled between Bali and Sumatra, and the coaster skippers hauling sandalwood and vanilla into Jakarta and Telukbetung never knew they were being watched from darkness.

With the coming of the dawn, she would withdraw into

the open ocean, hiding from patrol aircraft and passing sea traffic in the misty lair of a squall line or thunderhead, drifting with the movements of sea and storm.

But come the night, she would emerge to hunt again.

Inside the Southern Approaches   **2320 Hours, Zone Time:**
  to the Sunda Strait   **August 10, 2008**

With all topside lights blacked out and with her screws turning just fast enough to maintain steerage, the USS *Cunningham* circled beyond the established Straits shipping channel.

Atop the cruiser's superstructure, Stone Quillain looked down from the weatherdeck rail, his night-adapted vision making out the faint flickers of light swirling in the ocean.

The minimal wake and bow wave glowed with a thin blue-green bioluminescence as uncountable billions of minute sea creatures protested the ship's passage through their realm. Deeper beneath the oily surface, amorphous glowing things darted and pulsed. With the passing of the sun, the beasts of the wet dark were rising into the shallows to feed.

Above the surface, there were other illuminations. A golden half moon hovered in the sky, outlining the distant, rugged mountain spine of Sumatra. The running lights of numerous coasters and small craft twinkled within the Sunda Straits themselves, and distant shore lights could be made out on both the Sumatran and Javanese sides of the passage.

Intermittently, one of the smaller vessels would approach too closely and the Duke's engines would awake, the darkened warship turning away, slipping deeper into the night.

There was also an odd skyglow that Stone had noted but couldn't put a name to. A pulsing orange radiance against the clouds well back up in the Sumatran mountains. Different from fire, city lights, or lightning, the Marine found it somehow strangely disturbing.

"Hello, Stone. You can't sleep either, I see." The top strap of the nylon rail swayed as Amanda Garrett's weight came against it.

"Nope," he replied, glancing across to the shadow form beside him. "It's pretty thick belowdecks, even with the air-conditioning up. It's a little better up here, but I sure wish the Good Lord would hurry up and open the windows, so we can get a breath of decent breathin' air."

"Um-hum. I know what you mean."

They leaned there in companionable silence, listening to the soft turbine whine and wake hiss. Then, for the sake of saying something, Stone indicated the mysterious patch of skyglow he'd been watching. "Say, Skipper, you wouldn't happen to have any idea what that might be, would you? I've been studying on it for a while and I'd almost swear that's artillery fire."

"In a way, you aren't all that far off, Stone," Amanda mused. "I suspect that might be a volcanic crater in eruption. They're pretty common around here."

Stone cocked an eyebrow. "How common?"

"Very. Indonesia is the gemstone in the Pacific ring of fire. The archipelago has over seventy recognized active volcanoes. Fifteen over there on Sumatra alone."

"Seventy volcanoes? Skipper, you're puttin' me on!"

Amanda shook her head and Stone thought he caught the gleam of a smile. "Not a bit of it. According to the geologists, the Australian and Asian continental plates crashed together along here about fifteen million years ago. The resulting collision buckled up the oceanic mountain range that became the Indonesian archipelago. You can imagine the kind of energies involved. Earthquakes and volcanos aren't natural phenomena in Indonesia: They're a way of life."

"I'd guess. They ever have any really big bangs around here?"

"Only the largest in human history. When Mount Tambora on Sumbawa erupted in 1815, it ejected over fifty cubic miles of volcanic materials and killed over ninety thousand people. And then there was Krakatau."

"Uh, you mean like Krakatoa? I saw a movie about that once. Was it really that bad, or was that just Hollywood?"

"Krakatoa is the anglicized version of the Indonesian name. And no scriptwriter or special-effects man in the world could do justice to what actually happened."

"What's the straight dope?"

Amanda crossed her arms on the top strap of the railing and paused for a moment, marshalling the odds and ends of information she'd picked up over the years.

"Krakatau was a comparatively small volcanic islet," she began. "However, in 1883 it went into an exceptionally violent eruptive phase. The geologists theorize that the eruptions were so furious that the volcano partially emptied the magma chamber beneath it. Then the sides of the islet either blew out or collapsed inward, permitting the ocean to pour into the very heart of the open volcanic vent.

"The largest hydrogen bomb ever detonated couldn't come close to the force of the resulting steam explosion. The entire island was vaporized. All that remained was a blast crater almost a thousand feet deep in the sea floor.

"Two-hundred-foot tidal waves radiated outward from the explosion, devastating every coastline that faced the island. A hundred and sixty towns and villages were flattened, and oceangoing steamers were tossed inland like bits of driftwood. The death toll within the archipelago was incalculable. There were over thirty thousand known casualties on the island of Java alone.

"Debris from the explosion rained down on Madagascar, over on the other side of the Indian Ocean. The sound of the blast was heard as far away as Sydney, Australia, and the tidal waves were detected in the English Channel. The concussion circled the globe three times, and for three years afterwards the world's sunsets were bloodred from the volcanic dust blasted into the upper atmosphere."

"Lord a'mighty!" Stone was appalled and fascinated at the same time. "What happened next?"

"Krakatau went dormant for a while after the big blast, then returned to activity once more. The volcanic island rebuilt itself via a series of lesser eruptions and Anak Krakatau, the 'Son of Krakatoa,' rose from the sea. Today, the child bears a very strong resemblance to the parent."

"Jesus! You mean it could happen again?"

Amanda shrugged. "I gather there's no reason it couldn't."

"Uh, Skipper," Stone asked carefully, "just where is this Krakatau place anyhow?"

Amanda pointed off the *Cunningham*'s starboard bow. The reflection trail from the sinking moon silhouetted a gaunt basaltic cone rising from the center of Sunda Strait, multiple steam plumes trailing from its jagged crest.

"Right over there."

Inside the Southern Approaches to the Sunda Strait
0100 Hours, Zone Time: August 11, 2008

Javanese *dangdut* pop music flowed from the speaker of the cheap tape player, the softly wailing vocal counterpointing the heavy drum rhythm. The only other sound in the night was the thump and creak of the rafted motor launches as they butted together in the low swells. Aboard the small craft, the members of the Bugis raider party each found his own way of working off his pre-assault tensions.

The younger men checked and rechecked their weapons, jacking actions open and shut, thumbing clip-spring tensions, and giving knife edges a final unneeded honing. The older men, the veterans, their arms long before made ready, sat in the darkness puffing clove *kretek* cigarettes. Some studied the distant city skyglow over Balembeng on the southern tip of Sumatra, remembering past raids and past glories. Others lay across the boat thwarts and gazed up at the mariner's stars as their ancestors had done for a thousand years.

Hayam Mangkurat, the raid leader and prizemaster, sat in the stern of the lead boat and lifted a set of powerful Korean-made binoculars to his eyes and studied the running lights of the approaching freighter.

This one was nervous. It had veered sharply to the westward upon exiting from the Selat Sunda, leaving the standard shipping lanes. It was steaming hard now, hastening for the safety of the open ocean.

This captain had evaded interception twice before using these tactics, but now he had used them once too often. The eyes of the *raja samudra* were wide. Before Mangkurat's clan had sailed on this raid, the sea king's agents had whispered to them not only secrets of the freighter's cargo but of the course it would sail and where best the strike could be made.

Carefully, Mangkurat set the binoculars aside. After a lifetime at sea and a quarter century of raiding, his night vision was still keen and his sailor's judgment still solid. Still, it was easier to use the binoculars.

Much else was easier since the coming of the *raja samudra*. When he have sailed as a boy on his first raid, Mangkurat had carried nothing but a salt-rusted parang. Now there was a powerful new automatic pistol at his belt. There were new engines for the boats as well, and radios to link them together. There was food and medicine and other such luxuries for the village and money to buy peace from the *polisi* and military and respect from the Javanese politicians.

Most importantly, there was knowledge. Knowledge of which big ships have cargo worth claiming, and of where it could be sold for a decent profit. The sea king took his share, but the share was just for the return.

Mangkurat lifted the night glasses again. The target was holding its course and standing in closer steadily. He could make out the flash of white foam at the base of its cutwater now.

Could anything be gained by waiting further? No, it was time.

"Ayo!"

The play of the *dangdut* terminated abruptly. Mooring lines were cast off and the boats were shoved apart. Canvas covers were peeled back from the machine guns in the bows, and cartridge belts gleamed brassily. Electric starters whined and the primed and pre-warmed outboard engines snarled to life.

They stood in her dreams as they often did when action was in the offing: Erikson, Chief Tehoa, Snowy Banks, Fry Guy, Danno, the Marines from the decks of the *Bajara*. Telling her that another reckoning loomed. Speaking no recrimination, but reminding her of the price to be paid. Always reminding her . . .

Amanda's eyes opened and she looked into the blue-lit dimness of the cramped two-berth cabin. There was a momentary disorientation. She was back aboard the Duke, but these weren't her quarters.

Full recall came swiftly. She was an outsider aboard the *Cunningham* now, and the captain's suite belonged to Ken Hiro. After a long evening's wait for action, she had gone below to the transients' quarters assigned to her for a few hours of sleep.

Yet, what had brought her awake? What was happening with the ship? Maybe the Duke was no longer her personal command, but she still knew the feel of the cruiser down to the last pump resonance and plate vibration. Reaching down from her bunk, Amanda pressed her hand flat against the deck.

The power rooms were spooling up. The cruiser had gone to all ahead full and was coming hard about. Amanda could feel the lean of the hull. She was out of her berth and pulling on her slacks as the call to general quarters sounded.

"Battle stations, Aviation! All hands, stand by to launch aircraft! All aircrews and aircraft handling details lay to, on the double! Marine boarding detail, stand by to embark! All stations expedite! This is not a drill! I say again, this is not a drill!"

The cabin phone buzzed and Amanda snatched it from its cradle. "Go, Ken." She didn't have to ask who would be on the other end of the circuit.

"We've got one, Captain. The Russian RO/RO *Piskov* is

reporting she is under pirate attack and is being boarded at this time. She is requesting assistance."

"Whereaway?"

"In the Sunda approaches, fifty-four miles southwest of our current position. The *Piskov* reports she is taking fire from four Boghammer-type gunboats. As per the plan of engagement, we have gone to flank speed and are closing the range. Gunships and boarding helos are prepping to launch. Do you have further orders at this time, ma'am?"

"Very good, Captain Hiro." Amanda wedged the phone between her head and shoulder as she fumbled the buttons of her shirt closed. "Contact Global Hawk control and have them commence an expanding concentric search around the *Piskov*'s location. Those Bogs probably have a mother ship nearby. I want it spotted and tracked. Also, jam the *Piskov*'s distress call."

"Say again, ma'am?"

"You heard me, Ken. Jam the Russians' transmissions. Broad spectrum and full power. Take down all communications in this area. I don't want anyone else showing up for the party."

"Very good, ma'am."

"And notify Commander Richardson he'll be having a ride-along."

"Aye, aye."

She slammed the phone back into its cradle and reached for the equipment racked up beside the cabin door. First the pistol belt with its Navy Mark 4 survival knife, its clip pouches and the obsolete leather holster carrying the MEU Model .45 automatic. Then the Model 1-C combined flotation and flak vest, studded with survival gear. A touch at her throat made sure her dogtags were in place, and she was ready to face the night.

Topside, a warm gale whipped across the *Cunningham*'s decks as she gained way, the sea roaring in her wake as it boiled under the thrust of her hard-driving propellers.

On the helipad, aviation hands peeled the RAM shrouds

back from the two pre-spotted Seawolf Hueys. Rotors deployed for flight and dim blue-green instrument lights snapped on as flight crews raced through preflight checklists.

"Crank!" A voice yelled the single warning word through a cockpit window and the first turbine lit off.

"Hey, Skipper!" Over the rising clamor on deck, Amanda heard the shout. Stone loomed at her side, his considerable size enhanced by body armor and a load of personal electronics and ammunition. "The boarding party's loading down in the hangar now and the lift bird'll go on the elevator the second you guys clear the pad. We'll be five minutes behind ya!"

"Right. We'll fade back and let you close to two minutes' separation. Hear that, Cobra?"

"Two minutes." A third tall figure in a flight suit and helmet stood out of the shadows. "Got it."

"Just like in the planning sessions, gentlemen. The first pass drives off or destroys the pirate craft and traps the boarders on the ship. Second pass suppresses the deck and clears the way for our counter-boarders. Then we clean up the leftovers. Let's all remember the purpose of this exercise is hard intel and prisoners."

"Aye, aye!"

"This is our first fight of a new campaign. Good luck to us all!"

She lifted her hands palm out and received a matching pair of stinging high fives in return.

Quillain disappeared back into the superstructure while Amanda followed Richardson to the waiting Wolf One. As she climbed into the cabin and settled in the jumpseat behind the pilots, the crew chief passed her a flight helmet. Donning it, she jacked the combination power and intercom lead into the overhead connectors, testing both the integral headset and night-vision visor.

Wolf One's pair of armor-clad door gunners were the last crewmen aboard. With their heads grotesque in Head's-Up-Display targeting helmets and their bodies asymmetrically distorted by the MX-214 miniguns they lugged at their hips, they resembled the grim special-effects creations of some science-fiction filmmaker.

The reality was as strange as any fiction, however. These men were cyborg warriors, literally a physical merging of man and gun into a single weapons system.

One of the lessons learned during the long years of helicopter warfare in Vietnam had been that no fixed aircraft gun mount was as fast or as flexible to use as a weapon directly wielded by a human. Accordingly, the veteran airmobile gunners of that conflict learned to strap their machine guns to their bodies with a carrying harness, making themselves living gun mounts.

The Seawolves remembered the lesson.

Stiffly the door gunners lifted themselves into the bench seats that faced outward through the side hatches. Their monkey-harness straps were locked into overhead hardpoints, and feeder tracks connected the miniguns to the ammunition magazines built into the cabin roof. Powerlinks clicked home—intercom, laser sight, Helmet Mounted Display, gun drive. Systems cycled through checkout mode. Fighting men and fighting aircraft became one entity.

Amanda found the sequence a little chilling.

Flickering rotors occulted the stars, and Wolf One trembled on her skids. Cobra Richardson twisted around in the command pilot's seat, his rakish Errol Flynn mustache a dark smear across his paler features in the dim light. "Flight ready to launch, Captain. ETA over target approximately twenty minutes."

Lieutenant Commander Richard "Cobra" Richardson was a unique individual. Formerly of the Coast Guard's elite Caribbean-based drug interdiction gunship squadron, he had service-transferred to the Navy and to the Seawolves. His motivation had been the same as when he had previously made the jump from the U.S. Air Force's Air Commando Wing to the Coasties: an unending hunger to go where the action was.

Vince Arkady had recommended Richardson to Amanda.

"Cobra is made for your outfit, babe. He's a solid leader. He can fly any helo you can name right out to the limits, and he loves to operate. You'll just have to live with the fact that he's also just a little bit crazy."

Amanda smiled to herself. *Coming from you, Arkady, that's high praise indeed.*

"Get us in the air, Cobra," she said aloud.

"Aye, aye. *Cunningham* AIRBOSS, this is Wolf One. Executing departure now. Wolf Two, follow me out."

The tremble grew into a chest-deep vibration as the collective came back and the rotors caught air. Wolf One gingerly eased off the deck on the lift cushion of ground effect, the tight spotting on the cruiser's small helipad giving Cobra and his copilot barely an arm's span of clearance between their rotor tips and those of Wolf Two. Cobra coaxed the Super Huey into a hover, station keeping and bobbling slightly in the ship's slipstream, then he sheered away sharply. As they cleared the cruiser's deck and lost the ground-effect lift boost, the heavily laden helicopter fell out of the sky.

Amanda had been warned about this move, but her stomach still knotted through the dive and swoop almost to the wave crests as Cobra deftly exchanged his few feet of altitude for forward flight speed.

"No problems, ma'am," he commented without bothering to look back over his shoulder.

"I'll take your word for it, Commander." Twisting in her jump seat, Amanda looked aft out the open side door. Wolf Two had already tailed them into the air and now was jockeyed into formation. Flying without running lights, the gunship was a shadow against black velvet, only the faint, glowing smear of its cockpit instrumentation marking its position.

Farther away astern, the *Cunningham* was momentarily outlined against the shimmering path of the setting moon; then she, too, was taken by the darkness. With their engines shrieking at full war power, the Seawolves put their noses down and loped into the night.

                          • • •

Another aircraft reacted to the emergency as well.

From where she circled at sixty thousand feet, the islands of the Indonesian archipelago were black velvet patches against a pewter sea, spangled with the glittering sparks of towns and villages. Global Hawk Teal-Niner was ten hours into her mission profile with another eight to go before her relief bird came in from Australia.

With her turbofan throttled back to minimum cruise, the recon drone had been lazing in a wide racetrack pattern over southern Sumatra and western Java, waiting for a reaction command. So the time on station would not be a waste, her programmers had instructed her to conduct a series of secondary missions while loitering. She had monitored maritime traffic patterns, conducted infrared and low-light scans of some of the more isolated island groups in the area, and maintained a signal intelligence sweep for unusual radio traffic. Nothing particularly challenging for Teal-Niner's onboard artificial intelligences.

As the data had been acquired, it had been encrypted, packaged for microburst transmission, and fired off through a MILSTAR communications link to Curtin Base and to the drone's secondary control node aboard the USS *Carlson*.

So far, nothing of exceptional import had been noted. Intermittently, the Global Hawk would be painted by Indonesian air defense radar, but this was not a matter of undue concern. The Indonesians had nothing that could reach her altitude, and at most, the stealthy drone was a faint, intermittent ghost at the extreme limits of their detection capacity, an easily disregarded UFO.

Abruptly, a command channel opened over the MILSTAR link, a distant human systems operator overriding the autonomous onboard computer. Spooling up to fast cruise, the drone broke away from its preplotted course and swooped toward a new objective. In its belly, sensor and camera turrets swiveled and panned downward, zooming in on a tiny cluster of lights isolated on the sea far below.

                          • • •

"Ah, be advised, TACBOSS, Seawolf Lead, and Dragon 6, this is Raven's Roost. We have a situational update. Stand by to copy." The intel officer's voice sounded in Cobra Richardson's earphones, tersely clipping off the data.

"Target ship is Russian motor vessel *Piskov,* twenty-four thousand tons displacement, six hundred and ten feet in length. She is a Finnish-built roll-on/roll-off trailer carrier....Outbound from Vladivostok to Haifa, Naples, and Marseilles. All cargo decks loaded. Stern offside ramp, starboard side...high deckhouse aft...short mast at break of forecastle....Midships decks are clear except for a double row of ventilator housings....Vessel is dead in the water, but illuminated.

"We can see approximately eight armed hostiles topside....The crew is apparently being held below-decks....We have three Boghammers tied up alongside, starboard side aft....A fourth Bog is holding off the stern....Heaviest weapons apparent are assault rifles and light machine guns."

Richardson found himself grinning in an appropriately wolfish manner. It would be a challenging tactical setup, but a fair first bag.

Amanda Garrett, leaning forward between the pilots' seats, must have read his mind. "Remember, Cobra," she warned, "I want pieces to pick up afterwards."

He glanced across his shoulder at her. "Three out of four adequate?"

"I can live with that."

"Got it covered, then."

"And not too many holes in the Russian," she added. "I need her seaworthy."

Cobra shot another glance down his shoulder. "You do enjoy doing things the hard way, don't you, ma'am?"

She gave a wry grin. "If you wanted things easy, you could have stayed with the Air Commandos." Reaching up, she toggled her lip mike from Intercom to Radio. "Dragon 6, are you back there?"

"Roger that, Skipper," Stone Quillain's radio-filtered reply came back. "We got you on our FLIRS. We're about two miles astern of you."

"What do you think of the setup?"

"Sounds like we'll have to fastrope aboard. We're going to need a weatherdeck saturation with gas and flashbangs, then we'll go in amidships. Kinda tricky, but I think we can swing it okay. The big thing is fire suppression when the lift ship is in hover, especially from the freighter's deckhouse and bridge. We'll need the bad guys kept off of us for about thirty seconds."

Richardson thumbed the Transmit button on the end of his collective lever. "Consider that the least of your problems, buddy. The Wolves will be present and accounted for."

"Roger that. 'Preciate ya."

Amanda keyed her lip mike again. "Sounds like we have a plan, gentlemen. Raven's Roost, this is TACBOSS. Do you have any other suspicious surface traffic in the area?"

"Acknowledged, TACBOSS. We have what look like a pair of good-sized Bugis schooners loitering about eight miles astern of the *Piskov*. There's a high probability these are your pirate mother ships."

"I concur. They're holding off until the boarding parties have the target secure, then they'll close to take aboard the loot. Stay on those mother ships, Raven's Roost. They are your new top priorities. I want to know where they head after we intervene at the *Piskov*."

"We're not taking them down too, ma'am?" Richardson inquired.

Amanda shook her helmeted head. "Not this time, Co. I want the mother ships to run home to Papa."

"Ah, nuts."

At that moment, Wolf One's copilot lifted a hand and pointed beyond the windscreen. "Lights on the horizon. Bearing zero off the bow!"

Amanda glanced down at the Active GPU display, then she flipped down her nite-brite visor for a fast visual verification. "That's it. Target in sight. All strike elements, guns clear! Gentlemen, the show is yours!"

"You heard the lady. Wolf Two, heat 'em up. We're going downtown."

Cobra felt Wolf One bobble slightly as internal weight shifted. In his sideview mirrors, he saw his door gunners step out onto the small metal grid platforms mounted outside of the Huey's doors. Supported only by their monkey harnesses, they hunkered against the hurricane blast of the slipstream, targeting visors down and miniguns braced.

Ahead, the lights of the *Piskov* drew closer.

On the decks of the big Russian freighter, the pirate deck watch paced slowly, assault rifles slung. They were not lax, but they were relaxed. The difficult part of the night's work was over. The rest should be an often-practiced routine.

The boarding had gone well. A few bursts of machine-gun fire at the bridge had coerced the crew into stopping their engines. The Russian seamen had been herded into their quarters and safely locked away. Prizemaster Mangkurat and his cargo handlers were already below on the vehicle decks, prying open the locks on the trailers listed in his orders. Soon it would be time to call up the *pinisi* for loading. By the dawn, they would be sailing for home with wealth packed in their holds.

More than one man smiled at the thought of joyous families to greet, of young women to impress, of gifts to bestow.

And then came the thudding drone from out of the darkness, growing in intensity.

Cigarettes were flicked onto the deck. Rifles slid off of shoulders. Bolts ratcheted back. Dark seamen's eyes narrowed, seeking to pierce the wall of darkness beyond the freighter's deck lights.

There shouldn't be any threat or danger out there in the night. The *raja samudra* had promised it would be so.

Cobra keyed his lip mike. "Wolf Two, this is Wolf Lead. That one Bog trailing astern of the *Piskov* is yours. Kill him with a Hellfire. I'm taking the guys alongside. I will engage, overfly the freighter, then break left. You break right, cross behind me, and come down the freighter's starboard flank. Clean up anything I might miss."

"Roger D."

The Super Huey shuddered in its shallow dive, redlining just below rotor stall. The *Piskov* was no longer a glowing constellation on the horizon. Now she showed herself as a gaunt, long-lined freighter, outlined in the glare of her deck arc lights.

"Vajo," Richardson barked. "You got the twenty-five. Load lethal and arm for proximity airburst."

Wolf One's copilot lifted a hand to the overhead ordnance panel, calling up one of the two turret magazines for the grenade launcher and setting the system configurations. A computer graphics cartwheel sight materialized in front of his eyes, projected on the visor of his Helmets Up display.

As his head turned and his point of vision shifted, the chin turret indexed, the muzzle of the Crew Served Objective Weapon tracking on the death pip in the center of the helmet sight. The copilot stared at his target, his thumb flipping the combination safety guard and arming switch open on his pitch lever.

"Turret up! Proximity set! I got arming tone!"

"Acknowledged. Ten to range."

"This is Wolf Two," a voice interjected over the radio. "We are opening fire!"

Blue-orange flame glared from beyond the windscreen. A navalized Hellfire missile slid away from beneath one of Wolf Two's snub wings. Blazing toward the pirate gunboat loitering astern of the freighter, the hundred-pound PGM bobbled along the path pointed by its guidance laser.

The targeted Boghammer dissolved in a pulse of flame and spray. The fight was on.

A tracer stream arced up from alongside the Russian ship, a second and a third following as the pirate gunners engaged the airborne threat. Additional muzzle flashes sparked and danced along the freighter's rails as the boarding party joined the battle. For the moment, there wasn't much that could be done about the deckside riflemen, but it was definitely time to deal with those gunboats.

"We got range! Burn 'em!" Richardson roared.

The OCSW jackhammered, spewing high-velocity 25mm grenades. As each round was fired, the inductance coil wrapped around the barrel of the OCSW armed and programmed the proximity fuses of the deadly little projectiles for antipersonnel airburst.

The fire stream reached out for the row of moored Boghammers but didn't quite touch them. The grenades detonated a few feet short of their target, each round producing a focused blast of shrapnel. Holding down the trigger button, the copilot ran his eyes over the trio of pirate craft, brushing the life away with a whisk broom of high-velocity fragmentation.

Amanda saw the airbursts dance like popping flashbulbs above the gunboats. She also noted the shimmer of moonlit wavetops beneath the helo's skids. Trapped hair follicles ached under her helmet as she realized the racing aircraft was sinking below the level of the *Piskov*'s deck, the freighter's steel flank looming like a cliff before them.

"Cobra?" The cry was a half-strangled one.

The pitch and collective levers slammed back. Wolf One gathered herself and sprang like a Thoroughbred leaping a fence, a skid heel tracing a line across the sea for a split second.

For another split second, a stunned Bugis pirate looked in through the side hatch as the helicopter screamed across the *Piskov*'s deck between the deckhouse and the foremast.

Amanda's hands locked onto the jump-seat frame as the gunship flared up and over into an incredibly steep banking turn. All that could be seen outside of the left-hand door was the moonlit surface of the ocean. The door gunner, still standing on his platform outside of the aircraft, hung casually from his safety harness with the sangfroid of a commuter waiting at a bus stop.

With the *Piskov*'s superstructure deftly positioned to block the fire of the pirate deck gunners, the Super Huey snapped level again, racing away into the night.

"Did you say something back there, ma'am?" Cobra Richardson inquired, glancing back over his shoulder.

"Nothing important," Amanda replied, trying to make her aching fingers release their grip.

With his eyes and face shielded by his gas mask, Stone Quillain gripped a safety strap and leaned out of the open side door of the HH-60 Oceanhawk transport helicopter. As he studied the approaching objective, Amanda Garrett spoke through the tiny inductance speaker taped behind his ear.

"Dragon 6, we are positioning for deck suppression run. State your position."

"Ninety seconds out and inbound," he replied into his throat mike, his words relaying via the PRC 6725 Leprechaun transceiver clipped to his chest harness. "Looking good."

"I concur. It's your show now, Stone. Secure the ship and crew and get me prisoners!"

"Copy, Skipper. Lord a'mighty woman, I heard you the first time." Stone was careful to murmur the second phrase only after lifting his thumb off the Transmit key. Stone might have his doubts about some of this newfangled, non-lethal warfare gear they'd be using, but he could understand the need for human intelligence.

Rocking his thumb across the communications touch pad, he toggled over to the cigarette-pack–sized AN/PRC 6725F squad tactical radio clipped to the side of his helmet. "On final. Lock and load!"

Within the darkened fuselage of the helicopter, well-drilled hands fingered magazines out of harness pouches, socking them home into magazine wells, two per weapon. As did Stone himself, all members of the fifteen-man Marine Force Recon platoon carried the new Selectable Assault Battle Rifles.

Stone wasn't sure yet about all of the gee-whiz electronic gadgetry built into the new weapons, such as the laser-ranged proximity fusing system or the Heads Up display sighting link with their night vision visors. But Lord, he could sure appreciate the firepower.

The SABR was a composite weapons system, like the

old M-16 assault rifle/M-203 grenade launcher pairing. It mated two superb Heckler & Koch designs, the G-36 assault rifle and a 20mm grenade launcher variant of the CAWS semiautomatic combat shotgun, into a single, lethal whole.

The SABRs were perfect for the kind of work to come. All sorts of useful things could be fired out of those 20mm tubes beyond mere high explosives.

Leaning out of the open side hatch again, Stone refreshed his situational awareness. Shattered and half-sunken, the pirate gunboats trailed alongside the freighter on their mooring lines, their weapons silenced and their crews dead. The Bugis boarding party, denied their escape route, must be frantically trying to organize a defense. Even as he looked on, the *Piskov*'s deck lights abruptly went out, plunging the vessel into darkness.

"Why, thank you kindly gentlemen," Stone chuckled. Lifting his voice, he spoke over the tactical circuit. "Platoon! Vision up!"

With his free hand, he lowered his AI2 nite-brite visor, settling it into place over the lens interface of his gas mask. The world went bright in tones of luminescent green as the visor photomultipliers boosted the star and moon glow into the equivalency of broad daylight.

Now Quillain could pick out the two Seawolf Hueys converging on the *Piskov*, making their suppression run. As they got the range the 25mm turrets began to belch once more. This time, however, the gunships were firing anti-riot munitions. Stone's night-vision visor overloaded as a flickering wave of blinding light washed over the freighter's upperworks.

Aboard the *Piskov*, havoc rained from the sky. A barrage of proximity-fused flashbang grenades burst overhead, producing an eye-piercing magnesium glare and battering waves of concussion. Most of the topside gunners were thrown to the deck, the wind knocked out of them. And when they gasped for their lost breath, they found themselves inhaling a lung-scalding mixture of military-grade

CS teargas and capsicum dust. Gas grenades had alternated with the flashbangs in the OCSW belts.

In seconds, a choking cloud of chemical vapor engulfed the Russian freighter. With their eyes swelling shut, the stunned and agonized Indonesians staggered through the haze. Retching, weeping, and cursing, they were incapable of reacting effectively to anything, even to the growing roar of rotors overhead.

The big HH-60 flared out and went to hover over the midships weather deck of the freighter.

"Stand up!"

The assault platoon rose to their feet, hunching against the curve of the helicopter's fuselage.

"Rope out!"

The helo's crew chief rolled the carefully coiled fastrope out of the hatch. With one end connected to the boom of the helicopter's winch, the other snaked freely to the deck. Stone shot a last glance downward to verify that the aircraft wasn't drifting laterally and that the end of the cable had indeed touched down forty feet below.

"Go!"

He was the first man out of the hatch. Throwing his arms and legs around the cable, he slid down it like a fireman descending a fire station pole. It was a tricky move, and a missed grip could mean trouble, but it lived up to its name: fastrope.

Stone grabbed loose and dropped the last couple of feet to the deck. Unslinging his SABR, he ducked aside, clearing the way for the next man coming down two seconds behind him. Whipping his weapon to his shoulder, he scanned for threats, both to himself and to the Oceanhawk overhead. A good chalk, well trained in fastroping, could clear a hovering liftship in thirty seconds. But in a combat zone, that could be twenty-nine seconds too long.

Stone caught movement out of the corner of his eye. The rotorblast had momentarily dispersed the haze of riot gas, and Stone spotted a figure moving out on the wing of the *Piskov*'s bridge. Instantly the Marine recognized the dangerous straightness of a rifle barrel. Not incapacitated by the gas, thanks to his position high in the superstructure, a pirate leveled an AK-47 at the station-keeping helicopter.

Stone thumbed his fire selector to Autorifle and lined up on the target, but someone else beat him to the draw.

Wolf One lifted from behind the deckhouse. Her portside door gunner had also caught the move made by the Bugis boarder, and the multiple muzzles of his minigun swung to bear on target.

A powerful helium-neon laser sight had been married to the frame of the weapon. Its beam was invisible to normal human vision, but readily apparent in the gunner's Helmet Mounted Display visor. To aim, he pointed the finger of coherent light at his target. Where the beam touched, his bullets struck.

The door gunner brushed his firing switch, and the minigun sang its death song. It wasn't a clatter or a rattle but rather a brief, piercing tone, as from a giant tuning fork. The rotating gun barrels of the miniature Gatling gun blurred, a foot-wide ball of flame dancing before them. A needle-fine beam of light, visible to the eye this time like some science-fiction blaster bolt, lanced from the heart of this fireball, linking the weapon with its target.

Indeed, this was a kind of death ray. The light marked a stream of tracer bullets. Even firing at low rate, the MX-214 delivered four hundred rounds a minute, better than six rounds of 5.56mm NATO per second.

The human frame is not designed to have congress with such a concentration of kinetic energy. The pirate did not merely die. He exploded.

The last Marine hit the *Piskov*'s deck, and the lift helo nosed down and hauled away into the safety of the night, leaving the two smaller gunships to orbit watchfully.

Breaking down into two-man rifle teams, the Force Recon platoon dispersed. Each Marine had his SABR's grenade launcher loaded with nonlethal riot munitions, but each also had thirty rounds of 5.56mm NATO on call for an instant, deadly backup.

Helium-Neon targeting lasers probed unseen through the lingering smog of tear gas. Foam-soled combat boots scuffed lightly on deck plates. Filtered American voices whispered terse progress reports over the squad radiolink. Other voices, choking and pain-wracked, cried out in Bahasa Indonesia, cursing or calling for aid.

Contact was swift in coming.

With their night-vision systems and gas masks, the Marines had the edge, a small one. A pair of SABR launchers roared, with the hollowness denoting "jellybag" rounds going out. A pirate gagged as the high-velocity blobs of dense polymer caught him in the gut and slapped him off his feet. Seconds later, the Bugis's agony was compounded as nylon "disposacuffs" bit around his wrists. Then it was eased as a spring-loaded injector fired a potent dose of fast-acting barbiturate into his buttock.

"Bravo Team Two here. Hostile secured. Portside forward."

"Roger. One down."

Two figures in the murk recognized each other as enemy at almost the same second. Almost. The one in the Marine utilities brought the over-and-under barrels of his weapon up first. The one in the sun-faded denim caught the massive jet of concentrated capsicum powder full in the face. His assault rifle clattered to the deck and he followed, incapable of doing anything except scream.

"This is Charley One. Hostile secured at forecastle break. Forecastle clear. Working aft."

"Roger."

A sharp metallic *ping* sounded as a grenade safety lever flicked clear and a thumping rattle followed as a flashbang bounced across the deck. The two Bugis crouched in the theoretical shelter of a ventilator housing goggled at the little cardboard cylinder that rolled to stop at their feet.

WHAM!

"Double header. Portside quarter."

From somewhere aft, an Uzi machine pistol cut loose, spraying the night, the wild shooting of a panicked gunner seeking to suppress his own growing fear with fire and noise. A SABR snapped back an angry three-round burst in rifle mode.

"Able Two. Boloed one at the base of the deckhouse. Sorry 'bout that. Had to do him fast."

"Shit happens, Able Two. FIDO."

The front facing of the superstructure loomed through the dissipating gas screen. Quillain went flat against it. With his back against solid steel, he paused to regain his situational awareness. Over the next few seconds, Lieutenant Brice Donovan, the force recon platoon leader, his senior sergeant, and his communications specialist all scuttled in to join Stone against the bulkhead. A few feet away a body lay sprawled on the deck, the blood soaking the dead man's ragged shirt black in the nite-brite visors. Stone and the other Marines ignored the fallen pirate. They had other, more critical points of concern.

"How are we doing, Brice?" Quillain inquired through the speaking diaphragm of his mask.

"Looking good, sir," the younger man murmured back. "Weather-deck sweep completed and all personnel hatches padlocked for'rard. All fire teams positioning to enter the superstructure."

"Good 'nuff. Able takes the bridge. Charley goes for the engine room. Bravo goes for the crew's quarters. We'll try for officers' country from this side. Let's look lively. I bet somebody's thinkin' hostage about now."

"Aye, aye."

As Donovan relayed his orders over the squad circuit, Quillain cut over to the command channel on his Leprechaun transceiver, his own transmission paired down to the stark minimum of verbiage and a maximum of information. "Dragon Six to TACBOSS. Deck secured. Prisoners taken. No blue casualties. Going inboard."

"Acknowledged, Stone. Good luck," Amanda Garrett replied, taking the two-word luxury of a human concern.

An entry hatch was set into the superstructure bulkhead two meters outboard and to starboard of their position. Stone took a second to eject the jellyround magazine from the grenade launcher of his SABR, replacing it with half a dozen loads of good old-fashioned double-ought buckshot. Unhooking a flashbang from his harness, he glanced at the platoon sergeant and nodded toward the hatch.

Ducking low to stay out of the line of sight of the inset porthole, the noncom slithered along the bulkhead to the hatch. Flipping open the locking dogs, he crouched, ready to yank the hatch open and duck back.

"All teams ready to effect entry, sir," Donovan reported.

"Okay," Quillain replied, "we go on my mark. Three... two... one... mark!"

The sergeant flung the hatch open and Stone flipped his concussion grenade inside. Four seconds later the blaze and slam of the detonation made the steel of bulkheads ring. More hollow thuds reverberated through the ship's structure as the other assault teams opened their paths into the deckhouse.

Stone and his section instantly followed the flashbang in, SABRs shouldered and leveled.

Nothing. Stone flipped up his night-vision visor. The interior lights were still on and the grilled fixtures in the narrow passageway overhead revealed chipped green paint and oil-grimy linoleum decking. The ventilator fans had apparently been cut off along with the deck work lights, so the internal atmosphere of the ship was comparatively gas free.

Directly ahead, down the passage, a metal frame ladderway extended up to the next deck. And from that level came the sound of slamming doors and angered, frightened voices.

Lifting a hand, Stone issued a series of wordless commands, swift, concise gestures that silently deployed his team. All hands pressed back tightly against the sides of the passageway. While Donovan and his R/T covered the front aspect of the ladder, Stone and the platoon sergeant slithered along the bulkheads. Staying out of the field of view of anyone peering from the deck above, they positioned behind the open structure ladder.

The wait that followed was a brief one.

"You down there!" It was impossible to tell if the speaker using the unfamiliar English words was asking a question or making an accusation.

"You down there!" The Marines made no move. No sound. Instinct whispered that lives were at stake.

Suddenly a submachine gun raved from overhead, a stream of 9mm slugs and a rain of shell casings pouring down into the passageway. Bullets whined and screamed off steel, ricochets and metal fragmentation filling the air.

The Marines held. Stone smothered a grunt as a reflected projectile caught him under the ribs, the multiple layers of Kevlar in his interceptor vest reducing the death blow to a savage punch in the guts. Down the passage, the Marine radioman staggered, then caught himself, silently forcing his weight back onto his damaged limb, blood soaking the leg of his utilities.

The rattle of the autoweapon ceased as the magazine emptied.

Not a sound in the passageway, not the shift of a boot or the hiss of a breath. The platoon sergeant slowly lifted a hand and touched a flashbang, looking at Stone questioningly. Quillain shook his head. For the next few seconds, half measures wouldn't be adequate. Stone indicated the steel sphere of a fragmentation grenade. The noncom nodded and unhooked one of the deadly little hand bombs.

The ladderway creaked. A pair of seaboots and blue serge trousers appeared, descending the steps, their wearer moving awkwardly with his hands raised, a Caucasian, a ship's officer, four tarnished gold bars on the shoulder straps of his uniform shirt.

As the Russian captain's eyes came below the level of overhead, he saw the two Marines facing the ladder, and he hesitated. The sight must have been an unnerving one. Two big men, helmeted, camouflaged, bulked out in body armor, battlefield electronics, and load-bearing harness, both with exotic weapons leveled.

Urgently, Donovan gestured for the Russian to stand on. Comprehending, the ship's officer continued his descent to the passageway deck.

Again Donovan gestured. *Get forward! Get behind us!*

The Russian obeyed. As he passed beyond the field of view from the deck above, he tapped his chest, pointed upward, and held up three emphatic fingers. *Three more friendlies!*

The first, second, and third mates of the *Piskov* followed their captain down the ladder, the last being a stocky young blonde woman. However, the next set of legs to descend was thin, barefoot, and clad in ragged dungarees, the darkness of the skin marking the non-Slavic origin.

There was the softest of clicks as the sergeant pulled the pin from his grenade.

Stone caught the gleam of an Uzi barrel tracking the last officer down. Angling the SABR upward, Quillain slid the barrels between two of the ladder steps. Aiming at the back of the pirate's knee, he squeezed the 20mm trigger, conducting a very swift and violent amputation.

The roar of the grenade launcher and the scream of the falling pirate merged. As the Bugis plummeted the rest of the way to the deck, Stone snatched for the rags of Russian he knew.

"Spetsnaz!" he bellowed. *"Amerikanski spetsnaz!"* Whipping around the ladder, he aimed upward, hosing buckshot into the faces of the other startled hostage-takers. The safety lever of the platoon sergeant's grenade clattered on the deck, and Stone heard the noncom yell out his timing count. "One . . . two . . . three!"

At "three," the noncom hurled the frag up to the next level. Both he and Stone ducked back from the shrapnel that sprayed down the ladderway.

No further sound or action came from topside. Now the Marine R/T could swear savagely and sink down to the deck, clutching at his wounded calf. The pirate lay still in a pool of scarlet at the base of the ladder. With no chance to yank him clear of the grenade pattern, the fragmentation had finished what Stone's buckshot load had started.

Donovan and his sergeant rushed the ladder, climbing swiftly to secure the upper deck, their boots leaving blood marks on the treads.

As Stone socked a fresh magazine into the grenade launcher, he found himself surrounded by the Russian ship's officers, all of who had mistaken his one warning yell for a working knowledge of the Russian tongue.

"Yeah, whatever. *Dos vedanya,* y'all. Donovan, what's going on up there?"

"Two hostiles down. Officers' country and wardroom clear," the yell came back.

Waving the Russians back, Quillain keyed his commo pad. "Ship's officers secured. All elements, report status. Charley Team, c'mon back?"

"Charley Team here. Engine room secured. No contacts. But we got open hatches into the vehicle decks"

"Roger that. Hold position and keep 'em covered. Able Team, go."

"Bridge and radio room secured. Two hostiles. One up, one down. We also have the helo carrying the intel team orbiting and requesting instructions."

"Tell 'em to hold. We still got a party going on down here. Bravo, go."

"Crew's and engineer's quarters secured. According to the chief engineer, all hands are present and accounted for. Some of them are a little roughed up, but nothing major."

"Good 'nough. We're in the starboard deckhouse passageway, forward, on the main deck. We got the captain and the mates with us. Come and collect 'em, then move the crew to the fantail and hold 'em there. Also, signal the lift ship that we need a dustoff. Private Lingerman caught one..."

Stone glanced over at the wounded Marine. The *Piskov*'s female third mate, who was actually kind of cute, now that Stone had a second to study on it, was helping Lingerman apply a first-aid pack to his leg. The R/T's eyes showed the grin he wore behind his gas mask, and he gave Stone a thumbs-up.

"...not bad, though. No rush."

"Aye, aye, Skipper. Doin' it."

Stone switched back to his Leprechaun transceiver. Dialing through the alternate command channels, he found one that would induct through the steel bulkheads surrounding him. "Dragon Six to TACBOSS. You copy?"

"TACBOSS here, Stone. Go."

"Crew secured alive and well. Prisoners taken. One man lightly wounded. Superstructure, weatherdecks, and engine room secured. I think we still got hostiles on the vehicle decks. Starting to sweep now."

"Well done, Marine. Stand on. The prizemaster will likely be with the cargo. Get him alive for me, Stone."

"I'll discuss the matter with the gentleman, ma'am, and see what he has to say about it."

The *Piskov* was, in effect, a giant seagoing parking lot. She had been specially designed to carry her cargo preloaded onto semitrailer vans and flatbeds to expedite a rapid port turnaround. The open vehicle decks within her main hull were interconnected by ramps that permitted the cargo trailers to simply be driven aboard and spotted. Hence, the ship's nomenclature of RO/RO (roll on/roll off).

Peering forward from the open personnel hatch, Stone judged that this final phase of the ship clearing was going to be hell incarnate. The vehicle deck was a long, dimly lit steel cavern, the tightly packed ranks of semi-vans providing for a multitude of hiding places and point-blank ambush points for any hostiles that might be present.

And there were hostiles present. The listening watch posted at the access hatches had reported hearing sounds of movement forward in the trailer bays. The pirate prizemaster and his team had been trapped belowdecks by the Marine onslaught. They were in there somewhere, waiting.

Stone held out a hand, and one of the members of Bravo team passed him a loud hailer. Unsnapping his gas mask, Quillain aimed the megaphone through the hatch and held down the trigger switch. "Attention! Attention! This is Captain Stone Quillain of the United States Marine Corps. We have retaken this vessel. Your boats have been destroyed and the rest of your party has been taken prisoner. All deck hatches are locked and guarded. You cannot escape. Drop your weapons and come out with your hands up. You will not be harmed. I say again: Drop your weapons and come out with your hands up. You will not be harmed."

"Think they'll listen, sir?" the Bravo team leader asked.

"Nope," Stone resealed his mask. "Not even if they can understand what I'm saying. We'll give 'em five minutes anyway."

The creeping numbers on Stone's watch proved him right.

"Well, I guess we're going to have to go hunting," Quillain said philosophically after the sixth minute had passed.

"Should we call topside for more riot gas, sir?" the Bravo team leader inquired.

Quillain shook his head. "Nope. This tub's interior and cargo are not to be contaminated with a gas concentration unless absolutely necessary. Direct orders from the Lady."

"Christ! What's she got against doing things easy?"

"Generally, that gal has her reasons. Anyway, there's still some tricks we can pull." Stone keyed his throat mike. "All Dragon elements, this is Dragon Six. Stand by to go on night vision. Bravo Lead, you there?"

"Bravo Lead here, Cap'n."

"You got anything that looks like a master power panel in that engine room?"

"There's what looks like one over in the auxiliary compartment, sir."

"Good. Then get over there and start pulling the breakers. I'll tell you when to stop."

"Aye, aye, sir. On my way."

Stone lowered his nite-brite visor, switching the unit back on. "Get set, boys," he murmured to the other four members of the fire team. "Vision up and light 'em."

Reaching up, he pinched a small gray plastic tube attached to his MOLLE harness. Even the best photomultiplier in the world required some light to function, and in moments the interior of the *Piskov* would become as dark as the lower levels of Mammoth Cave. However, the special chemical lume-sticks the Marines were activating would provide more than enough brightness to permit the AI2 systems to function.

The luminescence involved was also filtered to a portion of the spectrum not visible to the unaided human eye, but readily usable by the nite-brite systems. The lumesticks would provide both vision and an instant IFF (identification friend or foe) reference for the Marines, while giving no aid to their enemies.

The freighter's interior lighting snapped off. To an observer not equipped with night vision, things went totally black, the darkness so dense that the hand literally couldn't be seen in front of the face. The Marines, however, merely reverted to the familiar green-lit world of night vision.

"Okay, Bravo Lead, that's got it. Keep those lights out till we give you the word," Quillain murmured. "Taylor, Smitty, you take the starboard side. You other two boys come with me. Able Team, you ready to go up there?"

"This is Able," the reply whispered back from the upper vehicle deck. "We're set."

"Okay, everybody. Let's go. Slow and easy now."

They moved out.

Each step was a miniature military evolution in itself. Scan the environment for hostile activity. Plot movement. Make sure of your footing and verify there would be no random noise-producing contacts with the bulkhead to one side or the trailers on the other. Lift one boot, then ease it down again. Refresh situational awareness. Repeat.

A random current of air would make a greater disturbance in its passage.

One member of each fire team scanned the roof edge of the trailers and the shadowed gap between the trailer tops and the overhead. The other sank into a crouch, sweeping his gun barrels across the space beneath each trailer and between the axle assemblies. Whispered words over the squad link kept the search teams coordinated.

Complicating each foot of movement was the network of steel cable and nylon strap tie-downs that bound the trailers to the decking, a thousand potential trips and falls for the individual who let his focus wander even for a moment.

Slow, slow work, performed with nerves stretched piano-wire taut.

A short distance on toward the bow, Stone and his party picked up signs of the others' presence. Locks had been broken. Metal-strip customs seals had been twisted off trailer door latches, and the doors themselves stood open. At one point the looting had already begun. Plastic-wrapped bales had been offloaded from one trailer and stood stacked on the deck, ready to be carried topside. Stone's probing hand disclosed an almost ethereal softness. Siberian sable furs, a small fortune's worth.

A battered, paper-stuffed clipboard sat atop the bales. Stone collected it. Squinting through his nite-brite visor, he made out the writing on the top sheet. Numbers. Neat computer-printed listings of trailer identification numbers and bill-of-lading cargo codes.

Score! Stone unzipped his interceptor vest and stuffed the papers, clipboard and all, inside. Resecuring his armor, he gestured on.

At the forward end of the vehicle deck, a half-spiral ramp climbed to the level above. Stone ordered a halt at the last trailer tier and the team went to cover, hunkering down behind the big tire trucks.

"Team Able, report your situation," Stone breathed into his mike.

"We're at the head of the bay. We have the head of the ramp covered. No sign of hostiles."

Stone scowled inside his mask. "Same here. We got the bottom end of the ramp under observation. We've got no contact, either."

"You think we missed 'em, Cap'n?"

"Christ, I hope not. Stand by, Able. Lieutenant Donovan, you by?"

"Roger that, sir."

"You got an English-speaking Russian back there?"

"Acknowledged. I have the chief engineer with me."

"Ask him if there's any way into the bow from the vehicle decks."

Impatiently, Stone crouched in the dark, waiting for the answer.

"Negative, sir. There's a heavy anticollision bulkhead just for'rard of the vehicle decks, separating them from the bow compartments. No personnel hatches. All access to the bow spaces is downward through the forecastle.

"But," the static spattered voice continued, "he says there is a small storage compartment underneath the vehicle ramp. It's used as a cable tier for storing the trailer tie-downs."

Peering around the tire, Stone noted a single man-size hatchway centered in the curved bulkhead beneath the ramp.

"Got it, Donovan, thanks. Able Team, hold position. Charley Team, let's check this out. Point men, go to port of that hatch on the forward bulkhead. I'll go to starboard. Cover men, cover us. Go!"

The three Marines rushed silently across the gap to the forward bulkhead, going to ground on either side of the hatchway. Stone had just pressed his back against the rust-gritty steel plating when the hatch gapped open and he found himself eye to eye with an Indonesian pirate at a range of barely three feet.

Instinct screamed to whip the SABR up for a snapshot. Discipline froze every muscle in place and seized up Stone's breathing.

Quillain realized that he and the Bugis raider were living in two different dimensions. Thanks to his night-vision system, Stone's world was as brightly lit as a summer twilight. The pirate stared out into a pitch darkness as deep as any night could ever be.

Unmoving, unblinking, Stone stared into the face of the Asian, a gaunt, scarred face with high cheekbones and a cruel twist to the thin mouth. Tracking downward, Stone could also make out the short sleeve of a worn cotton shirt, a thin, wire-muscled arm, and a gnarled fist clinched around the grip of a Beretta automatic. The Bugis's head was tilted, listening intently, responding to some trace of sound.

After possibly a century, the face withdrew and the hatch closed again.

Stone let his breath trickle out from between his clinched teeth. Enemy found and fixed. Now to finish them.

Lifting a hand, he waved the two cover men over to his side of the door. Touching one of the flashbangs attached to his harness, he held up two fingers in a V. Both men unclipped concussion grenades from their harnesses.

To the Marines across the hatch from his position, he made a hand gesture like the closing of a book and received responding nods.

In most military or quasimilitary organizations, the carrying of a pistol frequently denoted a position of authority or advanced rank. Stone theorized that the pistol carrier on the other side of the hatch was probably the leader of the pirate boarding party and the owner of the clipboard stowed inside his vest. If so, he was the prizemaster so intensely desired by Amanda Garrett. Stone staked the man out for his personal attention.

Quillain lifted his fist and pumped it once as an action notification. Then, shifting his SABR to his left hand, he reached down and tapped the butt sharply on the deck, just once.

Slowly, the hatch creaked open again.

For the Indonesian, it must have been a startling experience to have a hand lance out of the darkness to engulf his shirtfront. With an explosive heave, Stone yanked the pirate out of the hatchway. Hurling him sprawling to the deck, Quillain bellowed, "Do it!"

Coordinated by training and instinct, the grenadiers hurled their flashbangs into the confines of the small storage compartment. Then the second rifle team slammed the hatch shut, bracing the watertight door closed with their shoulders. Two deep, reverberating booms, like cherry bombs set off in an oil drum, echoed through the vehicle decks, and white light leaked from around the hatch edges as the door tried to kick open.

Another crash and flare followed as the prizemaster fired his pistol blindly at the blackness surrounding him. Then a size-twelve Danner combat boot smashed into his face. Stars burst behind the pirate's eyes and the darkness grew even deeper.

Following the flashbang detonations, Charlie team had rushed the interior of the storeroom, meeting no resistance. "Three more down in here, Skipper," the team leader reported. "Bleeding from the ears but livin'."

"This old boy too. He didn't really need that nose all that much anyway." Stone kicked the Beretta away from the pirate's flaccid hand. Rolling the man over with the toe of his boot, Stone knelt and applied a pair of disposacuffs. With that accomplished, he keyed his throat mike. "Bravo Lead. We got the last of 'em secured. You can turn the lights back on. The show's over."

With a riding-on-rails meticulousness, Cobra Richardson eased the Super Huey in over the *Piskov*'s amidships deck. Setting a single landing skid atop a ventilator housing, he held a stable hover.

Giving a farewell wave to the helo crew, Amanda hopped down to the top of the housing, then made the longer leap to the wet decks of the Russian freighter. The RO/RO's bos'n already had a work party sluicing the riot gas residue from the decks with a saltwater hose.

Amanda was pleased to see that. The *Piskov* was rapidly becoming a functional ship again.

Cobra's helicopter lifted and thundered away toward the cluster of deck lights standing off the freighter's bow. The *Cunningham* had arrived on scene a few minutes before. The big cruiser now loitered warily, ready to intercept and warn off any other inquisitive vessel that might approach.

Beyond the Russian work details, Amanda's own people were busy beneath the deck lights as well. Armed Marines encircled the band of captured pirates. The Bugis, drug groggy and sullen, squatted on the deck, their wrists bound behind them. Pharmacist's mates treated the wounded while intelligence section personnel searched for documents and personal papers. Another intelligence team worked stacking captured weapons and ammunition, identifying armament types and manufacturers, and recording serial numbers.

A third raven team worked from the *Cunningham*'s Rigid Inflatable Boats, examining the semisubmerged wrecks of the pirate launches moored alongside the freighter.

Amanda armed off her flight helmet and shook out her hair. So far, so good. With a little luck, they could be out of here before first light. Looking around, she noted a familiar figure striding toward her across the deck.

"Well done, Stone. Exceptionally well done."

The Marine shrugged. "Oh, pretty fair for make-it-up-as-you-go-along. We got you your prisoners, including the guy I guess is the prizemaster. He hasn't admitted the point yet, though. He hasn't said much of anything except to cuss us out in Sanskrit or whatever."

"We'll worry about that later. Are you ready to transfer them to the Duke?"

"Soon as the corpsmen are done. We'll sling lift the stretcher cases over by helo first, then move the unwounded."

"Okay. Sling lift all of them by helicopter, even if it takes a little extra time." Amanda started aft toward the deckhouse, Stone keeping at her side. "These Bugis are born seamen. If you even let them near a small boat, they may try something. On the other hand, helicopters are a bit outside of their experience. Dangling them underneath one on a cable should keep them spooked and amenable."

"Will do, Skipper. Anything else?"

"Yes, status of the freighter and its crew."

"Pretty much good. The Russkies have a few bangs and bruises, but they seem to be a pretty rough-and-ready bunch. They already have their bridge and engine room watches reset. The ship's in good shape too. No apparent engineering or navigational casualties and no water coming in. Most of the damage seems to be of the chipped-paint and busted-glass kind."

"Very good indeed. Where's her captain?"

"In his cabin, Skipper. He's looking forward to talking with you."

"That's good. I need to talk with him."

Captain Teodore Petreskovitch looked the way a Russian freighter captain should, stocky and bearlike with grizzled, gray-frosted hair and beard. Clad in blue uniform trousers and a sweat-stained white shirt, he reached across his battered desk to pour three fingers of a clear liquid into the water glass set before Amanda.

"Israeli vodka," he said sadly, taking care with his English. "Muck from my last voyage, but I have no better. I thank you, Captain, for the saving of my ship and cargo."

Amanda nodded and diplomatically lifted the glass to her lips, suppressing the wince as the liquid fire burned down her throat. "Speaking on behalf of the United States Navy, we're pleased we could help. I'm glad none of your crew were seriously injured in this event."

"As am I." Captain Petreskovitch casually tossed off his own drink. "In the merchant ships, we hear more and more of the pirates returning. You come through these waters, you know sooner or later you will have no luck. These damn monkeys will come for you."

"How did it happen?" Amanda was careful to keep her glass cradled in her hands to evade a refill.

The Russian shrugged. "One minute, nothing. The next, the damn little boats are all around us, shooting across the bow with machine guns and the rockets for killing tanks. We can do nothing except stop the engines. The owners will not let us carry guns. We have nothing to fight with except the deck hoses. We can only call for help by radio and watch them crawl over the rails.

"But then our luck returns and a most attractive American *devushka*, a lady, comes racing to our assistance." Israeli vodka or not, Petreskovitch poured himself another hefty hit from the bottle. "If there could be any way we might pay you back for your rescue, only ask."

"Actually, Captain, there is," Amanda replied carefully. "You see, my ship and I were not in these waters by coincidence. The decision has been made by higher powers to do something about the pirate threat. We're going after them, and you and your crew can be of great service to us in this matter."

Petreskovitch slapped the desktop. "Tell us what to do and it shall be done."

"Essentially, what we wish you to do is nothing." Amanda leaned forward in her chair. "Your ship is seaworthy and your crew is intact. We wish for you to get under way and continue on your voyage as if none of this had ever happened. Say nothing to anyone, not even your owners, until after you have returned to your home port. If you are contacted by the authorities concerning the distress call you sent, deny it: Say it was a hoax by someone. If there are problems about your broken cargo seals, have your agents speak with the United States embassy. Beyond that, say nothing to anyone."

A smile appeared in the midst of Petreskovitch's beard. "Ah," he nodded, "a *konspiratsia*. Russians understand such things. You have my word. We will deny this. It has not happened."

"Will you make this clear to your crew? Sailors love to talk in port, and our enemies may have ears anywhere."

"My crew is Russian as well," Petreskovitch said grimly. "They will know that if one word is said out of place, its speaker will swim back to Vladivostok."

The freighter skipper reached for the vodka once

more. "Another drink, Captain. To seal this pact of silence."

Amanda managed a polite smile and held up her glass.

Of the tourist and resort complexes that belt the southern coast of Bali, Nusa Dua is the most beautiful, the most upscale, and the most isolated from reality. Located four miles south of the mouth of Benoa Harbor on the Bukit Badung Peninsula, Nusa Dua lacks both the middle-class conviviality of Sanue Beach and the yeasty, surfers' boisterousness of Kuta Bay. Rather it is a place of peace, dignity, and wealth. Its dozen or so luxury hotels, none built taller than the palm trees that shaded them, as per Balinese custom, faced pristine white sand and glistening azure waters with the hawkers and overt kitsch of Bali's tourism invasion kept strictly at bay.

Here, too, were the business headquarters of Makara Limited, an ultramodern crescent of golden-tinted glass built on beach frontage worth one million dollars per linear meter. Harconan had little interest in its current worth. His father's family had purchased the land from the local raja in the sixteenth century for fifty muskets and an Amsterdam music box.

The signing of the Von Falken shipping contracts marched through the series of polite formalities mandated by corporate protocol in the conference room on the upper floor. Introductions were made, hands shaken, and coffee and light refreshments served in the lounge off the master conference room.

Makara Harconan and the Von Falken Far Eastern representatives wore the light, tailored safari outfits that were the uniform of choice for the archipelago businessman. The senior company officials from Hamburg, however, sweated in their conservative banker's suits, the dark clothing looking hot in the tropic sunlight pouring in through the glass wall that faced the sea.

Harconan aimed a wordless glance at an aide hovering unobtrusively at the perimeter of the meeting. Within moments, powered blinds purred down and angled, blocking the solar glare, and the faint whispering rumble of the air-conditioning deepened.

Polite compliments were offered about the Harconan business complex, and deprecating replies made. Hopes were expressed for a long and profitable joint venture between the two companies, and the thought was mechanically seconded by all present.

Makara Harconan maintained his expression of polite neutrality through it all, speaking the appropriate words, smiling the appropriate smiles, and concealing his boredom. He took no pleasure in these formalities, as ritualized in their way as a Ramayana ballet. This prize had already been pocketed. The challenge had been in seeking out the potentials of the deal and winning them on his terms. The mere documentation was something to be hurried through, freeing him to deal with more critical matters.

Tuning out the traveler's tale being told in labored English by the Von Falken vice president, Harconan's gaze crept back toward the narrow strips of dazzling blue that peeked through slatted blinds. Within days, the American Sea Fighter Task Force would be standing in to Benoa Harbor, figuratively under the guns of his stronghold, and his greatest challenge to date would begin.

Captain Amanda Lee Garrett of the United States Navy. What might he expect of her?

Over the past week, his corporate intelligence group had collected a dossier on her, a most impressive document that Harconan had studied assiduously.

Amanda Garrett appeared to be the epitome of the modern American "liberated woman," successfully assaulting a previously all-male bastion while earning the respect of her masculine peers. The daughter of an admiral and the heiress of an old Navy family, she had apparently bred true like an Arabian war mare, earning both her rank and a matching pair of Navy Crosses in combat. An objective assessment of her career indicated she was highly intelligent, extremely adaptive, and somewhat unconventional in her approaches to sea warfare. She was also apparently fearless on both the military and political battlefields.

This woman could be very dangerous, possibly one of the few truly dangerous individuals to challenge Harconan on his own ground in recent times. Was that why he also found the thought of her... stimulating?

Harconan snapped back to the moment and mouthed an appropriate platitude to the Von Falken VP. Detaching himself, he drifted loose across the lounge, desiring only the company of his own thoughts.

And then Mr. Lo appeared in the lounge doorway. He did not seek to speak to Harconan, nor did he send a message. The Straits Chinese merely allowed himself to be seen, then he vanished as silently as he had come.

It was enough. Harconan knew his factotum would not have made an appearance at this time unless some crisis had occurred requiring Harconan's immediate attention. Keeping his face calm, Harconan made his excuses and retired from the lounge.

Striding down the central corridor past the offices of his personal secretaries, he pressed his hand against the palm scanner that granted access to his private work suite at the southern tip of the building. Lo was the only other person to have his handprint registered with the security system. He waited within.

Harconan's personal office was a decisive contrast to the stark twenty-first-century Western modernism of the headquarters building. Teak bas-relief wall panels, hand-carved on Bali, flanked the inset bookshelves, and an ages-worn stone lion from the great Buddhist temple at Borobudur stood guard beside an antique dark oak desk brought from Holland some two centuries before.

Lo wasted no time. "We have just received word from Chief Adwar. There has been a catastrophic failure with the *Piskov* boarding operation."

The Chinese held in a stiff parade rest, a silhouette against the outer glass wall. For the perennially understated Lo to use a word like *catastrophic* underlined the urgency of the matter.

"What's the problem?"

"There rests the problem, sir: We do not know. The interception was made as per the operations plan, and the assault boats were launched. The boarding was apparently made successfully. Shortly thereafter, all communications with the boarding party was lost. The assault boats did not return, any of them. Their fate is not known."

"What about the mother ships?"

"Chief Adwar waited for the return of his attack boats until dawn, then he withdrew from the area. He reported no sign of unusual military or police activity except for some unusual flashes of light on the horizon. However, after sunrise, he observed a ship believed to be the target vessel. It was undamaged and under way, proceeding outbound for the Indian Ocean."

"What about our contacts in Jakarta? What do they have on the incident?"

"As arranged, there were no Indonesian naval forces within the immediate interception zone. A fragmentary distress call was received from the *Piskov,* indicating the vessel was under attack, then communication ceased. When the Regional Piracy Center later regained contact with the *Piskov* concerning her distress call, the vessel's master denied having made any such call and insisted all was well with his ship and that they had experienced no untoward events."

Harconan slowly crossed to his desk and leaned back against its scarred wood. "What could have happened out there, Bapak?"

"Two possibly associated events have been reported. With one, an Indonesian naval shore installation on the coast of western Java reported what was apparently intense radio jamming at the time of our boarding action. This may be the cause of our lost communications with our boarders and a clue to their fate."

"And the other?"

"The American Sea Fighter Task Force arrived in Singapore this morning—or, rather, part of it did. Our agents in Singapore initially reported that two American vessels were scheduled for replenishment at the American naval facility there. Only one, the auxiliary, made its appearance. The other vessel, the naval cruiser, did not. Its location is currently unknown."

"Damn it." Harconan let the curse escape, followed by a soft protracted hiss. Crossing his arms, he stared down at the floor, his thoughts racing. "I am a fool, Lo. I had the warning but I didn't see. *Damn it!*"

His fist smashed against the desk edge, the frustrated blow making the massive and venerable piece of furniture shudder. "The first touch of the blades and she draws our blood."

"Captain Garrett," Lo said quietly.

"Yes, Captain Garrett. She goes out of her way to politely give us her itinerary, her arrival times, exact information as to where she will be at a given date. And I'm fool enough to believe her. She's already in our waters, Lo. And she has already taken some of our people."

"There is no verification of that, sir. I have contacted our sources within both the International Piracy Center and the Indonesian government. There have been no reports filed concerning anti-piracy operations, the presence of U.S. naval vessels in Indonesian waters, or the arrest of Indonesian nationals by the United States. None of the conventions to be expected should such an event have occurred."

"Nor do I think there will be." Harconan straightened and began to pace slowly across the rich carpeting. "She has put us on notice, Lo. She does not intend to fight by convention. She will not play by the rules. This is not some politically expedient gesture being made, some flag-waving expedition. The Americans are here to destroy us."

"And how shall we respond, sir?" Lo inquired, studying his employer through impassive black eyes.

Harconan stopped pacing and gazed out toward the shimmering reach of the Badung Straits.

"We fight, Lo. Instead of letting ourselves be eaten up,

we fight. For a thousand years, these waters have, by rights, belonged to my people. Their tides flow in our heart, our spirit, our soul. It is time we remind the world of that fact—Washington, Jakarta, Singapore, even Amanda Garrett."

"Sir..." Lo hesitated for a long moment. "Initiating an overt confrontation at this time, when your greater plans are only approaching a state of readiness—do you perceive this as a... prudent course of action?"

Makara Harconan felt his lips curl into a slight, reckless smile. The multiplicity of gods who ruled these lands and waters must have sensed his hunger for new challenges. In their hunger for ironic divertissement, the deities had provided them, daring the mere mortal to react. In any such contest with the gods, a man had but two choices: to creep away in chastised humility or to draw steel and scream his defiance back to the heavens.

"No, Bapak, this is not a prudent course of action at this time. But it is the one I intend to follow."

Lo tilted his head in acknowledgment. "As long as you have recognized this, sir. What are your instructions?"

"Pass the word to all clan chiefs and support-group leaders. Until further notice, all raiding operations are to be shut down. However, all clans are to keep their fighting crews assembled and their ships ready to sail on my command. Clan resupply will continue, as will the combat training. Shift the arms and ammunition disbursements totally to our people. I want all clans up to peak fighting strength. We may need them."

"It will be done."

"Next, I want full intelligence collection on the task group: their intentions, their mode of operation, sabotage potentials. Focus on all of the vulnerabilities of the ships and their crews. Also, contact our clan leaders on Lombok and eastern Java. I want to start assembling a ground assault force here on Bali. Have them start infiltrating their best teams. Arrange for housing, funding, and equipment."

Lo nodded. "Very good, sir. A question, however, in relation to our discontinuing operations: Does that include the satellite project? The first of the foreign technical teams have arrived and are ready to proceed to the holding site. Should we abort?"

Harconan hesitated, balancing potentials. "No. Proceed with all possible speed. The sooner we can get the assessments done and the INDASAT parted out, the better. Also, contact our liaison with Morning Star separatists. I want our land security around the holding site reinforced heavily. Negotiate a suitable remuneration."

Lo frowned. "The more personnel we move into the area, the higher the probability of detection."

"It can't be helped. Garrett has stolen one march on me already. She won't steal two. I'm not running the risk of her simply popping in and walking away with this prize. If she wants it back, she must fight for it."

The Chinese inclined his head. "As you wish, sir. But might I suggest that we pre-position the *Harconan Flores* at the holding site in the event that a rapid evacuation becomes advisable."

"A good notion, Lo. Have her guns remounted as well."

"And finally, sir, might I also suggest that above and beyond our covert intelligence gathering operations against the Americans, we might bring a more overt methodology into play."

Harconan cocked his head. "How so?"

"It strikes me there might be a way to force your Captain Garrett to 'play by the rules,' sir. Covert operations within the Indonesian archipelago may prove more difficult if the American task group is kept under close surveillance by the Indonesian authorities."

Harconan snapped his fingers. "Excellent, Lo. It's time to get our money's worth on that retainer we've been paying to our dear friend Admiral Lukisan. Set up a meeting with him."

"As you wish, sir. Is there anything further at this time?"

For a few moments Harconan considered. "Yes," he said finally. "There is an old western military truism, Lo: 'Know your enemy.' To this, I would add a saying from my own people. 'To truly know your enemy, you must first look into his . . . or her, eyes.' We shall arrange for this."

In the year 1992, one of the most remarkable arms sales in history took place.

Following the collapse of the USSR and the reunification of Germany, the united German government inherited a massive stock of Soviet and Warsaw Pact armaments from the former East Germany. Urgently needing funds to help refurbish its prostrate ex-Communist eastern territories, Germany placed these unneeded weapons on the world market.

Indonesia, in turn, urgently needed seapower to defend and bind together its scattered archipelago territories. Taking advantage of this mammoth national garage sale, they purchased almost the entire East German navy, lock, stock, and barrel.

The Parchim-class frigate Wolf One, now orbited, had been part of that bulk buy of military might. Much had been changed, though, since the angular 250-foot warship had cruised the chill waters of the Baltic. Leaning out of the helicopter's side hatch, Amanda studied the modifications made to the frigate's weapons package with an intent, professional eye.

The old 30mm point defense mount and the two twelve-tube RBU antisubmarine mortars were gone from the forward gun deck, replaced by a Bofors modular 57mm cannon and by the angled launch cells of a quartet of Exocet antishipping missiles.

Triple sets of Bofors Type 43 torpedo tubes were carried amidships, while back aft, the old Russian Twin 57 and the SA-6 Grail launcher had been replaced by a second modular Swedish autocannon and a French Mistral SAM quad mount.

Jane's also indicated new Korean medium-speed diesels in the Parchim's engine room, and a full Japanese electronics refit. Over its series of rebuilds and updates, this old

Warsaw Pact subchaser had evolved into a fairly nasty little surface warfare platform, one that was paying far too much attention to Amanda's task force flagship for comfort.

Following the *Piskov* incident, the Duke had gone evasive, running first south and then east down the length of Java. Another night and day had been spent lurking off the Lombok and Atla straits on the off chance that one last pirate raider might not have gotten the word.

When one had obliged, CLA 79 had slipped through into the Java Sea and made herself apparent to the world once more, dropping her stealth and EMCON shields. Turning west again, she steamed to rejoin the *Carlson,* en route eastbound from Singapore.

Two hours prior, with Amanda Garrett onboard and with extended-range ferry tanks clipped to her hardpoints, Wolf One had departed the *Cunningham* to make an early rendezvous with the Sea Fighter base ship.

Upon arrival at the *Carlson*'s position Amanda had found that the LPD was not alone.

Cobra circled back for another pass over the Indonesian warship, and an officer, possibly the frigate's captain, stepped out onto the bridge wing. Clad in tropic whites, he stared up defiantly at the helicopter. Amanda met his gaze for a moment, wishing there were such a thing as mental telepathy.

"Okay, Cobra," she said into her lip mike. "I've had my look-around. Put us down on the *Carlson*."

"Doin' it."

Three minutes later the Super Huey settled onto the LPD's flight deck.

"Home, Captain," Richardson called back from the pilot's seat, as he and his copilot commenced the aircraft power-down. "Never mind about your gear. My people will get it up to your cabin."

"Thank you, and thanks for the lift and the good work. You and the Wolves didn't take long in proving yourselves."

"No strain, ma'am. Just give us something to shoot at every now and again and we're happy."

Leaving her cranial and lifejacket with the helo's crew chief, Amanda disembarked. Heading forward to the superstructure, she found herself noting the slower, more deliberate pitch and roll of the larger ship, so different than the Duke's decisive slice through the incoming rollers.

Admiral MacIntyre and Christine Rendino awaited her inside the open hangar bay doors, along with Captain Carberry and a handsome, intense Asian man in civilian clothes. He stood by impassively as Amanda honored the colors aft and exchanged salutes.

Admiral MacIntyre made the introductions. "Captain Garrett, this is Inspector Nguyen Tran of the Singapore National Police. He's the guide Miss Rendino promised us."

Amanda extended her hand and found it gripped in a solid western handshake. "I'm pleased to have you aboard, Inspector. We'll be needing your help."

"And I am pleased to be able to assist in this matter." The inspector's voice was deep, with a trace of the old formal British accent. "I am at your disposal."

"Uh, his presence aboard is also not known by his government or acknowledged by ours," Christine added. "The inspector's sort of the little man who wasn't there just now."

"He won't be alone in that status for long." Amanda glanced at Commander Carberry. "Commander, later this afternoon you'll be having a Seahawk coming in from the *Cunningham*. It will be carrying our...VIP passengers. Given the nosy Parker we have in the neighborhood, I suggest we do not unload said VIPs on the open flight deck. Bring the helo into the hangar and get the doors secured before disembarking them."

"Understood, Captain," Carberry replied. "As per Commander Rendino's instructions, ship's security has a holding area prepared."

"Very good. We can conduct the interrogations here aboard the *Carlson* a lot better than we can aboard the Duke. What we don't need at this juncture is for the Indonesian government to learn we're holding some of their citizens incommunicado, pirates or not."

"Not a problem, ma'am. By your leave, I'll make arrangements with my AIRBOSS."

"Carry on."

The rotund little officer strode briskly away, and Amanda turned back to the gray hull and snowy bow wave loitering beyond the LPD's wake. "And speaking of things we don't need, what's the word on our little puppy dog back there. What are the Indonesians up to?"

MacIntyre scowled and tilted his uniform cap back. "We're not exactly sure. This young sailor-me-lad picked us up as we cleared Singapore and he's been shadowing ever since. Inspector Tran has already developed one unpleasant theory about him."

"Which is, Inspector?"

"The piracy cartel has ordered their purchased officers within the Indonesian navy to monitor your operations," Tran replied. "I suspect also to interfere with those operations whenever possible."

Amanda's dark brows knit together. "The cartel has enough pull to do that?"

"They do, Captain. The proof follows behind us. Perhaps the greater question is, do they have enough 'pull,' as you say, to instigate the launching of an outright attack."

"Essentially it has been a search for a series of convergent factors," Tran stated to his small audience. He, Christine Rendino, Admiral MacIntyre, and the newly arrived Amanda Garrett had withdrawn to the *Carlson*'s wardroom. With his battered briefcase sitting before him on the tabletop, Tran began the presentation he had given so often in futility. "As it came clear a dedicated and effective support infrastructure was being developed for pirate operations in the archipelago, it also became clear certain specific elements must be involved."

"A very sophisticated fencing and money-laundering operation, for one," Captain Garrett commented. Frowning absently, she crossed to the miniature palm tree sitting in the corner of the compartment. Sinking to one knee, she tested the soil in its planter with a fingertip. "Pirating a high-value cargo is an act of futility unless you also have a secure method in place for reselling it on the world market and accounting for the money gained from it."

"Logistics and transport, for a second," MacIntyre added. The admiral sat half turned, facing Tran with his arm hooked over his chair back. "You'd have to be able to move your hijacked cargoes in to your sales points, and supplies and equipment out to your raider bases regularly and without arousing suspicion."

"We're also talking about a big-bucks business operation here," Christine Rendino added, booting up her laptop on the table across from Tran, "something you couldn't conduct in a waterfront dive. You'd have to be able to access some pretty rarified circles in the area of banking, international trade, and finance, as well as high-level regional government."

Captain Garrett crossed to the wardroom's sideboard and removed a water-filled spray bottle from one of the cupboards beneath it. "I would project, then, that our piracy cartel must control at least one legitimate maritime shipping line with regular traffic routes and ports of call both inside and out of Indonesian waters, an internationally rated bank, and a major trading house or brokerage. Am I correct?"

Returning to the little palm, she lightly misted its glossy leaves.

"Exactly correct, Captain," Tran replied. "However, there are two additional factors that narrow the field even further. Merely controlling these enterprises is not enough. They must be under tight, personal control, a rarity in these days of corporate entities. And finally, the driving force behind the cartel must be an individual who understands the culture of the Bugis sea clans in depth. He must be able to work with them and, most importantly, he must be trusted and respected by them. He cannot be an outsider."

Garrett set the spray bottle on the sideboard. "That should narrow the field considerably. How long is our list of suspects?"

"Suspect, Captain: singular. In my investigations I have

found only one man who seems to meet this convergence of factors."

Popping the latches on his briefcase, Tran removed a folder. Placing it on the wardroom table, he flipped the folder open, spreading out the eight-by-ten news file photographs he had collected from the archives of the *New Straits Times*.

"This man."

Captain Garrett returned to the table and joined her fellow officers in an examination of the pictures. She studied them for a long moment. "What's his name?" she inquired quietly.

"Harconan. Makara Harconan. His father was a member of one of the old Dutch colonial families that managed to hang on after Indonesian independence. His mother was the daughter of a major Bugis clan leader."

"Oh, yeah, Mommy," Christine murmured, glancing up at Amanda. "You can buy me one of these for my birthday."

Tran suppressed an ironic smile at the comment. As a police officer, Tran knew image rarely meshed with reality. Makara Harconan was an exception to the rule. He was the way a pirate king should be, very much in the classic Errol Flynn mold. Only the strength in those hard-lined features and the defiant boldness in those dark eyes were the real thing and not born from any school of acting.

Amanda Garrett slowly leafed through the photo file: Harconan in an evening jacket, escorting a prominent Singapore starlet; Harconan in a business suit, disembarking from an airliner; Harconan shirtless and smiling, leaning back against the rail of a Bugis schooner. Lightly she traced the curve of his jaw with a fingertip. "What's his story?"

"As I said, the Harconans were one of the old Dutch East Indies colonial families that stayed on after Indonesian independence. Apparently a very tough and stubborn lot, well versed in political infighting and in the accumulation of influence. They had to be, to survive both the Sukarno and the Suharto regimes.

"From his father's family, Makara inherited a number of assets, a small merchant's bank with branches in Jakarta and Singapore, several small coastal cargo vessels, and an interisland trading firm with outlets on the major Indonesian islands."

Captain Garrett tossed the file back on the tabletop. "There are your three major elements."

"The beginning of them at least," Tran replied. "However, what he inherited from his mother's side was perhaps more critical."

Captain Garrett leaned back against the table. "Go on."

"From what I have learned, Makara Harconan had no great bond with his Dutch father. I suspect that his parents' marriage was one of political expediency, an attempt to buy an 'in' with the Bugis clans. Be that as it may, the relationship between the father and the half-caste son never grew close.

"The same could not be said of the boy's feelings for his maternal grandfather. The mother's father took over the role of the male parent. As Makara grew toward adulthood, he spent the majority of his holidays aboard his grandfather's trading schooner, learning of his Bugis heritage as well as the ways of the sea. By the time he was fifteen, he was a master seaman capable of navigating a *pinisi* from here to New Guinea and back. I suspect he did so more than once."

Tran noted how Garrett smiled, her eyes distant. "What a marvelous childhood to have," she commented. "Most kids only get to dream of sailing away to the South Seas."

"Indeed. From all I can learn, Harconan and his grandfather developed a fierce affection for each other. There was only one drawback to the relationship."

"Which was?"

"The grandfather was also one of the most notorious and ruthless pirate captains in the archipelago," Tran replied. "The old renegade apparently schooled the boy in that as well. On this point, naturally enough, I have only the vaguest of coast rumors and supposition to go on. But in his teenage years, Harconan may actually have sailed on a number of raiding expeditions with his grandfather, very possibly being involved in the boarding and fighting. Also in the killing."

"Damnation," MacIntyre scowled. "I suppose you can say the boy came by it naturally. It's in his blood."

Tran lifted his hand in an open palm gesture. "More importantly, Admiral, it's in his mind. Makara Harconan is a man between two worlds, the world of the western-oriented twenty-first century and the more ancient and lawless realm of the Bugis sea gypsy. Being intelligent, aggressive, and educated to think outside of conventional morality, he has learned how to apply the tools and lessons gained in one world to the other.

"When he was eighteen, Harconan was sent to college in Europe for six years, first studying economics and business administration at the University of Amsterdam, and then attending the Dutch Maritime Academy, earning his merchant officer's ratings. Upon his returning home to Indonesia, he requested and obtained a placement aboard one of his father's coastal freighters. To no one's surprise, within a year he was commanding the ship.

"At that moment, almost to the day, the affairs of the Harconan family took a sudden dramatic upswing. Makara Harconan, it seemed, had a magic touch at nosing out profitable business, inevitably from islands with large Bugis colonies on them. It also seemed that his competitors were dogged with ill fortune. Some of them even had ships and cargo disappear completely."

MacIntyre glanced down at the photos on the tabletop. "Damn peculiar coincidence, that."

"Is it not? To proceed, by the time he was thirty, Harconan was the director of one of the strongest regional shipping lines in the archipelago. Harconan Seaways was also the premier moneymaker of the Harconan family holdings."

Garrett frowned and sank into a chair across the table from Tran. "How big of an operation are we talking about?"

Christine Rendino fielded the question. "Currently, Harconan Seaways flags a total of nine vessels. Six of them are good-sized motor coasters working a series of scheduled and unscheduled interisland routes from the Gulf of Thailand and the Andaman Sea clear across Indonesia and up into the Philippines.

"He also owns three big combined container and break bulk liners that work a couple of regular deepwater circuits. One is up the China coast with stops in Vietnam, the United Republics of Korea, and Russia. The other run circumnavigates the Indian Ocean, Bangladesh, India, Pakistan, a couple of the Persian Gulf states, and the African Horn. Harconan focuses on the trade out of some of the rougher secondary ports the bigger lines shy clear of."

"The smugglers ports, you mean? The ones with iffier customs coverage?"

The blonde intel quirked an eyebrow. "A judgmental and suspicious person might say that, Boss Ma'am.

Tran resumed the discourse. "In addition to their own vessels, Harconan Seaways operates an extensive charter and brokerage service. They may have several dozen *pinisi* under hire at any one time, moving cargo in and out of the lesser Indonesian ports."

"And does Harconan Seaways ever suffer from pirate attacks?"

Tran smiled. "Oh, yes, almost more so than the other regional shipping lines. Mr. Harconan has frequently stated his concerns about piracy in the archipelago. While he has not lost ships or personnel, his cargo losses are quite extensive every year. Cargo like maritime diesel power plants, outboard motors, radio and radar equipment—all never recovered. It is fortunate he always keeps his ships and the loads they carry well insured."

"A wise businessman," Captain Garrett agreed.

"He is." Tran continued with the story. "When his father died, leaving Makara as his sole heir, he was very much, as you Americans say, 'in the catbird seat.'

"He bought out the remaining holdings of the last few Harconan relations and investors with a surprisingly large personal cash reserve, assuming full control not only of the shipping line but of the Jakarta Trans-Asian Bank, and of Harconan Trade and Brokerage. He united all three as divisions of a holding company called Makara Limited, with a company headquarters established on Bali."

"There's your personal control," Amanda commented.

"Quite so," Tran agreed. "He has refused to place Makara Limited stock on the open market, keeping his own hand solely on the tiller. In spite of that, Makara Limited has boomed. It is a multi–hundred-million-dollar operation currently, and Harconan is a name to be strongly reckoned with among the new taipans of the Far East."

"That's rather peculiar, isn't it?" MacIntyre commented, his craggy features thoughtful. "If the man's made his pile, why continue with these piracy operations? Why keep risking it all? Why not do what the old Mafia dons did— go legitimate and sit back in the sun for the rest of his life?"

"Two reasons, I believe, Admiral. For one, I suspect that Harconan has an agenda beyond mere monetary gain. The wealth Harconan is acquiring through his piracy operations is being channeled back to the Bugis. He is making piracy attractively profitable for the sea clans again, luring the men away from fishing and trading and shoreside employment and encouraging the old raiders' ways.

"As the men return, he hones their fighting skills giving them better ships, better weapons, and better training. Soon they will no longer be pirates. They will be a navy."

"A navy that owes a secret allegiance to Makara Harconan," Amanda Garrett interjected.

"You got it, Boss Ma'am." Christine Rendino looked up from her laptop. "We saw this mechanism once before, in West Africa. A sufficiently charismatic and effective leader can turn a tribal culture into an empire practically overnight. He just has to prove he's a winner."

"'Charismatic and effective' very much describes Makara Harconan," Tran agreed. "Among the Bugis colonies he is already a known and respected man. He maintains a number of private philanthropic operations within the archipelago, providing aid and assistance to the Bugis. Things such as schools, better medical care, better housing. Many Bugis already say he has done more for them than Jakarta ever managed."

Tran hesitated before continuing. "If you know where to listen, there are already whispers of the coming of a *raja samudra,* a 'sea king' who will restore the glories of the ancient Bone Empire of Sulawesi, the apex of Bugis power within the archipelago. No name has yet to be attached to the title—publicly, at any rate."

"The restoration of some mythic 'golden age' or 'shining time' has set more than one culture on the road to war," Amanda commented grimly. "Where does our 'sea king' have his current throne?"

Christine took over the flow of the briefing. "Makara Limited's corporate headquarters are located in the coastal town of Nusa Dua, near Benoa Harbor. I suppose you could call Nusa Dua a suburb of the island capital of Denpasar. However, Harconan's personal headquarters are located on another smaller island off the northwestern tip of Bali, near the approaches to the Bali Strait."

Christine rotated her laptop's screen on its pivot point, displaying a chart call-up. "It's called Palau Piri, Island of the Princes, appropriately enough. Harconan owns the whole damn island outright. Apparently it's been in the family for centuries. Access by personal invitation only."

Amanda whistled softly. "Interesting. He must like privacy and borders both. And he must have picked Bali for his headquarters for the same reason we did: its strategic central location. Have the G-Hawks had a look at this place, Chris?"

"Oh, yeah, very impressive." The intel called up a high-altitude photo file. "About two square miles in area. As you can see, it's heavily forested with black-sand beaches all the way around. Reefs to the north and west with a small breakwater harbor and a set of piers on the south side."

On the screen, a window formed around the small group of structures near the piers, the image zooming up to fill the screen. Reaching around, Christine conducted a guided tour with a pencil tip.

"The only structures are the half-dozen inside the Harconan compound, the rest of the island is maintained as a nature preserve. That very impressive single-story building on the bottom left is the Harconan mansion. That's a helipad next to it, with the pontoon-equipped EC365 Eurocopter that Harconan uses as a personal executive shuttle."

The pencil tapped another point on the screen. "This is a boathouse. Beyond a couple of utility launches, you've got a Magnum VI open-ocean racing boat in there, a dope runner's special. According to the builders in Florida, it's equipped with a triple set of turbo-charged 454-cubic-inch Chevy engines and extended-range fuel tanks. It can walk away from just about anything afloat, even a Sea Fighter, and it has a five-hundred-mile range at a ninety-knot cruise."

"How about the other big building with the beach apron?" Amanda inquired.

"It's what it looks like, a seaplane hangar for the Makara corporate aircraft, a Canadair CL215-T twin turboprop amphibian, again with extended-range tanks. It could take you anywhere from Cooktown to Shanghai without refueling."

"Give this man two spare seconds and he could vanish off the face of the earth," MacIntyre commented, leaning closer to the screen.

"Pretty much so, Admiral, sir," Christine replied. "Note how the compound is energy-independent, with solar cell arrays on the roofs and a couple of wind turbines here and here. You can also see the multiple satellite dishes. The place is wired like a NASA ground station, with direct access to all major satcom information nets. It's also guarded like Fort Knox. There's a permanent forty-person staff in residence, half of whom are armed guards."

"Nung Chinese mercenaries, to be specific," Tran added. "The best in Asia, equipped with automatic weapons and night-vision systems. You also have a sea-and-air–capable radar system, low-light television monitors covering the beaches, and a charged and sensor-wired perimeter fence around the compound itself."

"What? No surface-to-air missiles?" MacIntyre inquired archly.

Tran held up a pair of fingers. "Two French Mistral shoulder-fired launchers issued to Harconan's security forces by the Indonesian army as an 'anti-terrorist' precaution."

"I should have guessed."

Amanda Garrett rose and started to pace slowly around the table, her hands on her hips, her lower lip lightly bitten in thought.

"Excuse me, Captain Garrett," Tran said apologetically. "But that particular posture you have assumed, the hands on the hips, is considered very insulting by the Indonesians. It's how their Dutch overseers would stand in the fields back in the colonial days."

Startled, she dropped her hands to her sides. "Thank you for the tip, Inspector," she smiled. "If you catch us performing any other local faux pas, please bring it to our attention."

She picked up one of Harconan's photographs again, studying it. "This is all very good material, Inspector, but it's also essentially circumstantial. We're going to need more hard evidence linking this man and the piracy operations."

"I regret I can provide none," Tran replied. "Makara Harconan is a most intelligent and capable individual, and he has built a most formidable machine. One that I, operating alone and in my spare time, have not been able to breach. In my heart, I know he is our pirate king. All my instincts and all available information point in his direction. But the proof you require must be gained through your resources."

"Then we'd best get about it." Captain Garrett let the photograph glide back to the tabletop. "Our first possible access point will be the prisoners and hard intelligence we collected from the *Piskov* attack. Inspector, I trust you'll be assisting Commander Rendino and our intelligence section with the interrogations and analysis?"

Tran nodded. "Of course, Captain."

"Thank you." She shifted her gaze to Christine. "Okay, Chris, I heard the transfer Oceanhawk come in a little bit ago, so your subjects are aboard. Wring 'em out as needed, but don't damage them. Are we still maintaining track on the pirate mother ships?"

"Fa' sure, Boss Ma'am. They headed north through the Sunda Strait and are now standing toward western Sulawesi, probably heading for one of the Bugis coastal villages."

"Excellent. Tonight, before we turn south for Bali, I intend to spin off a Sea Fighter microforce. We'll pre-position it on the Sulawesi coast with orders to penetrate and recon the pirate base as soon as we can get a fix on it. Our shadower will complicate matters, but I think we can work around him."

She glanced at MacIntyre. "That is, with your permission, sir?"

A rueful smile cut across MacIntyre's sea-tanned features. "*Micromanagement* is a dirty word, Captain. I gave you your job. Get it done. I'll just sit back in the shade and take the credit."

"That sounds like a deal, sir," Amanda Garrett replied, matching smiles. "I think this operation is well under way. What we need next is an approach that can get us closer to this Makara Harconan."

MacIntyre's grin faded, and he removed a message flimsy from the pocket of his wash khaki shirt. "Funny thing. I received a communication from our embassy in Jakarta this afternoon. It seems that a local business firm desires to sponsor a goodwill reception for the task force's senior officers during our port call in Bali. The usual cocktails, light refreshments, and local social and diplomatic elite."

The admiral held the flimsy up between his fore- and middle fingers. "Makara Limited is extending the invitation."

Somewhere Aboard the USS *Carlson*   **Zone Time unknown: 2008**

Hayam Mangkurat could not say if it was day or night, or how many days or nights might have passed since his capture. The bright electric light in the overhead burned continuously.

The Bugis prizemaster had seen neither the sun nor darkness since his capture aboard the *Piskov*. He had been moved from captivity on one ship to a second, he was certain of that. There had been the long helicopter flight, and this vessel rode the waves differently than the first.

He had been kept hooded throughout the transfer, and the gray steel walls of this cabin were all but identical to those of the other.

When Mangkurat had regained consciousness aboard the first vessel, he had sworn to himself by the Holy Name of God that he would not be broken. He was a Bugis sea raider, son of a hundred generations of sea raiders and a veteran of forty years' voyaging. He would place his trust in Allah and keep faith with his clan and the sea king. Beyond his courage and will, he had the promise of the *raja samudra* himself. "Should you fall into the hands of our enemies, you will be remembered. Keep silent in all things and you will be freed."

He had steeled himself for what was sure to come: the interrogation, the beating, the demands for information. His people had defied the Dutch, the Japanese, the Communists, the swaggering Javanese *polisi*. What could these American—at least, he believed they were American—*bule* do?

But what they did was nothing. His wounds had been treated with care, and he had been placed alone in that first metal room. The mattress on the bunk was comfortable. Sleep would have been easy were it not for the incessant glare of the light in the overhead. There was water to be had at the turn of a tap, and frequently food was brought. Bland fish and rice, but it was plentiful, brought three times a day . . . he thought.

He wasn't sure. The timing of the meals never seemed to be the same. The food was never brought at the same time . . . he didn't think. Sometimes he had to wait until his stomach growled. At other times the meals seemed only minutes apart. It was unsettling.

And the big men who brought the food. The men in the green uniforms who wore the black hoods that let only their eyes show. They never lifted a hand against him. They never threatened or questioned. They never spoke a word at all.

There were only the ship sounds. The padding footsteps beyond the locked steel door, the occasional squawk of a muffled voice over a loudspeaker, and the whisper of the air in the ventilator ducts that began to sound like a woman's whisper after a while.

And then they did come for him. Two of the green uniforms. They slipped the hood over his head and they guided him out of the narrow door, one on either side. Mangkurat thought for a moment about fighting, about making a break. But then the hands on his arms tightened as his guards read his mind.

A stumbling walk followed, up steep ladders and over shin-cracking hatch sills. Then the Bugis found himself forced down onto a low metal stool. The hood was whisked away, but Mangkurat saw only more blackness. He could not see his guards, but they were still there. Still close by.

Abruptly, dazzling white light exploded in his face, and Mangkurat's muscles spasmed in fright. Frantically he tried to drag his cloak of stoicism back around himself. He was Bugis! He was not afraid! They could not break him!

"Siapa nama saudara?" What is your name?

For the first time in days—how many?—he heard a human voice. It came out of the impenetrable shadow beyond the light focused in his eyes. A man's voice, quiet and level, the tongue Bahasa Indonesia, spoken with the ease and fluidity of a native.

"What is your name?" the voice repeated.

And yet again, "What is your name?"

Mangkurat kept silent and braced himself for the blow that must lash out of the darkness, be it a fist, whip, or club.

But the blow never fell.

"What is your name?"

"What is your name?"

"What is your name?"

A pause.

"Understand this," the voice went on after a moment. "We already know what you are. You are Bugis. You are a pirate who sailed away one day to rob a ship and who never returned. No one knows what happened to you. Not your captain. Not your family. Not your village. Not even the *raja samudra* himself."

Mangkurat struggled to keep his stoicism. They knew of the sea king. They must also know of his promise.

The voice continued quietly, hypnotically level. "No one knows where you are, so you are nowhere. You are a nonentity, a ghost, nothing. Tell us your name so you can be a man again."

"What is your name?"

"What is your name?"

"What is your name?"

There was only the darkness and the light and the voice and hard edges of the stool biting into his buttocks.

That and the one question.

"What is your name?"

"What is your name?"

"What is your name?"

Slowly, Mangkurat's folded legs began to go numb. Dryness crept down his throat and his eyes burned from the light. Even when he closed them, the glare seeped redly through his eyelids. And the question, hammering at him, becoming meaningless as time drew on.

"What is your name?"

His startled jump almost toppled Mangkurat to the deck. A second voice had asked the question, a woman's voice, still speaking Indonesian, but with the sharp-edged inflections of a westerner.

"What is your name?"

"What is your name?"

"What is your name?"

The voice was new, different. He had to listen to it again! It had meaning once more!

"What is your name?"

"What is your name?"

"What is your name?"

How many times did the two voices switch off? Five times, ten, a dozen? Mangkurat lost the count. He lost track of everything but that one hammering demand.

"What is your name?"

"What is your name?"

"What is your name?"

Once Mangkurat tried to spring up. He strove to hurl himself beyond the light at that hateful, insistent, eternal query, but his legs buckled beneath him. The guards materialized out of the darkness, catching him by the arms and restraining him as he writhed and hoarsely screamed curses. They did not strike. They did not beat. They refused to offer even a scrap of pain to hold and treasure as a charm against the eternal, nagging question.

When Mangkurat went limp and silent in their grasp, they lowered him gently back down onto the stool. And never once did that voice change its timbre or rhythm or request.

"What is your name?"

"What is your name?"

"What is your name?"

He would not tell them.

"What is your name?"

His name was his soul. He would not give it away.

"What is your name?"

They would not steal his treasure.

"What is your name?"

He was Bugis! He was Mangkurat of the Bugis! He would not weaken.

"What is your name?"

He was Mangkurat.

"What is your name?"

Mangkurat!

"What is your name?"

Mangkurat!

"What is your name?"

"Mangkurat."

"Mangkurat . . . thank you, Mangkurat."

Instantly they were upon him. They lifted him in their arms and the stool was kicked away. He was lowered into a chair, metal, but its smooth, cool contours soothed his cramped body like the finest silk. A cup was being held to his lips. Water! Icy sweet water! They let him drain the cup, and a second was offered.

He collapsed back in the chair, his ragged shirt sodden with sweat and spillage.

"Mangkurat," the voice repeated from beyond the light.

How could they know his name now? He hadn't told them. He hadn't . . . he didn't think. No, he had said nothing . . . nothing! They must have known all along. Fooling him. How many other secrets did they know?

"Now, Mangkurat," the voice continued, "what is the name of your village?"

"What is the name of your village?"

"What is the name of your village?"

Java Sea,   **0119 Hours, Zone Time:**
Approaching the Rass Island Group   **August 15, 2008**

The golden horn of the moon dipped into shimmering sea. As it sank steadily lower, the thin scattering of clouds in the tropic night darkened, losing its reflected light.

And then it was gone.

"Right. That's it." Amanda turned to the cluster of officers sharing the *Carlson*'s portside bridge wing. "Commander Carberry, your ship's status?"

"Ready to proceed, Captain," the little man replied crisply. "Crew at air and sea launch stations. Ready to initiate countermeasures and hangar bay blackout."

"And the latest from Commander Hiro?"

"He is paralleling us to the north at an eight-mile range at full stealth and limited EMCON. He reports he is ready to commence a high-speed convergence upon your command."

"Very good, Captain. Cobra, how about you?"

The aviator was even more succinct. "I'm good. Ready to launch."

"Remember your tasking parameters. Go in fast. Get out fast. You're a pest, not a provocation."

"I got the picture, ma'am. Aye, aye."

"Steamer?"

The Sea Fighter commander settled his baseball cap lower over his eyes. "*Queen of the West* and *Manassas* are ready to start engines. Fuel blivits embarked. Recon party going aboard. We're good to go."

"Christine find you your initial hide?"

"Yeah, a good little nowhere up in the Laut Kecils. Nobody around for miles, crappy access, and good cover. We can get to it and get buried well before oh-light-hundred."

"Very well. We'll have an underway replenishment set up with Curtin by tomorrow night. You shouldn't really need it with your blivits aboard, but I want you to go in with a maneuvering reserve, just in case." Amanda smiled and extended a hand. "An independent command, Steamer. You won't have a rusty old four-bar hanging over your shoulder. Good luck."

"I don't know, ma'am. You're kind of handy to have around sometimes," he replied, exchanging a brief, strong grip with her. "We'll see you in a few days."

"Maybe sooner than that, if we don't pull this off. Gentlemen, let's proceed."

Two miles astern of the USS *Carlson,* Lieutenant Commander Hasan Basry, captain of the Indonesian navy frigate *Sutanto,* swore into his pillow as the interphone at the head of his bunk buzzed . . . again.

He clawed the offending instrument from its cradle. "Yes?"

"I'm sorry, Captain," the watch officer said apologetically, "but it's the Americans. They are doing something...odd, sir."

"They have been doing odd things ever since they left Singapore, Lieutenant. What is it now?"

"They have launched a helicopter, sir."

"Ships that carry helicopters frequently do," Basry snapped. "What is so unusual about this particular exercise?"

"Immediately after launching their aircraft, the Americans cut off their running lights. The amphibious ship is now running fully blacked out."

Basry hesitated for several heartbeats. He wasn't certain why he and his ship had been ordered to abort a portside refit to keep the Americans under surveillance. Admiral Lukisan had merely said "for reasons of national security," a statement that covered a great deal of territory.

Just what were the Yankees up to in Indonesia's home waters? And what about the second American vessel, the major surface combatant that supposedly was to have escorted the LPD? First it had failed to appear at Singapore, then this morning it had materialized in the middle of the Java Sea, much to the consternation of Basry's superiors.

This evening it had vanished again, this time off of the radar screens of the naval surveillance Nomad attempting to keep it under observation. Could it be moving in?

"All right," he said into the interphone. "I'm coming up."

On the *Carlson*'s bridge, Amanda bent over the tactical display, studying the glowing graphics chart and the various position hacks like a chess master studying a game board. As per the ops plan, the *Carlson* was in the lead, with her shadower, the Indonesian frigate, trailing two miles astern. The *Cunningham* was steaming parallel to the LPD, but off to port at effective stealth range, invisible to the Indonesian's search radar.

A single bat-shaped aircraft hack circled in a close holding pattern over the *Carlson,* the recently launched Wolf One.

The task group was rapidly closing with the tail end of the Rass island group, an uninhabited and nameless patch of coral and sand that would be passing to starboard at a distance of five miles.

Amanda made a final check for merchant vessels shipping. Clear within a twenty-mile range.

All was ready. She touched the mike key of her command headset. "All task group elements, this is the TACBOSS. We are at Point Item. All elements prepare for breakaway. Wolf One, you are cleared to initiate audial and visual screening."

The Wolf One air hack fell back and occulted the symbol of the pursuing Indonesian frigate.

A hurricane blast of wind ripped across the decks of the *Sutanto,* and a dazzling blue white glare illuminated every inch of the frigate's weatherdeck. Clutching the bridge wing rail, Commander Basry squinted into both, and was able to make out the silhouette of a Huey helicopter hovering broadside on, just off the bow of his ship.

Sidling ahead of the Indonesian vessel, the helicopter had a battery of what appeared to be aircraft landing lights aimed out of its side hatch, trained full into the eyes and night-vision systems of the bridge watch.

"What are the Americans doing, sir?" the watch officer yelled over the rotor thunder.

"Something they obviously don't wish us to see," Basry yelled back.

The hangar bay ventilator fans raced at full power, pumping a flood of outside air into the space, air that was greedily devoured by the gas turbines of the hovering Sea Fighters.

"Prelaunch checklists complete," Chief Petty Officer Sandra "Scrounger" Caitlin reported from the *Queen of the West*'s copilot's seat. Glancing down from the cockpit windows, she noted the bay apes dragging the last tie-down strap clear. The same was being done for the *Manassas,* at her spot forward of the *Queen,* leaving both hovercraft bobbing on their inflated plenum skirts.

"Moorings clear," she continued. "We are free to maneuver."

"Roger, that," Steamer Lane replied. "Going to active station keeping." With one hand on the puff port controller, he held the PGAC in place against the pitch and roll of her mother ship. "Internal station status?"

"Boards green. All stations report secure and ready for sea," Caitlin replied "Power rooms indicate they are drawing on the blivit. We got good fuel flow."

Below, in the main hull, the other seven members of the hovercraft crew stood to at the weapons-control stations and in the power rooms. The seven Force Recon Marines and the pharmacist's mate that made up the *Queen*'s share of the land recon party were strapped into the fold-down benches along the bulkheads of the main bay. They shared this confined space with what resembled a gigantic gray slug.

The small Rigid Inflatable raider boat and the harpoon missile cells that usually occupied the Sea Fighters' central bay had been unshipped and replaced with a fuel blivet, a flexible Fiberglas-and-plastic fuel bladder that effectively doubled the hovercraft's 750-mile operational radius.

The hover commander thumbed the mike button on the air rudder control yoke. "BAYBOSS, this is Royalty. Tie-downs clear and ready to take departure."

"BAYBOSS, this is Rebel," Lieutenant Tony Marlin's intent voice joined in from the *Manassas.* "Make that two to go."

"BAYBOSS to hovers, acknowledged."

Through the open cockpit side windows, the MC-1 speakers bellowed over the turbine shriek and fan moan. *"Attention in the hangar bay. Stand by to launch hovercraft. All hands proceed forward of the deck safety lines. Set hangar blackout protocols. Extinguish all portable light sources. All hands go to night vision or stand fast in secure positions. Ten count to blackout . . . ten . . . nine . . . eight . . ."*

At the count of one, the hangar bay plunged into total darkness. Steamer and Scrounge flipped down the nite-brite visors of their helmets.

"Stern ramp opening."

In the *Queen*'s sideview mirrors, they watched the wall of steel behind them crack open to admit the night.

"Sea Fighters ready to launch, Captain," Carberry murmured at Amanda's side.

"Very well," she replied absently, intent on the developing picture on the tactical display. The angles were looking good. Very soon Steamer would have an optimum departure heading. But even though the Sea Fighters were very stealthy vehicles, they weren't totally radar-invisible at close range. Nor was the *Cunningham,* should it need to be.

"Let's take out their radars, Commander. The RBOCs now, please. Curtain pattern astern. Bring up your jammers, full spectrum."

"Aye, aye, ma'am. Jammers coming up. Firing a pattern."

At the aft corners of the *Carlson*'s deckhouse, the mortar tubes of the Rapid Blooming Overhead Chaff systems coughed hollowly. In a manner similar to a Fourth of July fireworks display, the charges they hurled arced high over the sea aft of the LPD. However, upon bursting, instead of a shower of multicolored stars, these charges dispersed clouds of metal foil strips.

On the bridge of the Indonesian frigate, the watch officer yelled over the aggravating hammer of Wolf One's rotors. "Captain, look at the tactical display. The Americans are launching chaff."

Captain Basry swore fervently and raced to the console screen.

Truly enough, a curtain of radar-jamming foil was being drawn across his ship's line of advance, the American flagship fading from detection beyond it. Intermixed with the chaff wall came the jittering blobs and strobing effect of active radar jamming.

This was intolerable! First the Americans blind his eyes, and now his radar!

"All engines ahead flank!" Basry roared. "Close the range!"

"Chaff deployed, ma'am."

"Very good, Commander. We have it on tactical. Good disbursement. I don't think we'll need another dose for the moment."

On the *Carlson*'s bridge, the chaff curtain existed only as an oblong graphics box on the tactical display, showing its area of effect on the Indonesian systems. For the United States vessel, the countermeasures cloud was as transparent as glass.

Chaff's effectiveness was dependent upon matching the length of the scattered foil strips to the wavelength of the radar being jammed. These loads had been carefully cut to leave a frequency "window" open that could be used by the U.S. systems, a window beyond the operational spectrum of the earlier-gen Indonesian radars. Much the same kind of peephole existed in the barrage of electronic noise being thrown up by the active jammers.

The *Carlson* was very close to the breakaway point now. But the range numbers that glowed beside the Indonesian frigate's position hack began to flick downward. They were increasing speed, overtaking the LPD.

"Captain Carberry, all engines ahead full, and give us a second chaff launch, please."

"Very well, ma'am. Lee helm, all engines ahead full. Make turns for twenty-five knots. CIC, countermeasures, launch RBOC pattern two."

Time to put her knight into play. Again, Amanda keyed her headset mike. "Talk between ships, please. Commander Hiro aboard the *Cunningham*."

Hiro's voice came back a moment later. "Right here, Captain."

"Ken, our Indonesian friend is being difficult. He's closing with us and I don't need him underfoot at the moment. Give him the shoulder, please. As we discussed."

"Understood. Executing."

On the bridge of the *Cunningham,* Hiro moved to stand behind the helm control stations. "Helm, come right to one nine zero, convergent course with the Indonesian. Lee Helm, all power rooms to full output. All engines ahead flank. Make turns for thirty-five knots."

As the *Cunningham*'s bow started to come around, a red warning tile flashed on the helm console's Navicom board and a computer-synthesized voice chanted from a speaker grill. "Collision bearing! Collision bearing! Collision bearing!"

Hiro leaned forward and hit the override, squelching the audile warning. "Yeah," he murmured under his breath, "it certainly is!"

Minutes passed, and the *Sutanto* plowed ahead through a glittering metallic snowstorm.

"Lieutenant, have you worked through this damn crap and corruption they're laying down yet?"

"Not yet, Captain." The sweating radar officer looked up from where he crouched beside his senior systems operator. "The Americans continue to deploy chaff, and their active jammers keep jumping with our radar frequency shifts."

"Keep working it. I must know what's going on out there. Quartermaster, switch to GPU navigation and watch your fathometer. We've got some shoals out there to port." Basry squinted into the glare pouring in through the bridge windscreen. "Communications! Warn that damn helicopter off immediately!"

"We've been trying, sir," a second junior officer called back from the radio shack aft of the wheelhouse. "We are calling on all standard channels . . ."

The radio officer's voice cut off with the blaze of the floodlights. Going dark, Wolf One broke out of its holding pattern beyond the frigate's bow. Climbing, the Super

Huey started to circle overhead, the beating of its rotors still drowning out all sounds less than a shout. But just getting the night back was a relief.

Basry strove to blink the pinkish dazzle blobs from his vision. "That's something, at any rate. Maybe now...*Allah's prophet! Hard right rudder! All engines back emergency!*"

A second bank of floodlights blasted out of the darkness, these set closer to the water than those mounted on the helicopter. The running lights of a ship snapped on as well, a very large ship, very close off the *Sutanto*'s starboard bow. Basry caught the impression of a huge razor-edged prow looming out of the night, seeming to aim at his vessel's vulnerable flank. Dual-toned air horns blared an imperious warning.

Without orders, the *Sutanto*'s quartermaster wrenched down on the horn cord and the frigate screamed in terror. Frantically the helmsman spun his brass-mounted wheel until it locked against its stops. The deck tilted as the frigate skidded into a minimum-radius turn away from the impending collision.

As the Duke pulled alongside the Indonesian man-of-war, Ken Hiro peered down from the starboard bridge wing, expertly gauging the narrow strip of water that boiled between the rails of the two warships. "Okay, helm, steady...steady...slack her off...slack her off...*slack her off*...! Okay, steady as she goes...."

A mile ahead, on the bridge of the *Carlson,* the moment came.

"Sea Fighters, this is the TACBOSS. Launch and execute breakaway!"

Steamer Lane came back hard on the puff port controller. The *Queen of the West*'s forward thrusters roared, shoving the Sea Fighter backward. Her rearward motion accelerated as she slid down the *Carlson*'s stern ramp, traversing from the darkness of the hangar bay to the darkness of the night. With an explosion of spray, she hit the water, bucking through the turbulence of the LPD's wake.

Steamer shifted his grip from the controller to the steering yoke. "Power!"

Scrounger Caitlin knew that her captain wanted it all. She shoved first the propeller controls, then the drive throttles, hard ahead to their stops. The airscrews, which had been feathered at idling power, angled their blades and blurred into shimmering disks within their duct shrouds. The wave crests flattened behind her under the surge of thrust, and the *Queen* lunged ahead, gathering speed.

Steamer sidestepped the stern of the LPD, racing the hovercraft gunboat up the left flank of the larger vessel. The *Manassas* followed them down the ramp a few moments later. Chasing her squadron leader, the second PGAC dropped into a line behind the *Queen*.

Clear of the *Carlson*'s bow, Steamer paid off in a wide turn, aiming the Sea Fighter column dead on toward the nameless island to port.

"Go...go...go!" Lane chanted.

Scrounger's eyes raked across the engine readouts on her instrumentation displays. Playing the power levers the way a master pianist might play a vintage Steinway, she kept the temperature bars well up in the yellow, not quite letting them touch red.

A turbine tech by training, Scrounger had come up from the *Queen*'s power rooms. She'd earned her nickname primping and petting those big Lycomings, using her deft skills at "midnight requisitioning" to acquire the best of the best for them, just for moments like this.

The wave patterns flickered past in Steamer Lane's nitebrite visor, vanishing under the Sea Fighter's blunt nose. The *Queen* was running balls to the wall, gobbling the range to her island target.

"Terry, gimme the MMS."

"Aye, aye, sir," Ensign Terrence Wilder, the *Queen*'s executive officer, barked from the navigator's station. "Activating mast-mounted sighting system...low-light television is imaging on your primary screen now, sir."

Both Lane and Caitlin grinned to themselves, even under the tension of the moment. Terry Wilder was new, both to the fleet and to the *Queen*. They'd both been bringing him along with how things were done in the gunboat Navy, but Wilder still suffered from Annapolis flashbacks in times of stress.

Flipping up his nite-brite visor, Lane swapped the fuzzy green luminosity of the AI2 system for the sharply defined gray tones of the more powerful low-light television pod atop the *Queen*'s snub mast.

The nameless landfall lay a few thousand yards ahead now, a low, dark mass rising only a few feet above the sea. More important, however, was the wavering white line even closer, the surf breaking over the reefs that circled the islet.

As a true hovercraft, the *Queen of the West* drew no water at all. But coming in as she was, like a bat out of hell, snagging a plenum-chamber skirt on a protruding coral head could prove catastrophic. Lane rocked his control yoke, fishtailing the Sea Fighter and swinging his camera arc, watching for the dark line in the pale surf that would denote a "shoulder" of a reef break, a tongue of deeper, smoother water showing the way through the jagged teeth of the coral.

He relied not on any training provided by the Navy but on the wave-honed instincts gained in an adolescence spent surf-bumming up and down the California coast. Those instincts had served him well before; they did again now.

"Yeah, I got it! We got a hole! Rebel, Rebel, this is Royalty! Hey, Tony, maintain line astern! Follow me in!"

The *Queen* screamed through the gap in the reef at almost seventy knots, the *Manassas* hot on her tail. Sand loomed ahead.

"Snowy! All back! Reverse props!"

Scrounger Caitlin slammed the propeller controls to reverse, inverting the blade angles on the airscrews, changing them from a driving "push" to a braking "pull." Lane shifted his right hand to the T-grip puff port controller in the center of the console, shoving it full forward. The bow puff ports, vents in the front edge of the plenum chamber, snapped open, the released jets of high-pressure air serving as retro-rockets to help slow the hurtling Sea Fighter.

The backing propellers and ports wouldn't quite be enough, however.

Lane mashed down the interphone button on the control yoke. "Hang on!" he bellowed to all hands.

The decelerating Sea Fighter hit the beach in an explosion of spray and a tornado of sand. A low dune at the head of the beach launched the huge war machine into the air for a breathless, weightless second before they crashed into an inland brush patch. The *Manassas* plowed to a halt alongside the *Queen* a moment later.

Without requiring the order, Scrounger hit the kill switches, letting the Sea Fighter settle off cushion.

"Yeah, well, we're here," Lane commented.

On the tactical display, Amanda looked on as the microforce reached the islet, the faint skin tracks of the Sea Fighters disappearing with the land return.

"Combat Information Center, we have breakaway. How did that look to you?" she inquired.

"Looked good, ma'am. No RCM reflection on the Indonesian radar frequencies, and except for a degree of screaming about being run down by the crazy Americans, we have no radio traffic out of the frigate. No indication they spotted the launch. Our guys are outa here."

"Very good, CIC. All task group elements, breakaway achieved. Secure chaff and jamming. Wolf One, you may recover at your discretion. All ships return to standard cruise protocols and proceed on course. Well done."

On the bridge of the *Cunningham*, Ken Hiro watched the *Sutanto* stagger away into the darkness. Like a cow pony with a recalcitrant calf, the Duke had herded the smaller Indonesian vessel through a full 180-degree turn.

Hiro took a deep, deliberate breath. The Lady still could make things interesting, even when she wasn't in the captain's chair. "Quartermaster, secure the searchlights. Helm, commence station keeping on the *Carlson*. Lee helm, all engines ahead standard."

"This is intolerable!" Basry raged, stalking the *Sutanto*'s bridge. "Intolerable. Radio room, get me the American commander immediately! I will demand an apology for this outrage!"

"Captain . . ."

"Immediately!"

"But Captain," the communications officer pleaded, "we already have a message from the American task group commander, designated for you personally."

Basry paused in his stalking. "What? What does he say?"

"Uh, 'To the commanding officer Indonesian warship *Sutanto*. We regret that you elected to close the range with our formation at an inopportune moment. We were conducting an antimissile exercise with which you accidentally became involved. Please accept our strongest possible apologies for your dis-accommodation.'"

The communications officer looked up from the message flimsy. "Signature Captain Amanda Lee Garrett, USN, Commander, Sea Fighter Task Force."

Captain Basry opened his mouth, then shut it again as he realized he had nothing to say. A woman. On top of everything else, it had been done to him by a woman.

Basry had no idea of just what all had happened here, or why, or what he had not seen. There was only the deepening suspicion he had been made a fool of.

Powered down and silent, the *Queen* and the *Manassas* lay huddled on the nameless islet. Peering seaward over the low dunes, their MMS systems tracked the departure of the trio of larger ships. Presently, when the task force and its shadower were out of sight beyond the horizon, they would light off their turbines again and take their own departure. From here they would make their way to another hide on yet another nameless islet, dashing and crouching their way across the Indonesian archipelago like a pair of infantrymen sprinting from cover to cover.

This was what they had been made for.

For the moment, though, their crews and passengers could take a breather and a cold can of Coke be sipped. All hatches and cockpit windows gaped wide to admit the errant, cooling puffs of the night breeze and the sound of the breaking waves.

"Real interesting departure, Snowy," Steamer Lane said softly.

Scrounger Caitlin's attention quirked at the murmur. The Skipper did that every now and then. Just like he'd back-slip and use Miss Banks's name every now and again when things got hot.

Ensign Sandra "Snowy" Banks had been the *Queen*'s first exec, and she'd ridden right seat for Mr. Lane for a lot of sea miles. That had been back when, before West Africa. Before they'd had to send Miss Banks back to her warrior's rest in that quiet St. Louis cemetery. The skipper still remembered, though. Chief Caitlin did too.

Sometimes she wasn't sure if it was just a slip of the tongue or if maybe Mr. Lane really was talking to the *Queen*'s old exec. Scrounger didn't mind particularly either way. In fact, it would be kind of nice if Miss Banks could drop by every now and again, just so she could see that everything was being kept shipshape on the old *Queen*.

Scrounger smiled into the dark. "We're taking care of business, ma'am," she whispered.

"That was a most interesting evolution, Captain," Commander Carberry commented with grave formality. With the old school's dread of commenting on a superior officer's performance, it was as close as he could come to a compliment.

Amanda gave an acknowledging tilt of her head in the screenglow. "The task force performed quite well. I'm pleased. When should we be in at Benoa Harbor? Around ten hundred?"

The chunky amphib commander didn't even glance up at the navigation display. "We will be tying up at ten hundred hours exactly, ma'am."

Amanda suppressed a smile. She would be willing to wager that the lines would be going over the side within one minute of that call. "Very well, then, I'll stand down for a while. Keep me notified of any new developments."

"Understood, Captain. Will do."

Carberry faced forward, intent on the night beyond the bow of his ship. Amanda took a final look around the quiet, red-lit orderliness of the bridge and started aft.

A shadow detached from the bulkhead near the entry-way. "Lucas couldn't say it, but I can. A slickly executed double-shuffle, Amanda. I bet that poor bastard of a Parchim skipper is still wondering what hit him."

"Hmm, that will just make him that harder to fool next time, Admiral," Amanda replied. "Remember, sooner or later we're going to have to sneak Steamer and his gang back aboard again."

"Sufficient is the evil unto the day, Captain. We'll worry about that later. In the meantime, would you care to join me for midrats in the wardroom before you turn in?"

"I'd love to, sir. Being sneaky gives me an appetite."

"Midrats," or midnight rations, is the fourth meal of the day for the United States Navy, either a final settling bite before turning in, or a starting jolt to the blood sugar, depending upon which end of the watch bill one is posted at.

With the *Carlson* standing down from action stations, a dozen other task force officers were present in the wardroom, making their selections from the trays of sandwiches, fruit, and fresh baked goods set out along the serving board.

A small napkin-covered plate had been placed behind the larger sandwich tray with a neatly lettered RESERVED FOR THE TACBOSS card set atop it. Amanda flipped the napkin back with appreciative anticipation. Welch's grape jelly and Jif extra crunchy peanut butter on French bread. With the telepathy required of a truly first-class member of his rating, the *Carlson*'s senior mess steward had one of her favorites waiting.

"Coffee, milk, or bug juice?" MacIntyre inquired from the beverage dispenser.

"Milk, please. A tall cold one," Amanda replied. "Anything else would be like serving red wine with fish. Hasn't your daughter ever taught you the proper aesthetics of peanut butter and jelly?"

"She's never had the chance, I suppose," MacIntyre replied, filling a glass for Amanda. "You know how it is with the trade."

"Very much so," she replied, accepting the beverage. "How are things going with Judy?"

"Fine." A hint of enthusiasm crept into MacIntyre's voice. Amanda had learned he enjoyed speaking about his "Daddy's girl." "She's getting on well at school, her grades are good, and she's growing into quite the young lady. She's going to be as beautiful as her mother."

MacIntyre tossed a roast beef on whole wheat onto his own plate and hesitated. "That's the one regret I've ever had with the Navy. I've missed so much with my kids, with Judy and with her brothers. Sometimes I worry about their forgiving me for being gone so often."

He glanced at her. "You were a Navy brat, Amanda. How did you take it with Wils?"

Amanda tilted her head in consideration. "Not too bad, really," she said after a moment. "But then, one of the first lessons my parents taught me was that you have to be willing to share. I also learned early on that I had just about the bravest, most loving, most wonderful dad in the whole world. When you're that lucky, you should be willing to be generous with it."

They moved to the nearest of the tables and took seats across from each other.

Amanda smiled at MacIntyre. "I wouldn't worry about it. Judy is a sensible young woman and she didn't seem to be the stingy type to me."

"No, she isn't. Not a bit of it. But still..." MacIntyre hesitated for a second. "Amanda, could I ask you a big favor?"

"Of course. What is it, sir?"

She was intrigued to find her solid and craggy CO looking faintly embarrassed. "Maybe when we get back from this cruise, you could take Judy somewhere and talk to her about me being gone so much. And maybe some other things, too, the kind of topics a sixteen-year-old girl might want to talk about to another woman instead of her father. I'd appreciate it," the admiral finished gruffly, "and I can't think of anyone else I'd rather ask to do it."

"I'll be happy to talk with Judy anytime, Admiral. I'm flattered you'd ask me." And Amanda genuinely was. "I will admit I haven't had much hands-on experience with that kind of thing, but I'll do my best. Tell me more about her."

Their conversation progressed little further that night, however. Christine Rendino literally staggered into the compartment, her appearance bringing Amanda and MacIntyre both to their feet.

"Chris, my God, are you all right?"

"Oh, sure, Boss Ma'am. I'm fine." Her face wan and her voice hoarse, Christine collapsed in the chair across from them. "I just need to toke a few tanna leaves and I'll be good to go again."

Reaching over, Chris procured and drained Amanda's glass of milk, then let her head thump down on her crossed arms. "It took us eleven straight hours, but Tran and I finally did it. We busted the prizemaster," she murmured.

Midrats were forgotten. Amanda, MacIntyre, and Christine withdrew at once to the security of Amanda's flag quarters.

"You've got him talking?" Amanda demanded as the soundproof door closed behind them.

"At the moment, we can't get him to shut up." Christine dropped onto the couch, rubbing her eyes. "The poor schmo didn't have a clue about effective anti-interrogation techniques. He tried to play the strong and silent type, and those guys are a cinch to break down. You just have to stay on 'em long enough."

"Please don't take this the wrong way, Commander," MacIntyre said, leaning back against Amanda's desk edge, "but if this interrogation's put you in this kind of shape, what's left of him? We are dealing with a foreign national here. One that we're going to have to give back sooner or later."

Christine grinned feebly. "We never laid a glove on him, sir. The last thing you want in a situation like this is to reenforce an anger-defiance scenario or to give your subject a solid pain point to focus on.

"While we had him on the Duke, we hit this guy with an isolation and temporal disorientation program to soften him up. Then, when we got him here aboard the *Carlson*, we hammered him with a repetitive, sequential-point interrogation with positive feedback anytime we gained ground."

"Hmm," MacIntyre grunted. "I'll take your word for it."

Amanda looked at her friend with concern. "Are you going to have to go through this with all of the prisoners?"

"Oh, no, not even close, Boss Ma'am. We can pick keywords like place and personal names out of the prizemaster's interrogation—his is Hayam Mangkurat by the way—and use them against the other prisoners. Once we can show that somebody else has already blabbed, the others should follow along pretty easily. Getting the first one to talk is the toughie."

"Will he recover?" Amanda asked.

"Oh, sure," Christine stretched. "We'll give him his day-and-night cycle back and he'll sleep it all off in a couple of days. He'll be fine."

"At least until his boss and the rest of his clan figure out that he spilled," MacIntyre commented grimly.

Christine waved the thought away. "No problem. I'm keeping the other prisoners isolated and under temporal disorientation until after the first round of interrogations. The way I'm going to double-shuffle the questioning, nobody's ever going to know who talked first. Not even old Mangkurat himself. Piece of cake."

"This time I'll take your word for it." Amanda crossed to the couch and tilted her friend's head back, studying the shadows under her eyes. "Wouldn't it have been easier to just hit him with a dose of scopolamine?"

"Babble juice does just that, makes 'em babble. When you break 'em down the old-fashioned way, you get to the straight skinny faster." Christine collapsed back on the couch, a faint smile on her face. "One thing's for sure: That Inspector Tran really knows his stuff. It's a real frickin' joy interrogating someone with him."

Amanda and MacIntyre exchanged glances. They both had come to rely on and implicitly trust Christine Rendino. Each, in their own way, had become very fond of the little blonde. But they both held to the old-line officer's adage that intels were always just a little bit strange.

"What have you got out of him so far?" MacIntyre inquired.

"That whoever is running this show, be it Harconan or whoever, has this place *organized*," Christine said emphatically. "Hayam Mangkurat's ship is one of half a dozen raider schooners that stage out of a Bugis colony on the western peninsula of Sulawesi. It's a village north of Parepare on Mandar Bay called Adat Tanjung. Apparently it's a major pirate port and operating base, but if we went storming in there tomorrow, we wouldn't find a single trace of a stolen cargo, an out-of-place weapon, or even a single rupiah that couldn't be accounted for."

Amanda sank down on the couch beside Christine. "How are they pulling it off, Chris?"

"They take advantage of the fact that there are about ten gajillion little islands, bays, and inlets out there, many of which have never been accurately charted. Apparently nothing incriminating is ever brought into the village area itself. The raider *pinisi* are decontaminated before they return to base. All weapons are secured in cache sites, and the hijacked cargoes are delivered to prearranged dropoff points. The pirates themselves never see who recovers the loot.

"A reverse procedure occurs when they need to re-outfit. They're given a pickup point along the coast or on a nearby island, and the gear they need—weapons, ammo, engine parts, whatever—is sitting there under camouflage, waiting for them. They never see who delivers it."

"How's this all coordinated?" MacIntyre demanded. "How do they set the pickup and delivery points?"

"It's so ingenious it hurts, Admiral, sir," Christine replied. "Every raider skipper is given two things: a garden-variety digital wristwatch with a month's memory, and a hand-held Global Positioning Unit—two items that wouldn't arouse any suspicion at all on an interisland trader. Each skipper is also given a place around his home village area where he leaves his wristwatch and GPU unit at a specific time once a month. When he picks them up again, the watch has been programmed with a set of pickup and delivery times and the GPU with drop and recovery point coordinates. There's also a block of raiding intelligence on ships and high-value cargoes passing within a given range of the clan villages. The raider captains themselves divvy up the pie according to what's within their capabilities. The only decrees from the sea king are fair shares for all and no poaching in another clan's territory. Break the rules and the support stops coming."

Christine smothered a yawn with her palm. "The raider captains and the village elders all know that one of their number is the chosen agent of the *raja samudra,* but nobody knows who. It's a classic cell security system. You can't leak what you don't know. There's no overt chain of command to follow to the higher echelons of the organization."

"How do the pirates get their payback?" Amanda asked.

"Any number of different ways; through material, for one: The pirate skipper leaves a wish list at his monthly drop, and the gear he needs is at his next pickup point.

"As far as cash goes, Indonesia isn't all that primitive anymore. It's the most natural thing in the world for the skipper of a *pinisi* to have a bank account on one of the interisland chain banks. Intermittently money is deposited in that account under his name, random amounts at erratic intervals. Money that can be explained away as a good haul of fish or a rich charter."

"And what about those Bugis aid programs Harconan sponsors?" MacIntyre added. "What do you want to bet that the clans that most support the sea king get the plumpest support packages?"

"No bets taken," Amanda replied. "And remember those so-called pirate raids on Harconan's shipping line? That will be another mode of payoff and resupply he can use while maintaining the front of being just another harassed shipowner."

She crossed to the porthole and stared out into the night. "He's careful, Admiral, and so cunning it hurts. He's subtly herding the Bugis clans under his control, building an association between the *raja samudra* and wealth, comfort, empowerment, and dignity. And so far he's asked for little in return. Someday, though, he will. He'll lead, and they'll follow. The question is, where?"

MacIntyre gave an ironic chuckle. "It's grown a bit from a satellite recovery mission, hasn't it."

"Too true, sir. Sometimes you have to tip the rock over before you can see what-all's hiding underneath. I think the secretary of state and the National Command Authority will agree that this is a very definite and growing freedom-of-the-seas concern."

"Tomorrow I'll get on the horn to Foggy Bottom and brief the secretary of state on the new permutations we're kicking up out here. I think he'll agree this is very much a case of 'Damn the torpedoes, full speed ahead.' Until we at least develop a clearer image of how far this plan of Harconan's has progressed. After that, we'll see who gets to throw the monkey wrench into the works, us or the Indonesians."

"Let's hope they'll believe us when the time comes." Amanda turned from the port and came to lean back against the desk beside MacIntyre. "At any rate, we have a better idea of what to look for now, and we know where to aim Steamer and the microforce. Maybe they can find us the next step up the ladder."

A soft snore came from the direction of the office couch. Collapsed in an inelegant but comfortable posture, Christine Rendino sprawled, asleep.

Amanda and the admiral swapped grins. "That reminds me"—Amanda lowered her voice to a whisper—"we'd all better get our beauty rest. We've got a party to go to tomorrow night."

It is said that Bali is the largest outpost of the Hindu religion outside of India; yet, this is not quite true. The religion of the Balinese, Agama Hindu Dharma (the Religion of the Holy Water) is unique unto and of itself, tempered with the ancient mysticism of the first peoples of the archipelago.

God- and demon-haunted, seemingly as delicate as a mountain mist or a butterfly's wing, this religion/philosophy/way of life has endured through the centuries with the resiliency of tempered steel.

To Bali the Brahman priests and scholars of the lost golden Majapahit Empire retreated in the fifteenth century, and here they made their stand against the Islamic invasion from the West. Here they held, the followers of Mohammed breaking like the waves against the stark coastal cliffs of the little island.

Here, also, the Dutch came in 1846, Bali being the last free holdout in the archipelago against Holland's colonial empire. Sixty years of savage resistance would follow before the last battle was fought, and yet, all the Dutch could claim were the towns and villages, never Bali's soul.

In the late twentieth century came the most insidious invasion of all, the twentieth century itself, with its tourists and commercialization and a government in Jakarta with decided ideas of what should be done "for Bali's own good."

And yet, the Balinese stand. Perhaps it is because the Followers of the Holy Water have an advantage over every other religion in the world: It is said they know what heaven actually looks like.

Like Bali.

The Sea Fighter Task Force arrived with the growing heat of the day, standing in through the mouth of Benoa Harbor, past Serangan (Turtle) Island and the tip of Cape Benoa.

The expected reception committee awaited them at the Port: an Indonesian army band and honor guard from the local garrison force and a small cluster of civil and military officials to say the appropriate words of welcome and to put the brightest possible spin on this visitation from the United States.

Others awaited the Sea Fighters' arrival as well.

Cape Benoa   2019 Hours, Zone Time: August 15, 2008

Makara Harconan wheeled the Bentley Challenger convertible into the harbor overlook, parking at the far end, well away from the guided-tour van and the clusters of rented motor scooters.

The sunset was flaming magnificently to the west beyond the Bukit Badung Peninsula with a flight of elaborate Balinese kites dancing against it, the excited voices of their young pilots shrill and happy in the growing dusk.

At another time, Harconan would have enjoyed watching the sky-borne dance. Tonight, though, he had other affairs to tend. Thoughtfully he studied the vast cluster of glowing work lights that seemed to float in the center of the bay.

Supporting the island's capital of Denpasar, Benoa Harbor has historically been the most important port in southern Bali.

Yet the great crescent-shaped indentation in the island's southern peninsula had also been chronically cursed with shallows and building sandbars. The Dutch colonial government, confronted with the problem, elected to make lemonade.

Setting aside their role as a colonial taskmaster, the old Hollanders were master engineers with a vast amount of experience at wrestling land out of a resistant sea. Taking advantage of the shallows, they built a two-kilometer-long causeway out onto the center of the harbor from its swamp-rimmed northern edge. At the end of this causeway they built a kilometer-square artificial island to serve as their port facility.

Here, as well as the required water depth, were the tank farms and warehouses, the container cranes and loading docks, needed to service the shipping of the world. One of his cargo liners, the *Harconan Sumatra,* was over there now, discharging.

The ships of his foes were present as well.

Reaching over to the Bentley's glove box, he removed a pair of folding sports binoculars. Snapping them open, he aimed them across at the port complex.

In the fading light he could just make out the two great gray shapes, stern on and bow on between the eastern port piers, the American stealth cruiser, long and low and ominous, and the big slab-sided amphibious warfare ship with who knew how many deadly secrets hidden inside its belly.

Harconan could feel the gods looking over his shoulder and smiling.

They come for you, O King of the Sea. What shall you do now? Give us divertissement.

The car's cellular phone purred softly, and Harconan lifted it to his ear. Bapak Lo spoke quietly. "Our guests will be arriving shortly, Mr. Harconan."

"I know, Lo. In fact, I'm paying my respects to some of them now."

White-gloved and with the red glare of the deck lights glinting off the gold of his saber hilt, Captain Stone Quillain worked down the line of the Sea Dragon's honor squad, a gimlet eye scanning for the slightest imperfection in uniform or demeanor. The twelve Marines held rigidly at attention, eyes level, statues in dress blues.

Stone could find no real fault; yet, here and there he tugged a white-enameled bayonet sheath even straighter or ran a finger along a rifle barrel seeking for a nonexistent smear of excess gun oil. These boys were just fine, just as he knew they'd be, but it wouldn't pay to let 'em think the old man was getting sloppy.

"They'll do, Sergeant," Stone grunted to the squad leader. "At ease till we're ready to embark."

"Very good, sir! Squad! Stand at ease!"

There was the faintest scuffle of shoes on the antiskid decking, any relaxation on the part of the honor squad being purely nominal.

A few feet farther forward on the *Carlson*'s flight deck, the Special Boat Squadron commander, Lieutenant Labelle Nichols, was putting her white-uniformed RIB crews through the same kind of meticulous formal inspection in preparation for the night's events. Farther forward, the detachment's two eleven-meter Rigid Inflatable raider craft, polished, primped, and gleaming, rested in the LPD's midships boat cradles, ready to launch.

Stone gave his own sword belt an unneeded settling tug. Even though Stone did enjoy doing a little saber fencing now and again, the Wilkinson Marine officer's sword at his waist was essentially ceremonial. The same could not be said of the Randall combat knife strapped to his left forearm under his blouse sleeve, nor of the SIG Sauer P226 automatic in his concealed "Superman carry" shoulder holster.

The skipper had been emphatic about it: "Until further notice, ladies and gentlemen, this command is fangs out. Even in polite society."

Stone wouldn't think of arguing the point. That was why he looked up so sharply as a computer-synthesized voice thundered in the night, powerful loudspeakers barking out a sharp-edged phrase first in Bahasa Indonesia and then Bahasa Bali.

A local motor *prahu* had meandered too close to the *Carlson*'s stern, triggering the automatic-proximity warning.

Long before the Port Aden tragedy, the Navy had been aware that its ships were never more vulnerable than when they were resting at anchor in port. Since the Aden attack, even more attention and technology had been focused on the problem.

The task force now had a number of advantages over the ill-fated *Cole.*

The Voice Proximity Alarm was the first line of defense. Programmable with the primary local languages, it vastly reduced the risk of killing an innocent Third World national who couldn't understand the meaning of "Get the hell away from here."

Nonlethal ordnance constituted the second line.

Forward, at each corner of the *Carlson*'s superstructure, the dish antenna of the LPD's SMADS—Ship-Mounted Area Denial System—had deployed flowerlike from their box mounts. Euphemistically called "antiriot directed energy projectors," the SMADS units were, in truth, microwave cannon carefully tuned to generate extreme discomfort but little physical injury.

Given a short-term exposure, at any rate.

Stone shuddered as he recalled the light brush he'd taken from a vehicle-mounted VMADS beam during the system orientation training. It was safe to say that anyone who stood on in the face of that brand of concentrated agony had to be either very desperate or very dedicated. Such focused individuals could be safely met with more decisive measures.

The *Carlson*'s four point-defense turrets were still retracted inboard, but gunners were at station in the 30mm chain gun mounts, scanning both the harbor and the dockside through their powerful night optics. Those were further augmented by the joint Marine and ship security deck patrols, the Marine half of each team carrying a loaded SABR, the Navy hand backing a squad automatic weapon with a full fifty-round magazine.

Like defenses were in place aboard the *Cunningham.*

Stone would have also liked OCSW grenade launchers mounted and manned at bow and stern and on the bridge wings, but Admiral MacIntyre had pointed out that at least some diplomatic niceties had to be maintained.

Other precautions had been taken, however. Both the *Carlson* and the *Cunningham* had "Mediterranean moored." Instead of lying alongside the quay, the Duke had tied up with her stern to the seawall, held in place by a broad V of spring lines. The LPD had done the reverse: moored bow on so her stern ramp faced open water, leaving her free to conduct launching and recovery operations.

Developed by the Sixth Fleet during the old Cold War days, the Med moor allowed a ship to cast off and scald out of port rapidly without the need of backing and filling or tug assist.

Both ships had emergency engine room and sea and anchor details held ready to get under way at a moment's notice. Both had anti-SCUBA tactical hydrophones deployed, and both had armed Seawolf gunships spotted on deck, ready to launch.

These bristling defenses were unneeded this time around. The startled motor junk veered away from the anchorage, scurrying away into the evening's darkness.

Lieutenant Nichols wrapped up her own inspection. Standing her people down, she crossed to where Stone lingered at the rail. Nichols wore skirted tropic whites complete with gloves and pumps and the Sea Fighters' black beret. Stone had to note that the tall and muscular young woman looked decisively sharp this night.

"Ready to go in the bandbox, Marine?" she inquired in a bantering tone.

"Oh, hell, we were born ready." Stone had found the Special Boat officer to be both a fellow Georgian and a fellow bass-fishing fanatic, making her more than a worthwhile companion. "How about yourself? Get all that spittin' and polishin' done?"

"Barely. I don't mind that the Lady is using my Raiders as liberty launches. But the way she's had me set them up ... there's something funny going on."

Stone nodded an agreement. "I know what you mean. It's the same with me and my boys. The Lady's got some kind of notion goin' in that red head of hers. The thing is, I've done a cruise with Captain Garrett before, and she always has a reason for everything she does. When she's ready, she'll let us in on it."

"I'll take your word for it." Even with her height and her heels, Nichols had to look up into Quillain's face. "So, Captain"—she impishly let a touch of the Old South creep into her voice—"y'all goin' to save me a dance on your card?"

Quillain pretended to think. "I dunno, woman. Those local gals likely haven't seen anything as pretty as me come down the pike in a long time. But if the Duchess of Argyle stands me up, I reckon I might even let you have two."

Nichols laughed, the brightness of her smile a pleasing contrast to the warm dark brown of her skin.

Amanda Garrett closed her makeup kit, satisfied with the results of that last careful dab of eyeliner. Stepping back as far as she could within the confines of her sleeping cabin, she critically examined as much of herself as possible in the small door mirror.

She was a naval officer to the core and she was proud of her nation's uniform, but she was also adequately feminine to savor dressing up when the opportunity presented itself. Her silken cream-colored blouse was long-sleeved and military-cut, and her formal length skirt was of lightweight black velvet, with a slash just high enough to be interesting. She was pleased with the effect.

Removing her small jewelry box from a wall locker, she sought for a final touch. Simple golden disk earrings and...a necklace? She pondered for a moment. No, something else. She selected a thin, coiled black velvet ribbon from the box. Vince Arkady had given that to her on one occasion, telling her it was one of the three most stimulating things a woman could wear.

He had refused to elaborate on why, or what the other two articles were, though. Amanda smiled at the memory as she looped the ribbon around her throat. Someday, when some suitable male was available, she'd have to make further inquiries.

Finally, she removed the Navy Command insignia pin from the box and secured it to her lapel. A little thing, but a reminder to others and to herself about who she was and that this night was still business.

She slipped her feet into a pair of rubber-soled deck shoes and caught up her evening bag and the pair of evening sandals she'd switch to before hitting the beach. Stiletto heels were definitely not designed for the ladderways of a man-of-war.

Ready.

She nodded to the sentry on duty outside her cabin door. The young Marine gave her a split second's worth of gawk before catching himself and refreezing at a neutral-faced parade rest. Amanda smiled to herself. Yes, this outfit would do.

The other task force officers attending the reception awaited her in the wardroom. The low murmur of conversation trailed off as she appeared in the entryway.

Christine was present, the only other female officer to opt for civilian dress, in her case a short, golden-sequined sheath, outrageous enough to suit her. Amanda noted with interest that her friend was lingering close to Inspector Tran in a rather nonprofessional matter. And understandably, the Singapore police officer cut a very dashing figure in his white evening jacket.

Captain Carberry had been standing near the entry. "Good evening, Captain..." he began formally, then hesitated. The old-school Navy didn't provide for moments like this with one's commanding officer. Then the faintest hint of a smile touched Carberry's face. "You're looking lovely tonight, ma'am."

"Thank you, Commander." Amanda was pleased to find that she remembered how to curtsy.

And then Admiral Elliot MacIntyre stood before her in razor-creased whites, his uniform cap tucked under his arm. Somehow he looked younger than his years and rank, much as he must have as an Academy midshipman. And there was something in the gaze of his dark eyes.

An unexpected shiver rippled down her spine, and she found herself extending her hand without intending it. Then his fingers closed around hers and he, too, was bowing.

"Amanda."

"Admiral." His name had come to her lips first, but she could not use it here. Nor could she permit this moment to last any longer.

Flustered, she made herself look away, slipping her hand free. She also made a note to take Christine Rendino aside sometime soon to slap that smug, knowing expression off the intel's face.

"Good evening, ladies and gentlemen," Amanda said. "Our transportation is ready to depart, I believe. I think we can expect an interesting night."

The shore parties filed topside to the *Carlson*'s boat stations.

The LPD couldn't spare the topside space or weight for conventional whaleboats or captain's gigs. Her boat cradles and powered davits had been dedicated to the assault craft of the task force's Special Boat detachment.

The eleven-meter rigid inflatable Raiders of the Special Boat Squadrons were the Navy's answer to the Boghammer gunboat. Powered by diesel-driven hydrojet propulsors, they were lightweight, swift, and heavily armed for their size. Capable of carrying eight passengers plus a three-person crew, the little gunboats were superb for their primary mission, delivering special-operations detachments to and from hostile shores. They were not, however, a typical mode of transportation to a diplomatic reception.

That suited Amanda's purposes quite well.

"Detachment ready to load and launch, Captain," Lieutenant Nichols reported crisply. "The Marine landing force is already embarked aboard Raider One as instructed."

"Honor guard, Lieutenant," Amanda corrected, standing in the scarlet glow of the deck lights. "Let's maintain the niceties. Are we ready to make our debut?"

The SB officer broke into a grin. "We're going to knock their eyes out, ma'am."

"Very good, Lieutenant. My intention exactly. Let's get them in the water."

Hydraulics howled as the power davits lifted the Raider over the side, lowering them smoothly and swiftly to the sea. The twin turbo-charged engines kicked over the instant water reached their cooling intake, and the bow and stern shackles were cast off. As Raider Two paid off and half-circled away from the quay and the ship, Amanda took a final judgmental look aft, checking the silhouettes of the security watch along the rails.

What had she overlooked? What else could be done? Nothing more here; it was time to refocus. Time to orient herself for this night's battle.

Trailing Raider One, Raider Two planed out and around the tip of Cape Benoa, turning south for the five-kilometer run down the coast to the Makara Limited headquarters at Nusa Dua. The big RIB was commodious but crowded this night, carrying in the first group of shorebound officers. Amanda sat beside Admiral MacIntyre on one of the fold-out bench seats in the cockpit, not particularly minding the warm touch at hip and shoulder. Across from them, she could see the shimmer of Christine's dress and the paleness of Tran's jacket in the glow of the console lights.

Amanda lifted her voice over the rumble of the diesels. "I'm glad you decided to accept Christine's invitation, Inspector. Your presence tonight should induce some useful effects."

Tran chuckled lowly. "As the saying goes, Captain, I wouldn't miss this party for the world."

MacIntyre shifted at her side. "All right, Amanda, this is scarcely your average liberty party we're taking ashore with us. You and your henchwoman over there have had your heads together all afternoon, assembling some kind of plot. Isn't it about time you let the boss in on the action?"

"It's about mind games, Admiral," said Amanda. "Harconan was playing one when he issued his invitation. He wants to get a close look at us, to learn how much we suspect, what our intentions are, and how we intend to play this out. All while we are effectively disarmed and out of balance at this supposedly innocent reception."

MacIntyre thumped his fist on his knee. "Ha! Now I get the dog-and-pony show. You're turning the game around on him."

Amanda's responding smile was grim. "I'm told that's one of my specialties. Harconan made a bold move with this reception. You counter boldness with boldness."

Makara Limited Harbor Court
2105 Hours, Zone Time:
August 15, 2008

"I must admit," Harconan commented, "I've been looking forward to this evening. I've heard a great deal about your navy's Captain Garrett. I'm very interested in meeting her."

Randolph Goodyard frowned thoughtfully. "I daresay we all have heard a great deal about Captain Garrett."

Harconan caught the accenting of Goodyard's words. "Is there some difficulty, Ambassador? If I may ask, that is?"

And Harconan knew he could. This was why he had invited America's ambassador from his posting in Jakarta to this function. Above and beyond the credentials he provided, Goodyard was a malleable source of information.

The two men spoke over the soft brassy flow of the jazz quintet and the murmur of voices. Taking advantage of the mellow tropic night, the fleet reception was being held outdoors in the artfully landscaped courtyard between the concave front face of the Makara Limited headquarters building and the beach. Almost as many guests came by boat as by car, the waterborne arrivals unloading at the modernistic J-shaped private pier centered on the court.

Hypersonic insect repellers kept insectoid night marauders at bay. Tray-bearing waiters moved with silent efficiency, and golden indirect lighting underlit the surrounding palm grove, half revealing the couples and clusters of people who conversed and occasionally laughed in the night.

"There's not a problem, really, Mr. Harconan," Goodyard continued as the two men paced slowly along the tiled walk atop the beach. "It's only that Captain Garrett and our Naval Special Forces as a whole have developed a certain . . . reputation."

"Reputation? How so, Ambassador? Oh, and please, call me Makara."

Goodyard glanced around for any of his staffers. The ambassador didn't fancy being overheard airing State Department dirty laundry off his own turf.

Lowering his voice: "It's only that some of us within the diplomatic community consider Captain Garrett and the current Naval Special Forces commander, Admiral Elliot MacIntyre, to be somewhat . . . destabilizing, if you understand my meaning. Mind you, they're both very capable officers, but Garrett is prone to precipitous and unilateral actions beyond the genuine level of her authority, and MacIntyre gives her carte blanche to get away with it. Some of us feel too many corners have been cut on more than one occasion."

The ambassador paused to finish the last of his excellent champagne cocktail, and he failed to note the minute flick of Harconan's head that summoned a waiter with a tray of replacements.

"The Foreign Ministry in Jakarta is acting as if they have a rebellion under every bush," Goodyard continued, a replenished glass in hand. "Nothing your government can't deal with, I'm sure. But given the current delicacy of the situation in this region, we don't need any cowboys—or cowgirls—in the area just now."

Harconan smiled behind the studied sobriety of his expression. "I understand that the task force's visit to Singapore and Indonesia is primarily intended as a goodwill mission. Might there be anything more to it than that?" The taipan laughed lightly. "If you can say, of course. I've heard there's been a degree of concern over the satellite that was lost over in the Arafura."

Goodyard grimaced. "Oh, that damn thing. No, that turned out to be something of a tempest in a teapot. It was all we heard about from Washington for a while, but the subject seems to be petering out. I think the secretary of state became a little embarrassed over the fuss the special interests made over the matter. I've been instructed to do a little fence-mending with your people over that."

Harconan nodded and sipped from his tulip glass of mineral water. Interesting. But then, intelligence sources such as Goodyard were always a two-edged dagger. On the one edge, the ambassador was telling him exactly what he wanted to hear. On the other, the ambassador *might* be telling him exactly what the ambassador wanted him to hear. One could never truly judge how good a liar a man could be until the point was proven. The more capable of sophistry the individual was, the more credible they would appear.

Goodyard seemed to be the innocent, but still . . .

Harconan glanced to seaward. "So we can expect no grand Garrett adventures in the near future? A pity, I was rather hoping to see the lady in action."

"Knock on wood." Goodyard grinned. "Not unless something breaks out while she's in the neighborhood. Then you might see the house blown up to put out the fire. I'm sorry to disappoint you, ah, Makara, but I don't need a visit from Rambo on my watch. Things look brittle enough as is."

Harconan nodded and smiled at the diplomatic understatement. The concept of *Bhinneka tunggal ika*, "Many are one," was the proclaimed ideal of the Indonesian government. The reality was that, for decades, Jakarta had engaged in a frantic juggling match with Indonesia's myriad of political and religious factions, balancing one against the other in the hope that, eventually, a true Indonesian identity would take hold within its population. To date, only an erratic and jingoistic nationalism had emerged within certain groups, such as the military.

Sooner or later, the juggler would miss a ball, or have it knocked aside. Once that occurred, it would be time for something new. Harconan's smile deepened at the thought.

"It appears you have some new guests arriving."

The ambassador's comment drew Harconan back to the

JAMES H. COBB

here and now. Looking northward along the coast, he noted a double set of running lights inbound toward the Makara Limited pier.

"So it would seem, Ambassador. Excuse me, please: I have a host's duties to attend to."

Lengthening his stride, Harconan proceeded to the pier deck that extended outward from the beach walk.

The curving end of the pier with its integral surf break created a patch of sheltered water within its inner curve. A small-craft float lay within this shelter, linked by sliding ramp to the pier deck. A pair of line handlers, rather incongruously clad in white dinner jackets, were already standing by on the float. Reception guests from Bali's diplomatic and business communities were drifting out along the pier, looking on with interest. The word had spread that the launches from the American task force, the guests of honor, were arriving.

Powerful marine diesels rumbled out of the night, and the first Navy craft moved into the zone of light cast by the pier arcs.

It was no mere launch from the task force: It was a unit of the task force itself. A rakish miniature gunboat swept out of the darkness. Its mottled gray-tone camouflage paint had been touched up flawlessly. The few small hints of brass and chrome had been burnished bright, and the workaday nylon strap safety rails around its gunwales had been replaced by dazzling white nylon cord, hauled taut and tied with elaborate seamen's knots.

Water boiled as hydrojet propulsors backed with a hiss. With absolute precision the assault boat curved into the float, the last of its wake dissipating just as its flank touched the side of the dock, the Raider's crew merely handing the mooring lines across to the pier-side handlers.

The uniforms of the SB hands were frost-white as well, white with the distinctive black beret of the Sea Fighter Task Force tugged low over one eye. Gunners stood at parade rest at the 25mm OCSW grenade launcher at the bow and at the pintle-mounted Barrett .50-caliber anti-material rifles amidships, riding with the motion of their small, deadly craft with the practiced ease of the Special Boat crewman.

A short aluminum gangway had been mounted upright on the gunwale of the craft. Now, with a single yank of a release pin, its outboard end dropped to the float's decking.

"Honor Guard..." a powerful baritone voice roared, "disembark!"

Half a dozen American Marines clattered down the short gangway, spacing out in a double row between its foot and the base of the float access ramp. Snapping to a stiff-spine parade rest, each stood with an obsolete M-14 rifle at his side, its white enameled wooden stock buffed to a satiny sheen.

A seventh Marine, an officer, taller, more powerful, more resplendent, paced slowly down between the short double row of his fellows. Pausing at the head of the guard, his dark hawkish eyes swept across Harconan and the other reception guests now looking on silently from the pier.

The Marine's lips pursed as if he saw nothing that impressed him. He pivoted machinelike into line with the honor guard.

The gangway swung back aboard, and mooring lines were snatched back from the pier handlers. The Raider blasted away back into the night on its water jets, curving back toward the distant Navy moorage for its next load of passengers.

"Honor Guard..." the Marine officer's voice rang again. "Fix bayonets!"

Polished black blades rasped from belt sheaths and clicked into place on underbarrel mounting lugs.

"Honor Guard...attention!"

Heels crashed on the pier decking.

A second Navy RIB came in out of the night, docking with the same deftness as the first. A second gangway dropped.

"Present arms!"

Rifles clattered and lifted, white-gloved hands slapping on polished stocks.

The Marine officer's sword screamed out of its sheath,

the glittering silver blade whipping to the vertical before his face.

"Commandant...United States Naval Special Forces... arriving!"

An officer strode down the short gangway and between the double row of the honor guard. An older man, graying, weathered but not aged. Not as tall as Harconan, but as broad-shouldered, with an almost defiant air of solidity, as if an earthquake might level all around him and yet he would stand.

Harconan descended the pier ramp, extending his hand. He had been briefed about this man. "Admiral MacIntyre, welcome to Bali."

"Mr. Harconan." The handshake was strong, the voice noncommittal. So the admiral had been briefed on him as well.

The Marine officer roared again. "Commander...Sea Fighter Task Force...arriving!"

She appeared at the head of the gangway. Blood royal rather than a military officer, yet totally at ease amid the hard-edged backdrop of combat technology. Slightly lifting her long skirt with her hands in an archaic, elegantly feminine gesture, she descended to the float.

Amanda Garrett was not truly tall—at best she was of average height without heels—yet, she radiated the impression of tallness, her head lifted in instinctive pride, her bearing regal by nature.

Makara Harconan had known and savored many women in his life, some of whom had been considered among the most beautiful in the world, but he had never before encountered any female so totally arresting. He could not say why. There had been models more perfectly featured, actresses more lushly endowed, but no one so inherently dynamic.

She paced past the honor guard and flowed to a halt at Admiral MacIntyre's side. A pair of large golden eyes glowed at Harconan and she extended her hand...palm down.

I have come for you, O King of the Sea, those eyes spoke silently. *Bow to me.*

Harconan vowed he would possess this woman. Closing his fingers around hers, he inclined over her hand, but only slightly.

"Captain Garrett."

She inclined her head. "Mr. Harconan. On behalf of the Sea Fighter Task Force, I thank you for this warm welcome to your home waters. May I introduce one of my officers and her escort. Lieutenant Commander Christine Rendino and Inspector Nguyen Tran of the Singapore National Police."

Harconan was jerked back to reality, turning to the couple who had disembarked while he had been fixated on Amanda Garrett.

Tran? Could this be the same Singapore gadfly he'd been forced to quash last year with a series of exorbitant payoffs? What was he doing here with the Americans? *Damn you, Harconan, forget the woman and look to business!*

Tran nodded to him, with the faintest of smiles on his angular features. "A pleasure, Mr. Harconan. We have never before had the opportunity to meet . . . in person."

The little blonde on Tran's arm said sweetly, "But the inspector has been able to tell us so much about you."

What was happening here? As Harconan mouthed the appropriate platitudes, his eyes swept the boarding stage. What sort of threat could this group pose?

He caught the slight bulge of a side arm under Tran's evening jacket, a factor that might be expected with a police officer. But then, there were matching bulges under the uniform coats of both MacIntyre and the Marine captain overseeing the honor guard, the same with every naval officer disembarking from the Raider craft.

The Marines of the honor guard still held a rigid attention, but their eyes were moving and alert.

And the rifles they were carrying. Harconan knew that the M-14 was long obsolete in American service, relegated to ceremonial usage. But these specific weapons were not mere ceremonial accouterments with welded actions. Harconan's second look revealed that they were still fully

194   JAMES H. COBB

functional and fully loaded, a twenty-round magazine of 7.62 NATO protruding from each magazine well. Each honor guard also had a white leather pouch at his belt that was not issue to the U.S. Marine dress uniform, but which was just the right size for a pair of reloads.

And the bayonets: Each black steel blade had a thin, silvery band along its point and cutting edge, the sheen of a razor sharpening.

Aboard the assault boat, every crewman and -woman wore a polished side arm holster and Brasso'ed ammunition belts gleamed in the gun mounts.

Amanda Garrett had not merely come to a party. She was landing a military expeditionary force.

Harconan had his own security elements discreetly deployed around the reception area. But nothing to match this potential concentration of firepower.

What had Ambassador Goodyard called this woman? "A cowgirl...prone to precipitous and unilateral actions..."

What in all hell was going on here?

Amanda Garrett wore the same slight, damnably knowing smile as Tran. It was as if he could feel her reading his every thought, every emotion.

Damn it, how long had it been since anyone had made him so apprehensive?

"I'm looking forward to talking with you, Mr. Harconan. I'm sure we have many things to discuss."

Then she turned away. Accepting MacIntyre's arm, she ascended the ramp to the top of the pier and the waiting reception line.

Java Sea,   **2205 Hours, Zone Time:**
Northeast of the Laut Kecil Island Group   **August 15, 2008**

Three hundred miles to the north, another carefully choreographed military evolution was under way.

To many, a visualization of the Indonesian archipelago would bring to mind tightly clustered green islands under a tropic sun, their azure waters busy with a multitude of small craft going about their affairs.

And so it was, in places.

Elsewhere, there are 'tween island straits broad enough to warrant the name of sea. No hint of land save for a cloud-bank on a far horizon, no shipping, no movement save for the waves and the wheeling of a weary seabird in transit.

In the center of one such emptiness, the Sea Fighters came to rest. Coming off the pad, the PGACs powered down and settled to the surface of the sea, drifting silently beneath the ten million and one stars of the tropic night.

Steamer Lane slid open the cockpit side window, admitting a puff of sea-fresh air and the sound of waves lapping against the hull.

"Position check," he called.

Ensign Terrence Wilder, the *Queen of the West*'s junior officer, thumbed a display call-up on the navigator's console. "Sir, Navicom indicates we are on station for rendezvous," he reported crisply. "I show matching coordinates on both Global Positioning Systems."

Lane slipped his helmet off and balanced it on the bow of the instrument panel. "That's good, Terr, we have arrived. Time check, Scrounge?"

"On the line, Skipper," Caitlin replied. "Fifteen minutes to rendezvous if the Air 'Farce' is up to it."

"Super good." Lane donned the earphones of the Digital Walkman he had clipped to the sun visor. "Terry, you have the con. Position the *Queen* and Reb for the drop reception...quietly. I'm going to catch a fast forty. Gimme a yell when we have the replenishment bird in sight."

Startled, Wilder looked forward from the Nav station. "Aye, aye, sir."

A twangy whisper of California surf rock drifted across the cockpit as Lane reclined against the back of his seat. With a developed warrior's knack, he was asleep in seconds, snatching the opportunity for brief refreshment.

Wilder hesitated, wrestling with his pride. But, as he was in fact an intelligent and capable young officer, he twisted his seat around to face the copilot's station.

"Hey, Chief," he whispered. "Could you help walk me

through this? I've never handled a drop replenishment at sea before."

"That's okay, Mr. Wilder," Scrounger Caitlin replied cheerfully, pulling a ring-bound procedures manual from the rack by her knee. "Nobody else has either."

Fifty miles to the south, Lieutenant Colonel Edwina Mirkle, United States Air Force, looked forward, first through the night-vision visor of her flight helmet, then through the nite-brite–attuned Heads Up display, and finally out through the windscreen of her MC-130J. Her knuckles clinched white on the control yoke, and her eyes burned dryly from her fixed stare.

She was not tense in the conventional sense of the term. This was simply how one flew a Combat Talon when one was so low the six-bladed Allison turboprops kicked rooster-tails off the wave tops and spume rattled against the nose. One stayed focused. Very, very focused.

After departing Curtin Field, the Air Commando transport had flown north conventionally from Australia until its sensitive IDECM (Integrated Defensive Electronic Countermeasures) arrays had sensed the Indonesian air defense net. The Talon had "gone tactical" then, staging incrementally lower and lower to stay under the radar net until they were literally skimming the surface of the sea.

The island of Flores had risen like a wall before them, and the MC-130 had climbed just enough to snake through one of the narrow passes in the central volcanic range, an unidentifiable black shadow blasting low over the isolated mountain villages.

The tension had risen incrementally when the Global Hawk drone, riding shotgun high overhead, had downlinked the warning of an interceptor scramble from an Indonesian air force base near Jakarta. However, the bewildered Anghkatan Udara Eurofighters soon turned back, the fragmentary radar track that had launched them having disappeared amid the lava crags.

Reaching water once more, the Talon returned to the

deck, racing out over the Flores Sea, its stealthed radar cross section blurring into the surface return.

That had been two hundred over-ocean miles ago. The altimeters had read zero continuously ever since. For the Air Commandos of the U.S. Air Force's First Special Operations Wing, the mission stank of the routine.

"Course correction," Colonel Mirkle's navigator murmured. "Come right five degrees to zero . . . one . . . two."

Mirkle eased down on her right foot pedal, nudging the big plane into a slow skidding turn on the rudder alone, keeping the wings fixed dead level by the artificial horizon. A conventional bank would put a prop arc into the water, cartwheeling the Talon across the sea in a spectacular crash.

"Steering zero . . . one . . . two," she read back.

"On the beam, ma'am. Ten minutes out. Global Hawk link verifies our customers are on station and waiting for us."

"Thanks, Johnny. Ed, tell the chief to rig for payload extraction."

As her copilot relayed the command to the loadmaster, Mirkle eased back minutely on the control yoke. The chief was going to be walking around back in the cargo bay, and the aircraft might bobble with the weight shift. Best to take her up a little.

Within the First Spec Ops Wing, Mirkle had a reputation as a cautious veteran pilot. Neither a hot dog nor a cowgirl, she recognized her own limitations and preferred leaving a margin for error.

The Talon climbed to a solid twenty-five feet and leveled off once more.

Maneuvering on their electric propulsors, the *Queen of the West* and the *Manassas* positioned a quarter of a mile apart, nose on to the wind and sea. Mast-Mounted Sighting Systems panned along the horizon, low-light television intently scanning for intruders, while ECM monitors suspiciously sniffed the ether.

Inboard, the auxiliary fuel blivets in the central bays of the hovercraft were flat and flaccid. The kerosene they had carried had either been consumed or transferred into the Sea Fighter's integral tankage. With an assist from the Marines, the gunboat crews rolled and lashed the empty bladders into compact bundles for storage, making room for their replacements.

In the *Queen*'s cockpit, Ensign Wilder reached forward and touched Steamer Lane on the shoulder. "Sir, we have established a datalink with the replenishment aircraft. They're on approach. Five minutes out. We are positioned for drop reception."

Steamer came awake and functional as swiftly as he had dozed off. "Good work Terr," he said snapping off the Walkman and returning his seat to an upright state. "What's the environment, Scrounge?"

"Sterile water and clean threat boards," Caitlin reported. "Wind direction and sea states are steady."

Steamer glanced at his tactical display, verifying the setup. "Lookin' good. Link to the transport we're standing by and are go for drop. Beacons are going active. Then buzz the Rebel and tell 'em to light it up."

Reaching up to the overhead control panel, Steamer adjusted the multimode navigational strobe atop the *Queen*'s stub mast to its infrared setting and switched it on.

Aboard the Combat Talon, the opening of the tail ramp fully admitted the thunder of the turboprops and the roar of the slipstream. Voices could no longer be heard without the medium of the intercom system.

Colonel Mirkle's copilot called out the sighting. "Surface strobes off the bow. We have acquired the drop site. Bearing looks good. Approach looks good. Little Pig Lead reports ready to accept delivery."

"Acknowledged." She skid-turned the aircraft again, aiming precisely for the centerline between the two flashing points of light that had appeared in her night-vision visor. The IR strobes pulsing on the Navy gunboats would give her the base and depth line she would need for the coming LAPES extraction.

"ECM Officer, threat status."

"Green boards, ma'am. Tactical environment reads secure."

"Cargomaster, load status?"

"Chocks clear." A wind-battered voice came back from the cargo bay. "Ramp clear. Drop station manned. Ready for extraction."

"Very well." Mirkle's thumb depressed the drop light switch on her control yoke. "Red Ready light is on." Loadmaster, stand by for cargo release on green.... Copilot, configure for LAPES. Coming back on power.... Flaps down fifteen...."

The avalanche of noise issuing from the engines softened comparatively as Mirkle came back on the Talon's throttles. Easing the nose up, she faded the massive aircraft back toward its minimal sustainable speed in level flight. Mirkle's eyes danced in a last data acquisition sweep: engine readout, flight instrumentation, the seaborne beacon lights rushing toward them. She felt the first uneasy tremor in the control yoke hinting at the approaching stall limits.

"Stand by..." she murmured. Once more, her thumb lifted over the drop light switch.

Through their night-vision systems, the observers aboard the *Queen of the West* saw a massive chunk of shadow tear loose from the sky near the horizon. The shadow configured into a massive, high-winged transport aircraft that skimmed the wave crests. Nose high and with its quadruple propellers turning so slowly the blades could almost be counted, it seemed to float more than fly as it ghosted down upon them.

This was what they had been expecting. This was what they were here for. And yet, the Combat Talon's abrupt materialization in the night proved startling.

Just as the airspeed indicator wound down to a dangerously low level, the MC-130 swept over the centerline between the two strobes on the ocean's surface.

The marker strobes edged out of the vision field of her nite-brite visor, and Colonel Mirkle's thumb came down on the drop-light switch, snapping the drop lights from red to green.

"Drop now! Drop now! Drop now!"

A ribbon chute streamed out behind the Combat Talon. Blossoming in the roaring night, it dragged the first full fuel blivet down the load tracks and out of the Talon's tailgate.

This was LAPES, the Low-Altitude Precision Extraction System, the most expedient method conceivable of delivering cargo from an aircraft to the earth's surface: Simply fly very low and kick it out the door. Stabilized and slowed by its drogue parachute, the hoped-for shock-resistant payload would then touch down and skid to a halt across the selected landing ground.

More specifically, this was LAPES-MD the Low-Altitude Precision Extraction System–Maritime Derivation. Instead of the collapsible cargo pallet used in a standard land-bound LAPES drop, the payload rode a Fiberglas hydrosled that would absorb the initial contact shock and prevent the payload from digging into the water and diving under.

In theory at least.

As the sled-mounted fuel blivet touched down, the sea exploded in a towering fan of glittering spray, lifting higher than the tail of the drop aircraft. The load sled burst through the spray wall a stalled heartbeat later, its multiton mass skipping across the wavecrests like a stone thrown by a titan, until the combined drag of the water and the parachute decelerated the mass.

With a final buck and wallow like a fighting bass, the blivet came to a halt, afloat and intact.

Cries of victory were screamed, and shoulders were pounded in the *Queen*'s cockpit.

The second loaded hydrosled followed the first out of the transport's tail ramp, and then the Combat Talon was away, the shadow merging back with the night in a growing roar of departing power.

• • •

"Cargo away!" the load master cried. "We got clean drops!"

Colonel Mirkle disregarded the woman's jubilant call. She came forward hard on her throttles, regaining her airspeed. Once the payload was out of her aircraft, it was somebody else's concern. With a warrior pilot's inbred dislike for flying too long in a straight line, she conducted another random skid turn.

"Flaps full up! Countermeasures, how are we looking?"

"We're good, Colonel. No radar paint above return levels. Boards are clean."

Mirkle didn't exactly sigh with relief, but she did acknowledge the fading of a tension level. The load was on the ground . . . or in this case water. Now there was nothing to worry about except for getting themselves home.

The chest-vibrating rumble of the engines muted as the tail ramp closed and they settled back at cruise power. From the drop zone, they'd slip through the Makassar Strait between Borneo and Sulawesi and exit into the Celebes Sea. In less than an hour, they could go non-tac and pull up to conventional altitudes. From there it would be a simple transit hop to their turnaround base in the Philippines and then back to Australia. They'd be eating lunch at Curtin tomorrow noon.

"Want me to take it for a while, ma'am?" her copilot inquired.

"Sure, Ed. You have the aircraft."

Colonel Mirkle unclipped her chin strap and lifted the flight helmet off her graying blonde hair. Lounging back in the instrument-lit darkness of the cockpit, she watched the wavetops shimmer past below the Talon's nose. A good night's work, but hopefully next time out they'd be given something more interesting to do than a milk run for the squiddies.

The fuel blivets wallowed in the low waves, supported by the inherent buoyancy of the kerosene they carried, a double row of infrared lume sticks marking their position.

The *Queen of the West* and the *Manassas* converged on

them. Dropping their tail ramps, the PGAC backed into recovery position. Shotgun-armed antishark guards appeared on the upper decks of the hovercraft while skivvy-clad crewhands dove into the warm waters to jettison the load sleds and parachute harnesses and to connect the recovery cables.

Winch motors moaned and the fuel blivets, like gigantic marine cephalopods, crawled out of the sea and into the bellies of the Sea Fighters, sliding up the Teflon-slicked tarpaulins that had been unrolled down the ramps to receive them. Checks were made for kerosene leakage, tie-down straps were secured, and glad-hand connectors linked, accessing the new fuel reserve.

With refueling complete, lift and drive turbines lit off with a rising whine.

"We're only eight minutes long, sir," Caitlin reported as the *Queen* came up on her inflating skirt.

"Well, damn. We can tell the Lady another of her screwball ideas wasn't so screwball after all. Terry, you get the replenishment confirmation off to the task force?"

"Aye, aye, sir. I just got the microburst off. We're getting a data dump from the *Carlson*. It looks like a mission update."

"They got tomorrow's hide for us?" Lane inquired, coming forward on the airscrew throttles.

"That's an affirmative, sir. It looks like a mangrove swamp on the Kelantan coast of Borneo. Coordinates coming up on your Navicom display now. We're instructed not to attempt the transit of Makassar Strait until tomorrow night."

"Gotcha. Anything else?"

"Yes, sir." Wilder's voice lifted in excitement. "We're getting targeting data! Intel has an objective for us, sir. A village called Adat Tanjung on the western Sulawesi peninsula. We're receiving a bunch of stuff on the place."

"Right." Steamer checked the iron log, watching their surface speed climb toward good cruise. "Put it on hard copy, then let's call our pet leatherneck up here and start making medicine."

Amanda Garrett loved to dance. Thus she established her command post on the tiled dance floor set up in the center of the Makara Limited forecourt. The position gave her a mobile overview of the entire reception area as well as an excellent cover for discreet conversation with members of the shore party.

Or at least the masculine ones.

As she fell in step with Elliot MacIntyre and felt his strong hand curve to her waist, she mused at the wisdom of combining pleasure with business.

"How are you finding the reception, Admiral?"

"Very illuminating," he replied, guiding her slowly to the updated strains of an old Bobby Troop lounge piece. "Did you notice a certain chill when you spoke with our Indonesian Ambassador Goodyard?"

She shot a glance toward the ambassador's table. "Unusual for the tropics, wasn't it?"

"The word is that Goodyard has been seen glad-handing with our host."

Amanda lifted an eyebrow. "In the pocket?"

"Not yet, but watch this space," the admiral replied, steering them to the emptier corner of the floor. "Remember handshaking with Brigadier General Bradley Inger, our Indonesian defense attaché? I attended the General Staff War College with him. I got Brad over to one side and we swapped scuttlebutt over a couple of drinks.

"According to him, Goodyard is your typical political appointee. He doesn't have a clue about international affairs, and he's scared to death he might actually have to do something out here."

"And the Harconan connection?" A distracted corner of Amanda's mind wondered at the delicacy of MacIntyre's embrace. Damn it, it wasn't as if she were going to break.

"Harconan has volunteered himself to serve as Goodyard's sea daddy and font of local information. Harconan's already had him out to Palau Piri a couple of times."

Amanda frowned. "Interesting. Could the ambassador be in Harconan's pocket already?"

"Brad doesn't think so. Not in the monetary sense, anyway. Goodyard's not an overt sellout. He's just green and a sucker for a good line. It's not going to be easy to convince him that Harconan's the root of all evil."

Amanda considered, moving automatically to the music and to MacIntyre's guidance. "Hmm, it's always good to know about potential broken reeds before you might have to lean on them. Do you think you could have the secretary of state whisper in Goodyard's ear over this matter?"

The admiral shook his head, his chin lightly brushing her bangs. "I'd have to be able to give Harry something solid on Harconan first. This man is a major player down here. Telling tales on this gentleman without the absolute proof to back it up will not endear us to either the State Department or the Indonesian government."

"I see. Catch-22 rides again. Was your friend able to give us anything else under the table?"

"Just that Makara Harconan seems to work very hard at being scrupulously honest, or at least in giving that appearance. He won't even touch the routine business high jinks expected of your average Asian trader. Enough to make Brad suspicious of a 'hole in the water' scenario."

"A smart bird doesn't make a mess in his own nest. Do you have any other friends here, sir?"

"One other. Theoretically he's an Australian trade attaché attached to their consulate here in Bali. However, when I knew the gentleman up in the Gulf, he was commanding a squadron of their Special Air Service Regiment and talking about a career change to intelligence work. We shall see."

The quintet completed the piece and the music trailed away, followed by a polite scattering of applause from the other dancers.

"Thank you for the dance." He looked down at her, that surprising trace of boyishness showing again in his smile.

"My pleasure, sir."

MacIntyre escorted her to the edge of the floor. There

was a moment's hesitation before he released her hand, then he was moving off toward a caucusing cluster of foreign-office types. Amanda followed him with her eyes. The embrace on the dance floor had not been...what it could have, but that last clasp of her hand had been firm and warm.

Smiling, she set that aside and looked to another of the surrounding tables, the one shared by Cobra Richardson and Stone Quillain and a growing accumulation of Bintang lager bottles.

Given the flailing hands of the aviator and the maps being fingertip-sketched on the tablecloth by the Marine, a major assault landing was well under way.

She crossed to the developing battle. Both officers broke off the engagement and stood at the approach of a lady.

"Good evening, gentlemen," she said, nodding in greeting. "Stone, I find myself lacking a partner and we haven't danced yet tonight."

Good Lord, was it possible for a Marine to blush?

"Uh, no, ma'am, we haven't. But then, I'm not much of a hand for slow dancing."

Amanda extended her hand. "The proper response, Captain, is 'I'm not acquainted with the evolution, ma'am, but I am prepared to learn.'"

If Eddie Mac had treated her like a spun-glass statue, her landing force commander taught her how to dance like a live land mine. "Begging the Captain's pardon," Quillain growled under his breath as he gingerly steered her across the floor, "but if she gets a busted foot out of this, it's her own damn fault."

"Understood, Stone. However, it is permissible to move that hand at least somewhat lower than my shoulder blade. Good grief, didn't you even dance with your girl at your senior prom?"

"Why, sure. We did some fine line dancing in between the fistfights. It's just I never danced with my CO before. Feels funny."

"Let me guess. You wore your best Stetson with your rented tux?"

"Doesn't ever'body?"

Amanda chuckled. "If they switch to country-western later in the evening, I know where to come. In the meantime you're doing fine. Have you picked up anything interesting so far?"

"Words with the lieutenant commanding the embassy Marine security detail. He's got a suspicion some of their Indonesian staffers might be taking home two paychecks. He's not sure who's signing the other one, though. It doesn't seem to be one of the usual suspect governments, so our guys figure it may be a private party. That'd play with what we're working on, wouldn't it?"

"It certainly would. What about Chris and Tran?"

"They're keepin' it fluid," the Marine replied. "They'll buzz us on the pager net when they jump off. I've already got the exterior security mapped. Nothin' we didn't expect."

Amanda glanced toward the headquarters building. "We can't say the same about the inside yet. Are the emergency extraction protocols in place?"

"Oh, yeah. We got a real nice little terrorist bomb all set to go off if we need it. Out in the trees on the north end of the court. Just cover your face with that special hanky I issued you and head for the boat dock. I'll see Miss Rendino and Mr. Tran get clear okay."

"Uh, Stone," Amanda asked cautiously, "you didn't get too enthusiastic with the bomb, did you?"

She felt the rumble of laughter in Stone's broad chest. "Oh, hell, no. Just a little old radio detonated flashbang in a Baggie full of CS teargas powder. Everybody likes a good cry now and again."

"But not if we can avoid it."

"That part's out of our hands, ma'am."

The dance came to its end, and Stone released her and stepped back with a degree of visible relief.

"Was it really that bad?" Amanda inquired archly.

"Purely the circumstances, ma'am." He grinned down on her. "You come back to Georgia sometime. We'll get us some decent music and this ol' boy will show you some dancin' that is dancin'!"

Amanda returned the grin. "Consider it a date, Captain."

Letting the Marine return to face the amiable ridicule of his tablemates, Amanda drifted along the edge of the dance floor, acquiring and pretending to sip from a glass of champagne. Unobtrusively she scanned for the golden sheen of Christine Rendino's dress and hair. So far their counterforce operation against Harconan had worked quite well. Shortly, her intel would be executing the most audacious facet of the night's game plan. The most risky as well.

Lost in that consideration, she was startled by the deep and resonant voice that spoke from behind her. "Good evening, Captain."

Turning swiftly, she found herself face-to-face with the enemy.

"I've been remiss as a host," Harconan continued soberly. "You are my guest of honor, and yet, I've been able to devote almost none of my time to you. I apologize."

Amanda's voice caught in her throat for a moment, then she continued smoothly. "No apologies are required, Mr. Harconan. It's a lovely evening and a wonderful welcome to this part of the world."

"A gesture." He shrugged. "I've noted you on the dance floor, availing yourself of our entertainment. I trust the music has been to your liking?"

"Excellent," she replied. *You may be a pirate, Makara Harconan,* she added silently, *but you do know how to throw a party.*

"I'm pleased." He held out his hand to her. "Then, shall we enjoy it together?"

The silent pager clipped to the inside of her skirt waistband vibrated a three-ring burst. Chris's signal her op was starting.

Amanda smiled and set her glass down on a table. "I'd love to," she replied, moving into Harconan's arms.

With the action notification sent over the silent pager net, Christine Rendino tapped a second number into her phone.

Keying the call into the local cellular system, she waited.

The call was picked up on the first ring. "Yes?" A guarded voice answered.

"Authenticator Victoria George," Christine murmured. "Execute. T minus two. Duration five."

"Acknowledged. T minus two. Duration five." The connection broke.

Christine snapped the phone shut, tucking it away in her evening bag. Glancing up into Inspector Tran's face, she stated. "I have a sudden overwhelming urge to go tinkle."

"And when one has to go..." Tran deactivated the miniaturized "bug sniffer" he had used to ensure their concealing pocket of shadows had been free of security microphones. Together they started toward the courtyard entrance of the Makara Limited headquarters building.

Makara Limited was a decisively security-conscious firm. They had hired a major Singapore-based private security agency to wrap their operations in multiple layers of high-tech corporate defense. Literally the best money could buy shielded the Makara headquarters building.

But that was its vulnerability as well. What could be bought once could be bought again, and Christine and Tran were eager purchasers.

The "acquisition of cooperation" is an art form in Asia, and Christine Rendino and Nguyen Tran were artists each in their own medium. For Tran, it was in the deft use of his National Police identification card and the hinted-at power of the all-encompassing Singapore national government. For Christine, it was in the deft use of a smile and access to NAVSPECFORCE's "special contingency" funds.

During the days before the *Carlson*'s departure from Singapore, they had mapped out the Makara security network, bit by bit and contractor by contractor.

Layer one would be building access. After business hours, all exterior doors in the climate-controlled building were locked and alarmed. Access was possible only through the use of both an employee's computer-coded key card and clearance through the internal security station.

Oddly enough, the reception itself breached this first barrier. One simply could not ask the wife of the French ambassador to use a port-a-potty. The courtyard entry of the headquarters building had been left open to permit access to the ground floor rest rooms.

A stolid Nung Chinese security guard stood at parade rest next to the open courtyard doors. As Christine and Tran brushed past him, he nodded politely, then refocused his attention to the outside building approaches. What happened inside was someone else's responsibility.

The entry lobby and the corridor beyond it were done in muted tans with framed batik panels intermittently adding flares of dramatic color. The indirect lighting had been toned down and their footfalls were silent on the fitted carpeting.

Directly ahead at the T intersection with the central building corridor, a small dark glass dome had been inset into the ceiling. Christine felt another set of eyes regarding her.

Harconan's interior defense line would present a far greater obstacle. Low-light–capable security cameras, like the one at the intersection, monitored every hallway, stairwell, and public area. Every interior office door was alarm-locked and every office space blanketed by radar-type motion sensors.

Multiply redundant, with an independent power backup instantly available, this was no Hollywood movie security system that could be deactivated by the snipping of a few convenient wires.

Christine and Tran had concluded the system to be almost impenetrable by conventional means. Fortunately, they had far more than conventional means available to them.

Seven kilometers away, at Benoa Port, Commander Ken Hiro returned the cellular-linked interphone to its cradle. He'd passed on the reception tonight, preferring to personally oversee a different round of "festivities" from shipboard. Turning, he crossed the screen-lit dimness of the

Cunningham's hexagon-shaped Combat Information Center, passing from the radio shack, starboard side forward, to the electronic warfare bay, portside aft.

Beneath his rubber-soled shoes, the Duke's deck trembled lightly. Down in the power rooms, one of the cruiser's three massive turbine/electric generator sets was spooling up to feed the upcoming load demand.

In the EW bay, the systems operators looked up from their workstations with anticipation. Tonight was going to be an interesting challenge. They would be applying the awesome power of their electronic arsenal in a way not exactly intended, or ever before used.

"Links set with the *Carlson*?" Hiro inquired.

"Yes, sir, *Carlson* reports go and we have joint control through our boards."

The LPD's countermeasures arrays were fully as potent as the *Cunningham*'s, and both formidable systems had been harnessed in tandem through the joint-engagement matrix.

Hiro glanced at his wristwatch. "All right, ladies and gentlemen, the word is go in ninety seconds. Duration is still five minutes by the action plan. Heat 'em up."

"Aye, aye, sir."

The primary jammers came on line, the powerbars crawling up the display scales marked CLA-79 and LPD-26. The senior SO chuckled evilly. "Boy, the local couch potatoes are gonna hate our guts."

Seated at the main console of the Makara headquarters security office, Chiang Long leaned back in his chair and yawned enormously, aiming yet another drowsy curse at his relief man.

Long's proper guard shift was the treasured nine-to-five daytime, befitting his years of seniority within Makara Limited's security division. But this afternoon, just short of the end of his shift, he'd received a call from his division chief. The man supposed to cover the board during the five-to-one shift had called in unavailable. Somehow the idiot had gotten himself mugged and rolled, and now he was in hospital with a sprained shoulder. Long would have to cover the evening watch as well.

He didn't object too strenuously to the overtime, but his wife was fixing unfried spring rolls and *hokken mee* noodles for dinner—his favorite. The packet of shrimp crisps from the lounge vending machine had been a poor substitute. Beyond that was the sheer boredom of night duty.

During the day, one could at least spy on the better-looking office ladies via the scanner cameras. After hours, there was nothing to watch but the empty hallways.

This evening, at least, there was the reception going on in the courtyard. That was outside of Long's coverage sector: The special-team boys had that duty, the bastards. But at least the access corridor from the courtyard lobby to the rest rooms was open. The occasional low-cut evening gown made an interesting change from the usual heels and business suits on the day watch. Long had taken one of his six console monitors out of the rotational camera cycle and had left it permanently linked with the entry corridor camera. All in the interest of security, of course.

The courtyard lobby doors, the ones whose lock and alarm systems currently read DISENGAGED on the status boards, opened now, and a couple entered Long's field of view. The man was only a man, one of the fat cats invited to the reception, but the woman was worth consideration.

She was Caucasian—a blonde, no less—maybe a little skinny for Long's taste, but the tits were good. Reaching for the joystick of the camera scan override, he zoomed in on her for an inch-by-inch examination.

Hmmm, maybe not too skinny after all.

Long followed the couple down the entry hall to the rest room entries. They paused before the door to the women's lounge, facing each other and conversing for a moment. Then, much to Long's growing interest, the little blonde slipped her arms around the man's neck and a most impressive kiss followed. As she came up on her toes, the pleasantly short skirt of her dress lifted until one could... almost...see...

Pah! The kiss ended and the skirt settled. Smiling, the

blonde disappeared through the ladies' lounge door, the one barrier in the building sacrosanct to Long's hungry cameras.

Long yawned again and rubbed his gritty eyes. The show was over until she finished her business....

"Three...two...one...Jammers are active, sir."

The task force's electron warriors had spent all day consulting with stateside specialists in their field and modifying their systems for this attack. A waveform had been sculpted with the care of a Michelangelo, an intangible etheric sword designed to cut precisely across certain portions of the electromagnetic spectrum.

The ships' planar arrays had also been aligned to blanket only the quadrant to the southeast. The island capital of Denpasar and its suburbs, as well as the Ngurah Rai Airport, would be uninvolved. "Brute force" electrical systems such as landline telephone, lighting, and power would also be safe enough, as would most computer systems. "Frequency windows" had been carefully programmed into the strike that would leave processors and memory unaffected. Still, in an expanding cone-shaped zone engulfing Cape Benoa and the resort communities strung out along it, certain electronic devices convulsed.

When Long looked up again, all six of his camera monitors shimmered blankly in a cascade of snow.

Long sat erect, his boredom evaporating. As his eyes tracked across the console displays, the status board delivered another shock. Every motion sensor in the building had gone off simultaneously.

What in the hell...? He'd never seen anything like this before, even in the training programs. The hard-lock sensors hadn't gone berserk, at least. All doors still read secure, as did the elevators, the safes, and the confidential hard-copy files.

But could he trust the readouts? What else might be going wrong?

Hastily, Long turned to the screen of the security office

computer terminal, calling up the systems diagnostics display.

Green boards on both the television and the internal alarms. According to this damn thing, all systems were testing fully functional.

Long glanced uneasily at the red panic button, the one with the guard flipped down over it. A press on that would sound an alarm at the regional *polisi* headquarters, bringing outside assistance. But Long knew that his employers didn't like outsiders, particularly from the local government, within the building—not unless there was a very good reason for it. That was why the manual man-break had been incorporated into the system. Indeed, that was why Long's security cadre had been hired and brought in from Singapore. Best to keep things in the house until he had a grip on what was happening.

Long reached for the Motorola walkie-talkie plugged into its charger atop the console, intent on contacting the head of the outside security team. There was no response to his call, and when Long lifted his thumb from the transmit button, static sizzled angrily in his ear.

So, it was a problem from outside of the building. An electrical storm, perhaps, or some kind of sunspot interference like they'd had last year. A check of the landline phones showed they were still working.

Long glanced at the panic button again. If this was just some kind of natural phenomenon and he called in the police needlessly, he could be looking at empty corridors until his retirement. Likewise, his division chief enjoyed his sleep and didn't appreciate unsubstantiated emergency calls. The smart move might be to just wait it out.

But what if it wasn't some natural phenomenon?

Long stood up, loosening the Beretta automatic pistol in his shoulder holster. He was a capable security man and nobody's fool. Before he did anything else, he would pull in a couple of the outside special force guards and have them institute an interior patrol. Then he'd see about sorting these systems out.

Donning his suit jacket, he deactivated the security office hard-lock alarms from the main console. Stepping to the entry, he released the dead bolt and swung open the heavy steel fire door. He started to make a visual sweep of the half-lit central corridor beyond.

Before he could complete the move, something silver flicked from left to right across his field of vision, a polished coin that bounced down the beige carpeting.

Long couldn't stop the instinctive turn of his head to follow the flash of movement. But then he froze entirely, feeling the circular coolness of a gun barrel pressing against the back of his neck.

"Continue turning, please," a masculine voice said in flawless Straits Chinese. "All the way to your right. Raise your hands, then step forward, just three paces. Do not look back over your shoulder. It would not be wise."

Karate-trained, Long tensed, readying to try for a spin, block, and strike. Before he could act, however, the gun barrel was withdrawn as his ambusher stepped back, denying Long his positioning mark. Whoever this man was, he was not an amateur.

Long completed his turn to the right and lifted his hands, taking the three steps down the corridor as ordered. The pistol was not removed from his shoulder holster; both Long and the man standing behind him knew it was an irrelevance at the moment.

The guard strained his ears, catching the hint of another footfall, a suggestion someone had just passed into the security office. Who else was here? What did they want and might it include his life?

"How is your family in China faring, Long?"

Those words snatched up the guard's attention. What could this man know of his family? And how?

"Your elder brother in Singapore is working hard to get your mother out of China," the voice continued evenly. "Your mother, your cousin and his wife, their children. Things are hard after a civil war has ravaged a nation. There is little work in Guangxi Zhuangzu region, where

they live. Food is scarce, medicine is hard to come by....
Your grandmother is ailing, is she not, Long? I know both
you and your brother have been trying to bring them to
safety to Singapore. But getting the immigration permits is
difficult . . . so difficult."

Long felt a slight tug at the side of his coat.

"There is a card in your pocket, Long. It has a name on
it, an official in the Ministry of Immigration. This official
could be of great use to you in your quest to bring your
family to safety and prosperity. There is also a date and a
time for an appointment with this official. He has your
brother's name and will be expecting him. Truly, this may
be your best chance for obtaining the permits you require.
It would be such a pity if an . . . untoward incident should
lead to the cancellation of this appointment and the loss of
this opportunity. . . ."

Inside the security office Christine Rendino, skintight rubber gloves drawn on over her hands, slipped into the still-
warm chair behind the systems console.

This was the last line of defense to overcome: the cybernetic guards overwatching the Makara Limited internal
computer network. Here, too, no expense had been spared.
Christine had greased copies of Makara Limited's purchas-
ing orders from a junior clerk in the office of their
corporate software provider. Specifically the ones involving computer security.

Even she was impressed. There would be no easy way to
batter past the firewalls and virus screens erected around
Makara Limited's secrets. Nor, once inside, would there be
any way to quickly and easily find a way through the maze
of in-company encryption barricades that had been deployed.

Even the physical use of a Makara network terminal required both a company key card and a personal access
code recognized by the system . . . unless, of course, one
could get access to an already active terminal, such as this
one in the security office.

Leaning in over the keyboard, Christine made no effort to penetrate deeper into the network. There was no time and far too many chances of tripping an internal watchdog program. Instead, she called up the Internet provider used by Makara Limited, typing in the Web address of Sony Business Security Systems Division.

From the main menu, she windowed up the USER TROUBLESHOOTING Web page. She went to the STATE PROBLEM window and typed in a memorized eight-digit code.

A FILE READY TO DOWNLOAD prompt appeared on her screen and she moused over and double-tapped, initiating it.

That was the interesting thing about computer firewalls: They were one-dimensional, keeping intruders out. However, as with a vampire, if something was invited in, all bets were off.

The programmers at Sony Security would not have recognized the link Christine had just keyed off of their Web site. They had not incorporated it into their system. It had not even existed twenty minutes before, and after this single use, it would disappear as rapidly as it had materialized, leaving no trace of its brief presence. All involved security and provider logs would register only a routine information request to a reputable host within proper business-use parameters.

Likewise, the Makara antivirus screens would not recognize the sophisticated espionage program caging itself over their operating systems. Until further notice, the combat hackers at NAVSPECFORCE's computer warfare center in San Diego would have an open back door into the Makara business net.

Minutes crept past, a small eternity of them. Chiang Long heard nothing more from behind him; no more words, no more traces of sound. His jaw knotted, the tension within building. Long didn't consciously plan and trigger the move; his muscles simply exploded, hurling him to the far side of the corridor, spinning him around, snapping his hand to the butt of his pistol.

There was no one. The half-lit hallway was empty, the door to the security office gaping open.

With gun in hand, Long peered around the door frame. An almost eerie sense of normalcy reigned in the security office. The motion-sensor board had reset and now glowed an unperturbed green. The television monitors cycled placidly through their interior views of an empty building. The set monitor covering the entry hallway showed the blonde of Long's prior lustful focus emerging from the ladies' lounge to take the arm of her escort.

It was if nothing had happened. Long might pass it all off as some freak of imagination...if he wished.

His hand dipped into his jacket pocket. A business card with the name of a Singapore Ministry of Immigration official, one higher up the ladder than his brother had ever been able to reach, with a date and time written on its back. This at least was real...if he wanted it to be.

Long closed the security office door, carefully securing the dead bolt.

Back in their shadowy corner of the courtyard, Christine palmed her cellular phone. Flipping it open, she verified that the unit was accessing service, a verification that the electronic barrage from the *Cunningham* was over. Over the sound of the dance music the distant metallic hee-haw of police sirens could be heard, a *polisi* patrol unit futilely responding to tripped burglar alarms elsewhere along the cape.

Tran chuckled softly. "I fear we've created a lot of paperwork for the local law enforcement."

"Fa' sure." Christine returned the phone to her bag. Exchanging it for Kleenex, she reached up and lightly dabbed a smudge of lipstick from Tran's mouth. "Excuse my familiarity, Inspector," she said, grinning, "but I thought we should put on a decent show for our friend Mr. Camera back there."

"Indeed, Commander." Tran's words were sober, but his grin matched the intel's, his hands coming up to rest on her slim shoulders. "A good police officer must be prepared to make sacrifices for the cause."

"Oh, very true, Inspector. Since nobody's shooting at us or sounding a hue and cry, I'd guess everything went pretty well, including our buy-off of Harconan's security man. Do you think your little gift will hold him?"

"It is difficult to say. The Nung Chinese have a centuries-old tradition of serving as loyal retainers and bodyguards. Your own military used them as such in my former homeland. But there is one thing a Nung or any other Chinese values even over a word given to an employer."

"Family?"

"Precisely. My contact at our Ministry of Immigration says that our guard is having certain difficulties in this area. Hopefully the coin I've offered him will be adequate to buy his silence."

"In that case," Christine said, "I can only see one small factor that I overlooked."

"And what's that?"

"Now I really do have to go to the bathroom."

They shared the laugh and Christine lifted onto her toes once more and the intel and the inspector shared a second kiss, this one on their own time.

They separated, and a satisfied sigh later, Tran glanced across at the dance floor. "Look, it appears as if progress is being made elsewhere."

Amanda Garrett still danced with Makara Harconan.

Amanda recalled a line from an old movie. Something about "Have you ever danced with the Devil in the pale moonlight?"

It was a novel sensation.

Likewise novel were the subtle differences between dancing with Makara Harconan and with one of her fellow officers. Certain intangible barriers born out of rank and professionalism did not exist. When this man held her, he might see her as an enemy but also as a woman. That she could recognize. There was no fear of the impropriety of his drawing her closer or shifting a hand with the hint of a caress.

There was a sensation of nakedness involved, of being stripped of layers of defense. Yet, as she moved in easy rhythm with the tall Eurasian, Amanda found this vulnerability only enhancing her own defiance. If one was going to dance with the Devil, one might as well savor the experience.

"Thank you again, Captain," Harconan said as the music concluded. "Would you care to sit out this next set with a drink?"

"I'd like that."

Amanda allowed herself to be guided to Harconan's personal table, noting that they would be alone save for the waiter already standing by.

Around Makara Harconan, things didn't have to be asked or called for: They seemed to simply happen effortlessly. Nothing ever just "happened," of course. Deft organizational skills were at play here, as well as a meticulous attention to the smallest detail.

This was something to remember. A warrior often fought as he lived. She wondered what her own actions might reveal to Harconan.

The taipan held her chair, then took the seat across from her. Without a word being spoken, the waiter set a tall tulip glass at her place. Thanking him, she reached for it, then froze, her fingers not quite touching the glass.

It was a sherry and soda, her favored cocktail beverage, a fact she had mentioned to no one at the reception.

Harconan watched from across the snowy tablecloth, smiling slightly.

She broke her hesitation and took up the glass. "And thank you."

She sipped. Yes, it was even her favorite brand of sherry. She admired the intelligence-gathering.

"My pleasure, Captain, and my honor." Harconan took up his own drink, mineral water with lemon. Religion or strategy? Amanda wondered. Had he adopted the Islamic ways of the Bugis, or did he simply desire a clear head at all times? The taipan's personal beliefs were something on which even Inspector Tran had no insight.

"When I learned you were coming to the archipelago," he continued, "I knew I wanted you as my guest. You are a most remarkable individual."

Amanda chuckled. "Why would you say that?"

It was Harconan's turn to chuckle. "Would you deny your record of rather extraordinary accomplishments?"

Amanda frowned in thought. "Yes and no. I've been fortunate to command some excellent crews, and not so fortunate in that I've had to take them into harm's way on occasion to serve my nation's interests. Any number of other officers within my service could have done as well. Honor goes to the personnel I lead. As for myself, I am most extraordinarily average."

Harconan laughed aloud this time, a genuine laugh, his even white teeth flashing. "Captain Garrett, we both know your charming humility is a polite fiction. You are a most unique woman, and we are both fully aware of that fact."

Amanda couldn't keep from smiling in response or lifting her head in challenge. "Why? Because I'm a woman and a naval officer? There's nothing particularly remarkable about that anymore."

"Agreed on that point," he replied. "However, it is inconceivable that you could have ever become anything else."

"How so?" Amanda inquired. This scenario was an intriguing one, as was the man. In her career she'd faced off against a number of strong and dynamic male opponents, but always across a battle theater, and never like this: eyes meeting across a table.

"There are many reasons," Harconan continued. "For one, you are a warrior's child, born of a line of warriors. The warrior's flame burns true through the generations. Your father, Admiral Wilson Garrett, had no grown son to whom he could pass the spark, so it passed into your hands."

Amanda felt her brows rise. Just how much did this man know about her?

Harconan touched the rim of his glass to his lips and answered her unspoken question. "Yet again: You are a sailor born of a line of sailors. You look to the sea to earn your living and to find your life's duty. You also look to the sea for your pleasure. You scuba dive, you fish, you own a cruising sloop, and you've competed in offshore powerboat races."

His voice softened, growing level, almost hypnotic. "You have never lived more than two miles away from the ocean in your life. You never will. You are physically and psychologically incapable of doing so. You would suffocate like a fish cast out on the land. The sea is in your blood. More than that, it *is* your blood."

He leaned back in his chair. "This is something I can understand. I am this way myself."

"You know a great deal about me." Amanda said slowly. "What have I done to warrant this attention?"

Harconan shrugged. "You interest me, Captain, and I learn about things that interest me."

"Apparently." She was almost afraid to ask the next question, but she couldn't not ask it. "What else have you learned?"

"One further critical factor: You command."

"An aspect of my profession, Mr. Harconan."

"Wrong!"

He put just enough sharpness into the word to startle her. He lifted a hand and aimed a finger at her heart. "You command as kismet demands that you command. Your profession merely takes advantage of the fact. Command is as much a part of you as the fire and the water. You are, by nature and by destiny, meant to rule and lead in the same way as the majority are meant obey and follow."

His voice softened to that hypnotic evenness again. "In the world where democracy is the current fad, that leaves you with either the military or commerce for your empire-building. By fastidious instinct, you dislike the miry waters of moneymaking, so you chose the clean cutting blade of the military. Save for one other potential, you have no other choice."

Amanda noticed for the first time that Harconan had the eyes of his father's people. They were dark gray and penetrating, and the way he used them on her put a wary but stimulating tingle down her spine. Damn, damn, damn, but she found she had to make one more pass closer to the flame.

"Interesting. I've never had my life assessed in quite that way before, Mr. Harconan. What's the other potential career choice you believe I have?"

Harconan smile deepened.

"Queen," he replied, and lifted his glass to her in salute.

"A port visit to Jakarta might have served us a little better, Admiral. Showing the flag at the real seat of power, you understand. But I can't blame you for wanting a shore leave on Bali," Ambassador Goodyard added with a forced attempt at humor.

"I'm sure our port call here will prove to be very productive, Mr. Ambassador." *More so than this conversation, at any rate,* MacIntyre added silently. "Following our layover here, we intend to conduct some further training in these waters. We'll give the Indonesians a good look at us."

He and the ambassador were sharing a table for the mandatory protocol drink. It had come late in the game. The reception was on its downslope, with the first guests taking their departure.

The task force's officers were rapidly approaching their own extraction time. They had come, they had seen, and if they had yet to conquer, they had at least conducted a successful probe into enemy territory.

Christine Rendino had given him the high sign about the successful insertion of the invader program into the Makara net. Even now, the combat hackers at cyberwar should be ravaging their way through Harconan's business files for useful and incriminating intelligence. What the end result would be, only time would tell.

Likewise with Amanda's psywar assault on Harconan. Would their applied pressure flush him out of his successful businessman persona into a more overtly confrontational mode? Again, time would tell.

MacIntyre glanced across the dance floor again. Amanda

was still seated at Harconan's table. She'd spent a great deal of her time during the latter half of the reception there or on the dance floor with the man.

If they'd shaken him with their challenging arrival, he'd recovered well. The taipan had proven to be the most charming of hosts. Could this be an indication that the suave son of a bitch was rising to the dare? Or did it mean they'd missed the call and he wasn't their pirate king after all?

The admiral tasted the ice-weakened rye whiskey in his glass and scowled to himself. No. As Christine would put it, there must be "bad vibes" radiating off Harconan at an instinctive level. Why else would it put his teeth so on edge to see Amanda close to the man?

"...Admiral?"

MacIntyre snapped back into himself. "Excuse me, Ambassador, I was distracted for a moment. What were you saying?"

"The Indonesian naval ministry is very interested in your, ah, Sea Fighter task force," Goodyard repeated. "They seem to think there's a good deal they could learn from your people in relation to—what do you call it?—littoral warfare. As an aspect of your goodwill cruise, they've formally requested a number of their naval officers be allowed to come aboard your vessels as observers during your stay in Indonesian waters. I thought I'd run the idea past you before kicking it upstairs. I think it's an excellent notion myself, both for them and for us."

MacIntyre set his glass on the tabletop. "I'm sorry, Mr. Ambassador, but we'll have to say no. Here in port, we'll be glad to have Indonesian military personnel tour our vessels and we'll be glad to make briefing officers available to the Ankatan Laut to discuss littoral doctrine. However, taking foreign observers aboard the task force at this time will be quite impossible."

The diplomat frowned, his voice growing pointed. "Admiral Lukisan at the naval ministry has indicated a strong interest in this particular matter. He seems to feel the observers would promote...positive relations between your services and our governments. I must agree. The admiral also informed me that one misunderstanding has already taken place between elements of the Indonesian navy and your ships. We don't really need any more of them. Onboard liaison officers would help in ensuring we would have no further such incidents."

MacIntyre nodded. "I agree, Mr. Ambassador, on that one point. We don't need any further conflicts with the Indonesians. That's why I would suggest you advise Admiral Lukisan to withdraw the warship of his command that has been shadowing my task force. Either that, or have him instruct his shadower's commander to stand off at a prudent distance in the future.

"As for onboard observers, as I have stated, that's impossible due to national security concerns involving certain systems and procedures being tested by the Sea Fighter task force at this time. The matter is closed. Please give my apologies to the naval ministry."

Goodyard's eyes narrowed and his lips pursed. Since his appointment to ambassadorship, he had grown unaccustomed to being spoken to with such decisiveness.

"Let's put our cards on the table, Admiral," he challenged. "Why are you really here? Is this, in fact, just a goodwill mission or is something else going on? Dammit, this is my territory! I have a right to know and I have a right to know the truth!"

MacIntyre suppressed a snort. By the great Lord Harry, this man was a tyro, and one who obviously hadn't been listening during the lecture series on basic State Department security. The admiral didn't care whose campaign this man had done favors for, he should have been left in the Midwest, kissing babies.

"Mr. Ambassador, I will be pleased to show you the orders, issued to NAVSPECFORCE by the chief of Naval Operations, instructing the deployment of the Sea Fighter task force to the Indonesian archipelago on a goodwill cruise in support of our relations with the Jakarta government. Beyond that, sir, I can only suggest that you refer to the CNO or the Secretary of State. They may have some information on this matter not available to this command."

"As you say, Admiral." Goodyard stood abruptly. "I may very well do just that, concerning both this matter and others. In the meantime, I do not want to hear of any further incidents or provocations taking place between your task force and the Indonesians while you are in my zone of responsibility."

The corner of MacIntyre's mouth quirked as he rose to bid Goodyard farewell. "Understood, Mr. Ambassador. I give you my personal assurance. You aren't going to hear another word."

Raider Two pulled away from the Makara Limited pier float. Lifting onto plane, it ran northward past the glittering lights of the resorts, bearing home the same party it had carried ashore hours before.

"As we had hoped, it was a most interesting evening," Tran commented.

MacIntyre gave an acknowledging grunt over the rumble and hiss of the diesel propulsors.

"I'd say so," Amanda commented, drawing herself in against the cooling slipstream that flowed around the cockpit control station. "I'd say very much so."

"What do you mean, Boss Ma'am?" In the darkness of the cockpit, Amanda didn't notice the intent way in which Christine stared at her.

"We don't know what cyberwar may pick up from your probe yet, Chris. And we didn't pick up on anything overt beyond Harconan having all of the appropriate connections and trappings of power. But I did learn something that convinces me that Inspector Tran, here, has us on the right track about Harconan."

"Which is . . . ?" MacIntyre murmured.

"The man is capable of doing what the inspector says he is. That's not saying that he's doing it, but he has the personal capability to be our pirate king."

"Where do you get that assessment, Captain?" MacIntyre asked stiffly.

"A combination of gut instinct, intuition, and personal experience, sir. I've been in the service long enough to rec-

226   JAMES H. COBB

ognize a born leader, the genuine article, when I see one. Harconan has the charisma and dynamism—the mystique, if you will—to draw followers and control situations. He also has the intelligence to effectively use this potential as a tool. Obviously he has used this talent to become an effective force in the business world. Just as easily, he could use it to become a national leader or a military commander. Remember General Belewa, Chris? He had the same touch."

"And our old buddy Sparza in South America," the intel agreed. "Harconan is not only the man on the white horse, but he was born in the saddle. Yeah, I agree. If that's where his head is, he could do it. I could feel it too."

"Feelings are all well and good," MacIntyre growled. "But we're going to need a hell of a lot more than that to bring this man down. We need hard evidence linking Harconan to the pirate operations, and still, all we have is rumortel. We need to find that damned industrial satellite and a way to connect Harconan to its theft. That's the only way we're ever going to justify direct U.S. action against him."

"We'll have a couple of shots at it tomorrow, sir," Christine replied. "Cyberwar should start to produce on his computer net, and the microforce is going to recon the pirate base on Sulawesi."

"We'll get a third shot as well, Chris," Amanda said, letting a hint of rueful amusement creep into her voice. "How fast do you think you could train me into being an effective Mata Hari?"

She felt Admiral MacIntyre twist abruptly on the bench seat beside her. "What in all hell are you talking about, Amanda?"

"Just that Makara Harconan extended me a personal invitation to visit his private island tomorrow. I accepted."

2012 Hours, Zone Time:
"Officers' Country," USS *Evans F. Carlson* August 16, 2008

Nguyen Tran closed the door of his assigned guest cabin. Spartan in its outfitting, the windowless Navy gray cubicle contained a set of lockers, two surprisingly large and comfortable bunks, and a built-in bulkhead desk, a small connecting head its sole luxury.

Somehow, the solid steel bulkheads and bristling defenses of the American warship seemed more conducive to a sound sleep this night. Even at this moment Tran knew his name would be going onto a number of potentially dangerous lists.

Still, it had been worth it, to fling a glove into the face of the formerly unreachable Makara Harconan. To make him fear, even for an instant, his own destiny, the way a terrified eight-year-old had done, clinging to a drifting hulk in the South China Sea. With good fortune and the aid of these new allies, perhaps this seed of fear could be made to flourish and grow. A pleasant thought.

Tran had just tugged open his tie when a soft knock sounded at the door.

"Come in."

Christine Rendino, still in her evening dress and heels, stepped into the cabin, flipping the door lock behind her. "Hi," she said, tossing a rolled khaki uniform, a small makeup bag, and a command headset onto the upper bunk. Turning her back to Tran, she inquired, "Want to unzip me?"

Tran hesitated, startled. Given the fiery kisses he had shared with the ebullient little blonde, it was a ridiculous question, but one he hadn't expected to answer quite so soon.

Christine glanced back over her shoulder and whistled a double note softly. "Zipper?"

Tran hastily ran the offending object down to the base of her spine. "My apologies, I was ... assessing the situation."

"Understandable under the circumstances." The intel shrugged her dress from her shoulders allowing it to slip down to her ankles.

Very sheer panty hose and very brief golden silk panties and bra were apparently considered a needless complication. Christine turned to face him again. "I know that in the Islands the gentlemen generally take the lead in such

228   JAMES H. COBB

things, but we have some time constraints going, and frankly, we can't afford for you to be a gentleman."

"We can't?"

She shook her head decisively. "Nope."

She kicked off her pumps and hooked her thumbs under the waistband of panty and panty hose alike, slipping both down with a wriggle and a relieved sigh. "I mean, it would be great if we could tack a little chrome onto this thing. You know, the traditional waltzing until dawn and gazing deep into each other's eyes for hours on end and that kind of thing, but I'm afraid we're not going to have that kind of leisure over the next few days."

A pity, too, for those large gray blue eyes were worth gazing into. "And after that?"

She smiled a soft, regretful smile and stepped out of her pooled undergarments to stand before him, a golden tanned statue, nude and untroubled. "And after that, no promise asked or given. I get very good vibes off of you, Tran, and I know from the sparks that happen when we kiss, the feeling is mutual. But I also know we both have other places to go and other things to do. That's the problem with being a cop or a spy. We know too much."

She rested a small hand on his chest. "Look, if you have a serious lady you haven't mentioned or if you'd just rather not, it's okay. I'll get dressed and get out of here with no harm done. But if the two of us are going to have anything at all, it has to be here and now, and we can't waste any more time."

Tran had heard stories about these forthright American women. How delightful to learn they were true.

"I quite agree, my colleague. I shouldn't want to be wasteful." He gathered Christine to him. Lifting the warm, satin-skinned form in his arms, he placed her in the lower bunk.

Half a thousand miles away, the replenished Sea Fighters of the microforce raced on through the early morning darkness, sprinting from cover point to cover point like an infantry rifle team.

Within their hulls, off-watch Marines and sailors dozed atop the fresh fuel blivet, as cool and comfortable a resting place as any waterbed.

Sitting on the edge of her bunk, Amanda studied the two holstered pistols lying atop the taut blanket: the big Marine-issue MEU Model .45 that Stone Quillain had issued her from the landing-force arsenal and her personally owned Ruger SP-101 revolver. Glancing over at the shoulder bag hanging from a hook on the opposite bulkhead, she considered.

Amanda was equally proficient with both handguns; Stone saw to that in his odd moments. The massive Marine captain hated the thought of being around anyone not weapons-capable. And the weight of either pistol in her bag might be of comfort in the day ahead. Maybe. . . .

Amanda gave a derisive snort. If she thought she might need a gun on Harconan's island, she shouldn't go in the first place. And if she had miscalculated and this was a trap, a pistol wasn't going to get her out of it. On the other hand, packing iron wasn't the act of a woman setting out for a pleasant rendezvous with a handsome gentleman. It could ruin her chance of getting close enough to Harconan to actually learn something useful.

Her decision made, she knelt and stacked the automatic and revolver back into the cabin safe under the head of her bunk, giving the combination dial a scrambling spin. Standing, she gave her tropic-weight uniform slacks a careful straightening tug.

Damn, damn, damn, this was a deadly serious business. So why did she keep getting flashbacks of pacing around her bedroom in high school, waiting for her date to show up?

Maybe because, black-hearted pirate or not, Makara Harconan was an extremely attractive and dynamic man.

And for Amanda Garrett, there had always been something about the legend of the buccaneer.

Amanda sat on the edge of the bunk and reached across to the built-in bookcase for an old and treasured friend, Lowell Thomas's *Count Luckner, the Sea Devil,* the biography of Count Hugo von Luckner. The tale of the dashing Imperial German Navy sea raider and his epic voyage in command of the last sail-powered man-of-war had always fascinated her, especially when she had been on the cusp of adolescence, providing her with her first romantic fantasies.

Perhaps they were right when they said that you always stayed just a little bit in love with the first one to touch your heart. Maybe that explained the tug she'd felt when she'd set eyes on Makara Harconan....

Amanda snorted again, at herself. Fantasies were all well and good for a fourteen-year-old, but she was a grown woman living in the all-too-real world. The buccaneers of legend and the pirates of reality were two very different breeds. Even her beloved count had in actuality been a naval officer of a proper and chivalrous age, and not a true sea marauder.

Glancing down at the worn volume in her lap, Amanda noticed a bookmark she didn't recognize. Admiral MacIntyre must have started reading about the count when he'd occupied her quarters. For some reason that pleased her, rather like the thought of two old friends hitting it off.

In the real world, a man like Elliot MacIntyre would be a far more sensible and worthy subject for a romantic fantasy: a solid and honorable man of proven courage, intelligence, and humanity. But what would a fourteen-year-old girl know?

The corner of Amanda's mouth quirked up. Or, for that matter, a thirty-eight-year-old woman?

Someone knocked on the outer cabin door. Amanda tossed the book onto the bunk and stood up. Taking her shoulder bag and Sea Fighter beret from their respective hooks, she stepped out into the office space.

"Come in."

Christine entered the office, a file folder of hard copy tucked under one arm. "Hi, Boss Ma'am. I have the latest situation reports assembled. I'll be going over them with Admiral MacIntyre while you're off ship."

"Good. Anything I need to know before I take off?"

The intel hesitated and then shook her head. "Nothing that can't wait."

"Leave them on my desk, then. I'll play catch-up . . . probably tomorrow morning, it looks like now. Any change in the situation with the microforce?"

"Negative." The intel set the file on the desktop and sank into one of the office chairs. "They're in the pre-mission hide. They're secure, and no situational changes are reported in the zone of interest. They'll start moving at 2300 and should be launching the op by 0100 as per the mission profile."

"I'll be back well before then," Amanda mused, "although it might be interesting to be on Palau Piri when we start putting some moves on one of our pirate king's bases."

The small khaki-clad figure in the office chair strangled something down under her breath, and Amanda noted the intel's exceptionally broody expression.

"All right, Chris," she said, parking her hip against the edge of the desk. "What's going on?"

"Request permission to speak freely to the Captain?"

Amanda sighed. She was in for it now. Military formality was dangerous, coming from Christine Rendino. "You've always had it, Chris. You know that."

Christine looked up, eyes glinting angrily. "Then may I remind the Captain that she is merely a line officer in the United States Navy, not frickin' Modesty Blaise!"

Amanda chuckled softly. "By that, I gather you still disapprove of my excursion to Harconan's island?"

"That's right, I do." Christine aimed an emphatic finger at Amanda. "You are going to be walking into the heart of the goddamn enemy camp alone. There's not going to be a soul around who can help you or even witness what might happen to you."

"Very true," Amanda acknowledged. "But I thought we agreed last night that the probability of Harconan taking any overt action against me was small. It would be too obvious. The death or disappearance of a senior American military officer on his home ground is just the kind of thing he'd want to avoid, especially now."

Chris lowered her eyes, her lower lip protruding stubbornly. "We might be wrong. It could be made to look like an accident. Maybe his buy-offs extend deeper into the local governments than we know. Maybe . . . anything. This guy has got to know you're after him, Boss Ma'am."

"The Navy is after him, Chris," Amanda replied quietly. "And I'm a very small and readily replaceable part of that organization. At the moment I'm unique in only one way: I'm the one he's invited into his home. It's our chance to get a closer look at how he thinks and operates. It's my best chance to get inside his head. I need to learn how to read him. That's going to be important."

"Well, maybe," Christine conceded grudgingly. "But maybe some of us feel you aren't all that replaceable. Maybe some of us, in fact, figure you're pretty damn unique in a lot of ways, and if anything happened to you, we'd be pretty damn unhappy."

Amanda tilted her head back and laughed. "I'd miss you, too, Chris. I promise nothing fancy. I'll just go in, sip tea with the taipan, and then I'm out of there. . . . But now that I think about it, would there be any kind of bug or hidden microphone or something I could smuggle in there with me . . . ?"

Christine collapsed forward melodramatically, catching her face in her hands. "Aaaaaagh! She watches an old James Bond flick on Site TV and she thinks she's a superspy."

"Just kidding, Mother! Just kidding!"

Christine looked up again. "I'm not. If you insist, try this soft probe, okay! Probably—I say again, probably—

Harconan will be willing to maintain this polite fiction you two have going for a while longer. He's probably still as curious about your intentions as you are about his, and he's likely going to try and pump you just as hard as you are him. Act dumb, but don't be stupid! They are going to be waiting for you to try something. Disappoint them! Please!"

Her friend's open distress brought Amanda back from her moment of levity. "I understand, Chris. I'll be on a knife edge. I know it. I'll watch myself."

The desk phone buzzed and Amanda leaned across to scoop the handset out of its cradle. "Garrett here.... All right. I'll be right up. Thank you."

She hung up the phone. "That was our AIRBOSS. It appears my ride is here."

Permitting a foreign civil aircraft to land on a U.S. naval vessel was strictly non-SOP. Accordingly, the Harconan Limited helicopter flared out and touched down in a corner of the quay parking lot, apparently unconcerned with the views of the harbormaster on the subject.

The quayside had been a busy place before the arrival of the sleek, dark-blue Eurocopter. A double row of buses was parked, both discharging and taking aboard passengers.

The discharging buses carried Balinese civilians, curious townspeople from the capital of Denpasar and the other surrounding communities, taking advantage of the "open house" program being offered aboard the American warships. Ushered aboard in small groups, friendly American sailors would then take each party on a brief tour of certain less critical areas of the cruiser and LPD, all part of the Navy's "Ambassadors of Goodwill" program.

But being an Ambassador of Goodwill did not mean being a fool. As each group climbed the pierced aluminum gangway to board each vessel, the more curious might have noted the soft purr of an electric fan under their feet. Chemical-sensitive bomb-sniffer units were at work, ready to flash a warning to ship's security.

The second, shorter row of buses loaded sailors and Marines for land-side tours and shopping expeditions. It would look strange if none of the task force personnel hit the beach while in Bali. All hands had been given very specific orders, however: Stay in groups. Stay in better-class public areas. No carousing, and all hands back aboard by nightfall.

Standing on the *Carlson*'s forecastle, waiting for the gangway to clear, Amanda and Christine watched as the copter's pilot dismounted from the idling aircraft. Both instantly recognized the tall tanned figure in the safari suit and sunglasses. He recognized them as well, throwing a hand up in a casual wave.

"The man himself," Amanda murmured. "I'm honored."

"Well," Christine responded sourly, "at least that eliminates the worry of a suicide pilot or five pounds of plastique under your seat."

Amanda waved the intel off. "I promise I won't sit in the back row in the movie, and if he claims he's run out of gas, I'll remember to hit him where you told me. See you tonight, Chris."

"Oh, really? You think?"

Feeling exceedingly antsy, Christine looked on as her friend checked off ship with the *Carlson*'s OOD and descended the gangway. Harconan awaited Amanda at the quayside, and even at a distance he looked hellishly handsome. Beyond listening range, the intel read the exchange of gesture body language that followed. Harconan's air of flamboyant gallantry, which would have seemed forced in another man, flowed naturally, and Amanda, with the blood of her Virginia belle ancestors, could flirt with the best when she put her mind to it.

"You look worried, Little One."

Nguyen Tran had come up beside her on the forecastle, keeping his voice low so as to not be overheard by the gangway watch.

On the dock Amanda and Harconan were walking away toward the waiting helo. "I am," Christine murmured.

"Please tell me I am stuffed full of blueberry muffins to think that somehow this is a really bad idea?"

"I'm not sure." Tran's eyes narrowed as he followed Amanda and the taipan with his gaze. "I doubt that Harconan would be foolish enough to harm your captain or do anything to draw suspicion onto himself. Still...do you know what the name Makara means?"

"No, what?"

"In Indonesia, the Makara is a legendary sea creature with two facets to its being: It has the beauty and grace of the dolphin, but the teeth...and soul...of the shark."

The Eurocopter lifted off and cut across the waters of Benoa Harbor and the narrow spit of the Bukit Badung Peninsula before turning northwest to parallel the coast. Amanda, who was not a pilot herself but who had spent a great deal of time in the company of aviators, noted the surety of the suntanned hands on the helicopter's controls and the way Harconan seemed to merge with the aircraft in flight. Again she had to be impressed.

The tangle of cheap surfing resorts and coastal tourist villages thinned out rapidly, the cliffs lifting along the seaside and the great central mountains of the island interior rising as they headed inland. Soon a green and elegant terrain was passing beneath the helo's pontoons, the valleys and even hillsides sculpted for rice cultivation, the flowing webwork of interlocking terraces seemingly made for aesthetics as well as for practicality. Interspersed among the fields were the farming communities, at the center of each the *pura desa,* the village temple, the *bale agung,* the village assembly ground, and the sacred banyan tree.

"This is more like what I thought Bali would be about," Amanda commented into her interphone headset.

"It is," Harconan replied. "This is the real Bali. The sprawl on the southern peninsula is someone else's idea."

"Whose?"

"Let me give you a hint. One of Bali's former Javanese

governors had the nickname Ida Bagus, or Okay, for his propensity for authorizing any development project that would bring in fast tourist dollars."

"And the Balinese have nothing to say about it?"

Harconan arched a dark eyebrow behind his sunglasses. "Of course they do. Just as much any other non-Javanese in Indonesia. 'We are many, but all are one,' as our national motto says. Only somehow the one from Jakarta always seems to end up giving the orders to the many."

"And this status quo is accepted?" Amanda probed.

"For the moment. The Balinese are by nature a mystic people, spiritual and artistic, until the gods tell them to be otherwise."

"The gods?"

"Quite so. Look back over your right shoulder: See that tallest mountain to the northeast?"

Amanda studied the impressive volcano with its snowy cloud cap through the cockpit bubble. "Yes, it's beautiful. What about it?"

"It's called Gungung Agung. Back in 1965, during the last days of the Sukarno regime, a great religious ceremony was held here on Bali, the Eka Dasa Rudra, purification and balancing to bring man and nature into harmony. It is only supposed to be held once precisely every one hundred years. However, Sukarno, in order to impress a convention of travel agents, ordered the ritual be held ten years early.

"In the middle of the ceremonies, Gungung Agung over there exploded in its most violent eruption in six hundred years, killing sixteen hundred people and devastating one quarter of the island. The Balinese saw it as a sign that Shiva was displeased with them for allowing outsiders—in this instance, the island's Communist faction—to come among them and disrupt the ways of the gods.

"In September of that year, when the coup was attempted and the Communist party of Indonesia was outlawed, the Balinese turned on them as well. But here it was unique. Here it wasn't a political massacre; it was an exorcism of demons as ritualized as any temple ceremony. For the most part there was no rampage, no mass slaughter in the streets, as there was elsewhere in the islands. The Communists were allowed to bathe and don white ceremonial clothing and were led politely and without hate to their execution. Fifty thousand of them out of a population of two million."

"My God, and you think it could happen again?" Amanda's own words reminded her of the conversation she had shared with Stone Quillain about Krakatau a few days before.

"Let's put it this way, my good Captain," Harconan replied. "Were I a Javanese official, a Chinese hotel owner, or an Australian tourist, I would look hastily to my plane reservations should old Gungung start rumbling again."

He banked the helicopter out over the sea. "I'm taking us out over the ocean. We're coming up on the West Bali National Park, and I don't like to disturb the bird sanctuaries."

A few minutes later they rounded Cape Lampumerah, at the northwestern tip of Bali. Two islands could be seen then off the north coast, emeralds in a sapphire sea. "The one to the east is Menjangan," Harconan pronounced. "It's part of the National Park. The one ahead is Palau Piri, and it is my home."

The Island of Princes was far more impressive in real life than in aerial photography. As the helo angled toward the flashing reception beacons of the island helipad, Amanda could only gaze awestruck as the complex of elegantly modern buildings and golf-course-smooth lawns rose toward her. *Ian Fleming should have seen this,* she thought wryly.

An elderly yet straight-spined Chinese in a black business suit awaited them in the ivory-tiled entry foyer of the main house. "Welcome home, Mr. Harconan," he said with a slight inclination of his head in a faultless and accent-free English. "And welcome to you, Captain Garrett. You honor

House Harconan with your presence. May your stay with us be a pleasant one."

"Thank you." Amanda suddenly wished she were wearing a skirt instead of slacks: A curtsy seemed the only appropriate response to such a welcome.

"Amanda, I would like you to meet Mr. Lan Lo," Harconan said with real affection in his voice. "My factotum, main functionary, and the only reason I'm a millionaire."

The expression of repose on Lo's face didn't alter. "That is, of course, a gracious exaggeration, Captain."

"Never argue with your employer, Lo. I say you are indispensable. Has everything been prepared for our guest?"

"Of course, sir. Luncheon will be ready in forty-five minutes." Lo turned slightly to face Amanda. "Would you care to bathe first, Captain?"

It would have been a rather startling pronouncement anywhere but in Indonesia. However, Amanda had studied the task force's cultural database enough to know that the Indonesians were both one of the cleanest of people as well as the best-versed in maintaining comfort in a tropic environment. Offering a visitor a chance to bathe after a journey was a courtesy. And the ride under the Eurocopter's plastic bubble had been a hot and sticky one.

"Thank you. That would be very nice."

If Amanda had been expecting one of the traditional Indonesian *mandi* scoop baths, she would have been disappointed. The sun-gold and ivory European-style bathroom she was shown to was alone larger than her entire flag quarters aboard the *Carlson,* and it opened off a dressing room and bedroom that were far larger yet. Amanda suspected that the cost of the furnishings and fabrics involved in the elegant guest suite probably could have effortlessly absorbed several years of her salary.

The suite also came complete with two pretty, skilled, and silent Chinese maids. It was the first time in many years that Amanda had allowed anyone to undress her, except for recreational purposes. However, the only way to maintain one's dignity in such a situation is to flow with it. Amanda relaxed and accepted the pampering.

The bath products were Guerlain, the tub large enough to float in. Appreciative of a good deep soaking, Amanda could have luxuriated for a far longer period, but her maids were standing by with fluffy sheet-size towels, and her host awaited.

At the dressing table she found an array of expensive, tasteful cosmetics matched to her complexion, and she found that one of the maids also doubled as a skilled hairdresser.

She didn't realize the trap that had been sprung until she returned, towel-wrapped, to the bedroom. Her uniform and every other stitch she had worn had been taken, no doubt for cleaning. Replacing them were a set of ice-blue lounging pajamas, obviously from one of Bali's finest fashion houses and made of silk so fine that it flowed like water. It made a person feel cool merely to look at them.

Amanda recognized the deft move. She could make a fuss by yelling for her own clothes back or she could wear this elegant, expensive, and exotic outfit, no doubt chosen by Harconan himself, that was simply screaming to be tried on.

Two minutes later she was examining herself in the triangular mirror. The effect worked well with her amber hair and golden eyes. It worked very well indeed. And the incredible feel of the silk . . . Just wearing these garments was an erotic experience.

There was a discrete knock at the bedroom door, and Amanda nodded to one of the maids. It was amazing how rapidly a person got used to having such handy individuals around.

It was Lo. "Luncheon is ready, Captain."

"Thank you, Mr. Lo. I think I'm ready as well." She slipped her feet into the soft golden sandals that had been provided with the outfit, shot a final glance into the mirror, and set forth.

"Understood, Frank. I agree with Admiral Sonderburg that getting a sound profile on the new Indian nuclear attack sub is important. I just disagree about how important."

The distant voice of MacIntyre's chief of staff sounded in his ear. The admiral's chair creaked as he tilted it back to stare at the cable clusters overhead. Beyond the Sea Fighter task force and its current mission, he still had the remainder of Naval Special Forces to run. Today, with the Lady away, he made use of Amanda's office and workstation for his daily bout of teleconferencing with NAVSPECFORCE headquarters.

"You can point out to the admiral that currently I have two—count them, two—dedicated Raven subs in the Pacific," he replied into the phone. "If COMSUBPAC wants to park one of his own attack boats off Madras for the next six months, fine, I wish him luck. I've got too many other missions for my hulls to leave them loitering around in the Bay of Bengal, waiting for New Delhi to run trials with their new nuke. Hell, Frank, we can track this guy down and lift a sound profile on him after he's operational and at sea. . . . I'll do better than that, Frank, I'll say I'm sure Admiral Sonderburg isn't going to like it, but that's my call."

A knock at the door straightened him up behind the desk. "Enter."

Christine Rendino hesitated in the entryway, a file folder of hard copy under one arm. MacIntyre gestured her into the chair across the desk from him as he finished his call. "Right . . . that should just about do it. Forward me the after action report on the last SEAL ops cycle in northern China and lean on the yard problems with the PC rebuilds. I'll catch you tomorrow at oh-eight for the morning sitrep. Later, Frank."

He returned the phone to the desk communications deck and swiveled the chair around to face the intel. "What do you have for me, Chris?"

She held up the hard-copy file. "Latest operational intelligence updates. Would you like the file or would you prefer a fast verbal?"

"Both. Let's start with the latest from the dungeons below. What's the status on our prisoners, and have you gotten anything more out of them on the location of the INDASAT?"

"They're doing fine, sir. We've got them out of isolation and time disorientation. They're eating like horses and watching *Baywatch* reruns in six different languages. When they go back to their village, they aren't going to be able to live without satellite television. As for intel, we're getting all sorts of casual stuff on routine raider operations. I can already give you the names of half a dozen other major base villages on Sulawesi and Ambon and maybe twice that many raider schooners and their captains. Apparently Sulawesi is a hotbed of both piracy and Raja Samudra nationalism. No surprises there. But so far we've picked up nothing on the upper cartel echelons or the INDASAT."

"Any explanation for that?" MacIntyre grunted.

"Supercompartmentalization. Harconan understands his people and the tribal culture form. He knows the propensity for gossip to disseminate rapidly within a fluid, mobile culture like the Bugis.

"If the INDASAT were being held at one of the Bugis colonies on Sulawesi, our prisoners probably would have at least a hint of something especially big going on. As we aren't seeing this, it suggests that Harconan's probably keeping our satellite in the hands of a special team of somewhat more sophisticated personnel at a location outside of the usual Bugis operating areas."

"In other words, the damn thing could be anywhere."

Christine perked up. "No, sir, the satellite is still somewhere in the Indonesian archipelago. It is in Harconan's hands and he is in the process of selling it off to the highest international bidder."

MacIntyre brought his chair upright. "What have you got?"

"We scored on our systems invasion of Makara Limited,

sir. Just a little bitty bit of a score, but it's given us six critical names."

She opened a hard-copy file and selected a sheet from it, passing it across the desk to MacIntyre. "Dr. Chong Rei," he read aloud. "Mr. Hiung Wa, Mr. Jamal Kalil, Mr. Hamad Hammik, Professor Namgay Sonoo, and Dr. Joseph Valdechesfsky.

"Who are these gentlemen when they're up and dressed?" MacIntyre inquired, looking up from the paper.

"Aerospace specialists, sir, satellite operations, cybernetics, space industrialization, the best their respective corporate entities can field. Rei and Wa are with the Yan Song combine out of Korea. Hammik and Kalil are with the new Falaud Industrial Development Group based in Saudi Arabia and the UAE, and Sonoo and Valdechesfsky, an expat Russian, are with India's Marutt-Goa. All of these guys have enough of a reputation in their technologies to be worth the NSA keeping an eye on them. All six of them have arrived in Singapore within the last seventy-two hours."

"What's the tie-in with Harconan?" MacIntyre demanded.

"All six of their names were pulled out of a Makara Limited data file. Not out of one of the primary business or accounting blocks: There's no mention of them or of their parent firms in any of the Makara primary files. We lifted these names out of the day work log of Makara Limited's director of public relations. She hard-linked her palm pad computer into her workstation terminal at just the right time, for us anyway. We have a list of flight arrivals, hotel reservations, limo service, meal and entertainment expenses, all the nickel-and-dime stuff that goes along with wining and dining a body of valued corporate clients."

Christine held up a finger. "Here is where it gets interesting. Inspector Tran has confirmed the arrival of these men through Singapore customs. We have also verified that rooms are being held in their names at various four- and five-star hotels across the island. But the listing of entertainment and support expenses cuts off abruptly about twenty-four hours ago."

"Have they left the island?"

"Not according to Singapore customs, but the expense trail ends cold. Harconan Limited has stopped spending money on them, at least in Singapore."

Christine produced a second sheet of hard copy. "I had cyberwar service the problem from an Indonesian angle. Their government systems are steam-age stuff, a walk in the park to hack."

"And?"

"And yesterday the Indonesian customs station at Pekanbaru in the Rau Island group listed two Koreans, two UAE nationals, one Indian, and a Russian coming in from Kuala Lumpur, Malaysia, on a passenger hydrofoil. The names are different, but the racial grouping and the physical descriptions match.

"The Indonesian *polisi* at Pekanbaru also issued these individuals with extensive *surat jalan* letters of passage, a kind of an internal Indonesian visa granting them free passage to just about anywhere in the archipelago."

MacIntyre scowled. "Any chance we could be looking at a coincidence?"

Christine shook her head decisively. "Uh-uh, not when you consider that a quick dip into the Malaysian customs-control database indicates they they've never heard of any of these guys, at least as listed. It's questionable if they were even on that hydrofoil. They just needed some kind of official entry mode to list on the paperwork.

"To me, Admiral, sir, it's apparent these three major international industrial combines, Yan Song, Falaud, and Marutt-Goa, have taken Harconan up on the INDASAT offer and he's ghosting their inspection teams into Indonesia to look over the merchandise."

"Is there any way for us to track them?"

The intel shook her head. "I'd doubt it. I suspect they're already long gone en route to the location of the satellite base. Harconan is probably moving the inspection teams covertly via his own ships and aircraft. They probably won't be a blip on anybody's scope until they magically reappear in Singapore, ready for extraction."

MacIntyre studied the hard-copy sheets, finding no point of disagreement with the intel's assessment. "Well, this was something, at any rate. It's a hint we aren't barking up the wrong tree, but it's also not a smoking gun. It wouldn't be hard to come up with a justification for those expense accounts. What else do you have?"

"Two other factors, sir," Christine replied, "both of which are really interesting."

"Explain."

"For one, we've completed the analysis on the weapons we captured from the *Piskov* boarding party. The report has a disturbing bottom line—to me, anyway."

"Disturb me, Commander."

Christine took a deep breath. "Okay, sir, but this is sort of complex. I have to walk you through it. First, there was no big surprise with the Uzi machine pistols we captured. They were license-produced Uzi clones manufactured here in Singapore, part of a two-hundred-gun shipment to the Philippine government taken by pirates about two years ago.

"The automatic pistol we took from the prizemaster was a different matter. It was an inexpensive Beretta 92-F knockoff produced by Helwan of Egypt. The serial number indicates it was one of a five-hundred-unit shipment supposedly bought and paid for by the government of Vietnam for their national police. However, the Vietnamese claim to know nothing about buying or paying for such a shipment of handguns."

"Go on."

"The medium machine guns mounted on the Bugis Boghammers were South African MG-4s, an unlicensed 7.62 NATO variant of the old American Browning M1919. We have no idea where they came from, except they all have similar series ID numbers, and one of our specialists thinks he recognizes Israeli-style refurbishment work.

"Things really get interesting with the assault rifles. They were a short-barreled folding-stock variant of the

AK-47, ex–Hungarian army issue. A few years back, when Hungary went to NATO standard with their small arms, they took all of their old 7.62mm Warsaw Pact stuff, refurbished it, and put it on the international arms market for resale. Last year a Thai arms dealer purchased a block of six thousand rifles, theoretically on speculation. The paper trail on that arms shipment leads from Budapest to Bangkok, where the weapons are supposedly sitting in a locked warehouse, gathering dust."

"And the reality?"

"All that's left in the warehouse is the dust. The arms and the arms dealer have both disappeared. Six thousand assault rifles, Admiral. Enough to equip two entire infantry brigades."

"I know my unit strengths, Commander. What's your disturbing bottom line?"

Christine passed across the new sheaf of hard copy. "Admiral, the sizes and diverse origins of these arms shipments suggests to me that Harconan is covertly acquiring and moving a lot of firepower from a large number of diverse sources—much more than he'd need to simply supply his pirate fleet."

"What could he be doing with it?"

She shrugged and sat back. "That's just it. I don't know, unless he could be gunrunning for some of the other rebel factions within Indonesia. Fa' sure, there's enough of them and he has the transport network for it. The problem is, none of the extremist groups like the Morning Star separatists on New Guinea or the Muslim Aceh separatists on Sumatra have shown any indication of being up-gunned lately. If Harconan is arms trading, who's getting the stuff and what's it going to be used for?"

"Think cyberwar will be able to dig up the answers for us?"

He saw the regretful shake of Christine's head. "Not unless we get another lucky break like that leaky palm pad. That's the other interesting factor: Harconan Limited has two entirely different levels of communications going."

"Go on."

"On one level, there are the day-to-day business transactions. Cyberwar indicates we are in with that data flow. It all seems to be pretty standard corporate stuff: buy, sell, trade, ship routings, etc. It's commercially encrypted but we can bust it, no problem. The second level is a different story. Not much of it shows up in the Makara Limited corporate net, and when it does, zip, it's routed straight over to Palau Piri Island. I suspect a lot more is going in direct to Harconan through his satellite links. This is presumably the hot dope on his piracy operations and arms deals. Unfortunately, we can't read any of it."

MacIntyre looked perturbed. "With all of the funding we've been channeling into cyberwar, we can't crack a commercial encryption package?"

"It's not that simple, sir. Contrary to what the Reverend Dr. Gates up in Seattle would have his corporate purchasers think, there isn't any encryption program you can't break eventually with a large enough baseline, a fast enough computer, and a degree of time to work the problem. Harconan's aware of this, so he's had someone run him up a computerized variant of the old single-use, tear pad cipher.

"He's not using one code, he's using thousands of them, all essentially simple word and number substitutions, none of which is ever used more than once. For example, in one message the letter *e* could be signified by a multidigit number, say five six eight four. In the next, it's signified with a word set, like 'cheese,' 'basketball,' 'Thursday,' 'Mormon,' but no two ever the same."

"I understand how a tear pad works," MacIntyre said. "There's never a large enough baseline to analyze for decryption. You can't transmit the *Encyclopaedia Britannica* or a digital breakdown of the roof of the Sistine Chapel using one, but it's good enough for basic messaging."

"And good enough for Harconan's needs," Christine agreed. "He must have a computer program that generates huge batches of these code sets. Then he distributes a bunch of inexpensive laptops to his key agents, all of them preprogrammed with an individual set of codes for that specific agent. The code sets are likely designed to sequentially roll over after each use, with the previous code being erased.

"The laptops will be stand-alones that probably have been physically modified so they can't be networked, guaranteeing man-breaks in the system. After encryption, a message has to be downloaded onto a data disk or card and then physically inserted into a second computer for transmission over the Internet.

"To make things even tougher, according to the transmission addresses, none of this second-level stuff ever comes out of a Harconan Limited office or a personal computer. It inevitably dumps and loads through a public Internet access like a library, a post office, or a business services center at a big hotel. Even if we could track down the holder of one of these boxes and pulled the code set, it would only give us the communications string for that specific agent."

"Presumably when an agent runs low on codes, he gets sent a new laptop."

"Exactly, sir. There will only be one master program, with all of the code sets assigned to all of the agents. That will be a stand-alone mainframe on Palau Piri. You can bet it will be isolated and impossible to hack from any outside access, and it will be physically guarded like Fort Knox."

"Enigma rides again," MacIntyre grunted. He swiveled his chair away from the intel for a moment, staring toward the open porthole in the bulkhead, then turned back. "Tell me, Chris. Does Amanda—Captain Garrett—know about this encryption system of Harconan's? Did you brief her on it before she went out to Palau Piri?"

It was Christine's turn to look away. "No, sir, I didn't. I was waiting for confirmation from cyberwar on certain aspects of the system before discussing the matter with Captain Garrett."

"Translation," MacIntyre stated flatly. "You didn't want to risk her poking around after that mainframe."

Something hot and angry flared in Christine's eyes as she looked up. "No, sir, I did not. She's running a big enough risk as is, being out there with Harconan. I didn't want her stretching the envelope."

MacIntyre put an edge on his voice. "And you don't think Captain Garrett is capable of executing her own good judgment in this matter, Commander?"

"No sir! I do not!" The words slipped out without her meaning them to. Christine mentally floundered for a way to recall them. Shit, MacIntyre was the only person who'd ever had the knack of flipping her open like that.

The admiral's soft chuckle eased her. "Stand easy, Chris. I fully concur with your decision. If you had told her about this damn thing, you, I, and God all know she'd make a try for it."

Somber-eyed, Christine studied the admiral. At one time she'd thought she had this blocky, plain-spoken man figured. Of late, though, she'd started to sense well-hidden subtleties and a capacity for perception that could be a little unnerving at times.

Such as now.

"You're worried about her being around Harconan, aren't you?" he continued.

"Of course, sir. Who wouldn't be?"

MacIntyre's eyes narrowed. "But you're talking about something more than just a tricky tactical situation here, Chris. You've assessed something that you don't like, but you don't want to speak about it. That suggests to me it's not professional, it's personal."

"Did you ever serve a tour with Intelligence, sir?" Christine asked ruefully.

"No, but I am raising a teenage daughter. The skills required are similar. I've found that if something's making you jumpy, it should be talked about. There are only two of us here. Now, what's going on?"

Christine sighed and hesitated a final second. Damn, did this have to come out with this man? "I'm afraid Captain Garrett... Amanda... might be getting in over her head in this situation in ways she doesn't understand herself."

Christine stalled again, groping to put instincts into words, to give verbalization to deeply personal thoughts.

"Just say it," MacIntyre said patiently.

"Admiral, Amanda Garrett is a nun!"

MacIntyre's eyebrows shot up! "What?"

Christine let the words free flow. "I mean, in her way, Amanda has lived a very closed existence. For all of her life she's been married to the Navy in the same way a nun is married to the Church. It's her world. Even before she attended Annapolis she was brought up in a Navy environment. As her friend, I can say for a fact that the last time she had a major personal relationship outside of the Navy was in high school."

"And your point?" MacIntyre asked, puzzled.

Christine took a deep breath. "My point is, she has never had exposure to a man like Makara Harconan or to his ultra–high-roller kind of world. Right now she is way the hell off her playing field, involved in a game she doesn't really understand, and I'm scared spitless that she won't realize it until it's too late."

MacIntyre stared from across the desk. "You can't mean... Good God, Chris. Are you seriously proposing that this pirate could... turn Amanda's head?"

Christine shook her head. "Not to fall in love, sir. Not the genuine article. Not the kind of thing that would ever make her deliberately betray the task force or the Navy. But she might be knocked off her feet enough to be blinded to some personal risks, physical or emotional. We aren't the ones in danger here, Admiral: Amanda is."

MacIntyre shot out of his chair and paced off the length of the limited office space. "That's ridiculous, Commander. That's just... flatly... ridiculous!"

"Sir, I wish to God it was!" Christine exclaimed, turning in her chair to follow him. "But shit of that nature happens, and with alarming frequency. How many times have you heard of some male officer totally screwing up his life with some chickiepoo not worth the powder to blow her to hell?"

MacIntyre didn't reply immediately, but the expression on his face indicated he was thinking of any number of prime examples. "But not Amanda," he said finally. "She has too much common sense to do anything like that."

"Sir, trust me. When glands override brains, women can be just as gonzo as men." Christine popped the center of her forehead with the heel of her hand. "Jeez, this is intense woman stuff. How do I say it? Females can be drawn to men of power. Anthropologists say it's because our instinct is to seek out strong genes and good providers for our children. Be that as it may, certain supermasculine types can sometimes really trip our switches. Makara Harconan is one of those types. He is a total package. He's highly intelligent, he is highly successful, he is personable, intensely dynamic, and, if you're a woman, he is drop-dead gorgeous!

"I felt the effect the first time I saw his picture," Christine concluded. "Just about any conventionally aligned female would. I'd say he's maybe one in a hundred thousand in that area."

MacIntyre stared at a pine-paneled bulkhead. "I see. One in a hundred thousand? And how would that apply . . . tactically?"

"Does the phrase 'clubbing baby seals' bring anything to mind, sir?"

Palau Piri Island   1233 Hours, Zone Time: August 16, 2008

Luncheon was served al fresco in the mansion's central garden, the palm shade and Amanda's air-light clothing nullifying the tropical warmth of the day. The meal itself was superb. Simple yet subtle, prawns in a butter and garlic sauce, *sate,* savory barbecued meat impaled on skewers of sugarcane served with a firy *sambal* peanut sauce made with chilies, peanuts, and coconut cream. Steamed white rice served to mellow the spices and, oddly enough, the solid Dutch-style Anker lager served with the meal perfectly counterpointed the food.

Amanda noted that on this occasion Harconan drank and enjoyed the beer as much as she. Not a Muslim, then, or maybe more just his own man. She had ten thousand questions about this individual, born out of what Tran had told her about him. But she dared not ask too many. She could only catch the scraps of information he offered.

The Chinese server who bore in the dessert tray offered the chance for one such insight.

"I notice that most of your staff here are Chinese," she commented. "Is there a reason or is it just coincidence?"

"A reason," Harconan replied. "I suppose you could say it's for security's sake. Most of the Chinese here in Indonesia are...apart from the main flow of the island culture. They are overlaid on top of it, as it were—hardworking, successful, and prosperous for the most part, but envied and held in suspicion and distrust by many Indonesians. One could call them the Jews of Southeast Asia, I suppose."

Harconan took a sip of his beer. "Here in House Harconan, as part of my staff, they receive a good salary and are treated with the respect due good employees. Thus their allegiance is to me, without my having to worry about an excessive number of outside entanglements."

"You make it sound almost like a feudal society."

He flashed her a grin and lightly brushed his mustache with a knuckle. "There is no almost about it, Amanda. That's exactly what it is and I'm quite content with it. That's what being wealthy can do for a person. It not only permits you to live where you wish, but when as well."

Over dessert, he introduced her to the local fruits, insisting upon personally wielding the silver fruit knife and skewers himself. She found herself sampling things she'd never even heard of before. The *tuih* and the *zirzak,* the *blimbing* and the honey-flavored *sawo,* the snake fruit that by Indonesian legend was the true apple in the Garden of Eden, and the durian that smells like an open cesspit and tastes like a blend of onion and caramel and, once sampled, is strangely addictive. Harconan let her consume half a dozen slices before casually mentioning that the durian is also supposedly an extremely potent natural aphrodisiac.

Superb chilled champagne was served with the fruit, and Amanda found the laughter and relaxed conversation flowing easily. Bit by bit her guard came down as Harconan seemed to work at diverting topics away from the task force and anything that resembled politics or world affairs. They agreed that wood was the only decent and proper material to build a sailing boat with, and they compared the points of Indonesian, European, and American design, verbally sketching out a compromise craft that incorporated the best of all three worlds.

The shadows sundialed around the lanai as they forgot time; they were reminded of it by the reappearance of Lo.

"Excuse me, Mr. Harconan, but I fear I must remind you of that conference call." Harconan started and glanced at his black-faced Rolex diver's watch. "Damnation, is it that time already? Amanda, you must excuse me. Duty calls in a shrill, unpleasant voice."

Amanda found she was genuinely disappointed to have the day ending. "That's a call I recognize all too well. Don't worry about it. Do you have a pilot who can fly me back to the ship."

"Nonsense, it's barely two. The day is young. This will take me forty-five minutes, an hour at the most. Why don't you have a swim and a sun on the east beach while I deal with this call? I'll have a word with my chief of security and he'll ensure you complete peace and privacy. I'll join you there as soon as I can."

"That sounds wonderful. Do you have a suit I can borrow?"

Harconan shrugged. "If you feel the need for one."

A swimsuit, a French-cut backless one piece in pale green satin, awaited her in the guest room along with a short terry-cloth beach jacket and a pair of sandals. Amanda was not surprised when it, too, fit to perfection.

It must be nice to own a magic wand, she mused with irony. Beyond that, there was again the somewhat eerie sensation that her mind or at least her life was being read. If Harconan could even conjure up her clothing sizes when he wished, what else did he have in his hands?

The hundred-yard walk to the east beach followed a meticulously groomed but meandering lava gravel path through the island's palm groves. The walk itself was an experience. Amanda had visited world-class botanical gardens that didn't have the beauty of Palau Piri's wild ground cover. She recognized bougainvillea, jasmine, poinsettias, and marigolds growing in their natural home environment, and a hundred more she couldn't begin to put a name to.

The air, perfumed with its myriad scents, was almost dizzying. The atmosphere was filled with birdsong and gecko chirp as well, the birds as dazzling as mobile flowers, catching and flaring bursts of the sunlight that leaked past the palm shade, the lizards skittering explosively across the paths and up the striated palm trunks.

It was all a little overwhelming. Amanda found herself wondering just when Bob Hope and Bing Crosby were going to show up.

And then the path wound toward a brightness beyond the trees, and she found herself at the beach. Amanda brought herself up short. The walk had been overwhelming, but this was awe-inspiring.

It was real.

All the legends, all the images, all the fantasies, conjured by the whisper of "the South Seas" were real. One only had to search until one found the Island of the Princes.

Black velvet sand with snow-colored surf curling against it. A sea and sky two different grades of sapphire, clouds as white as the surf piling against the peak of Propat Agung on the Bali mainland, and the mainland itself and the more distant Menjangang island burning a vivid living green under the sun. A single great crested tern circled offshore.

If she slept a hundred years, Amanda couldn't imagine ever dreaming of anything this perfect. For long minutes she stood and drank it all in, only to want more.

Eventually she blinked and came back into herself. Glancing around, she noted a pair of comfortable-looking chaise longues drawn back into the shade at the head of the sand, separated by a small drinks table with a cooler set ready at its feet.

Amanda could only grin in sheer admiration. The man was still ahead of her.

She noted something else as well: something tree-tall

but not organic in the palm line was set a short distance back from the beach. Curious, she moved closer.

It was a security-camera mount. A gray steel pole with a remote scanning head, part of the island defenses Chris had mentioned. Currently, however, the unit had a nylon cover drawn over its camera. As Harconan had promised, she would have her privacy here.

Amanda returned to the open beach, walking a few more yards farther down. Kicking off her sandals, she found the sand was soft and pleasantly hot under the sun. Shedding her beach jacket, she took a step toward the surf. Then she hesitated, glancing down at herself.

Damn that man!

She remembered the lazy, condescending smile he had given her when she had asked about borrowing a suit. "If you feel the need for one."

This beach, the setup, putting her alone like this.

The bastard was daring her!

Aloud, she gave an angry, frustrated yip.

If she did, he would have won yet again, maneuvering her into it. And if she didn't, she'd lose for not having the nerve to accept the challenge.

Damn, damn, damn the man!

She fought the battle for a minute more, then the sun and the brush of the warm wind on her skin won. Her hands came up and crossed, slipping the straps from her shoulders. The discarded satin whispered off her body and pooled at her feet. Stepping out of the suit, she yielded to the pleasure and freedom of her nudity and ran down to the sea.

Plunging into the blood-temperature water, she reveled in the infinite difference between swimming in even the most minimal of clothing and swimming in nothing at all, wondering if it were possible for Harconan to have learned of her secret passion for skinny-dipping.

There was a reef some twenty yards offshore and she swam parallel with it, keeping a safe distance from its jagged coral and defending army of spiny sea urchins, yet diving intermittently to sightsee the brilliant swarms of reef fish that flickered and danced among the multicolored sea fans. She should have forgotten about the suit and asked for swim fins and a face mask. Next time, that's how she would do it.

Next time?

Before Amanda realized, she had swum a quarter mile up the beach and noticed that early-warning glow of too much skin, sun, and salt water exposure. Paddling ashore, she sought the shelter of the shade line at the head of the sand. She was going to have to walk back to her suit bare, but that prospect wasn't particularly unpleasant. She picked wild-growing scarlet hibiscus and tucked it into her hair as she ambled back toward the path.

She was so deep in daydreaming that she overshot the mark. She looked back in puzzlement. No, she couldn't be mistaken: There were her sandals. This was the place she had left her suit. The beach jacket too.

They were gone, and suddenly Amanda found herself no longer merely nude but naked.

He'd done it to her again! Amanda's hands started to move in the two classic gestures of a female caught in the predicament. Angrily she straightened and forced them down to her sides. It was not as if he had not already seen everything that was available. She was not going to lose her dignity on top of her clothing.

"Makara!" she yelled at the top of her lungs.

"Yes," he replied casually coming down out of the deeper shade of the seaside grove. He was barefoot and wearing a beach jacket, and his gray eyes studied her with frank and open appreciation. Instinctively she started to cover herself again, catching herself once more. Angrily, she snapped at herself that this was just like having her clothes taken in escape-and-evasion training.

Only it wasn't and she was fully aware of it.

"All right, Makara, what happened to my suit?"

"Nothing happened to it," he said matter-of-factly. "You neither needed it nor wanted it anymore so I simply sent it back to the house. You are very lovely as you are now and I intend to keep you this way for a time."

"That was a dirty trick!"

He sighed as if explaining something to an obstinate child. "Amanda, be reasonable, nobody tricked you except yourself."

"Are you going to deny you set this whole thing, and me, up?"

"I admit to recognizing a potential," he replied, grinning. "Recognizing potential is what I do best. Be fair: At most I can be accused of opening a series of doors for you, and in each case you stepped through of your volition, of your own desire."

"I did not!"

"Of course you did. You could have stopped my stripping you like this at any time. Have you been forced, coerced, had a hand lifted against you? I think not. Even now it's not too late. We can lie and say that this is something neither of us want. You may have my beach jacket to walk back to the house in."

He lifted a hand now, to reach out and brush the petal of the flower in her hair against her cheek. She found her knees trembling, and her own hands came up, trying vainly to shield herself, to hide the hardening of her nipples and the other signs of the growing, uncontrollable fire within her.

"Makara, please," she whispered. "I'm naked out here."

The back of his fingers caressed her cheek directly this time. "Of course you are. Naked and very beautiful and vulnerable and helpless, as you wished to be, just for a little while."

The sunset was awesome in its gold and flame grandeur. They watched it together on the scratch bed made out of the lounge mattresses. They lay on their sides, spoon fashion, Makara's right arm under her head as a pillow, his face buried in her slightly salt-sticky hair. Both of them finally satiated after an almost frightening time when neither of them could seem to have enough of the other. And yet, the hunger for more still lived, the fires banked by sheer exhaustion.

"You're right," Amanda said, the first conscious word she

had spoken in many hours. "I did want this, but I don't know why."

"I could take that as an insult, you know," Harconan replied his voice slurring slightly as he kissed the back of her neck.

"That's not what I mean, love," she replied wryly, reaching back to administer a caress. "I'll acknowledge that your very obvious charms impressed me from the beginning. I mean, why was I drawn to this particular scenario you set up? I'm usually more . . . straightforward about such things."

"Must you always be so analytical?" he inquired, delivering a nip to her shoulder blade.

"Yes," Amanda replied honestly, starting to move the backs of her thighs in a gentle massaging motion.

"Mmm, well, I'd tell you my theory, but I don't want to interrupt what you are doing."

"I'll stop cold right now if you don't, mister."

"I hear the captain coming back already. Very well, woman, here is my theory. You fell into my trap because you wished to do so. You wanted to dice with the Devil and be defeated. You wanted to lose the game and quite literally be stripped of all your control, all of your considerable power, to be left as you are now, naked and helpless. In short, you wished to lose."

She stopped moving her hips and looked back over her shoulder, her eyes wide. "That's crazy."

"No, it's not. Not for people like you and me." Harconan closed both of his arms around her, drawing her back against him in a fond hug. "Losing is a natural human experience, a part of living. We learn from it. But you and I are different from the normal herd."

"How so?"

"We are, as they say in your country, high rollers. We live large and the stakes are high when we gamble. When we lose, the losses are great, in money, in policy, and in lives. We *must* win—anyway we can, whenever we step to the table. Thus, the battlefields where we dare to lose are few and far between. You found one on my beach this day. I hope the experience was interesting for you."

"Yes . . . very. Makara?"

"What, beauty?"

"I must be back at the ship soon. Before I go, do you think you could . . . defeat me one more time?"

Twin shadows ran in echelon formation through the night, not with the shriek of turbines and the billowing spray of lift fans, but with the all but inaudible mutter of silenced auxiliary diesels and the lap of waves against displacing hulls.

The *Queen of the West* and her sister craft, the *Manassas,* crept in toward the river estuary that served Adat Tanjung as a harbor. The ECM threat boards had sensed no trace of radar, and the only stealth ranges the Sea Fighters needed to be concerned with were the ancient ones of sight and sound.

At the "shoulders" of each broad hull, just aft and to either side of the cockpit, weapons pedestals elevated into firing position, rocket pods and twin-barreled 30mm autocannon locking into place and panning across the darkness. The snub barrels of OCSW grenade launchers supplemented the primary armament, peering from the open side hatches.

Normally, a third grenade launcher would have been mounted aft, to fire out the opened tailgate. On this night however, a small team of SOC Marines made use of that space to inflate and equip their small CRRC (Combat Rubber Raiding Craft).

With the hull hatches open, the *Queen*'s air conditioners couldn't cope with the inrush of steaming warm night air. Sweat prickled under interceptor vests and Kevlar K-Pot combat helmets. Steamer Lane bounced his attention between the graphics chart of the estuary on his Navicom display and what was visible through the windscreen via his night-vision visor.

"Okay," he commented, "that's the western point. We

get around that and we should see the village on the eastern bank of the river mouth."

"Uh-huh." Scrounger Caitlin looked up from the console screen she was using to access the more powerful low-light television camera in the Mast-Mounted Sighting System. "Better keep us at least two klicks off the point, sir. I'm seeing some fish traps and some small-boat activity off the beach. Locals night fishing, I guess."

"Will do. How about that coaster passing astern of us?"

The sensor pod atop the snub mast swiveled around to peer aft.

"Almost over the horizon, sir. No longer a factor."

"Good enough." Lane chuckled softly. "I can see a real nice break over the bar across that river mouth. You know, if you had a strong southerly wind building out here, you could probably catch a wave on that bar and ride it a good mile up the bay."

"Begging the Commander's pardon, but I don't think my guys and I want to try that tonight."

It was a try at levity from the young Marine officer riding the cockpit passenger seat. It didn't quite come off. Tonight would be the first hot mission for Second Lieutenant Lincoln Ives, USMC (SOC).

Steamer Lane and Scrounger Caitlin knew the feeling and empathized. They had been there themselves. It wouldn't really help Ives to explain that the knotting gut and dry mouth would always be there. Experience just allowed you to hide the symptoms better.

"Don't worry, Lieutenant," Caitlin called back over her shoulder. "It's going to be a cakewalk, you'll see."

"Thanks for the vote of confidence, Chief," Ives replied wryly.

"Vote nothing, sir, a statement of fact. I *know* tonight's run is going to be good for you."

Ives looked up from adjusting his MOLLE harness for the tenth time. "You know? What do you mean?"

"Just that. I know. I got the Touch, sir."

"The Touch..." the Marine's voice trailed off. He'd

heard the stories. Every combat hand does sooner or later. The military urban legends about certain individuals who seem to have the ability to sense the future, specifically concerning fate, life, and death, warriors who have accurately predicted the loss in combat of others or themselves. Ives had always tossed off such stories as just that, stories. They couldn't be true, no matter how matter of factly the *Queen*'s chief of the boat spoke. Could they?

"Believe her, Lieutenant," Steamer Lane said quietly. "This is a genuine no-shitter. If the Scrounge says you're going to be okay, you are."

At that moment Lincoln Ives had wanted nothing more in the world than for someone to say, "Hey, it's going to be all right," with enough conviction to make him believe it.

"If you say so, Commander." He grinned. "Thanks for the word, Chief. I'll pass it along."

There was a thump and scuff from overhead, and Ensign Wilder slid down through the open hatch in the cockpit overhead. "Cipher drone tie-downs are cleared for launch, sir," he reported, sliding into the navigator's seat.

"Good enough, Terr. Get us a status update from the *Manassas* and then let the *Carlson* know we're on station and ready to open the ball."

"Aye, aye, sir."

"I'd better check on how my guys are coming down in the main hull." Ives levered himself out of the jump seat and started down the cockpit ladderway.

Lane let him drop out of sight before glancing over at his copilot. Steamer would no more doubt Sandra Caitlin's gift than he would one of the *Queen*'s instrument readouts. After "the Touch" had foretold the deaths of some people very close to them both, he and Caitlin had spent many long nights considering the complex morality involved in such a power.

"So was that a square count on tonight's run?" he asked.

She returned his gaze and gave an ominous shrug.

The Combat Information Center, or CIC, of a modern warship is by nature windowless, being located deep within the vessel's hull or superstructure. But here, surrounded by arrays of increasingly sophisticated sensors, communications systems, and intelligence-gathering assets, a commander can truly "see" what is going on in the surrounding combat environment.

Befitting the complex nature of her amphibious warfare mission, the *Carlson* had more than one such facility. The *Carlson*'s CIC proper controlled the offensive and defensive posture and actions of the LPD, and, through the data links of the Joint Battle Management System, the task group as a whole when she was acting as command ship of the formation.

The second facility, the joint information center, oversaw the operation of the task force's "Raven" assets, its strategic, operational, and tactical intelligence-gathering capacity. Here flowed the electronic and signal intercepts, the recon satellite and drone downloads, the sit reps from the National Security Agency and Defense Intelligence—even the latest off the wire from CNN—all to be assessed, correlated, and passed on to the task force decision makers.

Thirdly there was the landing force operations center, or LFOC, mission control for the embarked Marine detachment.

The LFOC had a comforting familiarity for Amanda, the low cable strung overhead, the triple row of workstations facing a bulkhead paneled with large screen displays, the quiet efficiency of the duty crew in the CRT-lit dimness. Some were in Navy officers' khaki or enlisted denim, others in Marine-green utilities.

Amanda had fought her first wars in places like this.

"What's our latest on Indonesian air and naval deployments, Stone?" Amanda inquired, standing behind the force commander's workstation in the rear row of consoles.

With a headset settled over his close-cropped brush of dark hair, Stone Quillain brought up a regional area map of western Sulawesi and its maritime surroundings on the main bulkhead flatscreen. Using the joystick controller with only a hint of unfamiliarity, he highlighted the key points amid the sprinkling of civilian traffic hacks on the 120-inch display.

"Well, we got us a maritime *polisi* launch at Parepare. That's a good forty miles to the south. She's currently off patrol and standing down at her slip. I don't think we have to worry about her much. The nearest Indonesian air is a C-160 transport over the Makassar Strait about thirty miles to the west in the standard ATF corridor to Balikpapan. Nothing to worry about there, either. The nearest major surface element is a training frigate, the *Hajar Dewan*...something or other, way down here off Selayar Island. No helo embarked at this time. Another no-problem."

"How fresh is this intel?" Amanda inquired.

"JIC says it's hot out of the oven, Skipper. They're direct linking with both the Global Hawk we have over the target area and the Oceansat recon net. If somebody steps outside of his hut to take a leak, we'll hear the splash."

"Do tell," Amanda replied wryly. She sank into the chair behind the adjacent workstation and plugged her command headset into the communications hardlink. "Stone, do you ever feel obsolescence sneaking up behind you? I like to consider myself innovative, but the technology just keeps pulling away."

The Marine cut his eyes at her and chuckled, a baritone *huh, huh, huh* in his chest. "That's for you button pushers to worry about. I'm still a bayonet-and-bullet man. They're going to be needing me around for a long time to come."

"Hmmm, consider where you're sitting at the moment, Stone," Amanda smiled back. "Consider where you're sitting."

The big shadow beside her grumbled something about women under his breath.

There was a flicker of corridor light in the cool CRT-lit dimness as the blackout curtain in the operations center entryway was brushed aside. Amanda felt a cluster of people pressing close behind her and her nose cataloged the scents added to the limited space: Admiral MacIntyre's old-fashioned bay rum, Christine Rendino's slightly musky cologne, and the clean lime bite of another aftershave that she didn't recognize at first. Then she recalled the scent signature of Nguyen Tran.

"Status?" MacIntyre inquired at her shoulder.

"The microforce is positioned," Amanda replied. "We should be getting the active link from the *Queen* momentarily."

As if prompted by her words, a second large screen display lit off, filling with the low-light image of the *Queen of the West*'s cockpit interior, the face of Steamer Lane's executive officer centered in the screen.

Ensign Wilder's lips moved. "Possum One, this is Royalty. We are at point of team departure, commencing live data stream. We are on the time line with green boards. Tactical situation appears nominal."

More flatscreens activated.

One was a computer-graphics overhead simulacra of the engagement area, a composite image built from the information flow from both the Sea Fighter's sensors and those of the orbiting Global Hawk drone, combined with the geointelligence database on the Adat coastal region.

Another screen filled with the low-light vista drawn from the *Queen*'s Mast Mounted Sight cameras.

Amanda lifted her voice. "Give us a pan across the village area."

A systems operator in the console row ahead accessed a system override and manipulated a miniature joystick.

Seven hundred and fifty miles away, the *Queen of the West*'s sensors responded to the command.

The village of Adat Tanjung lay before them, its fleet of oceangoing *pinisi* riding at anchor offshore, its smaller craft beached or moored alongside an accumulation of spindle-legged piers that extended into the estuary. Bare masts swayed with the wave action, and an occasional light glowed in a cabin or on a deck.

Extending to the northwest and southeast along the inlet beach was a further spidery entanglement of fish and crab farming pens, while beyond the piers were the streets of the village itself. Rows of traditional thatch-roofed Bugis dwellings, set high on stilt foundations, extended back into the verdant palm groves. Interspersed among them were a few low Western-style buildings, their corrugated-metal roofs catching and reflecting the starlight.

Many homes were fully illuminated, and lanterns and even torches burned in the streets.

"There's a lot of activity over there tonight." Amanda could hear the scowl in MacIntyre's voice.

"No," Tran replied from behind her other shoulder. "This was to be expected. It works in our favor."

"How so? What's happening?" Amanda asked over her shoulder.

"Ships have returned from a raid with lost crewmen," Tran answered softly. "The clan mourns. As with their neighboring people, the Toraja of the Sulawesi highlands, their feasts for the dead are quite elaborate and will last for several days and nights. All will attend, including the crews of the raiders. The ships should be unmanned."

For a moment Amanda considered the Bugis pirates still secured belowdecks aboard the *Carlson*. How would it be to return home to find yourself declared dead?

Christine Rendino had taken over the workstation on the far side of Stone Quillain. Now she conjured a targeting box around two of the schooners lying rafted together well off the beach. "See these guys? These are our two friends from the *Piskov*."

A second targeting box blinked up around a second rafted pair of ships. "These fellows also belong here: They base out of Adat Tanjung as well. These dudes"—a third set of schooners were designated—"came from a little farther up the coast. They came in and anchored here yesterday. See how all six of these schooners are larger than the other *pinisi* in the moorage? How they've tied up together, and how they're set off a little to one side from the other craft? That suggests an organization pattern."

"Teamed fighting units," MacIntyre replied.

"Uh-huh," Christine agreed. "All day today we've been seeing a lot of activity around these six ships, refueling and replenishment. There's something else kinda special as well."

"Which is?" Amanda inquired.

"According to our prisoner interrogations, standard operating procedure for the Bugis raiders is to download all armament at a weapons hide before returning to home base. Now we've been sitting right on top of the *Piskov* pair ever since we picked them up and they've come straight home. They haven't diverted anywhere or downloaded anything. They still have their guns aboard.

"The *Piskov* raiders must have received instructions en route to stay armed," Amanda murmured.

"Uh-huh. Betcha a pretty we're going to find these other guys have picked up their heat and are running heeled too."

"Somebody's assembling a strike force."

"You got it, Boss Ma'am. And I bet this tune is being replayed at just about every Bugis colony up and down the archipelago. These guys are gearing up for a fight."

Stone Quillain snorted. "You think these little pissants might be figuring on coming out after us? That'd be crazy."

"I don't know, Stone," Amanda replied in the darkness. "Remember our old General Belewa? That outboard motor navy of his gave us quite a fight off West Africa. As we don't know what Harconan is planning, we'll take this threat seriously."

She considered the prospects with the unique personal insight she had gained from her day with Makara Harconan. She strongly suspected there was nothing this man might not dare. And the motto of Great Britain's Special Air Service pointed out a great truth: "He who dares, wins."

The video link with the *Queen of the West* reactivated, filling with a different face, leaner, harder, more angular than Ensign Wilder's, yet in its own way as painfully young. The Marine's features were densely smeared with dark camou cream, and he wore a Kevlar K-Pot battle helmet with a camouflage cover. An AI-2 night-vision visor had been lifted onto the front helmet facing. Clipped to the right side of the K-Pot was his squad tactical radio; on the left was another cigarette-package-sized module, this one with a low-light television lens aiming forward.

"Possum One, this is Lieutenant Ives, Recon Able. We have the boats in the water, ready to move out on the line. Any further instructions?"

Stone keyed his mike. "Hi, Linc, this is Stone. Do it like you planned it, boy. You and your top go active on your helmet cams when you reach objective. We'll just ride along in your shirt pocket and enjoy the view."

The recon Marine's lips tightened in a brief, tense smile. "I hope it'll be a good ride, sir."

"All that counts is doing the job and getting yourself home again, Marine. Move out."

Stone went off circuit. "He's a good boy," he said almost to himself, "a real good boy. He just has to season some."

"That's so often the case," Amanda replied.

The communications carriers from the microforce hissed softly through the overhead speakers, an occasional curt low-voiced comment or command sketching out the departure. A pair of new blue "friendly" surface hacks appeared on the tactical display, drifting slowly inward toward the Bugis moorage. On the MMS monitor, two small, heavily laden inflatables could be seen pulling away from the hovercraft, driven by silent electric outboards. Growing steadily less distinct, their humped outlines could be made out for a long time against the photo-multiplied glare of the village lights, then they were gone.

MacIntyre paced and Christine found a seat. Tran stood erect and silent by her side, sipping smoke from a Player's cigarette.

"Drone Control," Amanda lifted her voice, "let's take another look at the target ships."

Sixty thousand feet above Adat Tanjung, a camera turret

swiveled and zoomed in. Yet another monitor lit off, showing the empty decks of a pair of rafted schooners, the image changing angle slowly and shimmering a little from atmospheric distortion.

"No situational change. No electronic or thermal emissions detected."

The image jumped from schooner set to schooner set.

"No situational changes. No electronic or thermal emissions." The SO murmured repetitively.

"All right. Let's have a look at the village itself."

The camera panned across the bay refocusing on the streets of Adat Tanjung.

Fires burned in the forecourts of many of the houses, people clustering about them. Around some, men stood, hands linked, swaying to an unheard song, women sitting in a wider circle beyond, moving to a different rhythm.

"What's happening here, Nguyen?" Christine inquired.

"A lament is being sung in the memory of the dead, and the story of their lives is being retold for their friends and family. The Bugis are primarily Muslim, but many of the old ways and the old ceremonies live on." Tran took a light draw on his cigarette. "The village has taken a hard hit with this raid. Nearly every family must have taken a loss."

"How will they explain the losses to the authorities?" Amanda inquired.

"They won't. This is of the tribe and the Bugis. The authorities will be Javanese. This will not be considered their affair. The Bugis are a proud people, fast to anger at intrusions. The island administrators generally recognize this and leave them to themselves. They remember Kahar Muzakkar too well."

Stone Quillain glanced around. "Kahar who?"

"A Bugis teacher and soldier who led a guerrilla-warfare campaign for Sulawesi independence. He and his followers battled with the Jakarta government for a decade and a half, from 1950 until his death in 1965. Sulawesi venerates his memory. The government fears it."

On the tactical display, symbols for the two CRRCs separated, one moving toward each of the outermost pairs of rafted schooners.

"Nah, that's not how you should be doing it, Linc," Quillain murmured aloud. "You ought to get that inshore pair first." The Marine started to reach for the Transmit key on the communications pad. Then he hesitated and reluctantly lowered his hand.

MacIntyre chuckled without mirth but not without sympathy. "Welcome to the upper echelons, Stone. All of this fabulous new C3I gear they keep coming up with lets us sit right on top of our people out in the field. One of the most important and toughest things we have to learn is how to sit back, shut up, and let 'em do the job their way."

"Yeah, guess so." Quillain drew his hand across his chin, the day's whiskers rasping. "Does it get any better as you get up there a little more?"

The slim shadow seated beside Quillain answered the question. "No," Amanda said, "just worse."

A communications specialist spoke up from the console row ahead. "We're getting helmet cam streams from Lieutenant Ives and his platoon sergeant."

"Put 'em on Monitor Two. Split-screen it."

Flickering low-light images filled the designated screen, the sterns of the two rafted sets of Bugis schooners looming out of the night. They were seeing what the two Marine boarding-team leaders were observing as it happened.

"This is just too goddamn weird," Stone whispered.

More images. The side of a schooner...the rungs of a boarding ladder flowing past...shadowy shapes moving across a silver-gray deck, a whispered commentary flowing from the overhead speakers.

"This is section A, we're aboard schooners One and Two....Corby, Franklin, set the lookout....You guys start working the other ship....Section B boarding...all okay so far on Three and Four, Lieutenant....Nobody aboard....That's good. We're good too. Start scanning, let's go...."

Through their headsets, Christine and Tran fed their own

careful prompts back over the communications loop. "Lieutenant Ives, this is Commander Rendino. Don't forget to get the serial numbers off the engine block. . . . Gentlemen, on some *pinisi* the captain's quarters will be nothing more than a patch of deck. Check any personal belongings you may see lying about. . . ."

The feedback began.

"Mr. Tran, this is Sergeant Patterson with B Section. We're just over the keel of the Number Three schooner and our mine detector is reading right off the scale. Do these guys use scrap metal for ballast?"

"Negative, Sergeant," he replied. "They use stone. Metal is too valuable. Start looking for signs of concealed fasteners or a hidden door of some kind in the decking."

Wood scraped. Breath hissed, men swore silently. Then: "Yeah, yeah, we got it! We got guns! Man, this orange crate has some kind of teeth!"

Video images of heavy automatic weapons and recoilless rifles were recorded. Serial numbers were taken. The minutes marched past. Eyes flicked to the time hacks in the corners of the displays more and more often.

Finally: "*Carlson, Carlson*. This is Ives. We got the first four schooners pretty much covered. We confirm they all are armed. We've turned some documents, pretty standard stuff, bills of lading and so forth. There is no sign of a Global Positioning Unit on any of these ships. No navigational material at all except for regular ship's charts."

"Shit," Christine hissed. "The captains probably took their GPUs ashore with them. Ives, make sure you get some high-definition photography of those charts. There might be some markings that will be useful."

"Wilco," the reply hissed back.

"There's still those last two schooners left," Stone commented.

"Very true." MacIntyre scowled in the screenglow. "But they've been out there a long time."

On distant Sulawesi, Ives read their minds. "Captain Quillain, request instructions. Should we extract at this time or move on to the next pair of ships?"

Amanda looked back to Tran. "What about it, Inspector? How much longer will those ceremonies ashore continue?"

"An excellent question, Captain, for which I wish I had an answer. They could end in the next three minutes or go on all night."

No one else had anything to add.

Quillain keyed his mike. "Linc, this is Stone. You're the man out there, son. Make the call and we'll go with whatever you decide."

The circuit was silent for a minute. Then: "We're going for it, sir. We'll secure things here, then I'm taking both parties across to Five and Six. Stand by."

Moving with quiet haste, the Marines erased all traces of their boarding the schooners. In the LFOC there was brief consideration of the weapons in the concealed gun lockers. They could be aimed at U.S. sailors in the near future, and the temptation to attempt a little sabotage was strong. It was agreed that the risk of discovery was too great.

Taking departure from the first two sets of gunships, the Marine Force Recon platoon converged on the third. This time the boarders had gained experience with their environment: Disembarking from their rafts, they knew what they were looking for this time. They moved faster and with more confidence. Amanda began to hope that they might pull it off.

The helmet cam of Lieutenant Ives panned around the interior of a small cabin. They watched his gloved hands open lockers and dip into drawers, probing under carelessly folded clothing, shoving aside a hodgepodge of cheap personal effects.

"Hold it! Hold it! Hold it!" Christine Rendino squealed into her lip mike. "You got one!"

In the center of the monitor, the Marine held up a brick-size and -shaped plastic unit with a small CRT screen, a retractable antenna, and a keypad.

Christine clawed through a hard-copy file. "Ives, listen to me. I can see that's a Fuji model Globemaster III. Read me off the serial number."

"You got it, ma'am." The unit was turned in the Ma-

rine's hand. "One...six...six...seven...oh...nine...
oh...Foxtrot...Golf."

"Okay, good." Christine spoke in an aside to the others
in the operations center. "Score! That's one of eighty units
lifted off a Harconan freighter. Okay, Ives, turn it on. The
disk switch is on the right side....Now hit Memory."

The little screen of the GPU lit up, the numerals and letters displaying ghost-white on the low-light monitor. Ives
scrolled the memory and a long string of latitudes and lon-
gitudes flowed past. Places the *pinisi* had visited or was
bound for. Amanda noted that a few of the coordinate sets
had a star symbol marking them.

"Jeez, are we going to have fun with that," Christine
whispered.

"All elements, all elements," Steamer Lane's voice
barked from the overhead speaker. "Be advised we have
movement in the moorage area."

All eyes snapped over the tactical display. A small-craft
symbol was moving among the other anchored vessels of
the village.

"Steamer, where did he come from?" Amanda demanded.

"He took off from one of the other moored schooners. It
looks like a small motor dinghy. I don't think it's big
enough for more than two or three guys. It's heading out
toward the gunships!"

"We see it," Amanda snapped. "Steamer, stand by to
start engines! Ives, get those schooners cleaned up and get
out of there."

"We're on it, ma'am. What about this GPU?"

"Shit!" Christine yipped. "We can't take it! It'll blow the
whole deal!"

"We can't leave it, either," Amanda said grimly. "We
need those position fixes. Lieutenant Ives, hold the screen
of that GPU up to your helmet camera. Scroll through the
memory slowly, several times. Somebody, make sure this
is being recorded!"

A babble of softly shouted orders sounded over the Marine tactical channel as the recon men scrambled to evacu-

ate, the number and letter clusters jerking past on Ives' helmet cam feed. The platoon sergeant was on deck, his camera view sweeping the moorage area. The temperature seemed to skyrocket in the LFOC.

"*Carlson,* I confirm that dinghy is headed for the gunship moorage. You got about two minutes."

"This is going bad," Quillain said lowly. "They aren't going to make it. We can't get 'em clear in time to not be spotted."

"Options," MacIntyre demanded.

"Take 'em prisoner if they board Five and Six. Burn 'em if they hit for the other schooners. Our guys got silenced weapons."

"Those could simply be innocent fishermen, Captain," Tran pointed out.

"We got nothin' else, Mr. Tran. A couple of fishermen spotting us aboard one of those ships will blow this soft probe sky-high."

"So will a couple of shot-up corpses or vanished villagers." Christine shook her head, her blond bangs glinting silver in the blue battle lights. "We are so screwed."

Amanda stayed silent. Mentally she visualized the possible shattering of her plan, rearranging the fragments that might survive it, seeing how to make a new successful pattern of them. The concept that she might "lose" in this situation did not occur to her; there was only the hunt for a different way to win.

Onscreen, Ives deactivated the pirate GPU. Throwing it back in the drawer, he slammed the drawer shut and raced topside.

It was too late. In his sergeant's helmet cam, the dinghy could be made out, a black blotch on a gray sea, the chugging of its single-cylinder outboard caught by the earphone pickups. Silhouetted in the background village glare, three figures could be made out huddled in the rowboat. It was apparent now that the Bugis were headed for one of the other pairs of rafted gunships and that they would cross the bow of the vessels occupied by the Marines by about a dozen yards.

Ives whispered orders to his men. Marines carrying MP-5 submachine guns with the bloated cylinders of silencers screwed to their barrels moved forward.

Amanda's fingertip touched her Transmit key. "Lieutenant Ives, this is the TACBOSS. Lay low and hold your fire. Ultra-hush. They might not notice your boats tied up alongside in the shadows and they might...just...go...on past...."

Frozen in place, the Marines crouched unmoving behind the gunwales and high bows of the *pinisi,* Ives lifting his head just enough to track the dinghy with his helmet cam.

For a moment they thought they might make it. The small boat chugged past ten yards...twenty, then the onboards picked up the hint of a shout. Someone in the dinghy pointed back at the rubber raider craft tied up alongside the schooners. The outboard motor revved and the boat turned sharply toward the beach.

Quillain threw a pen down angrily in the console. "That's it. Show's over."

"Carlson, we have been spotted," Ives called excitedly. "Do you want us to engage?"

This time Amanda slammed her hand down on her keypad. "Negative, negative, negative. Do not engage! We have a change in the ops plan! Go back and grab that GPU and any charts you saw lying around, then disembark and stand by for pickup. Expedite!"

"Aye, aye, ma'am!"

She toggled over to the command channel. "Steamer, are you still there?"

"Right here, ma'am."

"Execute an immediate pickup on the Marines! Fast and dirty. Start engines and go in on the pad! Move it!"

"Roger that! Executing engine start now. We'll be there in a super-short."

"Amanda, what in the hell are you thinking?" MacIntyre demanded. "We've got the only military hovercraft around here. If you take those Sea Fighters in there like that, you'll be telegraphing Harconan that we're on to him."

Amanda twisted around in her chair to face the admiral,

speaking hastily. "That's irrelevant, sir. Any kind of unusual activity at any of his bases will be attributed to us. Harconan will assume we have penetrated his security and will act accordingly, changing his ops plan. Accordingly, we change our plans first. We turn this soft recon probe into an attack mission. We use this opportunity to take out the strike force he's assembled here."

On the monitor, the Marines were piling into their raider craft in preparation for casting off. An enterprising drone controller had moved the *Queen*'s prowling Cipher into position to cover the village waterfront. On his displays, the dinghy could be seen grounding on the beach, its passengers running toward the lights of Adat Tanjung.

"Damn it, Amanda," MacIntyre exploded, "a recon probe is one thing; so is intervening in an active pirate attack. Calling in an overt anti-shipping strike on a group of Indonesian vessels is another, even if we can prove they were illegally armed. This will pull the Indonesian government down on us!"

Amanda shook her head decisively. "No, sir, it will not. Harconan will cover it up for us."

On the tactical display, the position hacks of the microforce hovercraft began to sweep toward the moorage. At Adat Tanjung the sound of their lift fans and turbines would be rolling in over the village, the drumming and laments trailing off at the strange, frightening sound coming from the darkened sea.

In the LFOC, the lower rank kept silent as the TACBOSS and the CINCNAVSPECFORCE butted heads.

"Dammit, Elliot, think! Harconan doesn't own the entire Indonesian government or military. Having questions asked and official inquiries launched about a U.S. Navy attack on a Bugis village is just exactly what he doesn't want either! Like Tran was saying, the island administration doesn't like messing with the Bugis. These are Harconan's people, and what he says, goes."

Neither Amanda nor MacIntyre noted her use of his first name. It wouldn't register on either of them for some time. "We have a chance to salvage a major material and psychological victory here," she went on forcing her point. "We can cost Harconan ships and weapons without causing Indonesian casualties, we can make him lose enormous face with his own people, and we can make him do the cleanup work for us. This can work! I'll take full responsibility for this."

MacIntyre gritted his teeth. Trying to run a hand through his hair, he snagged his headset. Impatiently he tore it off. He'd been here before with this woman, off the China coast and in northwestern Africa. The Pentagon flag officer he'd been for the past few years was instinctively appalled at kicking the book over the side this way. But the Special Boat driver he'd been in the times before said, *Yes, she's right, roll the dice!*

"You're the TACBOSS, Captain. Carry on."

She slapped her palm on the console. "Yes! Thank you, sir!" She spun back to face her workstation and the bulkhead displays, her features blade keen and beautiful in her fierce exultation.

MacIntyre looked at Amanda's back and the fall of silken shoulder-length hair and felt suddenly old. There had been a time he wouldn't have had to fight himself to make that call.

On the helmet cams the *Queen of the West* and the *Manassas* materialized, braking hard with their forward puff ports. Spinning about, still on their air cushions, they presented their opening stern gates to the Marine raider craft. A wave of spray broke over the camera lenses blurring them out, but the voices still could be heard over the tactical loop yelling over the roaring howl of the lift fans.

"Put her on the ramp....Put her on the ramp, come on....Where is the goddamn shackle! Over the bow!... Move it! Ferkin'...ah, shit!...Go! Go! Go!...Yeah! We're in! We're in! Ramp coming up!"

The command circuit overrode the overhead speakers. "TACBOSS, this is Royalty! Fourteen out, fourteen back! Full recovery verified. All reconners aboard. Requesting instructions."

"Well done, Steamer," Amanda replied. "Here's your reward. Take out the pirate ships. I say again, take out the pirate ships."

"Eeeeeeyyyyyyyyaaaahooooo!" The scream overloaded the loudspeaker.

"I believe he approves," Tran commented.

The real-time download from the Cipher showed the villagers streaming down to the beaches and wharves. There was nothing they could do, save to rage helplessly. Their heavy weapons were aboard the flotilla of anchored gunships, and even the boldest pirate was disinclined to put out in a small boat to challenge the screaming sea monsters that had invaded their harbor.

Steamer Lane danced the *Queen* around until she was between the rafted ships and the shore, ensuring that his misses would scream out over the open ocean and not inland toward the village.

"*Manassas*, you got Five and Six," he directed. "I'll take Three and Four."

"Rog' that," Tony Marlin replied in his earphones. "I am in position, ready to fire. Bet mine are on the bottom first."

"Steak dinner. Taken. Gunners, cannon, fire!"

The *Queen of the West* hovered bow to bow with her targets, fifty yards separating them: point-blank range for the twin sets of 30mm autocannon she carried in her shoulder-mount weapons pedestals. These were the same Hughes M-230 series chain guns carried in the chin turret of the Apache attack helicopter. Weapons designed to kill armored fighting vehicles, not wooden-hulled schooners.

The cannon jackhammered, spewing their multiple shell streams. The rounds alternated between armor-piercing and high-explosive incendiary. The HE/I rounds ripped away timbers and planking, spraying white phosphorus fragments among the splinters that remained. The AP rounds simply tore through the entire length of the hundred-foot-plus-long hulls of the schooners. In the parlance of the old broadside Navy, this was called "raking fire," and it was considered the most devastating. What was true then was still true now, especially as the concealed arms lockers and engine room fuel tanks of the pirate *pinisi* became involved.

The rakish vessels began to settle rapidly by the bow, flames boiling out of their deck hatches and climbing their rigging. After half a dozen long bursts, the 30-millimeters checked fire, barrel overheat warnings sounding at the gunners' stations.

Scrounger Caitlin looked judgmentally between the two sets of sinking hulks. "I'd call it a draw," she said.

"Looks like," Lane agreed. "Tony and I'll buy you the steak instead. Rebel, Rebel, let's move it out of here. Set departure heading and form up on me. All ahead... good cruise. Door gunners, finish off the leftovers."

The hovercraft surged past the burning ships, gaining speed, their OCSW 25mm crews in the side hatches pumping a final few dozen "make sure" grenades into the wrecks.

"Royalty, this is the Reb. What about the last two?" Marlin inquired.

"Missile drill. Hellfires. One off each pedestal. Our guys don't get a chance to do enough live-fire with those. Let's not miss the opportunity."

"Roger that. Hellfires on the rails."

The Sea Fighters' weapons pedestals snapped vertical, loading arms slicing down into the gun tubs to acquire and lift the stumpy sleek shapes of Hellfire laser-guided missiles onto the launching rails that ran above the autocannon barrels. The Hellfire was yet another antitank weapon successfully converted to a naval application. It, too, was intended to kill steel and not wood.

The pedestals swiveled and trained aft. Designation lasers lanced out from the Sea Fighters' mastheads, painting the targets as they fell away astern, pointing the way for the venom to follow.

The Hellfire salvos arced high on golden flame and dove in. The last two pirate vessels dissolved.

"It's like the Fourth of July," Scrounger commented as

she studied the receding fires in her sideview mirror. "You always shoot off the big one last."

The people of Adat Tanjung stood on the beach, watching until the last flickering bit of floating wood extinguished itself. No one considered taking one of the village trucks to the nearest *polisi* post. No one considered appealing for aid to the nearest farm village inland. They were Bugis, and the clan affairs stayed in the clan, even the disasters.

All were silent as they withdrew to their darkened huts. The lament for the lost ships would begin tomorrow. The residents of Adat Tanjung were nominally Muslim, but the old gods stand close behind every Indonesian. First they had lost their men on the *Piskov* raid. Now their finest war *pinisi* had been eaten by a strange and terrible foe. It was as if the vested spirit of the sea had turned its back on the clan.

For a Bugis, nothing could be more fearful.

One among them hurried back to his chandler's shop and to the two-way radio concealed in the storeroom.

Landing Force Operations Center,   **0121 Hours, Zone Time:**
USS Carlson   **August 17, 2008**

"How do you want to work it with the microforce now, Skipper?" Quillain inquired. "Have 'em go into hide as per the old ops plan?"

"Yes . . . no, hold on that." Amanda was suddenly finding it very hard to think as she tipped back over the edge of the combat adrenaline rush. "Tell them to go stealth and to clear the area, avoiding contact with Indonesian surface traffic. Then bring them home. Tell Steamer to proceed directly to Benoa Harbor for recovery. He has enough fuel remaining for a direct transit."

The Marine nodded. "Might as well. The bad guys sure know they're out there now."

"Exactly: We're not going to gain any advantage in holding them out there. When Steamer shows up tomorrow morning, we'll tell the harbormaster they've been conducting training exercises in international waters. We'll let the Indonesians worry about just what that may mean."

The operations team in the LFOC were standing down, securing systems and preparing to hand things over to the skeleton duty watch. Standard white lighting snapped on, replacing blue battle illumination.

Amanda rubbed her burning eyes with her palms, a sense of unreality washing over her. Had Palau Piri been just that afternoon? It seemed like a different world altogether, a different reality, some incredible fantasy spun in a half dream state.

It had been real though, something to be confronted and lived with.

God, but she was so tired.

She sensed someone standing beside her. Admiral MacIntyre, stolid and impervious as always. Remembering the way she had spoken to him during the engagement made her suddenly feel like a very awkward little girl.

"I'm sorry, sir, for getting a bit emphatic back there. I apologize for getting out of line."

"You were running a combat engagement, Captain, and at that moment you didn't have the time to worry about the formalities. Getting the job done has the priority. I need to apologize for lagging on you for a second there. You were correct in your assessment. This was a good mission save and an acceptable calculated risk for the return."

"I hope so, sir."

He smiled at her. It was a good smile, sure and safe and approving. "Midrats?" he inquired.

"That sounds good. Last time, you were telling me about Judy."

Palau Piri Island   0725 Hours, Zone Time: August 17, 2008

Mr. Lan Lo stood waiting beside the breakfast table in the central lanai. He had known for an hour already of the night events at Adat Tanjung and of the loss of the fleet units, but he had kept the knowledge to himself. There was no immediate action that could be taken, and it would be better for Mr. Harconan to be centered from his morning swim and run before he was apprised.

It was unfortunate.

Lo was not a man of overt passions, but he did have a profound understanding of the human condition. His employer, Makara Harconan, was a man in the total and classical sense of the word. Thus he required a mate for completeness, the proper balancing of Yin and Yang. More than that, however, Mr. Harconan was a man of extraordinary capabilities. Such men frequently require extraordinary women to match them because they rapidly become bored and unsatisfied with the frivolous or the commonplace.

Over the past few days, Mr. Harconan had given every indication of having found one such extraordinary woman. Regrettably she was also his blood enemy, who was striving with her own considerable resources to destroy both him and his works.

Truly a tragedy on a par with any told in the *wayang* poems of the Ramayana. No doubt resolution would be... difficult.

Mr. Harconan strode into the inner garden looking enervated and happy with his world. Lo allowed him to take his chair and then related the events of the night, telling of the secrets presumed lost to the Americans and of the slash at the heart of the Bugis fleet.

When he was finished, Mr. Harconan stared at the tabletop. "She must have known," he said. "She must have had the entire attack set up and in motion before I brought her here. She looked me in the eyes and never a hint. Never a slip. Not even when..."

"Quite so, Mr. Harconan."

Port of Call Bali   **August 2008**

Three days passed for the Sea Fighter Task Force. Three days of sight-seeing temples under tropic skies and drinking beer on the beach at Kuta Bay. Three days of ushering curious Balinese around the decks of the *Carlson* and the

Cunningham. Three days playing the Bahasa Indonesia tour tapes provided by the Department of Defense School of Languages and of answering questions asked in hesitant English. Three days of performing their open mission, showing the flag, and demonstrating America's military presence on the Pacific Rim.

Three nights as well. Three nights of sitting behind closed-up defenses, watching the dark. Three nights of the Sea Fighters slipping out of the *Carlson*'s well deck to moan away beyond the Island of Turtles. Three nights of helicopters clattering away into the darkness to skim the wave crests at radar-evading altitudes. Three nights of the same explanation being offered to the port master and Bali ATC. "Units launching to conduct routine training exercises in international waters."

The Indonesian naval air and surface units that attempted to track the stealthed and evasive Yankees knew this to be a sophistry. Fragmentary fixes and sighting reports indicated the Sea Fighter elements to be plunging deeper into Indonesian territory. Yet, their commanding admiral dared not ask the question "What are the Americans up to?" either to his own government or to the United States. He feared being asked a question in return: "Who asked you to find out?"

Sabalana Island Group   **0143 Hours, Zone Time:**
Flores Sea, Indonesia   **August 20, 2008**

Even though the lonely coral spit lifted only a few feet above the surface of the sea, Cobra Richardson had to climb to avoid dragging Wolf One's skids across the beach. Whipping up a whirlwind of sand now instead of a wake, he eased the ground-effecting Super Huey forward at a walking pace, a Marine ground guide with a pair of infrared lumesticks spotting the smaller helo in beside the two larger grounded Cargohawks.

Its turbines spooling down, Wolf One's rotors slowed, whickering into silence. When all that remained was the sound of the breaking surf and the disturbed cries of the nesting terns, the helicopter's side hatches slid open and Amanda Garrett and Christine Rendino disembarked.

Stone Quillain's looming shadowy presence awaited them. "Evenin', Skipper. Evenin', Miss Rendino. We hit something funny out on this weapons hide. Sort of what Miss Rendino wanted us to keep an eye open for; I thought you might want to check it out for yourself."

"We do, Stone. Lead on."

The Marine headed inland, although there was little "inland" to this place. A double spine of sand dunes ran down the center of the spit. Even by starlight, the entire tiny island could be made out from either dune crest. There was no sign of life save for a whispy hint of salt grass and a scattering of birds' nests—no reason to land here at all unless one had a set of coordinates downloaded from a pirate captain's Global Positioning Unit.

"Which one is this?" Amanda asked as they trudged upslope through the feathery sand.

"We've coded it Star Bravo," Christine wheezed. "We've been wondering what the addition of the star symbol meant with the hide site designations we picked up at Adat Tanjung. Looks like our resident leatherneck found out for us."

A shallow hollow ran between the twin row of dunes, and the landing party was at labor at its bottom.

Amanda had an AI2 visor hung around her neck like a pair of binoculars. Taking a breather on the sand crest, she switched the visor on and studied the weapons hide.

At some time in the recent past, a long trench had been dug down the center of the hollow. Packing cases and bundles heavily wrapped in plastic sheeting and tightly tape-sealed had been stacked along its bottom. Once re-covered, the sea winds would have swiftly smoothed away all trace of its presence.

By the invisible light of IR lumes, the Marines were re-opening the trench, learning and exposing its secrets with engineer's probes and mine detectors.

"Were there any booby traps?" Amanda inquired as they shuffled down into the hollow.

"Naw, they just weren't figuring on anybody finding this place. No sense risking blowing up one of your own people by accident and maybe setting the whole shebang off. We got one of 'em fully set up over here."

Stone snapped on a white light flashlight and shined it on his prize, half smothering the beam with his hand.

It was a compact rocket artillery piece, twelve up-angled launcher tubes in three rows of four, mounted on a light two-wheeled trailer.

"I don't recognize the system offhand," Quillain commented. "It fires a four-point-two-inch spin-stabilized rocket, and all the case and weapon nomenclature and manuals look to be in Chinese. It's a secondhand piece. It's been fired and used in the field."

"It's a Type 63," Christine said, sinking down on her knees beside the launcher. "An older Chinese system, ex-PLA. How many launchers are there?"

"Four of 'em. Plus about a thousand rounds of HE and incendiary ammo. Plus a cache of what looks like maintenance gear and spare parts. It's a whole field artillery battery set to go."

Christine's fingertips brushed the launcher's tubes in a near caress. "This is what I've been wondering about. No way are these any kind of naval ordnance. Somebody's planning a land war."

"Boy howdy, I'll say. Let me show you this other stuff." Quillain stepped off into the darkness and returned dragging a couple of flat wooden cases.

"We got land mines here," he said, lowering the cases flat on the sand. "Oops, 'scuse me, Princess Diana, I mean 'area denial munitions.' These I do recognize. These here are good old Made-in-the-U.S.A. M-21s, heavy antitank mines that can give just about any armored fighting vehicle in the world a bellyache. These others are C3A1 Elsies, Canadian-made antipersonnel mines. Mean little buggers, too, impossible to pick up with a standard electromagnetic detector. The Canucks swore up, down, and sideways they'd disposed of 'em all. I guess they must have missed a few."

"How many mines in all, Stone?"

"We guess about fifty of the M-21 ATs. Maybe four hundred Elsies. We're still digging up cases."

"This has got to be what the stars mean," Christine insisted. "They denote hides that aren't Bugis resupply points. They're arms depots being built up for somebody else. But why? Harconan can't be doing this just because of his generous nature."

Amanda didn't reply; instead she turned away and walked a short distance up the hollow. With arms crossed, she looked up at the sky and the haze of glittering stars. *What are you planning, Makara? Who are you buying these armaments for? Who do you mean to kill?*

No answer came back to her save the hiss and caress of wind-blown sand particles flowing low over the dune surface. She had gone to Palau Piri hoping to learn the man. Instead the taipan had read her secrets while remaining as darkly enigmatic as his smile.

I lost to you on your beach that day, Makara, and accepted the defeat. I swear that will be the only time.

She moved back to the trench. "How are you coming with the site documentation?" she demanded.

"Best we can. We're collecting all the paper, manuals, logbooks, and such. We got low-light videos taken of the hide site and the ordnance, and we're recording all case and serial numbers."

"Good enough. Finish up and rig this place for demolition. Blow it all."

"Like the others?"

"Just like the others."

Five miles to the north of the coral spit, a small fishing *prahu* circled with slatting sails. The fishing here in these particular waters was not good, as the *prahu*'s three-man crew knew full well. Yet, they had loitered here at the trailing end of the Sabalana group for two full days.

A few hours before, the man on watch at the tiller had heard the faint flutter of helicopter rotors in the distance. He had awakened his comrades, and with fishermen's patience they had waited. Now they heard the flying machines echoing across the still waters, taking their departure.

Then came the prolonged flash like heat lightning on the horizon and the rumble like matching thunder.

The three Bugis seamen exchanged grim looks. It had been as the *raja samudra* had said it would be. The war had begun. The *prahu*'s captain brought the waterproof transceiver up from the tiny cabin along with its solar-charged battery and began setting up the antenna. The word must be sent.

On the lonely sand spit, the fires died down and the smoke plumes faded. The tireless trade wind began its task of refilling the smoldering trench and burying the myriad fragments of jagged metal one coral grain at a time. It would have a fair start on the job by dawn.

Palau Piri Island   0645 Hours, Zone Time: August 20, 2008

Makara Harconan pushed aside the half-emptied cup of coffee, regretting the way he had snapped at his servant for being slow with it. It was not the fault of the kitchen staff that he had come to the lanai early for breakfast. Breaking with routine, he had elected not to do his morning run and swim around the island. The east beach and the memories it invoked were too distracting.

Early or not, Lan Lo had been waiting for him, taking his straight-spine seat across the table from the taipan.

"Mr. Harconan, the depot at the south Sabalanas was destroyed last night."

"I know, just as were the replenishment sites at Bawean and Tana Jampea. The Americans probably got the locations of half a dozen other active hides in the Sulawesi operations area off the squadron at Adat Tanjung. They'll be sailing from Benoa tomorrow, probably to conduct a sweep of the remaining sites."

"Might I propose an evacuation of our assets?"

"Impossible, Bapak. If we move in a ship to evacuate our stores, American reconnaissance will backtrack it to its base and the cycle will begin again."

"Then what is lost is lost and we must accept and rebuild. The damage to our operations will not be excessive."

"I'm not so sure, Lo." Abruptly, Harconan drew the coffee cup back, taking a gulp from it. "The material losses we can live with, I agree. But we're being hit and we aren't hitting back. This isn't good for our people, Lo. Things have gone well for us and suddenly they aren't."

"The maintenance of one's aura of invulnerability is a difficult task."

Harconan looked up sharply at Lo. Was it conceivable that the weathered and staid Chinese was making his version of a joke?

Harconan would accept it as such. "Point well taken, Lo," he replied, smiling wryly. "A serious problem nonetheless. My people must keep their faith with me if we're to continue with the plan. To ensure that happens, I must keep faith with them. Have there been any reports from Jakarta concerning the people we lost in the *Piskov* raid?"

"No, sir, nothing from the *polisi* or the Defense Ministry."

"Then if any survive, they must be held aboard the American warships. When do they sail from Benoa?"

"Their scheduled departure time is eight-thirty tomorrow morning, sir."

"And the port assault force I ordered assembled?"

"Two hundred and forty-five Bugis assembled and equipped, Mr. Harconan, plus small craft and demolition materials. Also, should more sophisticated actions be required, we have a twelve-man Nung Special Operations team standing by."

"Excellent." Harconan hesitated a moment more before committing. "Lo, we're taking down the American task force tonight. We're going to eliminate them as a threat, and we're going to get our prisoners back."

There was only a flicker in Lo's dark eyes. "You have set yourself a formidable task, Mr. Harconan. We must assume the Americans will be prepared for diverse eventualities."

"Very true, Lo," Harconan replied, taking another sip of coffee and finding that he enjoyed it. As always the decision to attack, to take action, eased his tensions. "But it will only get worse if we let them get out to sea. This will be our best chance."

"Possibly, sir."

Harconan drained the cup. "Now, tell me this, Lo: As this will be their last night in port, are there any ceremonies or special events scheduled to take place as a farewell?"

"Yes, sir. The island governor is holding a farewell dinner and an exhibition of Balinese dance and performing arts tonight at the Taman Werdi Budaya Art Center, for the ships' officers."

Harconan lightly brushed his mustache in thought. "I see. And have I an invitation to this function?"

"Governor Tengarra always sends you an invitation to any such affair, sir."

"Excellent. You may inform the governor it will be my great pleasure to attend. Please notify the helipad that I'll want the helicopter in one hour. Have the pilot standing by as well: I think I'll want him along on this flight. Also, notify the unit leader of our special-operations team that I want him waiting in my office when I get in."

"As you wish, sir." Lo hesitated for a moment, his uncertainty very unusual. "Mr. Harconan, may I state that this is a decided . . . gamble we will be taking?"

Harconan looked fondly at his old retainer. "What hasn't been a gamble, Bapak? From the beginning and on to whatever the end will be, always there will be the gamble."

"This is understood, Mr. Harconan. But there is always the degree of the gamble. In a direct confrontation with the United States Navy, you will be taking on a foe such as never before challenged."

"A ship is a ship, Lo," Harconan replied jovially, "and all are prizes to be taken. You know how it is with the Americans: With a bit of luck, having two of their ships attacked in an Indonesian port will set their politicians to squabbling like a pack of village dogs. We'll be left in peace for years, or at least until their next election."

"Possibly, sir. But might I remind you of the words of a

Japanese admiral, Yamamoto, in a somewhat similar situation with the Americans. . . ."

Harconan sobered abruptly. "I recall, Bapak. 'We have awakened a sleeping giant that will destroy us all.'"

"We've had one major development since this afternoon's O Group." Clad in her pumps and going-ashore whites, Christine Rendino sat back on the flag office couch. "It seems that one of Mr. Harconan's ships is missing."

Standing beside the desk, Amanda Garrett looked up from the revolver she'd been checking. "Say again?"

"We can't find one of the Harconan Seaways ships, anywhere," Christine repeated insistently. "I ordered an assets inventory on the shipping line and we can't get a fix on one of his coasters."

"Which one, and how do you lose an entire ship?" Amanda spun the chambers, checking the five .38-caliber loads in the little weapon, then carefully pressed the cylinder closed. Once, on the firing range, she'd flipped the action shut like she'd seen done on television and Stone Quillain had almost taken her head off—something about distorting the cylinder crane. Amanda hadn't seen fit to question his call on the matter.

"The *Harconan Flores,* and that's what we'd like to know. She's not listed in at any of the regional ports, and we can't pick her up at sea with either the Oceansats or the Global Hawks. Either she's done a Bermuda Triangle on us or our boy Makara is running a swifty."

Amanda couldn't stop the frown that tugged at her mouth at the mention of the taipan's name, nor could she halt the burst of recent memories it released. Turning away from the intel to hide her expression, she slipped the handgun into the holster she'd had stitched inside her shoulder bag, verifying that the row of speedloaders were in their loops at its bottom.

The revolver in her bag and the automatic in Christine's were only an aspect of the security she'd ordered for their last evening in Bali. If she could exercise her own preference, no one, especially the task force's senior officers, would be leaving the ship tonight. But they had to maintain the pretense that this was still a routine goodwill port call, even though the enemy knew by now it was just a facade.

She wondered how he had taken it, the night after their day together. Had he reacted to her attack on his base with anger, or coldly, as if it were just another chess move in the game they were playing? Had it been enough of a slap in the face to draw him into an overt action against the task force? If it had been, he'd move tonight, before they sailed.

Amanda became aware of the voice behind her again. "Excuse me, Chris, what was that?"

"The *Harconan Flores* is a most interesting ship, Boss Ma'am," Christine repeated patiently. Amanda could sense an intent blue-eyed gaze aimed at the back of her neck. "She's an amphib, an ex–East German Frosche-class LSM, part of the same bulk buy as our old buddy the *Sutanto*. Harconan picked her up surplus a couple of years ago and had her refurbished for use as a small interisland RO/RO. Her beaching gear and bow ramp are still installed and operational, and I bet you and Harconan did it mare-and-stallion style a lot. He looks like the type."

Amanda spun around, an angry, wordless exclamation bursting from her. Christine sat on the couch, legs crossed, chin supported by her palm, calmly daring her friend and commanding officer to deny the charge.

After a long second Amanda let her held breath escape in a sigh. Denying it in this company would be an act of futility. "I didn't mean for it to happen, Chris, or maybe I did. I'm not sure myself."

Christine shot a beseeching glance at the overhead. "I knew it. Pow! The baby seal bites it!"

"What?"

"Nothing, just something I said when Admiral MacIntyre and I were talking about this situation."

"What!" Appalled, Amanda stared down at the intel.

"You were discussing Makara and me with the admiral?"

"Just the potential, not the reality. Don't have a cow, Amanda Lee: He wouldn't have a clue about that Little-Nell-done-wrong haze you've been wandering around in since you got back from Palau Piri. In most ways Eddie Mac's as big an innocent as you are."

Amanda crossed the room and sank down on the couch. "Damn, damn, damn, Chris. I don't know what to say other than it happened."

"Well, you can start by sketching in all the really juicy details. It must have been fantastic!"

Amanda glared. "Chris, I slept with the enemy, dammit! I let him, or rather I let myself . . ."

The little blonde glared back. "Was it or was it not fantastic?"

Amanda groped for the correct words for explanation or self-condemnation and could find neither. "Yes, it was!"

"Good! You're a classy lady, Boss Ma'am, and I figured that it would take somebody really, really special to make you feel like an idiot."

Amanda found that she could not help but smile sheepishly. "Thanks, I think. In one way the whole experience was incredible. I don't know how to describe it beyond saying that after a while I just forgot who Makara was and why I was there. We were just two . . . lovers on this incredibly beautiful island. Chris, assessment, please: Is there any way conceivable that Harconan might not be our pirate king? Any possibility at all?"

Almost sadly, the intel shook her head. "An assessment of all intelligence collected to date indicates that Makara Harconan is our target subject. No valid alternatives have presented themselves. None, and I've been looking—hard."

"Since when?"

"Since you fell a little bit in love with that swashbuckling pirate you've dreamed about since you were a little girl."

"Oh, damn, Chris." Amanda looked away.

"Can we quit doing Navy for a little bit, please?" Christine received a tight-throated nod in reply.

She slipped her arm around Amanda and rested her head

on her shoulder. "It seems like it's something we all do, you know?" she said softly. "Sooner or later we all meet that one really incredible guy who it's really, really dumb to get involved with. And we do it anyway and we get all smashed up over it. Then, if we're lucky, we get past it and go on. I had my turn in college and I thought I was going to die from it, but I didn't."

She rocked her friend slightly. "Because you're such a total, straight-edged square, it took longer for it to happen to you. That just makes it harder because you can't pass it off as kid-stupid."

She felt the soft fringe of Amanda's hair as it brushed the side of her face and she shook her head. "No, I can't pass it off, Chris. I made love with him and now I have to destroy him."

"Yep, Boss Ma'am, you sure do."

The rasp of the interphone startled them apart. Amanda straightened and rose to her feet, and Christine watched as she drew an almost visible shell of discipline and control about herself. Her voice was totally level as she picked up the handset.

"Garrett here. . . . All right, thank you. We'll be right down. Captain Carberry, the *Carlson* is now lead ship and you have the watch. Set all A-class security protocols now. We will maintain until we clear port tomorrow. Guns hot. Lethal force is authorized. Good night, Captain."

She returned the phone to its cradle. "Come along, Chris. Our coach awaits . . . and thank you."

The causeway road was a concrete ribbon across Benoa Harbor, linking the ordered arrays of golden work arcs at the port island with the scattered constellations of the shoreside villages. Half a dozen sets of headlights flowed along it, heading inland, the motorcade carrying the task force officers into the island capital.

Precautions had been taken. Cellular communication was being maintained with the ships, a pistol rode under every jacket and in every shoulder bag, and a Marine security guard sat beside the Balinese driver of each of the rented Toyota sedans, an ominously heavy briefcase in his lap.

However, others had taken precautions as well. As the Navy motorcade cleared the causeway road, a second group of vehicles also in contact with a central headquarters and also carrying a heavily armed party of men began to maintain an expert alternating front and rear tail on the convoy.

1830 Hours, Zone Time:
August 20, 2008

Taman Werdi Budaya Art Center

Located in the suburbs of the boisterous island capital of Denpasar, the Taman Werdi Budaya Center lingered as a preserve of the old Bali, a place of lotus ponds, delicate gardens, and fantastically decorated Balinese architecture.

Here gathered the elite of a race of artists, the sculptors, the painters, the actors, the musicians, and the dancers, especially the dancers, to perform for the world at the center's amphitheaters.

The prerequisite preliminary reception was held outside of the theater area in a garden lit by the flicker of oil lanterns. Elliot MacIntyre found the setting exotic and interesting, even while going through the appropriate political motions. Especially as he was in the company of Amanda Garrett.

In the last minutes before the opening of the night's performance, they found themselves walking slowly along a path that circled the garden's perimeter, a cool and darkened place away from the core of the talk and forced official joviality.

The unsecured environment made shop talk unwise, and MacIntyre was willing to take advantage of the fact.

"One of the problems I've found with the Navy is that while you do see the world, it's just in glimpses."

"I know what you mean," Amanda replied, trailing her fingertips over a piece of path-side statuary, its features half erased by time and exposure. "You catch a taste of something in passing, but the full flavor doesn't hit you until you've had the chance to think about it for a while. Only by then it's gone and you're moving on to the next mission, the next tour."

"There are other ways to live, I suppose." Eddie Mac hesitated for a moment. "Amanda, have you ever thought about what you're going to do after the Navy?"

It was her turn to hesitate, a thoughtful expression crossing her shadowed features. "For a time I was, but I sort of gave up on it when you gave me the Sea Fighters. I could never really come up with a solid idea of what I wanted. There were the superficialities, like maybe picking up a consultant's job somewhere or buying a real cruising boat, but no true vision ever jelled."

"What about a family?"

"It would be nice," she replied softly. "I envy you Judy and your sons. But I'm running out of time there. Pretty soon, having children won't be such a good idea."

MacIntyre snorted. "Nonsense! You're still a young woman, Amanda. There's no reason you couldn't start a family if you wanted one."

She chuckled. "Thank you. But there is still one complication: I'm old-fashioned in some ways. If I were to have a family, I'd want someone to have a family with. That hasn't jelled, either."

MacIntyre stopped walking. "I can't understand that. For someone like you . . ." He fumbled with the words, suddenly feeling awkward. "There must have been opportunities."

She gave an acknowledging tilt of her head. "Oh, yes, a couple of times, but never quite the right one at the right time. The luck of the draw."

"Some kind of luck, anyway." Elliot MacIntyre felt himself on the verge of doing something catastrophically wrong. His hand ached to reach up and brush aside the curtain of red brown hair from Amanda's cheek, and he hungered for the first time in many years for the feel of a woman's lips under his—this woman's.

"Amanda." It was another voice out of the night. A tall figure in a white evening jacket strode down the walk toward them. "Ah, and you as well, Admiral MacIntyre, good evening!"

"Good evening, Mr. Harconan." MacIntyre was pleased with the way he kept the snarl out of his voice, even as he watched the way Amanda looked up at the approaching taipan.

"Good evening, Makara." There was an odd timbre to Amanda's reply, a hesitation yet an excitement as well. "I wasn't expecting to see you again."

"And why should you think that? With your permission, Admiral, I'd like to invite Captain Garrett to sit with me this evening. I'd greatly appreciate the chance to share this performance with her."

"That's entirely her call, Mr. Harconan."

"Amanda?"

"Well..." She paused a moment more before accepting the arm offered her. "If you don't mind, sir?"

"Why should I, Captain? Enjoy yourself. I'll see you and Mr. Harconan after the show."

As he watched them start down the walk to the amphitheater entry, MacIntyre found that his hand still ached from the fist he had clenched.

Benoa Port, Bali   1859 Hours, Zone Time: August 20, 2008

It started with a breakdown on the causeway road. A heavily loaded tractor trailer truck swung across both traffic lanes and stalled, blocking all passage. The driver dismounted and tilted the truck cab forward, as if seeking for some mechanical fault.

"As if" because there was nothing wrong with the truck—at least, there hadn't been until he had completed his tampering. Seeing headlights approaching from landward, the driver ran a short distance farther down the causeway. Vaulting over the roadside rail, he scrambled down over the slimy breakwater boulders to where a fast outboard launch awaited him.

The launch carried three Bugis seamen, automatic weapons, and a pair of crude but effective magnetic limpet

mines built around fifty-pound charges of industrial dynamite.

Backing away from the causeway, the launch turned and
started to move toward the harbor island, one of half a
dozen such craft on the same mission.

On the artificial island itself, other men, men who had
been trickling out to the island all day long in one, twos
and threes, rendezvoused in the shadows of the warehouses
and collected weapons from a previously positioned cargo
container.

The roving *polisi* patrols that should have spotted the
growing accumulation of armed men had been called elsewhere. Likewise the sole Indonesian warship in port, the
frigate *Sutanto,* had been ordered to haul off and anchor in
the harbor away from the port facility, well away.

Stealthily, by land and water, the net began to close
around the Sea Fighter Task Force.

USS *Carlson*   1905 Hours, Zone Time: August 20, 2008

Commander Lucas Carberry had not minded catching the
senior-officer-afloat duty for the evening. In fact, he appreciated the opportunity. It gave him a chance to pursue one
of his own private passions.

Tonight's project was of a favorite ship of his: the old
protected cruiser USS *Olympia,* Dewey's flagship at
Manila Bay. The assembly wasn't excessively difficult.
Deftly filing and fitting the turrets and upper works was
second nature. But as with all of the Edwardian age,
pre–gray-camou naval vessels, the painting was the challenge, getting the white hull, buff upper works, and black
masts and funnels just right, with no bleedover, and applying those faintest of hints of silver and gilt in just the precise places.

And all on a model two inches long.

His den back home in Philadelphia was lined with the
dreadnought-age navies of the world, as well as with
dozens of first-place and best-of-show awards for naval

miniatures. Within the enthusiast's snug world of naval war-gaming, owning a Carberry miniature had come to mean something. They were never sold, only given away as gifts to close friends or to individuals who had defeated Carberry in a combat scenario.

There were few who could make the latter claim. Carberry, like his miniatures, was something of a legend in war-gaming circles as well. A chubby, cold-eyed legend who could win the battle of Jutland with either side with equal ease, who had sunk the *Bismarck* and *Prinz Eugen* both with the HMS *Hood*, and who had turned the Battle of Tsushima Strait into a Japanese rout.

Tenderly he eased his latest creation down onto the droplet of glue in the center of its black plastic mounting plate, allowing his desk phone to buzz twice before freeing a hand to answer it.

"This is the captain."

"This is the officer of the deck, sir." The voice on the other end of the line was tense. "We have unusual activity quayside. Possible hostiles."

Carberry's own voice was precise and emotionless. "Have all security stations been alerted?"

"Yes, sir, we are at flash yellow both here and aboard the *Cunningham.*"

"Very well. I'll be on the bridge momentarily."

Carberry started forward, wiping a dab of paint from his fingers with a Kleenex.

The view through the LPD's wide bridge windscreen presented no obvious call for alarm, only the broad concrete quay apron and the wall of gray and rust warehouses beyond it illuminated by a scattering of arc lights. Nothing moved, save for the foredeck security patrol and the gangway watch. However, the OOD and the Marine lieutenant serving as security officer of the watch both looked concerned as Carberry pushed past the light curtain.

"What do we have, gentlemen?"

"Sir, the task force moorage has been placed under observation, and we have detected the movement of a large unidentified body of men into the area. Their intent is unknown, but they appear to be deliberately staying under cover."

"When was the activity first noted?"

The security officer fielded the question. "About five minutes ago, sir. A gunner in one of the 30mm mounts spotted a man on a warehouse roof watching us through a set of night glasses. We have a deck camera locked on his position."

The Marine crossed to the console under the windscreen and called up an image on a brow monitor. On a magnified section of roof beside a ventilator box, gray-toned in the low-light television, a man's head could be made out peering over ridgeline binoculars set to its eyes. A second head bobbed up intermittently in the background.

"Our lookouts and the Duke's have picked up on three other OPs like this one, covering the whole moorage area."

Carberry nodded. "Interesting, and she's the USS *Cunningham,* Lieutenant, let's be precise. Now, what about the large bodies of men?"

"Uh, yes, sir, the *Cunningham,* sir. As for the large bodies of men, we have them located inside the warehouses on the mast-mounted sighting systems, FLIR mode."

The Marine switched imaging systems, accessing the Forward Looking Infrared scanners.

This set of cameras did not see images of light but of heat: Focusing on the thermal radiance of the environment, they could look through visual impediments like darkness, smoke, fog, and, to a degree, walls.

The front of a warehouse appeared on the screen, the outline of its facade and doors hazy and almost ectoplasmic in nature. A large number of amorphous blobs of light could be seen within the structure, some of them moving intermittently.

"We've spotted four groups of about fifty men each, not one of whom has let himself be seen."

"Anything on the radio watch?"

"We aren't sure, Captain," the OOD replied. "Signal intelligence indicates there may be something in the citizens-band ranges. Maybe just random make-and-break static of some kind, or maybe somebody doing a carrier click code on a number of walkie-talkies."

Another captain, such as Amanda Garrett, would have asked opinions at that stage, but not Carberry. His subordinates had given him the required data; it was up to him as senior-officer-on-station and captain-under-God to make the decision—in this case an effortless one. A false alarm would merely provide for a good training exercise, of which in Carberry's opinion there could not be too many.

"Officer of the Deck, bring the task force to general quarters. Hush mode. Prepare to repel boarders."

No alarm Klaxons clanged. No bellowing voices thundered over the MC-1. Interphones and command headsets buzzed all over the ship, and call to arms was passed by word of mouth, division officers swarming down from officers' country and CPOs from out of the goat lockers, yelling to seamen as they ran.

It was somewhat slower than a standard battle-stations call, but outwardly it left no sign of the explosion of activity within the hulls of the task force. On the *Carlson*'s bridge, the cruising watch stormed up the access ladder and manned their workstations. Light patterns began to shift on the consoles, going from the yellow of in-port standby to the green of ready for sea. Rows of monitor screens lit off, displaying ship's status of not only the *Carlson* but also the *Cunningham* as the Cooperative Engagement interlinks came up.

The standard deck patrols, alerted through their headsets, maintained their even pacing as per the ops plan, but other Marines appeared topside. Fully armed and armored, they snaked up through the vertical hatches and belly-crawled to their posts in the superstructure and along the deck edges, staying low and out of sight.

On the bridge, as per the call to general quarters, all hands had grabbed Kevlar helmets and combat/flotation vests en route to their battlestations. Now a female rating hurried forward from the arms locker, burdened with pistol belts and side arms. Distributing them, she went back for a second load of shell bandoliers and combat shotguns.

The task force bristled, awaiting assault. Any force launching a surprise attack on it would be met with a very nasty surprise. Which was the entire intent of the exercise.

"The task force is at general quarters, sir," the OOD stated from behind the master helm console. "Ships are ready to repel boarders and are ready in all aspects to commence power up and to get under way." He glanced over at a Marine demolition specialist standing by in the corner of the bridge. "Ready to execute emergency unmooring procedure."

"Very good, Mr. Johnson." Carberry stood stolidly, his hands clasped behind his back, helmet and flak vest stacked on the chart table beside him. "I think it's time we advise the task force commander about the situation."

Makara Harconan shot a careful glance down at his wristwatch. Soon...it would be soon. Seeking divertissement to keep himself relaxed, he returned his attention to the stage and the performance.

In honor of the guests from the task force and the accompanying government officialdom, the current resident troop at the center was performing the *Legong,* the most difficult and dazzling of the Balinese women's dances. Glittering costumes of silken brocade and gold leaf blazed on the stage as the youthful performers spun the tale of the beautiful kidnapped princess Rangkesari and her evil and arrogant suitor, the king of Lasem.

Even after a life lived in the archipelago and a hundred performances seen, Harconan could still lose himself in the elegance and perfection of the Balinese dance and the discordant yet flowing percussion of the gamelan orchestra. The woman beside him was totally enthralled.

Amanda Garrett leaned forward, eyes wide and intent, catching every gesture, every nuance. As a dancer in her own right, she must appreciate even more than the average patron the skills and training involved in developing this precision.

"God, I wish I could learn some of this," she whispered, never shifting her eyes from the stage.

"For the *Legong,* I fear it is too late," he replied under his breath, studying the fine line of her jaw and undercurl of her hair beneath it. "A *Legong* dancer begins her training when she is five and must retire with her first menstruation."

Amanda made a slight face. "I'm an inch too tall to be a ballerina, too."

"There is training you could take in other schools of the dance," Harconan encouraged. "It could be arranged with the proper instructor. It would take time—two years at a minimum."

"That would be nice, but the Navy doesn't provide for dance training sabbaticals."

"You aren't going to be in your Navy forever, Amanda."

"That's true," she answered absently, "but by the time I retire, I'll be too old for anything more demanding than a foxtrot."

A court-martial for losing your command could expedite that retirement, Harconan added silently. But would that be something she could ever forgive him for?

He sneaked another look at his watch. Two minutes more to the jump-off.

Abruptly, Amanda sat erect in her seat. Her hand darted into the bag at her side, drawing a cellular phone. Harconan realized that she must have received a prompt from a silent pager concealed somewhere on her person. He had to suppress the urge to slap the phone from her hand.

"This is Garrett." She held the phone tightly against her ear, her hand cupped around the mouthpiece to seal in her words and seal out the sound of the orchestra. And then she was looking at him, every hint of the dreaming dancer stricken from her face. Those molten gold eyes narrowing in rage like a mother whose child has been threatened.

"Execute immediate departure! Extraction Bravo!" Her voice lifted. "Get those ships out of there *now*!" She was on her feet, lifting her voice again, yelling over the orchestra. "Sea Fighters! Back to the task force! Move!"

The Gamelan musicians stalled and the dancers hesitated. Around the amphitheater white-uniformed naval officers and blue-jacketed Marines were hastening from their seats to the exits.

What the hell had happened? Had his people launched the attack early, or had they been spotted? Harconan had known the Americans would be alert, but he'd hoped for a few minutes of surprise or confusion. She must have been holding them coiled and poised to counterstrike like an angry cobra.

As she had been holding herself. Her face was cold and her eyes unreadable, her hand in her shoulder bag again as she stared down at him. "Call them off, Makara," she commanded. "For their sake, call them off!"

Then she was gone and the amphitheater was a mass of milling confusion. By the time Harconan could reach an area secure enough for him to use his own cellular, it was too late.

Benoa Port, Bali   1913 Hours, Zone Time: August 20, 2008

Like all sound plans for a military operation, the one for the Bugis assault was simple, relying on speed and shock effect. At the 1915 execution time, the dockside ground forces would open fire, raking the decks of the U.S. warships, suppressing or wiping out the topside security patrols. Then the mine launches would race in.

After planting their limpet mines against the hulls of the ships, the launch crews would set their timers and retreat. The resulting detonations would disable or possibly even start sinking the American vessels. In the confusion that would follow the mine attack, the land force would board the crippled vessels, completing the destruction of the ships and crews and, hopefully, finding and freeing some of their fellow Bugis who they had been told were being held aboard the task force.

The pirate clan leader commanding the ground strike force was confident. There was no reason the plan shouldn't work. The *polisi* had been bought off. His security was tight. There was no sign of unusual activity aboard the target ship, and he was two minutes away from ordering the assault. From his warehouse observation post, he peered through the crack in the door a final time.

And scowled.

The American gangway watches stationed on the quay apron, the first individuals scheduled to die in the attack, were scrambling hastily up to the bow of the LPD and the stern of the cruiser, ducking out of sight over the deck lip. In fact, suddenly no one was visible aboard either ship. The roving security patrols had disappeared as well.

There was a stillness that could only be called ominous. The dark-tinted bridge windscreen of the LPD looked down impassively on the quayside, and there was no sound except the lapping of the waves against the breakwater. Then came the hiss and rumble and the steady, rising whine of massive marine engines turning over.

The Americans were getting under way! One minute from the attack and the damn targets were preparing to sail!

The Bugis clan leader was stunned. He should have realized that the assault was blown and that his critical element of surprise was gone. No doubt, given a few more seconds to think, he would have reached this conclusion and aborted the operation. Unfortunately for him—for he would die shortly—and for the rest of his assault force, his hunter's instincts triggered first. His prey was escaping!

He screamed the order to attack.

The scream was magnified two hundred times over as the Bugis poured from concealment within the row of warehouses ... and ran headlong into a storm of automatic-weapons fire. The weatherdecks and upperworks of the ships blazed, Marines and Navy security opening up on the pirate force.

The Bugis were staggered by the ferocity of their reception, but they were Bugis: They scattered, taking cover behind the rows of cargo pallets that had been artfully positioned for them by port stevedores during the day. Shooting back, they strove to perform their initial mission. If they could not suppress the ships' defenses, maybe they could at least distract them enough for the mine launches to deliver their body blows.

Even this would not be easy. The battle was escalating, and the defenders were bringing heavier and more fearful weapons to bear. Grenades exploded over the heads of the Bugis gunners as they crouched behind what they thought was secure cover. Heavy tracer streams arced down from the corners of the *Carlson*'s forward deckhouse, autocannon shells chewing through and scattering pallets and men both. For just this kind of infighting, the LPD had been equipped with four of the same kind of Mark 46 30mm turrets carried by the new Marine Advanced Armored Assault Vehicle, a precaution that paid for itself now.

But there was something else, something the Bugis had never before encountered—something terrifying.

Pain, sporadic waves of terrible, burning, sourceless pain, as if the Bugis were being engulfed by invisible flames. Pain agonizing enough to make a brave man drop his weapon and scream.

The raiders were Bugis pirates, fearless in the face of other men and willing to dare the clean death of a bullet. But what man could fight this work of demons? Raiders began to slough away, fleeing for the safety of the cool, uncursed shadows.

Just off the *Carlson*'s Combat Information Center, in a cramped fire-control station colloquially known as "Zap Gun Alley," Lieutenant Linda Janovic looked over the shoulders of her "gunners" as they kept their weapons in play.

Janovic was the *Carlson*'s Ship-Mounted Area Denial Systems officer. She greatly enjoyed this career slot, not merely because it kept her on the cutting edge of technology, but also because while she was proud to serve in her nation's military, she didn't particularly enjoy the thought of having to kill people.

SMADS was the star of the new generation of nonlethal ordnance coming into service that theoretically permitted an enemy to be disabled and defeated without the application of outright death and destruction. The Area Denial System was literally a science fiction "ray gun" brought into reality, its parabolic emitters generating a focused beam of silent, invisible, microwave energy. While a short-term exposure was not physically damaging to a human being, the target underwent an experience that had been described as "having a hot light bulb pressed against every square inch of skin." Very distracting, if nothing else.

Through the Cooperative Engagement net, Lieutenant Janovic had gathered the *Cunningham*'s SMADS mounts under her control, splitting the tasking. The three emitters that could be brought to bear on the land battle—the Duke's stern mount and two forward superstructure mounts of the LPD—were under the direct guidance of her systems operators.

Leaning over the shoulders of her SOs, she watched through their sighting monitors as they put fire into the enemy. She was satisfied with what she saw. There were explosions or sprawled bodies accountable to her batteries, but wherever the crosshairs of her sighting systems were laid, the volume of enemy fire dropped immediately as their foes abandoned thoughts of aggression and focused on getting the hell somewhere else.

The remaining forward SMADS mount on the *Cunningham* and the aft emitters of the *Carlson* had been handed off to the Duke's controller. Their job was to assist with seaward security, and up to this moment they had not energized a beam. Now a voice sounded in Janovic's headset.

"*Carlson* control, this is Duke SMADS. We have unidentified small craft coming in fast! Multiple targets!"

Janovic slapped a hand down on the access pad of a secondary monitor, flipping through the imaging from the forward targeting cameras. Half a dozen small outboard launches were converging on the moorage, showing no lights or other identification. It didn't make sense for any of the local boatmen to come rushing into a firefight, but there was a chance these might be Indonesian police or military craft coming to assist the task force.

But then, that was the beauty of SMADS: If you made a mistake you could apologize to the victim afterward.

"Cook 'em," Janovic snapped. At the speed of light, the beams lashed out.

The SMADS projectors were state-of-the-art nonlethal projected-energy weapons. However, the dynamite mines aboard the Bugis attack launches were crude, simple explosive devices. As the two differing technologies encountered each other, odd, unintended things happened. The copper wiring between the timer and battery units and the industrial-grade blasting caps embedded in the explosives acted as a receiving antenna for the sudden massive surge of microwave energy. Induction currents resulted.

The lead mine launch vanished in a tremendous explosion.

Janovic recognized the mechanism and its meaning instantly. "Shit! Suicide boats! *Cunningham,* hose 'em! Hose 'em!"

Emitter dishes slammed from traverse stop to traverse stop, spraying the night with energy. As each boat was trapped in a beam, it disintegrated, its crew slain in bewilderment by their own weapons. Aboard the last of the six, someone must have had a realization. Frantically they tried to jettison their mines; they got one over the side in time but were a split-second late with the next.

Janovic's guts twisted sickeningly as the spray plumes of the explosions collapsed and the smoke clouds dissipated. It had been too much to hope for, that there might be a way to fight a war without the blood.

"Captain," the OOD yelled over the raging stammer of the gunfire. "All engine rooms report ready to answer bells!"

The bridge windscreen had taken hits heavy enough to blow two of the armor-glass panes out of their frames, letting in the full uproar of the battle along with the occasional ricocheting rifle slug. Still, Carberry stood immobile, his hands behind his back, disregarding the blood trickling from the cut on his forehead. If he was a legend within his war-gaming hobby, the little man was building another here.

"Very well. Signal the *Cunningham* to get under way." Somehow Carberry didn't find it necessary to lift his voice to be heard. "We'll hold departure until she's clear."

"Aye, aye."

A few moments later, a string of flashbulblike bursts danced along the flanks of the Duke, the crack of the mini-explosions lost amid the gunfire.

In planning for an emergency exit under fire, Amanda Garrett hadn't liked the notion of exposing a sea and anchor detail on the decks of her ships. Accordingly the broad V of hawsers and spring lines used in the Mediterranean-type mooring of the task force had been doctored for a rapid departure.

Foam rubber flotation cladding had been wrapped around the upper shipside ends of the lines, ensuring that they couldn't sink and foul a propeller, then a loop of explosive tape had been lapped around each hawser head. Wired for remote detonation, the ships could be cut free with the single push of a button.

The water boiled along the *Cunningham*'s flanks as the contra-rotating propellers of her propulsor pods cut water. As smoothly and almost as swiftly as an accelerating automobile, the cruiser hauled away from the seawall. Running blacked-out, she faded into the night in a matter of a few seconds.

"The *Cunningham* is away, Captain."

"Very well, Mr. Johnson. Clear our lines, please. Helm, steady as she goes. Lee helm, all engines back one third."

The Marine demo man hit his firing box and a second string of flashes danced around the perimeter of the LPD's deck, the hawsers falling away. Diesel powered and backing with conventional screws, the *Carlson*'s response wasn't as decisive, but she began to reverse, the gangplank crashing from her forecastle to hang vertically against the seawall.

The small-arms fire trailed off as the LPD opened the range, following her consort into the darkness. A pirate fired an antitank rocket at the ship in a final futile gesture. It streaked past the bridge, sputtering sparks like a malfunctioning firework, and fell wasted into the harbor waters. A point defense turret yammered a long, angry replying burst, having the last word. The battle of Benoa Port was over.

"Lee helm, port ahead one third. Continue backing starboard one third. Mr. Johnson, you may resume the conn. Ware her about and follow the *Cunningham* out through the Turtle Island channel. Maintain blackout topside until further orders, and procure the damage and casualty reports with all speed, please."

"Will do, sir."

"Order the Sea Fighter squadron to execute an immediate combat launch to recover the shore party at rendezvous point as per ops plan Bravo. Also, get some drone recon up and have two of the helicopter gunships spotted on five-minute ready alert."

"Will do, Captain. Uh, would you like someone to have a look at that cut, sir?"

Carberry unclasped his hands. He was past the trembling now. Reaching up, he touched the coagulating blood on his forehead. "Probably a good idea, Mr. Johnson. Have sick bay send a pharmacist's mate up should they have one free."

Not a bad action at all, Carberry thought. It had been rather good having the *Carlson* cover the cruiser's departure. It would remind the surface-warfare crowd that the amphibious forces were fighting ships as well.

"Mr. Johnson, another thing. Please inform the ship's company that I am satisfied with their performance tonight. No, on second thought, make that eminently satisfied."

The Marine security detail had already thrown up a security perimeter around the hired cars. The contents of their briefcases were now revealed as FN P-90 personal defense weapons, an odd-looking but lethal Belgian-made crossbreed of bull pup assault rifle and submachine gun. The hired Balinese drivers had also been relieved of their keys and pointedly told to get lost. From this point on, no one who was not in a U.S. Navy uniform was going to be trusted.

Her own weapon drawn, Amanda hurried down the path to the parking lot. Even though they were a good eight miles from the harbor, she could hear the sound of distant explosions.

Stone Quillain was already overseeing the loading, an automatic in his right hand, a cell phone held to his ear with his left.

"What's happening with the task force?" she demanded, hurrying to his side.

"They're hitting us," the Marine replied matter-of-factly, "but our guys were waiting for 'em. So far, so good. Captain Carberry's casting off and hauling out."

"Good. How about our people here?"

"All present and accounted for. Loading now."

"Right! Pull in your sentries and let's get to the pickup site. Is the point driver set to lead us out?"

"Corporal Smitson drove the route twice yesterday. He's good to go. Mount up, Skipper, the admiral's waiting on you."

"Negative, I'm taking the trailer. I'll see you at the rendezvous."

Before Quillain could raise an objection, Amanda was sliding into the front seat of the last sedan in line. Having been designated the emergency recovery vehicle in the advent of trouble with any of the other cars, it carried only a Marine driver, its passenger load having been divided among the rest of the motorcade.

"Take off, Stone," she yelled through the open window. "Expedite!"

From the shadows near the parking lot exit, Harconan watched the line of sedans swerve into the road and accelerate away with a chirping of tires. As he expected, he caught the sheen of red hair in the front seat of the last car. In this situation, her instinct would be to be the last one out, ensuring that all of her people were away and safe.

Harconan was already aware that his attack on the task force was a disaster. She had been waiting for him to strike at her ships. But perhaps the day was not totally lost. There was another prize to be taken, one she had left vulnerable.

Flipping his phone open, he called through to the team leader of his Nung special-forces unit, issuing specific instructions.

The liberty party's evacuation route did not run south toward the Benoa Harbor area. That had been calculated as too obvious and too much of an invitation to an ambush. Instead it ran eastward, passing under the urban core of Denpasar to the resort area of Sanur Beach. There a Sea Fighter would be waiting to return the officer cadre to the big ships waiting offshore.

It was a solid plan that should take only a matter of minutes to execute.

"What's the task force status, Stone?" MacIntyre demanded from the number-five car's rear seat, which he shared with Christine and Tran.

"They had to wax a bunch of Boghammers, but they're clear now, sir. Minimal damage," Quillain reported, riding with his phone still to his ear.

"Captain Garrett was correct in her assessment," Nguyen Tran commented. "Your actions are driving Harconan to adopt increasingly desperate measures."

"That'll sound a lot better when we're back aboard ship," Christine replied. She was twisted around in her seat, peering back through the rear window.

"Is she still back there?" MacIntyre demanded testily.

"Still hanging in, sir."

The Toyota executed a dry-pavement skid as it snaked around a tight corner on the narrow two-lane. The motorcade was thundering through a semirural area with truck-garden patches and palm groves interspersed with the close-set houses and shops of roadside villages. They were still out of the coastal resort strip, and lights and other vehicles were few and far between.

MacIntyre looked over his shoulder into the glare of the trailing headlights. "Damn it, Stone, why'd you let her take the trail car? That wasn't in the plan!"

"I know it, Admiral, and I wasn't happy about it either. If somebody had just given me a four-grade bump to brigadier general, I woulda been happy to do something about it."

"Then you should have called me, dammit!"

"Maybe so, sir. But we were kind of tight on time back there. Anyway, we're comin' up on Panjer village. Six more klicks and we got it beat."

But they didn't.

As they shot past a side road MacIntyre caught a glint of chrome from a blacked-out automobile. An instant later the headlights of Amanda's car were occulted as the black car cut it off. The crash of crumpling steel was cut through by Christine's scream.

"Brake!" Quillain roared, and the Toyota's tires sobbed on the potholed pavement. He caught up the P-90 and was rolling out of the passenger door before the sedan had reached a full stop.

"I'm coming with you," MacIntyre yelled, starting to open his door as well.

"The hell you are, sir." Quillain shouldered the door shut. He'd screwed up once tonight; he wasn't doing it again. "Take off, O'Malley, and don't you stop for anything, especially admirals!"

The sedan shot away, its tires smoking.

Standing six feet away, Nguyen Tran slid his Glock automatic out from under his evening jacket. "Will you permit me to assist you, Captain Quillain?"

Quillain wiped his mouth with the back of his free hand. "More'n that Mr. Tran, I'd appreciate you. Let's go!"

Their car had halted a good hundred yards from the crash site and the two men separated, working up the road through the scrub cover on either shoulder. Their instinct was to race back, but their wisdom said that would only lead to disaster. There would be waiting guns covering their approach, and stealth was their only chance.

But stealth took time.

The scent of hot metal and steam told them they were close. The Toyota had center-punched a large and elderly Mercedes-Benz station wagon. There were no other vehicles immediately in sight, but less than a minute later a rattletrap farm truck appeared, coming in from behind the wrecks. The illumination of its single headlight revealed no activity at all around the crash site.

Stone bit the bullet and charged.

Nothing.

The Toyota's air bags had worked, but the Marine driver was still sprawled behind the wheel, unconscious. The shattered driver's-side window and the bruise on the side of his head resembled rifle-butt work far more than it did a collision injury. As for Amanda Garrett, there was nothing except for her shoulder bag lying on the car floor.

"Elegantly done," Tran commented. He returned his pistol to its holster and went to calm the startled driver of the farm truck and to arrange for a lift.

Badung Strait   **1025 Hours, Zone Time: August 20, 2008**

With the PGACs deployed in an anti–small-craft screen, the task force steamed to the northeast, seeking for the open waters of the Bali Sea. The lights of the Bali coast faded to port as did those of Penida Island to starboard.

The green and red sparks of the *Sutanto*'s running lights trailed astern. The Indonesian warship, noteworthy in its uninvolvement in the fight at Benoa Port, had hastily sortied after the task force and resumed its shadowing. To the

Sea Fighters, its presence served only to magnify the sensation of being run out of town.

Stone Quillain stared down at the untouched mug of coffee on the wardroom table. "It's my fault, sir. I accept the responsibility for the loss of Captain Garrett."

Reembarked aboard the *Carlson,* the task force's senior command officers had immediately gone into an emergency operations group to assess their current catastrophe.

"No, cancel that, Stone." Passing behind his chair, MacIntyre clapped the Marine lightly on the shoulder of his dust-stained uniform blouse. "It's not a matter of anybody's fault. We thought we had all the bases covered, but Harconan got ahead of us. I gather we all agree that the gentleman is responsible for this action."

"Given the sophistication of the operation and the speed with which it was organized and executed, I would say almost undoubtedly," Tran replied. His evening wear also showed the signs of his brush-busting. "To the good, this was obviously not an open attack on the officers cadre or an assassination attempt. It was a kidnapping, targeted specifically against Captain Garrett. Thus we can assume she is still alive and a hostage, no doubt with the intent of using her as a bargaining chip of some nature."

Commander Ken Hiro, as the new Sea Fighter TAC-BOSS, scowled up at the inspector. "Okay, the captain's alive and that's great. What do we do about getting her back? Shouldn't we be on the horn to the authorities on Bali about this?"

Tran shrugged. "That's one of the conventional acts we can perform, Commander. However, I doubt we can expect much from that sector. As you had your evacuation route preplanned, so will Harconan. It's questionable if Captain Garrett is even on Bali any longer. Besides, it's apparent that any networking done with the local authorities will benefit Harconan more than us."

"He's right, Ken," MacIntyre said, continuing his slow pacing path around the table. "I'll be filing a report with the Indonesians concerning the attack on the task force. As an aspect of that, I'll put in a request that a search be made for any U.S. personnel who might have accidentally been left behind in our rapid departure. For the moment we'll keep Amanda's disappearance to ourselves and we'll work the problem ourselves. The moment we bring the governments in, theirs or ours, we're going to lose control of this. The more red tape we get snarled up in, the more it will work in Harconan's favor."

"Then that brings us back to my original question, sir," Hiro said hotly. "What do we do about getting the captain back?"

"We work the problem with our own secure assets, Commander. We count on what we can count on." MacIntyre's features were expressionless as he continued his slow, deliberate orbit of the table, as was his voice. Whatever he was feeling at the moment was locked within, as if he were fearful of letting it out. "We are going to find where he's taken her, and we are going to get her back, and to hell with everything else."

"Then, may I make a suggestion, sir?" Quillain said, looking up. "How about letting me and some of my boys pay a call on this guy's home base, this Palau-whatever-it-is. Let's kick a few doors down and see if we can get our hands on him. It won't take long to get some answers. I guarantee it."

"I doubt it would be that easy, my friend," Tran said. "I think it may be assumed that Harconan is not going to permit himself to be available to either us or the Indonesian authorities. I would say he'd likely disappear down the same escape-and-evasion route as he intended for Captain Garrett."

MacIntyre stopped his pacing. "Yes. He'll be with her. Wherever they're headed."

"East."

Up to that point, Christine Rendino had taken little part in the conference. She had drifted silently into the far corner of the wardroom and to the planter there, lightly caressing the leaves of the miniature palm tree with a fingertip. "It won't be either Java or Sumatra," she said, her voice oddly distant and detached. "Too civilized, too high a population density. It won't be Sulawesi, either: too expected, too close to a large Bugis population. It will be off in the eastern end of the archipelago somewhere, in the wild islands."

Amanda Garrett writhed through a protracted nightmare, reaching out for consciousness but never getting a solid grasp upon it. Pain...fragments of voices speaking in tongues she didn't know...a stranger's hands stripping away her clothing...a wetness being poured on her head...a protracted time with nothing but a vibration and a roar hammering at her dully aching mind...at last the deeper, safer darkness of true sleep.

Her eyes opened, and after a vague moment more she forced them to focus. She was in a small room—no, a cabin—on a boat or small ship. Her surroundings were moving and with wave rhythm and not just vertigo.

The cabin was maybe eight by eight, white-painted but grimy, with rice matting on the deck. She was lying on the cracked plastic cover of a foam rubber mattress in the lower of a double-decker bunk. There were no other furnishings or accouterments except for a cracked mirror and a number of heavy nails driven into the bulkhead to serve as clothing hooks.

And speaking of clothing, her own was gone. Her uniform replaced by a wraparound sarung of bright cheap cotton print, the almost universal garment of the archipelago. Her feet were bare, but a pair of woman's-size rubber sandals had been thrown on the deck.

Amanda sat up too quickly and had to fight an explosive surge of nausea. The side of her head throbbed, a result of the...she groped for memory...a result of the car wreck. There was also a less readily identifiable stinging on the inside of her left elbow.

Glancing down, she noticed the two needle punctures in her skin. Drugged on top of being knocked out. No wonder she felt like the wreck of the *Hesperus*. What else had been damaged? She pulled herself to her feet, using the bunk frame, and promptly lost the *sarung,* the securing tuck at its top having come undone. To hell with it: The cooler touch of air on her skin helped to clear her head. Lurching across to the mirror on the bulkhead, she peered at herself.

Someone else looked back.

The effect was momentarily startling. Her hair had been dyed jet black. After a moment, Amanda smiled grimly at the stranger. She'd always wondered what she might look like as a brunette.

There was nothing left in the room to examine, save a single porthole and the door. The porthole was open and latched back for air, but a heavy wooden bar had been screwed across it on the outside. Only open water, sunlight, and sky were visible beyond it.

The ship was wooden-hulled; Amanda strongly suspected it to be a Bugis *pinisi,* but the deck was vibrating to the drive of a propeller, and she could hear the rumble of a powerful marine diesel. They were under way under power with none of the steadying lean of a schooner under sail.

And that left the door.

She reclaimed the *sarung,* spent a few moments securing it, and slipped her feet into sandals. Crossing to the doorway, she carefully tried its tarnished brass handle.

Locked from the outside. That confirmed it. She was in enemy hands.

She returned to the mirror. A small wooden box had been bolted underneath it, and Amada recalled seeing half of a broken comb lying in it. Taking it up, she sat down on the bunk once more and, after carefully examining the comb for possible passengers, began to smooth and order her hair.

Amanda's motivation was simple: Do something to improve your situation *now*! Even if only combing your hair, it was a refusal to surrender to apathy and helplessness, a statement of control over one's destiny. It was never too early to start fighting that battle. As she worked on her snarled mop, she did the only other viable thing possible. She thought.

She was clearly a prisoner, taken in an action possibly tasked for that specific purpose. But she was also a "soft" prisoner. She was neither bound nor blindfolded, she was being permitted clothing and she was being held in fairly comfortable surroundings. This all pointed to a single specific conclusion as to who was responsible.

A positive factor, the potential for at least a slight degree of leverage. Amanda didn't fool herself into thinking it would be much, but even the poorest card can be built into a fighting hand.

She tore a strip from the inner hem of the *sarung* and used it to bind her hair back. Crossing to the mirror once more, she checked the result of her grooming. Deliberately she slapped herself twice across the face, pulling up a little color into her cheeks. Without a makeup kit, it was the best she could do.

Going to the cabin door, she pounded insistently on it with her palm, stepping back as she heard a bolt draw back on the far side.

Amanda found herself confronted with a Bugis seaman, an older man, gaunt, scarred, and lean, his naturally bronzed skin darkened from the salt baked into it by decades of tropical sun. He, too, wore a *sarung* around his waist and a bandanna binding his graying hair.

He also cradled a well-maintained L2 Sterling machine pistol under his arm. Cancel *seaman* and substitute *pirate*. He stared levelly at Amanda.

She met his gaze head-on, with no attempt at obsequiousness. This was Asia. Prisoner or not, she must set "face," establishing herself as a person of position, mandating respect. "I don't know if you can speak English or not," she said, "but you know who Harconan is. I want to see him, *now*!"

The Bugis schooner was a big one, a hundred-and-fifty-footer that had undergone a conversion into a motor coaster. A large combination deck and wheelhouse had been constructed atop the aft half of the hull, and the foremast had been shortened to serve as a kingpost for cargo handling.

The inside of the wheelhouse was spartan in the extreme, the wheel itself the control pedestal for the engine and a binnacle. No electronics were apparent, nor was there even a chart. For a Bugis skipper, such affairs would be irrelevant.

Harconan was there in the wheelhouse, sharing the watch with the Bugis helmsman. It was a very different Harconan than the one Amanda had so far known. He wore faded jeans and a disreputable dungaree shirt, half unbuttoned and with the sleeves rolled. Comfortable sandals were on his feet, and a broad sun-cracked leather belt was cinched in at his waist. He hadn't bothered with shaving. At the receptions and on Palau Piri he had looked suave, polished, and ineffably debonair. Here, leaning in the open wheelhouse window, with the trade winds ruffling his dark hair, he was merely magnificent.

Amanda sensed it was because her captor was truly himself now, at ease in what he must feel was his own environment. In spite of everything that had happened, Amanda felt her body stir in response.

He looked back at her and smiled. It seemed a genuine smile of greeting and pleasure at seeing her. "Good morning. I hope you're feeling well."

"A little hungover but good enough," she replied coolly. Ignoring the guard who had trailed her to the bridge, she moved forward to peer ahead off the bow. "Where are we?"

He issued a good-humored challenge: "You tell me."

She glanced around the half circle of horizon visible from the wheelhouse. There was nothing to be seen but a slow, rolling sea reflecting a piercing sun. The sky was sun-washed pale azure, with only a single mound of cloud off to the south. No other sea or air traffic was visible nor a solitary point of land.

"The Banda Sea," she said after a minute. "Given the lack of other shipping, it's the eastern Banda."

She pointed to the cloud mass to the south. "Off to starboard there is the Tayandu group. As we're standing on east-northeast, I'd say we're bound either for the Kai Island group or the western coast of New Guinea."

"Indeed, and why couldn't we be in the Arafura, standing on for Torres Strait, with Jervis Island to starboard?"

Amanda shrugged. "The wave action is wrong. The Arafura is open westward to the Indian Ocean and you get the longer, slower deepwater rollers there. We're still inside the archipelago. Besides, you wouldn't risk running the Torres Strait with me aboard. No doubt you know about the Australian navy corvette usually on station there."

Harconan threw his head back and laughed. "Ha! I knew you had to be a real sailor and not just a button-pusher. I'd give you one of my schooners to command any day."

"There's only one problem with that, Makara. I'm on the other side."

"I see." He grimaced slightly and rubbed the back of his neck. "Well, I suppose it is time we drop the sophistry. Our game of mutually pretended ignorance has worn a little thin. I trust, Amanda, you'll agree that a little honesty between us might be pleasant."

"I don't find any of this pleasant. Why am I being held prisoner?"

"Amanda, don't talk foolishness. Of course you know why you are here. You're a prisoner of war, taken honorably in combat. And while I confess that Makara Limited is not a signatory of the Geneva Convention, I can promise that you will be well treated. There is no reason for you to be afraid. No harm will come to you if you act reasonably."

"And what's the definition of 'reasonably'?"

Harconan nodded toward the guard, who stood at the rear of the wheelhouse. "Ask him."

Amanda noted that the old Bugis raider always stayed back a step or two, keeping himself more than a grab away and unobtrusively positioning so Harconan was out of his line of fire but she was not. The inference was plain.

"I see," she said.

"I'm glad you do, Amanda." He rested a hand on her shoulder. "I know that your instinct will be to attempt something heroic. Please don't. It won't succeed and I genuinely don't want you hurt or killed."

She jerked away angrily. "That doesn't ring particularly

true, Makara. If I'm a prisoner of war, then we are at war and you're the one aiming the gun at my back, even if one of your hired hands pulls the trigger!"

"Amanda, you're talking foolishness again. You know I don't want to harm you and why."

She lifted her head defiantly. "Because of what happened on your island? That was just a mutual reconnaissance mission and you know it."

"No!" His hand slashed the air saberlike in a gesture of denial. "Because of who we are and what we are, we have lied to each other since the first moment we met. I suspect we will continue to lie to each other for a long time to come. But we have had one moment of truth together, there on my beach at Palau Piri. You cannot deny that any more than I can. Let's at least acknowledge that. Maybe we can use it to find other truths."

He turned to stare back out to sea, a silence following as might have existed between two lovers in a quarrel— which, Amanda mused, was exactly what they were.

She looked forward over the tarped ranks of oil drums that constituted the coaster's deck cargo and on past the upcurved bow to where the flying fish skittered and gleamed as they fled the cutwater.

"Why did you have my hair dyed black?" she asked eventually.

"Oh, that? Call it protective coloration. I'm fully cognizant of the capabilities of your reconnaissance satellites and remotely piloted vehicles. There are few redheads riding about on Bugis *pinisi*. It was either make you look like one of us or keep you confined belowdecks until we reached our destination. That would have made it more . . . unpleasant for you."

"I see. Thank you. Where are we heading, anyway?"

"You'll see soon enough." He turned back to her with a tentative smile. "Our dress suits you well. You look lovely in it."

Now, lower the eyes, Amanda, and smile, just a little. "Thank you, it's very comfortable. . . . Makara, may I ask you something? And please, could we find some of that truth we were talking about?"

"Possibly."

"How badly did you hurt us last night? How many of my people were killed? Please tell me."

He sighed and paused before answering. "You cut us to pieces. You were waiting for us and I can see now it was madness even to try. But I took you as a prize and so I consider it a victory."

And so the task force was still in the fight. "I see. I appreciate you telling me, Makara. Now, may I go back to my cabin for a while? I'd like to lie down again."

Amanda stared at the plank overhead of the tiny cabin, but not seeing it, just as she did not hear the rumble of the diesel or the creak and give of its hull, or feel the perspiration prickle at her skin.

She was focused totally inward, assessing and reviewing her situation and seeking to develop a valid plan of action. Recriminations for allowing herself to be trapped like this were dismissed instantly as a critical waste of time and energy. What was done was done and only what came next mattered.

Amanda had always recognized that the risk of becoming a prisoner of war was inherent in her chosen profession. As such, she had prepared for it by taking part in a number of interservice POW and escape-and-evasion training courses, including the grueling and frighteningly realistic Mustang E&E program run by the U.S. Army's Special Forces.

The first rule all of these programs had taught was "Do something immediately." The sooner one could escape, the better.

But did she necessarily want to escape?

Abstractly assessing her situation as she might any other tactical problem, Amanda began to recognize potential. Gradually it occurred to her that at the moment she was perhaps at the best place she could possibly be, at the heart of the piracy cartel and in a position to collect intelligence on the organization. Also possibly to influence and affect its leader.

By no means did she consider herself indispensable to the Sea Fighter Task Force. There was any number of capable officers, from Admiral MacIntyre on down, who could take her place there. There was no one who could take her place here.

With that realization, Amanda ceased thinking of herself as a prisoner, jettisoning the last of the emotional shackles that went with the title. Likewise abandoned was any thought of escape. Replacing it was the concept of attack.

To win in any kind of military conflict, one had to attack. It was irrelevant if one was mistress of a multibillion-dollar ultratech warship or if one commanded nothing but a loaned cotton *sarung*; you used the assets available to do the maximum damage possible to your enemy.

How best to do so?

That part was simple: Let the task force know where Harconan was and where he was headed.

As she had projected in the wheelhouse, it either had to be for southwestern New Guinea or maybe the Kai Island group.

Chris had mentioned both areas as prime possible hide sites for the INDASAT. Logic would indicate Harconan was en route to that hide now. Excellent. Now, how to let the task force in on the fact?

Amanda rolled onto her side, exposure to the air generating a transitory burst of coolness down her spine. Given that the task force was operational, logic would indicate that they would be looking for her and Harconan with all resources available. Those resources would be extensive, from recon satellites on down. Camouflaging her as a Bugis woman had been a wise precaution, as Harconan couldn't be sure what might be looking over his shoulder. How best to deliberately draw the attention of one of those assets?

Radio? She had seen no sign of a ship-to-shore in the schooner's wheelhouse. Harconan no doubt had brought a very extensive portable communications suite with him. Also, no doubt, it was well secured, with no chance of her getting near any of it.

What about making a simple spark gap with a couple of wires? Something to produce enough coded static to register on a direction-finder array?

Amanda's eyes sought for the cabin light fixture. She found it, and smiled derisively. There was a lamp bracket on the wall, with a patch of kerosene soot on the overhead above it.

So much for electronics. What about visual scan?

It was highly doubtful that anyone was going to let her stand on deck heliographing to a Global Hawk with the cabin mirror.

Amanda was confronted with the conundrum of drawing attention to herself unobtrusively. She recalled a scene from one of Captain Edward Beach's excellent submarine warfare novels in which the hero marked his presence as a prisoner aboard an enemy vessel by reaching out of a port-hole to paint the name of his own ship on the hostile craft's side. The flare of the hull prevented the paint from being seen on deck.

Unfortunately, most of the searchers seeking for her would be overhead, and she didn't have access to a can of paint anyway.

She called up the mental catalog of the possible assets she had seen aboard the Bugis coaster, its outfitting and its cargo both. Using them like the pieces of a jigsaw puzzle, she tried to fit them together into a coherent pattern.

Wood ... canvas ... flags ... semaphore ... stupid! Metal ... radar ... radar beacon ... too big, too passive ... Some way to modulate it? ... Signal ... signal flares ... fire ... too obvious. Heat ... infrared ... a thermal pulse of some kind ... heat ... heat ... flame ... oil ... diesel ... oil ... oil ... oil. What was it about oil?

Amanda's head lifted abruptly off the pillow.

Oil.

There was one asset that hadn't been taken from her. Possibly ... probably ... as an act of kindness by Harconan she still possessed her Naval Academy class ring. Sitting up in the bunk, she tore it from her finger. In a matter of moments she was facing astern in the inner aft corner of the cabin, as close to the keel line of the ship as she could get.

Using her ring as a pendulum, she assembled a crude inclinometer. With a thread unraveled from the hem of her *sarung* she suspended the ring from one of the clothing-hook nails driven into the bulkhead. Intently she studied the sway of the pendulum to port and starboard, gauging the arc of each sweep as the *pinisi* gently rolled and pitched in the low swells.

No cargo ship, not even a large, modern freighter with gyrostablization and computerized ballast tanks could be trimmed to ride perfectly. There would inevitably be at least a slight list to port or starboard. This particular schooner seemed to favor her port side, by a couple of degrees. Not enough to affect her handling or to even be noticeable when one stood on the deck. But the list was definitely there.

Amanda needed to know that. Now she needed something else. The clothing hooks were too obvious. There was too much chance someone would notice one of the nails missing. Instead she began to scour the interior of the cabin, checking out every plank end and joining.

Once, the Bugis *pinisi* had been built entirely without metal, master shipwrights fitting the sleek craft together with wooden pegs that swelled with exposure to sea water, bonding the rakish schooner together almost into a composite whole. But with the passage of time and the coming of the engine age, the Bugis had yielded to the ease of screws, spikes, and nails.

Amanda found the lifted head of one such nail beneath a deck mat, slightly loosened by the working of the schooner's hull. Again she used her precious ring as a prying tool, backing the nail out of its hole in the deck, cursing silently at its stubbornness, swearing wordlessly at the tears and gouges in her fingers, dreading the sound of the cabin's door bolt snapping back.

After a minor eternity she succeeded. It was better than

she could have hoped for. The nail was almost ten-penny size. It would work well.

Carefully, Amanda sheathed it in the hem of her garment. Re-donning her scarred ring, she lay down on the bunk once more. Now, to wait for nightfall and to pray that her captor would be amenable to just a little manipulation.

The slant and fade of the light through the wooden-barred port told of the passing of time, as did the odor of cooking within the deckhouse. Harconan himself came with a quiet invitation to the evening meal.

Amanda had been hoping for this, but she strove for a proper balance of hesitation and resignation in her acceptance.

Served in the main cabin, the food was simple: rice, grilled fish, and tea. The only conversational ploy aimed in Amanda's direction came from Harconan. The other members of the schooner's taciturn crew, English-speaking or not, either kept their peace or spoke only to their companions in a low murmur, a decided difference from the curious, casual, and friendly extroversion that was the Indonesian norm.

It was readily apparent to Amanda that the hand of the *raja samudra* hovered over her. She was not to be a matter of consideration by the schooner's crew.

There was the one exception: the wiry, sun-darkened old sailor who guarded her. He took a seat on a bench diametrically across the cabin from her, his pristine Sterling machine pistol at his side. As he ate, his eyes never left her, monitoring every move she made, every gesture or shift of position, every morsel of food she lifted to her mouth. There was no lust in that gaze, just an intent and wary focus.

No doubt but that her watchdog had been personally selected by Harconan for his diligence and ability. His was the only firearm Amanda had seen overtly carried aboard the schooner.

Possibly Makara was still infatuated with her, but he was no fool. Amanda had no doubt as to what would happen if she made any threatening action against Harconan or the ship. There was also no doubt she would have to carry out her plan under her guard's unwavering stare.

Amanda ate slowly, drawing out her meal until she, Harconan, and the guard were the only ones remaining at the cabin table and full darkness had settled beyond the ports.

"I'm glad to see you have an appetite tonight," Harconan commented. "May I assume you are feeling better this evening?"

"As well as can be expected, I suppose," Amanda replied, wiping her right hand—her eating hand—clean with a moistened cloth. "A little fresh air would be appreciated, though. Would it be possible for me to go out on deck for a while?"

"Of course you may. Amanda, please believe that I have no desire to make this situation any more unpleasant for you than absolutely necessary. In fact, I'd like to make you an offer."

"What kind of offer?"

"One of parole, an ancient and respected military tradition," Harconan replied. "Give me your word that you will not attempt to escape or to interfere with my operations and I can promise you an even greater degree of comfort and freedom than you might otherwise enjoy. You will be betraying nothing because there is no chance of escape where we are going. Likewise, any action against us or attempt to communicate with your navy will fail."

He reached out and rested his hand on her wrist. "Also, under parole, I may be able to show more of what I am attempting to do, and why. I'm not just a pirate, Amanda. I'd like the chance to explain that to you."

Steady, Mandy, don't jump at it too fast. Softly, softly, catchee monkey.

"I'd have to think about it, Makara," she replied stiffly. "That and a lot of other things."

He nodded his acceptance. "That's understandable. Take all the time you need."

Amanda stood up from the table. "May I go on deck now, please?"

"Of course." He tried a smile. "I don't suppose you'd want some company."

"No. Not just now. I'd rather be alone for a while."

"As you wish."

A glance at the Southern Cross revealed that the *pinisi* was still eastering steadily, the almost waveless sea boiling beneath the upraked bow. The only deck illumination issued from the red and green running lights amidships and the glow of the binnacle in the wheelhouse—that and the glitter of a million tropic stars overhead. There was more than enough for Amanda to find her way to the portside rail and for her soft-footed guard to keep her under observation.

As was his way, he held back, staying in the shadows at the base of the deckhouse as Amanda idled her way forward toward the bow, pretending to be a person deep in thought.

In reality, the thinking had already been done and the decisions made. With her back to the guard, she slipped the nail she'd stolen from the cabin deck out of her *sarung*. Fitting it carefully into her hand with her thumb folded over the head, she found about half an inch protruded from the bottom of her fist. Perfect.

She was on the narrow strip of deck between the rail and the deck cargo, the lashed drums of diesel. She was also portside, just where she wanted to be. There was nothing to be gained by waiting.

She sank down to the deck, sitting with her back to the oil drums. As she drew her knees up under her chin, her right hand whipped back, behind the cover of her body, driving the nail into the lower face of the oil drum beside her.

This was the most critical moment. Would her guard have noted that single odd tinny thump, and would he investigate? Amanda paused in her breathing.

There was no movement from the base of the deckhouse. Forty feet aft, her guard was sitting cross-legged on the deck as well, content with keeping her in visual range and content that the noise must have been a harmless transitory.

Amanda had felt the slick splash of oil on her hand when she had struck her blow. Glancing down now, she saw a pencil-thin jet of diesel spew across the deck, forming into a dark stream that trickled into the scuppers. As she looked on, the stream's end disappeared over the side, drizzling into the sea.

Her homemade inclinometer had read true! There was a portside list! She was in business. Unobtrusively she flicked the nail away over the side. Silently she began to count, *One . . . two . . . three . . . four . . .*

Minutes crept by.

. . . two ninety-eight . . . two ninety-nine . . . three hundred.

Dropping her hand to her side, she pressed her finger into the hole in the oil drum, cutting off the flow.

Let's see, the space between the components of one character is one unit. Between characters should be three units. Here we go again. . . . One . . . two . . . three . . .

The numbers crawled by. Her arm ached. The stars wheeled in their arc across the sky. It was all a matter of time. There would be a chance if Harconan would give her enough of it. Two hours would do it. Two hours.

She held herself immobile, her body and the shadows the only shields she had between her actions and her guard. Occasionally she dared a look toward the deckhouse. Was his gaze still fixed on her? Or was his chin resting on his chest, the warm night wind and the steady slow pitching of the ship having taken its toll?

Then, beyond the cramping of her muscles and the numbing trudge of the numbers in her mind, Amanda heard the slamming of a hatch and the sound of Harconan's voice calling in Bahasa Indonesia up to the deckhouse.

She had almost finished the last unit. It would have to do. She stood up and moved forward hastily, stepping over the stain on the deck, moving away from it to the forepeak of the schooner's bow. As she walked she tried to wipe the diesel from her right hand onto the tarpaulins tied down over the oil drums.

Footsteps sounded on the wooden deck behind her.

"Amanda?"

"Don't worry," she replied. "I haven't thrown myself over the side yet."

She kept her eyes fixed forward into the velvet darkness, but she felt Harconan come up behind her. "I'm glad to hear it. And not just for the sake of your hostage value."

"I'm having a hard time believing that."

"Hmm, I agree, it is rather a bizarre situation, isn't it? And in honesty, I will confess that your presence here will prove useful in certain negotiations I intend to conduct with your government."

"So much for being a POW, then. I am a hostage in a terrorist scenario."

"Yes and no." He crossed his arms and leaned back against the stacked oil drums. "In appearance you will be, with a variety of dire threats hanging over your head. The reality is that while I intend to hold you for a time, it is my truest wish, on the body and soul of my grandfather, not to harm you."

"Why not, Makara?" She turned to face him. *All right, Mandy. Offer him his first name.* "Why not the real thing? Sending an amputated finger back with your demands is usually the first step, isn't it?"

"Amanda, come now, I'm being honest here with you. Be just and return the favor." He stood and rested his hands on her bare shoulders. "You know why I don't wish to harm you. I can understand your anger, your bitterness at being trapped like this. I can understand it very well because we are so alike in so many ways. Even at war with one another, the soul recognizes its mate and the instinct reaches out. Call me a liar. Tell me that what happened between us at Palau Piri wasn't real?"

She couldn't. He was right. It had been true, the true and honest passion of two eager and hungry animals drawn to each other for their hour of mating. The politics and posturing were a matter beyond that moment.

"No, for that you aren't lying."

It wasn't too difficult to let herself sink forward against

Harconan's chest. On one level there was much in what he had to say. She could acknowledge that, at least to herself. She could even accept the pleasure of having those powerful, muscular arms close around her.

"There," he whispered into her hair. "This is a truth. Give me a chance, Amanda. Give me a chance to show you about other things, other plans. There is so much more to what is happening here. Maybe we can find some other truths between us presently."

"Maybe," Amanda whispered.

"Have you thought about my offer of parole?" he inquired.

Amanda hesitated a few moments more, as if fighting the internal battle he might expect. The simple reality was that she would readily give her parole. She would also cold-bloodedly break it at whatever opportune moment might present itself. She had no problem with that at all within her personal code of morality. An oath and an allegiance could only be given once. Long ago she had given hers to her nation and her service. That was a truth as well.

"All right, Makara. I guess it doesn't make any sense not to. You have my parole."

His arms tightened around her. "A wise woman! No escape tries and no troublemaking? Agreed?"

"You have my word. No escape tries and no troublemaking." She let a hint of humor creep into her voice. "Just at the moment, I don't see too many openings for either one."

Harconan laughed. "You have none at all, my beautiful captive, none at all. Relax and enjoy captivity. Savor the adventure of it. Tomorrow will be an interesting day."

"What happens tomorrow?"

"You'll see. I have a surprise for you. I think you'll be impressed."

Amanda thought of the thin stream of oil trailing in the schooner's wake. *And I, my magnificent bastard, may have a surprise for you.*

BUMP THE ARAFURA RUN AND WESTERN NEW GUINEA TO
THE HEAD OF THE STACK THIS WATCH, LINDIE. MAX PRI-
ORITY.

Air Force Technical Sergeant Linda "Lindie" Peterson
swore and set aside her cup of drink-dispenser coffee and
breakfast Danish to answer the E-memo that had snapped
into existence on her workstation's secondary screen.
She'd just barely made it through the door of her cubicle
and her watch officer was already declaring a Chinese fire
drill.

"Go ahead," the imaging analyst muttered under her
breath. "Take the joint service assignment with the damned
Navy, Lindie. It's a good ticket to get punched and the kids
will love Hawaii."

Savagely she clattered a reply back into her keyboard.
EXCUSE ME, LIEUTENANT, BUT WE ALREADY HAVE MAX
PRIS ON BOTH THE NORTHERN CHINA AND BLACK SEA
RUNS. WHAT IS OUR EXACT TASKING ORDER?

The reply scrolled back across her screen. ALL INDONE-
SIA SWEEPS HAVE ULTIMATE MAX PRI UNTIL FURTHER NO-
TICE. THAT'S THE WORD FROM THE MAN, EDDIE MAC
HIMSELF. SAME FROM COMMANDER RENDINO. DO IT PER-
FECTLY YESTERDAY!

CAN I ASK WHAT WE'RE SUPPOSED TO BE LOOKING FOR,
LIEUTENANT? Lindie typed.

QUOTE "ANYTHING UNUSUAL." GET ON IT, SERGEANT.

She groaned and accessed the section tasking file. She
found that she had been assigned a multispectral comparison run on the easternmost peninsula of New Guinea using
an imaging block just downloaded from one of the big
NSA Keyhole 13 reconsats. In essence, her day's labor
would be to play a titanic game of "Compare these pictures" involving a half-million square miles, seeking for
terrain and environmental differences that might become
apparent as images taken at various levels of the infrared,
ultraviolet, and visible spectra were matched and com-

pared. Variances in the imaging under different light forms might reveal evidence of human activity not apparent to the naked eye. For example, dying vegetation that had been cut and deployed as camouflage would reflect light differently than undamaged living plant life.

It would be a finicky, time-consuming job that required the sharpness of the human eye and the flexibility of the human mind.

Lindie lit off the two big thirty-inch analysis screens that overlooked her workstation console. Pausing to snap a bite out of her Danish, she called up the first sector scan.

Some four hours later her uniform jacket was draped over the back of her chair, her blouse collar was undone, and the crumbs of her pastry-and-coffee breakfast had been replaced with the remnants of a canned-soda-and-cheese-sandwich lunch. With her eyes burning, she continued the analysis drill. Pull up a satellite photograph of a block of the New Guinea coast as seen from a high altitude baseline on her A screen, then pull up the same image in an alternative light spectrum on the B screen, matching the two for deviations. When one was found, it was coordinated for further investigation at a lower baseline.

Lindie had completed the sweep of her block at twenty-, ten-, and five-kilometer altitude equivalencies and had found nothing extraordinary. That merely meant that now she must re-grid her block to a smaller scale and start over again from one K.

Her eyes burned and she took a moment to rub some tear moisture back into them with the heels of her hands. Simply to look at something different for a moment, she called up the base scale image of her analysis zone on her screens; that was the view of eastern New Guinea as seen unmagnified from low-earth orbit.

And caught something.

The spectrum imaging on her A and B screens had been slaved together. When she had called up the standard spectrum view of New Guinea on her A screen, the B screen had pulled up an IR variant of the same image. And there was a differentiation.

An odd little broken streak cut across the bottom of the infrared image. Nothing was apparent on the visible light photo. Possibly it was just a transmission or processing flaw.

Then again, maybe it wasn't.

It was also far out of Lindie's tasked analysis block, being well out in the Banda Sea off the coast. That, however, was irrelevant. A good photoanalyst has mongoose blood, the instinctive need to go and find out. Using her computer mouse, she windowed around the irregularity, then blew it up to full-screen size.

Minutes later she was dialing her watch officer's office number. This wasn't a matter for an E-memo.

"Lieutenant Morgan, this is Sergeant Peterson. I think I may have stumbled across something pretty hot here. It's out of my area, but it is in the Indonesian operations zone.... Yes, sir, Southeast Asian quadrant four.... Sector I-A-9...Block 30.... Try altitude baseline 50K in the infrared.... Yes, sir, I concur, a definite surface reflectivity variant, and that has got to be an artificial pattern.... Yes, sir, I would say that counts as an 'anything unusual.'"

A kiss and a cupped hand over her right breast brought Amanda awake the next morning.

The bunk in the schooner's master cabin was wider and equipped with a better mattress. Amanda had enjoyed both amenities without shame, just as for long hours she had savored the fiery lovemaking of Makara Harconan.

She had allowed herself to be carried here the night before, surrendering after another round of perfunctory protests.

She returned the kiss and intimate caress, opening her eyes to Harconan's soft chuckle. "Good morning," he whispered, leaning in over her. "Is being a captive all that bad?"

"I'll let you know after I see what breakfast is like."

He laughed again and drew back from the bunk. Harconan had apparently been up and about for some time. He'd shaved and was clad in light khaki trousers and a short-sleeved military-cut shirt. Crossing to a wall locker, he removed a similar set of clothing.

"Here," he said, tossing the garments across to Amanda. "We're not going to have to be quite so security-conscious presently. I think you'll find these a bit more comfortable than a *sarung,* although you did look most charming yesterday."

"Thank you, sir," she replied, sitting up to catch the clothing. "Uh, excuse me, but how about underwear?"

"Women are never satisfied. You could be grateful that I was able to find pants and shirt aboard in your size. I might have decided to leave you in that *sarung* or, better yet, in just a pair of these." He flipped her sandals onto the deck beside the bunk.

Amanda softened her voice and looked away as she slipped the shirt on. "Excuse me, I forgot my place as your prisoner."

Harconan hesitated, then crossed to the bunk. Sitting on its edge, he slipped his arm around her. "I rather wish you would, Amanda. I wish that, for the next few days, you might consider yourself a guest of the Bugis people rather than a prisoner."

"I believe Saddam Hussein once used the same line." Keeping her eyes averted, Amanda could only hope she was not overplaying her role in either direction. With her strategy set, she must not seem to give ground too readily; yet on the other, she must appear to be vulnerable to a seduction over to Harconan's side.

She felt Harconan squeeze her shoulders. "Amanda, please, there are events taking place here that go far beyond piracy and the loss of your satellite. Things are going to change in this part of the world. For the sake of your nation and mine, I ask you only for an open mind."

Amanda counted to three and hesitantly looked back into Harconan's face. "Well, it never hurts to listen."

"It doesn't. Now, finish getting dressed, and hurry; there

is something you'll want to see. This morning you'll breakfast in the stronghold of the sea king."

With a final smile and a kiss on her forehead, he departed.

A bolt was still thrown on the other side of the cabin door, and Amanda sensed the presence of a guard in the passageway.

So far, Amanda mused as she pulled on her slacks, her act was holding her audience. Or at least to the extent that Harconan was willing to maintain his own façade.

Or could it be more than a façade?

As in her old cabin, a small salt-clouded mirror was bolted to one bulkhead. Amanda looked into it, still mildly startled at the dark-haired visage that looked back. She studied the high-cheekboned face with its start of horizon crows'-feet at the corner of the eyes. She acknowledged being reasonably good-looking and she'd been exceptionally fortunate in having some very attractive and dynamic men in her life, but she couldn't see how this visage could ever be a valid justification for the launching of a thousand ships. She couldn't see it, but then, there was no accounting for taste.

This was a duty quite different from any other she'd ever been called on to perform before. She had an instinctive dislike for both lying and for using a personal relationship in this way, even with a foe like Harconan. Stark feminine and military practicality pushed that aside, however.

Harconan had chosen the tune, but she would interpret the dance in her own way. If it required that she lie in his arms and accept his frankly delicious passion, so be it. If, for the moment, all she could do was to serve as a distraction, drawing Harconan's time and focus away from his confrontation with the task force, so be it. She would fight with whatever was in the shot locker.

One factor that helped keep the taste of betrayal out of her mouth was Makara's apparent assumption that she, Captain Amanda Lee Garrett, USN, could be seduced away from her life's worth of duty to her nation and the Navy.

She arched an eyebrow in the mirror. *Sorry, darling, it's very nice. But every man I've ever met has one.*

She found a rubber band suitable for binding her hair back. She did appreciate this offering of western-style clothing, though. But did he mean that deck security was no longer so critical?

She slipped her feet into the sandals and knocked on the louvered cabin door. Her old friend with the Sterling machine pistol pulled the bolt and fell back.

It was a dazzlingly bright morning, with the rising sun streaking across the oil-smooth surface of the sea. The bow wave boiled under the upswept stem of the *pinisi,* the spray kicking wide. The coaster was driving hard, its powerful diesel hammering at what must be close to full power. As Amanda came on deck, she couldn't help but look aft for any sign of possible pursuit. There was none, the sea and sky being devoid of any other traffic.

The *pinisi* was standing in toward a low green coast that extended out to the horizon mists to the eastward. Well inland, a cloud-capped mountain range, massive even by Indonesian standards, reared into the sky, and Amanda caught a hint of earth, corruption, and growing things on the wind.

New Guinea. It had to be.

Shading her eyes with her hand, Amanda could make out no sign of human habitation along the shore. There was, however, a narrow cape extruding from the bulk of the coastline. The coaster seemed to be steering for the tip of this headland.

Patiently her guard stood back on the deck, the Sterling casually aimed at the small of her back. Amanda continued up the exterior ladder to the schooner's wheelhouse.

Harconan was present, along with the Bugis skipper manning the wheel. Some of the other bronze-skinned crewmen were working on deck, rolling the tarpaulins off the deck cargo and preparing to clear the forward deck hatches.

"A beautiful morning," Harconan commented.

"It's going to be a hot one, though."

"They all are here. You'll get acclimated."

Amanda casually made her way to the port side of the wheelhouse. Looking forward, she checked to see if last night's deliberate oil stain stood out against the accidental deck scarring.

And that was another problem. From the look of things, they were getting ready to work cargo. Would they pass off one empty oil drum as a routine shipping loss, or might somebody figure it to be something else?

She shot a glance at Harconan. Makara was not stupid, but then, what she had tried with the oil was so totally off the wall that it should never occur to him.

Unfortunately, it might not occur to anyone in the task force either.

"We seem to be in a hurry to get somewhere," she commented, probing.

"Quite so. We have an appointment to not keep with one of your ocean surveillance satellites."

Amanda's brow knit. "You have an orbital traffic schedule for our recon sats?"

Harconan lifted his hands and gave a boyish grin. "What can I say: I have friends in high places. One of your Keyhole spy satellites will be coming over our horizon in perhaps another forty-five minutes. Best we're out of sight by then."

"That'll be a trick."

"One of many I possess. Watch and be amazed, my beautiful Amanda. I'm proud of this."

The tip of the cape grew steadily closer. Amanda could make out towering black lava cliffs with the distinctive columnar pattern of water-cooled basalt and obsidian, the facings at least three times the height of the schooner's masts. Another mast height of verdant jungle growth topped the cliffs, while waves broke to white foam at their feet.

As the range continued to close, Amanda could make out the moss streaks on the stone and the giant ferns overhanging the cliff edge. She frowned as she also made out the swirl of the sea around jagged lava outcroppings at the cliff base. They were working in fast and close, and this *pinisi* didn't seem to run to accessories such as a fathometer.

"Pardon me for asking you your business, Makara, but how much water do we have under us?"

He chuckled. "Enough for a supertanker. There's an almost sheer dropoff around the cape to a five-hundred-foot bottom."

She shook her head, her mariner's instincts kicking in. "It would be hell to be caught off of this thing in a bad easterly. No holding ground for anchors. If you didn't have the power to haul off shore, you'd be finished."

"Not if you know the secret, Amanda. Watch."

The *pinisi* skipper was paying off, cutting across the tip of the headland. As he did so, the stone cliffs seemed to move, to gape silently open. It was a startling effect until one realized it was an optical illusion.

The tip of the cape was actually bifurcated into two smaller peninsulas, a narrow inlet curving in between them. The cliffs on either side of the inlet were of uniform height and coloration: Given a little distance and heat shimmer, the passage between them was all but invisible from sea level.

The Bugis vessel was slowing and nosing into the inlet now, its skipper lifting one hand from the wheel to sound the air-horn in a sharp long-short-long.

"There's plenty of water here as well. We're in a dredged channel."

"A dredged channel. Who dredged it, and why?"

Harconan only smiled.

The passage might be four hundred feet wide, the channel itself extending perhaps a quarter mile into the heart of the peninsula before coming to a dead end at yet another cliff. The muttering idle of the schooner's engines reverberated between the inlet's walls, and the muggy heat was magnified with the loss of the sea breeze. Lost also was the smell of the sea, replaced totally by the musty organics of the landside jungle.

Amanda looked up from the open wheelhouse windows and studied the looming cliffs. She started as a human figure seemed to materialize on cliff edge, dispassionately looking down at the passing ship.

He wasn't Bugis. Amanda could tell that even from here. He was tall and slender and almost as dark as the lava rock of the cliffs, a Melanesian, one of the true New Guinea natives. He appeared naked save for a bandolier and an automatic rifle.

So, Harconan and his pirates had land-based allies.

As her perception adapted to the terrain, she began to make out other irregularities along the cliff edge: stacked lava-rock fortifications, deeply concealed in the vegetation, and the telltale straightness of gun barrels under camouflage netting.

"Look ahead." It was a two-word command from Harconan.

Amanda obeyed, glancing forward. And the hair on the back of her neck stood up as again the rock began to move.

Once more it was an optical illusion. This time a man-made one. Beneath a rocky overhang at the head of the inlet, the "cliffside" was parting like a theater curtain.

It *was* a curtain—a huge, masterfully painted camouflage tarpaulin retracting on a set of powered overhead tracks. Its parting revealed a rectangle of shadow marked with sparks of artificial light.

As the schooner drew closer, Amanda began to make out shapes within the shadow.

"Damn, damn, damn!" she murmured. "That's a ship in there!"

"Very much of a ship." Harconan agreed.

No mere *pinisi,* either, but at least three hundred feet of modern oceangoing transport. Amanda could make out a massive slab-sided stern house, the stern drive-through gate of an LST- or LSM-type amphib, and a distinctive flat-topped bow structure.

"The MV *Harconan Flores,* I presume," Amanda said with rueful respect. "No wonder we couldn't find her anywhere."

Harconan rested his hand on her shoulder. "You didn't know the right rocks to turn over."

The radar mast had been folded flat to permit the ship's entry into the cavern. Amanda noted another alteration as well—a restoration, actually. The ex–East German amphib's gun turrets had been remounted on their hardpoints. Twin 37mm autocannon stood bore-sighted down the inlet approaches.

The *pinisi* slid into the shadow of the cavern. Looking overhead, Amanda could make out a network of rusted cross girders helping to support the lava-rock ceiling. The cavern was apparently a combination of man-made and natural work, a sea cave almost as large as the Sea Lion Caves of the Oregon coast.

Wooden docking piers ran down either side of the cavern. The pilings were dark and ancient, but the deck planking showed the golden sheen of new wood. The *Harconan Flores* was moored on the right-hand dock, leaving a gap adequate for the *pinisi* to fit between its steel hull and the left-hand pier.

A second schooner already lay alongside that dock, leaving space astern for Amanda and Harconan's vessel. In a masterful display of ship handling, the Bugis skipper worked his craft into the remaining cramped slot. With a final burst of reversing power, he rang her down and brought her to a halt with her bowsprit overhanging the stern castle of the craft ahead and the flank of his ship just brushing the pier fenders. Mooring lines were passed off between the *pinisi*'s deckhands and the pier-side stevedores.

There were several dozen people visible within the cavern confines. Bugis, darker Melanesians, and even a few paler-skinned Caucasians. Cargo was being unloaded from the other docked schooner, deck work and maintenance was under way aboard the *Flores,* and a number of heavily armed guards prowled in the shadows. A sandbagged emplacement also stood at the head of the left-side pier. Amanda recognized the quad .50-caliber barrels of an old American-made M-55 antiaircraft mount supplementing the *Flores*'s guns in the defense of the stronghold.

The coaster's diesels clattered to a stop. Replacing the sound was the grinding whine of electric motors drawing the camouflage curtain closed, walling out the daylight. A chill touched Amanda as the cavern basalt leached the warmth out of the puff of tropic air that had entered with the *pinisi*.

"I am impressed, Makara," she said softly. "This is incredible. An old Japanese installation, isn't it?"

He nodded in the half-illumination of the cave's scattered work lights. "It was intended as a submarine pen but it was never used as such. The cape was cut off and isolated during the Allied counterinvasion. It was forgotten by the Japanese and never discovered by your forces. Come, let me show you around. The story is more incredible than you could even imagine."

They descended from the wheelhouse to the schooner's deck, Amanda's guard still trailing them wordlessly. A portable power crane had already moved into position at dockside and the first slingload of fuel drums was being lifted off the *pinisi*'s deck.

Harconan swept his hand toward the landing ship moored at the opposing dockside. "I'll have us moved into the master's cabin of the *Flores* tonight. Electric lights, a shower, and all the hot water you wish—and a real bed. Captain Onderdank won't be pleased, but after all, I am the owner."

"It sounds very nice, Makara." Amanda hooked her thumb back over her shoulder at her guard. "Will *he* be standing behind me in the shower too?"

Harconan grimaced and spoke a quick phrase to the guard. The seaman uncocked and slung his machine pistol and withdrew.

"I gave you my parole, Makara." Amanda didn't push to the point of trying to sound hurt, but she did soften her voice. "I'm not going anywhere."

"No, you are not. You are literally at the end of the world here, Amanda. Above and beyond my garrison here, you have better than a hundred kilometers of lethally inhospitable jungle between you and the nearest civilization. You wouldn't last a day."

Gauging carefully, she hardened her response. "I said I gave you my parole."

He sighed. "You have my apologies. But please recall your own rather formidable reputation."

"Well, I suppose you have a point there. But I assure you, I'm not Sheena, Queen of the Jungle." With ground won and with a hint more freedom of action gained, she disengaged blades with a smile. "Now, what's the story about this place?"

"Ah, as I said, the Japanese engineering unit constructing this facility was apparently cut off in 1943. Yet, they continued to work, constructing the tunnel complex and enlarging the main cavern, awaiting the day when they would reestablish contact with other Imperial Japanese forces."

Genuinely interested, Amanda listened as they descended the gangway to the cave-side pier.

"As far as I have been able to tell," Harconan continued, "they never learned the war ended. They just kept building and waiting."

"You mean they refused to give up even after the Japanese surrender, like the holdouts on Guam and in the Philippines?" She let her eyes play across the stack of cases on the pier that had been unloaded from the other schooner. Rifle cases maybe. And the labeling on them was either French or Belgian. And that was a stack of mortar base plates.

"Apparently they never even heard of the surrender," Harconan continued, "or they refused to believe it. There were a hundred and fifty men in the garrison, and they stayed on under Imperial military discipline, their ranks thinning out slowly under starvation and disease. A few desertions took place, but none apparently ever made it out."

"How long?" she inquired, looking up at the shadowed cavern roof with new respect for its builders.

"I found the commanding officer's log in a footlocker in what must have been his quarters in one of the lateral tunnels. The date of the last entry translated as March 17, 1979. He and four others were left and he was dying. His last words were an apology to the Emperor for his weakness."

"That was a soldier."

"He was," Harconan agreed. "I've preserved that log. One day, when it is possible, I will see that it is returned to his family. Such devotion deserves honor."

Amanda found that she could honestly give Harconan's hand a squeeze after that. There was so very much they stood at odds over, but he was right: There were also things that they could agree on as well.

The pier ended at a broad shelf cut out of the living rock that extended across the full width of the cavern head. The bow boarding ramp of the *Harconan Flores* had been lowered and rested on this shelf. Beyond the LSM's ramp, a large tentlike affair had been deployed. It glowed green, bright internal lighting burning through the thin fabric of its structure.

"Come," Harconan said. "It's time you had a look at what brought you here."

Air conditioners, dehumidifiers, and air-filtration units rumbled softly as they approached the structure, and Amanda realized that she was looking at an ad hoc "clean room," a contained and sterile artificial environment keeping at bay the hostile natural elements of the cavern.

Harconan opened the zippered door of a small side compartment.

Within was a bulging wall of transparent plastic and INDASAT 06.

Amanda could see now that it wasn't a "tent" in a classic sense but rather a positive-pressure inflatable structure. The pirated spacecraft lay cradled on a white painted lowboy trailer within this protective cocoon. A score or more of the service and access panels gaped open in its reentry-scoured outer shell, revealing gleaming systems and experiment bays. Half a dozen men clad in green surgical scrubs and white gauze masks worked around the massive lozenge-shaped hull, like coroners conducting an autopsy on a beached whale.

Even with their faces covered, Amanda had little difficulty matching the men to their names and photos she'd seen in the NAVSPECFORCE database. The two Asians would be Rei and Wa, the representatives from the Korean combine; the two Arabs must be Kalil and Hammik from the Gulf states. And the single East Indian and Slav would be Sonoo and Valdechesfsky for the Indian outfit.

It was Sonoo who noticed the presence of the two observers. He heaved his portly bulk up from behind the laptop he'd been addressing on a field desk and crossed to the plastic containment window. He gave a quick, nervous nod and spoke in a precise but accented English. "Mr. Harconan, it is good to see you again. Good. Have you received word yet from my superiors?"

"Yes, I have, Doctor," Harconan replied. "I have good news for all of you. Your superiors are impressed with your initial findings and are agreeable to the next phase of the operation. Once certain financial exchanges are dealt with, we'll be ready to proceed."

"Very good, excellent." The technologist gave another quick, birdlike bob of his head, the gesture out of place from a man of his dimension. "We have done very good work here. I have much to transmit. But we need improved facilities now, elsewhere from this place. This is understood?"

There was a questioning, almost a pleading, to the man's voice, matched by the expression in the dark eyes peering over the mask. Amanda sensed the East Indian was not enthralled with his current working environment.

"Don't worry, my friend," Harconan said jovially. "Things are proceeding and we'll have you and your associates under way for civilization shortly."

Sonoo glanced questioningly in Amanda's direction.

"Oh, excuse my manners," Harconan continued. "I should make a formal introduction at this time; however, I feel that under the circumstances we can all understand the wisdom of a degree of anonymity."

Amanda decided she had been playing passive long enough; it was time to put a shot into somebody's waterline. "Oh, I'm quite well acquainted with the work of both Dr.

Sonoo and with Dr. Valdechesfsky, his associate at Marutt-Goa." She locked eyes with the startled East Indian. "Taking part in an industrial hijacking is not going to look good on a résumé, Doctor."

Sonoo blanched. "Who is she, Harconan? Who is she?"

Harconan's jaw tightened in anger and his hand closed painfully about Amanda's upper arm. "No one you have to concern yourself with, Doctor. Continue with your work. I'll discuss departure preparations with the teams later."

Harconan dragged her out of the observation tent. Half a dozen rough shoves took her to the rock wall at the rear of the cavern. A steel-hard hand locked around her throat, pinning her back against the slime-damp stone. The pirate chief loomed over her, outlined in the glow of the work lights. Amanda glared back her own defiance.

"You gave me your word, Amanda," Harconan said, his voice dangerously soft. "You promised no trouble."

"That was before I realized that I was being lied to as well," she shot back, "by you."

"What are you talking about?"

"Remember who you're talking to, Makara. I'm not a fool! You told me you were holding me hostage, presumably to get Admiral MacIntyre and NAVSPECFORCE to back off and let you complete delivery of the INDASAT to your buyers. But then we came to this place, your prime base, you started giving me the grand tour. This cavern, your ship, the satellite, and the industrial technicians you have working on it. You've let me see way too much, Makara, from the moment I woke up. It was stupid of me not to see it before. You don't any intention of releasing me, do you, Makara? I'm never getting out of here alive, am I?"

For the duration of ten rapid heartbeats, Amanda thought that maybe she had overplayed her hand. Either that, or inadvertently she had blurted out the truth.

Harconan's hand slipped from her throat to her shoulder. "No, Amanda, you're wrong." The softness in his voice didn't have the steel behind it this time. "I have sworn to you that you will not be harmed unless you force me into it. You're correct, you aren't going to be released, at least not immediately. There are things I am trying to bring about. Things I am trying to do for the sake of all the peoples of Indonesia. I've brought you here to learn about them."

The taipan lifted his hand from her shoulder, holding it out to her beseechingly. "I want to explain my dreams, Amanda. So that someday, not too far in the future, you can go out and explain them to the world. You will be free again, Amanda, I promise. Free to go. Free to come back"—Harconan's voice sank to a whisper—"free to stay. Just give me time to explain!"

"It's going to take a lot of explaining, Makara, to the world and to me. Kidnapping, terrorism, piracy, the theft of other people's dreams..." She nodded toward the inflated containment module holding the INDASAT.

Harconan glanced over his shoulder. "That? That's just business, Amanda, just business. I steal it from *your* industrialists and sell it to *their* industrialists. They'll work on it for a while and make a few improvements, and then *your* industrialists will come along and steal it back again. In the long run everyone gains."

"What about the crew of the *INDASAT Starcatcher,* Makara?" she asked, verbally clawing at him with deliberation. "What did they gain?"

She heard the breath hiss between his teeth. His hand went past her head and he braced himself against the wall.

"How did you find out about Sonoo and the others?" he demanded, changing the subject.

"I can't tell you, Makara. You know that."

"How much more do you and your admiral know?"

"I can't tell you that, either. If you want me to understand you, Makara, you have to understand me." She was careful to invoke his first name again, careful to choose her words. "I will not betray my people, not even for you."

She trailed off that final hinted possibility.

Frustration edged Harconan's voice. "This isn't a game, Amanda! I have my people to think about as well."

"I'm aware of that."

His hand went back to her throat, thumb and middle finger digging in beneath her jaw. "Damn you, you could be made to talk! Everyone talks eventually."

"I'm aware of that, too, Makara," she replied calmly. She was leaning over the edge now. Deliberately testing. "But if you've studied me as much as you say you have, you'll know I'm a 'Mustang' graduate. You'll know what that means. I can hold out a long, long time before I break. After your people are finished, what's left won't be worth taking to bed."

"Damn it, Amanda! There are other ways...drugs..."

"I know about them too," She let a hint of sadness tinge her voice. "I know how to fight them as well. If you want to be sure of the answers you'll get, you're going to have to put me under so deep I probably won't come back. No is the only answer I can give, my love, so you decide and let's just get on with it."

She'd called him her love. Would that be her ticket back from the edge?

The pressure under her jaw eased and his hand dropped. He looked away, then lifted his voice, calling over a couple of the cavern security guards. Curtly he issued them a command.

"These men will take you to the cabin on the *Flores*. You'll be held there for now."

Amanda didn't reply.

As promised, the captain's cabin aboard the freighter had been modernized and given a comfortable civilian conversion, complete with mock teak-paneled bulkheads, a queen-size bed instead of bunks, air-conditioning, and an attached head.

The dogging nuts on the two exterior portholes were also torqued down to the point where they were immobile without a wrench, and the steel fire door had a newly added exterior bolt that was thrown after the door had closed behind her.

Amanda crossed to the cabin's built-in couch and sank down upon it, her arms crossed over her stomach in a self-embrace. For the first time in days she was cool, but that wasn't why she was shivering.

She'd pushed it close by scaring Sonoo that way, very close indeed. No doubt anonymity had been promised to both the technicians and the firms they'd represented. That their names were known on the outside was probably a very unpleasant surprise that would have those tech reps sweating and Harconan doing some tall explaining.

She'd had to do it, though. Harconan could read her too well. He was expecting some kind of fight from her. If she let herself be too submissive, too pliant—if she yielded on too many points too rapidly—he'd scent the falsehood.

On the other hand, dicing with kings could be a dangerous sport. Henry VIII had probably been quite fond of Anne Boleyn right up until she'd gotten mouthy that one time too often.

Amanda stood up abruptly. Crossing to the head, she checked the shower to see if she was within water hours. She was. Stripping off her single layer of clothing, she stepped under the water, turning it up as hot as she could stand.

When she emerged, sleek and steaming, a few minutes later, she was redheaded again, the dye having washed out. Somehow that made her feel better.

What did he really want from her? Why was he holding back? Why was he risking his kingdom? Could she actually be that attractive in Harconan's eyes? She couldn't be that good of a lay.

Was it truly something more?

"Damn, damn, damn," she murmured to the empty room. "I guess he's as big an idiot as I am."

The word didn't have to be passed when the priority data dump came in from NAVSPECFORCE HQ. In the face of the multiple layers of steel and sound insulation around the joint intelligence center, Christine Rendino's piercing scream of joy and triumph echoed through the *Carlson*'s passageways.

Five minutes later, Admiral MacIntyre was in JIC, studying an image on the central bulkhead flatscreen. To him it resembled a rather bizarre example of extremely esoteric modern art: a series of oblong blobs of a puckered yellow-orange curving across a light-green background.

"All right, Chris. What am I looking at?"

"Oil slicks, sir. Trace oil slicks in the Banda Sea as seen from low earth orbit. These were part of a multispectral reflectivity sweep of Indonesia taken this morning by an NIA Keyhole reconsat."

Obviously the image meant much more than that, because the little intel was on the verge of exploding. She was hugging herself, and tears glinted in the corners of her eyes. MacIntyre had never seen her grinning so before.

"And?" MacIntyre asked cautiously.

"And it's a message, sir. A message addressed to us."

Dubious, MacIntyre stared at the computer-enhanced blobs once more. "A message?"

"Yes, sir, a goddamn message! Jonesy, run the imaging correction program for wind and current drift."

The systems operator did so, and the oblong blobs snapped into a straight line. Suddenly it leaped off the screen into MacIntyre's face. "That's Morse code!"

"Yes, sir, with the exact three-to-one unit and character spacings: dot dash, *A,* break, dash dash dot, *G. A G,* Amanda Garrett! She's telling us where she is in a line of code fifteen miles long!"

"By God!" MacIntyre's fist lifted with deliberation, smashing down on the seat back of the workstation he was standing behind. "By God! How did she manage that?"

"Amanda must have remembered how we backtracked the *INDASAT Starcatcher* to her sinking point by her trace oil slick. She must have banked on us doing another multi-spectral sweep of the archipelago."

"What's the position on this thing?"

"The more important question is, sir, is: What was its position when it was laid? Jonesy, give us the chart on the eastern Banda Sea on Display Two, then designate the time- and drift-adjusted coordinates of the slick."

Christine continued excitedly, "The imaging center ran an analysis of the slick's pattern of dispersal and distortion, applying the Banda Sea current patterns from our oceanographic database and the regional weather states for the past forty-eight hours. Their best estimate is that the slick was generated sometime yesterday evening at this position: northeast of the Kai Island group, in the western approaches to New Guinea, about a hundred and seventy-five miles off the coast. They figure it was produced by a surface craft with a rate of advance of about ten to twelve knots, maintaining a heading of east by northeast."

"For how long, though?"

"A considerable distance, sir. Jonesy, back off imaging magnification by point five."

The multispectral view snapped back to half its size in the center of the display. Beyond the code-patterned section of the slick, a long, continuous streak of oil continued. Drift-adjusted, it pointed dead on toward the underside of New Guinea's Bomberai Peninsula.

"We were able to maintain the track to within eighty miles of the coast, sir, with no deviation in course or speed. We've always known New Guinea to be a prime potential site for the INDASAT hide, and this proves it out. That's probably where they're taking her right now."

MacIntyre studied the time hack at the corner of the screen. "Yesterday evening. That means they've had more than enough time to reach the hide and go to ground."

"But, Admiral," the intel protested, "at least we now know that Amanda has to be somewhere on that stretch of coast!"

"All too true, Chris," he replied, leaning on the seat back. "We know that she's somewhere on the wildest, least-known, most dangerous stretch of coast on the entire planet."

Crab's Claw Cape   1700 Hours, Zone Time: August 23, 2008

Amanda remained locked in the *Flores*'s captain's cabin for most of the day. Abstractedly, she wondered how long her banishment from the sea king's presence would last. Her deliberate revelation of how much the task force knew about Harconan's INDASAT clientele was bound to foment trouble among the "staff," as it were, and serve as yet a further drain on Harconan's time and energy. For her next go-round with him she had better be ready to do some contrite damage-control work on her relationship with him.

If he gave her the chance.

If he didn't, she hoped they'd use the truth drugs. Dying of a scopolamine overdose would be far more pleasant than being dissected alive. Either way, she wouldn't have much to say about it. Accordingly she rejected the worry and spent the afternoon napping and mentally composing an intelligence report on all she had seen and heard.

There was no clock in the cabin, and in the eternal dusk of the cavern she could only surmise that it was about sunset when Harconan himself came for her.

He looked tired as he opened the cabin door; apparently even pirate kings could have a hard day at the office. "I thought you might like a little fresh air."

"I would, thank you," she replied quietly, rising from the cabin couch.

"Then come. I'd like you to meet someone."

He led her off the ship and across the cavern floor, her silent guard falling in step behind them but holding back a respectful distance.

Harconan guided her into one of the two tunnels at the rear of the cavern, the right-hand one. Close to the cavern, the passage was concrete-lined, with lateral tunnels branching off to what must be storerooms and underground barracks. Amanda counted her steps. There were four such laterals on the right at about fifty-foot intervals, and one on the left about a hundred feet in, a crossover she suspected to the other main tunnel. Grilled work lights were spaced out along the ceiling, and the air was cool and damp, smelling of slime and diesel fumes.

Beyond this section the concrete lining ended, revealing bare lava-rock walls, and the tunnel began to angle toward the surface, a dot of green light ahead marking their objective. Amanda was surprised at the distance they had to climb.

The tunnel ended in a huge concrete bunker. A massive set of rusted steel blast doors lay on the ground before the entry. The door framing was fractured, showing where high explosives had been used to blow the hinges out of their setting.

Harconan gestured toward them. "When we found this place, these outside entrances were closed and barred from the inside. When they knew their show was playing out, the last survivors of the Japanese garrison must have sealed themselves in as a last gesture of obedience to their orders to hold until relieved."

"Impressive," Amanda murmured, looking around.

So were the rest of her surroundings. Red sunlight angled down through the dense stand of areca palms, prehistoric-looking ferns sprouting densely around the bases of their trunks. After the cool of the tunnels, heat lay over the land in a smothering blanket. So did the silence, unbroken save for the stroking of the surf along the flanks of the peninsula and the exotic call of some bird or reptile. The air smelled of charcoal smoke and orchids.

It was as if they had stepped through a magical doorway into some primeval wilderness. Amanda halfway expected to turn around and see a stegosaurus munching on a fern clump. Instead, a tall Melanesian warrior drifted past the overgrown bunker, unashamedly naked save for a *koteka* penis sheath; his bare feet were soundless. The only jarring note to the primitive image was the all-too-modern FALN assault rifle he carried.

"A friend of yours?" Amanda inquired.

Harconan smiled. "Of a fashion. Come, I want you to meet another."

They walked on to the southern cliffside of the peninsula to a point where a view could be had of both the sea and the New Guinea coast. There, another Melanesian awaited them, an older man; age had bent him and grayed his wiry hair. He wore the rags of a shirt and trousers, and yet, he radiated an immense dignity: Amanda sensed the leadership and wisdom in him. A very worn but well kept double-barreled shotgun of some indeterminate make leaned against the palm log on which he sat.

He nodded to them as they entered the clearing.

"Captain Garrett, this is my friend and my ally, Chief Akima of the Asmat. His tribes hold this stretch of coast."

"I am pleased to meet you, Captain," the Asmat replied gravely in good English, extending a hand.

Amanda accepted the firm, dry handshake. "And I am pleased to meet you, sir."

"Please, sit."

Amanda and Harconan accepted a log section across from the older man.

"Chief Akima is also a member of the Morning Star separatist movement," Harconan continued. "I trust you are acquainted with them."

"To a slight degree," Amanda replied, frowning. "I know that the Morning Star movement is a revolutionary group seeking independence for New Guinea from the Jakarta government. I also know that there has been a protracted low-grade guerrilla war ongoing between the Indonesians and the Morning Star movement for decades. I'm afraid that's all."

Chief Akima laughed. "Then, Captain, you know more than many, many people. Our people and our fight for freedom have been ignored by most of the world. We call ourselves the Operasi Papua Merdeka, the Free Papua Movement, although the Morning Stars is not a bad name. Papua is what we call our land, but we do not mind you to say New Guinea. It is better than what Sukarno named us:

Irian Jaya"—the chief's mouth twisted in distaste—"his 'victorious hot land rising from the sea.'"

"Bapak, would you tell the captain the story of the Morning Star?" Harconan asked. "It is best heard from your lips."

"If your lady would be interested."

"I would be," Amanda replied. "Very."

"As you wish." The chief nodded. "We are not of Indonesia or its peoples. Our skin is not their color. Our ways are not their ways. Our gods are not their gods. Nor do we wish them to be. Papua is our place, our land.

"In the last century, the Dutch came and planted their flag. But there were never many here, a few hundred. There was little to interest them, and they stayed in their trading posts along the coast, leaving our land to us in peace.

"Then came the great war, the World War Two, and the Japanese and your people came and fought here, many, many thousands. But you were like a wave breaking on a rock: You came and then you left again and still the land was ours and we were left in peace.

"But then the war ended and the Dutch tried to reclaim their colonies in Indonesia, but the time of colonies was past. Sukarno led a rebellion against them and the Dutch were driven out once more."

The chief gestured to the ground. "Everywhere but here. Here for a time they stayed. They knew by then that the age of colonies was past as well, and they began to work with our people, educating them, teaching them technical matters and administration. They said that soon they would be gone and we would be free, our own nation to find our own way. The Indonesians, Sukarno's government, claimed that Papua belonged to them. They used the promise of uniting Papua with the rest of Indonesia as a rallying cry to draw their people to them, promising them land and wealth— our land . . . our wealth!"

"Did they ever ask if you wanted to be united?" Amanda inquired.

The chief chuckled mirthlessly. "They launched their *konfrontasi* campaign against the Dutch with terrorism, propaganda, and political pressure against the Dutch 'colonialists.' In 1962 the Dutch went home and the Indonesians came to 'liberate' us. We were promised an 'Act of Free Choice,' a vote of our people on whether to join permanently with Indonesia or to become an independent nation. It was to happen in 1969, but when the time for the voting came, Sukarno decided we were too primitive, too savage and ignorant, to understand voting and to choose our own destiny. Instead, only special representative voters would take part in the election."

The chief held his leathery palm up flat. "As the Indonesians got to choose all of the representatives, is it a surprise that the vote was unanimous for joining with Indonesia?

"Since then we have found our brown-skinned colonial masters a heavier burden to bear than our former white ones. They tear open our mountains for the minerals there. Papua has the largest and richest copper mines in the world. The Indonesians share them with us. Jakarta takes the metal and the money and we get the poisons in our rivers.

"They share more, the *transmigrasi,* the surplus population from Java and their other islands. They gather them up and bring them here in their thousands every year, dreaming of the day when they will outnumber us. Walk in the coastal towns like Jayapura, Biak, and Wamena and look at the color of the skin of the shopkeepers and policemen and officials. Then look at the skin of those sweeping the streets, carrying the loads, and working as houseboys. Then you will see why the Morning Star has risen. Let the Dutch come back: We would greet them as brothers. But the Indonesians we will drive into the sea!"

The old man had never lifted his voice once. But his passion was plain.

"I can understand your cause. There is justice in it." Amanda glanced at the man sitting beside her. "But you are allies with Harconan, and he is an Indonesian."

The chief shrugged. "He hates Jakarta as much as we. He needs men to fight for him and to guard his bases here on Papua, and he pays us well with the supplies and arms we need for our battle. We shall be—what is the word?—yes, his *mercenaries,* for as long as it benefits us both."

She continued to gaze at Harconan. "Even if Harconan stands accused of being a pirate and criminal? It could damage your cause in the eyes of the world."

Chief Akima shrugged. "Harconan gives us guns, which is more than the world has given us."

"He tells quite a story, doesn't he?" Harconan said, standing with foot propped up on the palm log.

"He certainly does," Amanda replied, looking out to sea in the dimming light of the afternoon.

Akima had faded into his jungle, leaving the two alone on the cliff edge.

"Maybe you are willing to admit that things are not quite as simple as you think?"

Amanda sighed. "Makara, I've always been willing to admit that there is nothing simple in this part of the world. But I can't see how the murder of the crew of the *INDASAT Starcatcher* is justified by the Morning Star rebellion."

"In war there are casualties."

"And when did Australia and the United States declare war on you?"

"Damn it, Amanda"—Harconan took his foot off the log and paced a frustrated step or two—"you are a very frustrating woman."

"And you expected me not to ask these questions?"

"No...not at all. You're not stupid."

"Thank you for agreeing." She smiled.

"Then you agree there is a problem here—that something must be done!"

"I quite agree, Makara. Something must be done. But as a military officer, I must point out that war is a last best choice for the resolution of any problem. You are a man of great power in this part of the world: economic power, political power, personal power. If you want to help the Free Papua Movement you could do so in a hundred better ways than fomenting an escalation in what is bound to be an exceptionally bloody and ugly conflict."

"But it's not just the Morning Stars, Amanda; it's what is being done to the entire archipelago. Not just to New Guinea, but to all of the islands and all of the cultures here."

There was a fervor in Harconan's voice and an intent glint in his eye that told Amanda she was close to another truth with this man, the real motivation beyond mere wealth. She was coming close to where he lived.

"What is happening to them, Makara?" she prompted.

"They're being buried alive. You heard Chief Akima: The same story is being repeated with all the other islands as well. Indonesia has never been a representative government, it's always been Java-centric. The Javanese dominate the government and they want to dominate our cultures as well. Their battle cry is their national motto, 'Bhinneka tunggal ika,' 'The many are one'"—Harconan spat the phrase out—"but the only many that count are the Javanese, and the only one that rules is Jakarta. Is that a right thing, Amanda?"

"No, it isn't," she agreed somberly. "But what is there to take its place?"

The taipan sank down on the log beside her, lost in an image within his mind. "We go back to what Indonesia was before the coming of the Dutch and the Portuguese. Just islands in the sea. Each island independent unto itself, answerable to no one but itself. Each people and culture free to grow and develop in its own way."

"In some places that's called Balkanization, Makara. It's generally considered to be a bad thing."

"But not here, Amanda; this was how it was in Indonesia's golden age, and we could go back to what it once was."

He kept saying "we." What "we" was he speaking of? And the earnestness of him touched her. He wanted her to see his golden islands and revived glories as he did.

She covered one of his hands with hers. "I'm sorry, Makara, but a writer in my country once said that 'Paradise is inevitably either ahead, around the next corner, or back around the last.'"

"But it could be here and now, Amanda. If I had the right...*help* to do it. A confederacy of independent Indonesian states, each free in their own right but each united by..." He hesitated.

"Tell me, love, united by what?" Amanda challenged gently. "Or by whom?"

The moment was broken. Harconan stood abruptly. "It's getting on towards dark. We'd better get back down into the tunnels."

Amanda followed him silently. However, just before she entered the tunnel mouth, she looked back sharply over her shoulder. For a moment she had experienced that inexplicable but unnerving sensation of being stared at.

1732 Hours, Zone Time:
August 23, 2008

Joint Intelligence Center, USS *Carlson*

"Commander Rendino"—the systems operator at the drone control station lifted his VR-helmeted head, his voice sharp—"Curtin Base just tried to override me on G-Hawk Teal Deuce."

"Did you lose it?" Christine demanded, hurrying across the darkened center to lean down at the SO's shoulder.

"Nah, I got the signal strength on 'em. I jumped ops frequencies and regathered the aircraft. If those Air Force clowns keep screwing with us this way, they're going to dump us a bird."

"Is Teal Deuce still good with fuel?"

"I'm projecting we still have a good fifteen minutes to absolute bingo, ma'am."

"Then use all fifteen of them. I'll take care of the Air Force." She mashed her thumb down on the Transmit key of her headset belt unit. "Communications, patch me into the hot link to Curtin drone control! Expedite!"

From his seat across the compartment, Inspector Tran watched the fierce little blonde press the earphone tightly against the side of her head. It was interesting to see his irreverent and playful lover so transformed into the steel-willed warrior. A Hindu would say the shade of some past incarnation had come forward at need to guide her through her current crisis.

"Curtin, this is *Carlson* JIC. What in the hell are you guys playing at, aborting our search ops?... Screw the fuel reserves! We need every second of coverage we can pull with the Global Hawks.... Screw your standard operating procedure while you're about it! We'll cut your birds loose at absolute bingo and not one second before. Got that?... Glide 'em home if you have to!... Go ahead and call your squadron commander, Lieutenant. I'll see your lieutenant colonel and raise you a three-star admiral!"

She broke the connection. Noting Tran's level gaze, she grinned sheepishly. Brushing back her tousled bangs with her hand, she crossed to the inspector.

"God," she murmured, "you'd think I was some kind of a Navy puke or something."

"Easy, little one," he replied even more softly. "There is actually no real difficulty in, as you say, finding a needle in a haystack. Once you have ascertained the needle is there, everything else is merely a matter of patience."

"That's just it," Christine whispered back. "I'm beginning to wonder if the needle is in the haystack. All the evidence indicates Amanda is somewhere on the southern coast of New Guinea. That's where she pointed us to, but we still don't know for sure."

"Then work the possibility until you do know. Then, if required, move on to the next. That is the way of the investigator."

"I know, I know. " She put her back to the same bulkhead Tran had leaned against. "This should be like any other problem I've ever worked. It's only that..." Her words trailed off.

He rested his hand on her shoulder for a moment. "It's only that this time it involves someone who matters greatly to you. Thus, you must still do your job, but with a dagger driven into your heart."

Christine took an unsteady breath. "I wish it was appropriate to kiss you just now."

Tran smiled soberly. "In due course."

"Commander Rendino!" The call came from one of the real-time analysis tables. "We might have something here."

Christine and Tran were both across the center in an instant.

The analysis table was a horizontally mounted flatscreen display currently accessing the download being transmitted from one of the Global Hawk drones. The HDTV imaging was as clear and razor-sharp as a view downward through a window from five thousand feet.

A glance at the status hacks in the corner of the screen indicated the Remotely Piloted Vehicle was actually flying at eight times that altitude. Invisible from the earth's surface, it currently was cruising slowly southeastward along the New Guinea coast.

Approaching now along the RPV's track, a narrow peninsula jutted out from the New Guinea mainland. Perhaps a mile and a quarter in length, the tip of the peninsula was bifurcated by a narrow, curving inlet. Nguyen Tran thought it rather resembled the partially opened claw of a crab or lobster. The rampant greenness of the tropical forest covered the full length of the peninsula, while the surrounding waters were a deep and vivid blue, with little of the azure paleness that might denote shallows, even between the parting of the crab's claw.

"What do we have, Chief?" Christine demanded.

The female chief petty officer looked up from the screen. "A possible abnormality, ma'am. This imaging is from Teal Niner, currently between Jantan and Aiduna in that broken stretch of coast under the Bomberai Peninsula. In standard spectrum all you see are the treetops, but check out the thermographic scan."

The reconnaissance analyst tapped a sequence into the keyboard on the edge of the display table. The image of the little cape went to an inverted black and white, like a photographic negative. Now an entire constellation was revealed, glittering sparks of white light, dozens of them, scattered down the lengths of the crab's claw like a diamond incrustation.

"Open surface fires," Christine noted. "About the right size for cooking or mosquito smudges."

"Yes, ma'am," the analyst replied. "Enough for a good-sized village. But this isn't like any of the other coastal plain villages we've been seeing. Way too dispersed. More like a whole lot of independent camps in one general area."

"She's right," Tran commented. "There are no central village clearings and no outlying cleared areas for crop-raising. Also there is no easy access to the sea, no decent beaches, and there are cliffs all along the sides of the peninsula. They can't be fishermen or boatmen."

"Hunting parties?" Christine inquired.

"Not with that density," Tran replied. "The lowland jungles on Irian Jaya are very thick and lush, but they generally don't provide large amounts of food without cultivation. True hunter-gatherers would have to disperse more widely to survive. This concentration must be drawing on some other supply source than the local environment."

"If we have the average of eight to twelve people per fire, ma'am, we're looking at between three and four hundred people on that peninsula."

Christine lifted an eyebrow. "Nguyen, any suggestions about who these guys might be?"

Tran nodded. "My first thought would be we have stumbled upon a major staging base for the Morning Star separatist army. But why they'd be massing out here in the middle of nowhere is an open question."

Christine nodded. "Maybe. Chief, take us up to magnification ten."

A segment of the central peninsula windowed up to fill the display. Now each fire was a dancing crystalline dot surrounded by a hazy nimbus of radiant heat.

"Small cooking fires, ma'am, with the smoke dispersing under the tree cover," the recon analyst commented. "There are a couple of abnormalities here...here...and here."

Christine nodded. "Thermal plumes without a central

flame node. The fires there must be inside of buildings, with the heat escaping through a vent or a chimney."

"Yes, ma'am. That's what I thought," the analyst concurred. "And they must be pretty substantial buildings to damp the node that thoroughly. We're not talking about thatch-roofed huts here."

"This one appears different as well," Tran commented, pointing to a thermal trace at the bottom of the screen.

"It is," replied Christine. "Chief, window in on that and bring us up max mag."

Again the image expanded, the sensor turret on the distant drone swinging on the designated target.

"It seems to pulse regularly," Tran observed.

"Yeah," Christine agreed. "A definite thermal modulation. That's a diesel exhaust, and from a pretty big plant. There's no sign of anything like a road. It can't be a truck engine."

"No building or structure outline, either," the intelligence CPO commented. "More like its venting right out of the ground."

"Ain't that the truth, Chief. Shoot a thermocouple reading. What's the temperature of those exhaust gases at the emission point?"

A numeric data hack rezzed into existence beside the thermal trace. "One-forty-five Fahrenheit, ma'am. Cool."

"Which means a long exhaust pipe. Any sign of radar emissions in this sector? Any air traffic?"

"Negative, ma'am. Clean boards."

Christine hesitated for a moment, thinking. "All right. I want another run made over this peninsula, east to west this time, down the full length of it. It'll be active scan; we'll risk using the synthetic aperture radar. We'll also risk bringing the Hawk down to just above contrail height. Let's make it fast: We're coming up on sundown and I don't want to risk that drone being spotted because of underlighting."

"Aye, aye, ma'am! We're on it."

Christine looked into Tran's face, a hot glimmer of hope

in her eyes. "Keep reminding me about patience and the haystack."

Beyond the crab-claw–shaped cape, which had no name recognized by civilization, the sun touched the brooding bulk of the Jayawijaya range, the arched and buckled spine of New Guinea. Soon would come the night and the minute lessening of the day's smothering heat.

Around the perimeter of the peninsula, two-score pairs of eyes swept the jungle and the sea. The vision of some of these lookouts was augmented with powerful binoculars. With others, the only augmentation came from a hunter's instincts honed from a lifetime lived in this verdant and deadly environment.

Among this latter group, a few, like Amanda Garrett, felt a faint, passing uneasiness, a sourceless sensation of being intently studied by an unseen presence.

Like a hunting eagle, the Global Hawk drone transited the cape a second time. Its fan-jet was throttled back to the barest idling whisper, inaudible from the ground, and its nonreflective gray stealth paint melded with the sky.

As it ghosted down the length of the crab's claw, "smart skin" panels on the belly and underwings of the big RPV energized, becoming emitting and receptor arrays for its synthetic aperture radar system.

This was much the same kind of technology used by NASA geophysicists to survey and map ancient riverbeds, lakes, and trade routes long buried beneath the desert sands of the Sahara. It gave both the scientific researcher and the suspicious warfighter the ability to see things otherwise unrevealed.

Four hundred miles to the west, in the *Carlson*'s joint intelligence center, the task force's senior command staff crowded in behind Eddie Mac MacIntyre and Christine Rendino. All watched the radar imaging crawl past on the main bulkhead flatscreen. They had more than a professional interest. The Lady, their Lady, might be out there.

"See the swirl pattern of the bedrock," Christine commented. "Pahoehoe lava. You find this kind of image pattern all over around the Hawaiian Islands. A series of lava flows must have dumped into the sea at this point, building an extrusion outward from the coastline. This accounts for the steep dropoff and deep water on all sides. Bet you're going to have a lot of pillar basalt along those cliff edges."

Stone Quillain grunted. "Ain't that going to be fun to climb if somebody's at home and feeling cranky."

"We don't know if anybody's home yet," MacIntyre replied. "When will we, Commander Rendino?"

"Soon. Coming out over the peninsula now. There's the narrows at the neck...." Her fingertip stabbed at the screen. "There . . . we have a geometric!"

A small, neat, glowing rectangle began to crawl up the display.

Far away, over the crab's claw, the drone's probing radar was looking down through the trees, through the undergrowth, through the upper few feet of earth itself, to reveal what was hidden underneath. Nothing short of metal, solid rock, or its equivalent could stop and reflect the carefully modulated beam.

"There's more of them." Stone's blunt fingertip joined Christine's outlining the developments on the display. "An inverted chevron pattern facin' inland with interlocking fields of fire. Sure as hell, those are blockhouses. Hardpoints on a defense line."

"The genuine article too," Christine exclaimed. "To throw that kind of return, we gotta be talking poured concrete! See those fainter straight-line shadows connecting them? Those might be ground displacement effects. Tunnels and entrenchments. Copleigh, are you recording this?"

"Yes, ma'am," the SO replied decisively. "Double disks!"

A second chevron pattern appeared, then a third, each fortification placed with a mathematical precision.

"What are those smaller blips or whatever they are?" Cobra Richardson inquired, indicating a series of clustered sparks on the display.

"Weapons returns," Christine replied grimly. "That's about what you'd get if you bounce an SA beam off an infantryman packing a rifle and a load of ammunition. Copleigh, overlay of the thermal scan on this image."

The systems operator rattled a command into his keyboard and the thermographic and radar images merged.

"Yeah," Quillain commented. "Those gun returns are mostly grouped around the fires. Bet you got a series of squad-level camps dispersed all up and down the peninsula. I'd bet these smaller singleton returns along the cliff sides and across the shore-side neck are sentry posts and heavy-weapons emplacements. These old boys are taking care of business."

"And nothing showed on the visual sweeps?" MacIntyre demanded, his arms crossed.

Christine gave a shake of her head. "No, not a thing. Just what looks like virgin forest. I know what you're thinking, sir: Poured concrete would mean heavy construction gear, and there isn't a sign of it from the air."

"Mr. Tran, do you have any input on what we might be seeing here?"

"I have no idea, Admiral," the inspector replied. "The Bugis is a shipwright, not an engineer. And the Morning Star separatists are a mobile guerrilla army. They have no use for fortifications, or the means for building them."

The scan approached the outer third of the peninsula and the joint of the crab's pincers.

"Somebody's been doing some heavy work out here," Christine murmured, perplexed. "If those are bunkers, this peninsula has been converted into a fortress, but what's being...Oh, my God! Look at that! Look at that thing! Copleigh! Put a scale up beside that!"

To this point, the surface bunkers detected had been comparatively small, possibly the size of a two-car garage. This structure was titanic, a faint but definite outline just at the juncture of the claw at the head of the peninsula inlet. It didn't show the sharp return of the surface structures concealed only by earth and vegetation: This was deeper, within the living stone itself, its presence revealed by fracturing and subsidence within the geologic structure of the island.

Still, it displayed the unmistakable straight-line signature of a man-made artifact.

"That damn bunker or whatever has to be at least four hundred feet long and a quarter of that wide," Christine said in simple awe. "It's huge!"

"That's not all there is to it," MacIntyre added. "You've got more displacement shadows moving deeper inland. There's a network of lateral tunnels as well. And see those two other surface structures? I'll bet those are your surface entrances; they have to be a good hundred and fifty yards back from the primary complex and big enough to drive a truck through. Damm it, but I've seen something like this before!"

"Me too," Stone interjected. "When I was in Sweden doing a training exchange with the Swede marines. They've moved most of their naval basing underground, tunnelin' into the sides of those fjords or whatever you call 'em. You got sub pens and fast-attack docks sunk right under their coastal mountains. You couldn't even scratch 'em with a tac nuke."

"That's exactly what this structure is, Stone," MacIntyre asserted. "This is a sub pen or some other kind of bombproof dock. You can see where it opens into the head of the inlet. If you're careful with your pilotage, you could run a fair-sized ship in there: You'd have the water depth and the room for passage."

"You'd have a hell of a time doing it if they didn't want company, though," Steamer Lane spoke up. "Check out the cliff edges overlooking the inlet. More gun positions with a larger return. Heavy machine guns or light autocannon, I'll bet. Maybe even recoilless rifles. Anything coming up that inlet would be nailed by a three-way crossfire from the cliff tops and from the mouth of the pen."

The drone completed its transit of the peninsula, pulling out over the Banda Sea.

Christine turned to one of the other drone systems stations. "ELINT Monitor, did you get anything on that pass?"

"There's somebody in there all right, Miss Rendino," the SO replied, looking up from his console. "The iron in that black rock lava makes for a good natural Faraday screen, but we caught a couple of spikes just as we crossed over the inlet. Generator static and leakage off a small power grid."

"Understood. Drone Control, take her back up. Establish a sentry circuit and keep these coordinates under continuous surveillance." She turned back to the others. "Fa' sure, I think we've just zeroed Harconan's prime base."

Stone snorted. "Boy howdy, I'll call that a base. It's the Rock of Gibraltar West."

Tran shook his head, awed. "I knew Harconan had resources, but I never imagined he had enough to build an underground facility like this."

MacIntyre shook his head. "Harconan didn't build it, Inspector. At best, he's established squatter's rights in something that's been here for a long time."

Christine's eyebrows lifted. "The Second World War?"

An immediate operations group had been called, dedicated to assessing the discoveries made on what had been dubbed Crab's Claw Peninsula. MacIntyre, the intel, and the other element commanders had withdrawn from the cramped confines of the joint intelligence center to the relative comfort of the *Carlson*'s wardroom.

Christine's activated and interlinked laptop computer stood by, ready to grant access to the onboard intelligence files, while meter-size hard-copy images of the cape taken from both radar and visible spectrum covered the tables.

No one even made a pass at the coffee urn.

"That's where I've seen structures like this before," MacIntyre replied, tapping one of the radar prints. "Maps of the old underground fortifications at Corregidor and the Bonin Islands. I'll lay you odds this is an installation left over from the Japanese occupation."

"But there's nothing in the records about any facility like this along this stretch of coast," Christine objected. "There's nothing about it in the *Admiralty Pilot for the New Guinea Coast* or in any of the war records. We checked the Navy archives when we were assembling this database!"

"Then we may presume, Miss Rendino, that the Navy never knew it was there. And as for the *Admiralty Pilot,* I suspect the last time the Royal Navy's hydrographers ever really had a look at this coastline was well before World War Two. This site's natural isolation and security were why it was constructed in the first place. That and the fact that the underground structures here are probably not entirely man-made."

He tapped the radar print once more. "As you pointed out, this little cape is of volcanic origin, an outflow point for a series of lava flows. Well, one of them probably created a lava tube down the center of the peninsula, a natural cavern of considerable size that opened into the sea.

"During the Second World War, the Japanese were very much into building fortifications. Likely they stumbled across Crab's Claw and its lava tube and recognized its potential as a superb hardened basing site for submarines and small naval craft within strike range of the Australian coast. When they invaded the East Indies, a Japanese army or navy construction unit was landed on Crab's Claw to enlarge the natural core cavern and fortify the peninsula."

"Like they did up at Biak off the north coast of New Guinea," Stone grunted. I remember studyin' about a big old tunnel complex they had up that way."

"They called it the Sponge," MacIntyre acknowledged, "so named because of its ability to soak up Japanese troops and American blood. An entire six-thousand-man Japanese infantry brigade simply disappeared underground. Like Crab's Claw, here, it was a combination of man-made and natural tunnels. We were never able to learn just how extensive it was because it was invulnerable to any kind of conventional attack."

"Just out of curiosity, how'd we ever take that place out?" Labelle Nichols asked from her position astride a wardroom chair.

Stone Quillain shrugged. "In the end, MacArthur's boys ran a pipeline up into the mountains and pumped a couple of tankerloads of diesel and aviation gasoline into the tunnel air vents. Then somebody fired a flare gun into the main entrance. Blooie!"

The SB officer cocked a well-formed eyebrow. "That would have been something to see."

"Back then, we were lucky," MacIntyre continued. "Probably before Crab's Claw became fully operational, we counterattacked and retook New Guinea. The Japanese abandoned the facility."

"But you still would have found the base when you re-occupied the island, wouldn't you?" Nguyen Tran asked.

"Not necessarily, Mr. Tran," Stone Quillain said. "Because we never did occupy New Guinea in the way you're thinking. MacArthur was in charge of the showdown here during the war, and one of the notions old Dugout Doug came up with during one of his smart spells was island-hopping. He figured you don't have to dig out every little garrison and resistance point in an island archipelago, like you would block-clearing in a city. You just land and secure the main bases and you use air and sea power to isolate and starve out the smaller ones.

"He used the same tactic on New Guinea. He'd amphib his troops along the coast to take out the main Japanese installations, bypassing the smaller outposts. With their supply lines cut, and with the sea on one side and an impenetrable jungle on the other, the little guys were just left to die of disease or starvation."

Stone squinted at one of the high-altitude photoprints. "From the look of it, that's a mighty mean stretch of coast. If we didn't think there was a reason for it, we'd likely never land troops along it."

"I see," Tran agreed. "Much the same would apply after the war. The southwestern coast of Irian Jaya has its own special name, the Land of Lapping Death. If not from the saltwater crocodiles and the endemic diseases, then from the headhunters who contentedly followed their old tribal ways well into the twentieth century. A scion of one of your notable American families, Michael Rockefeller, disappeared along this coast not far from this location in the 1960's. It's widely suspected that his well-shrunken head still graces a native rooftree somewhere in the vicinity."

Tran joined Quillain in studying the visual spectrum prints. "During the conflict, the Japanese would no doubt have kept their base carefully camouflaged from air and sea observation. And afterwards, the jungle would have rapidly reclaimed it, erasing all overt trace of its existence. The only ones likely to stumble across it would be either the local natives or—"

"Or Bugis sea traders looking for safe anchorage along this coast," MacIntyre finished.

Tran nodded. "Precisely. Neither group being outgoing with their secrets."

Captain Carberry rose from one of the chairs he had claimed at the wardroom perimeter and leaned in over the table, studying one of the SA radar images. "Commander Rendino, I believe you mentioned that the primary chamber was some four hundred feet in length by one hundred wide?"

"Yes, sir. That's our best guess."

"Interesting," the stubby amphib commander mused. "I recall that an East German Frosch 1–class LSM has a length of three hundred twenty-one point five feet and a beam of thirty-six point four feet."

Christine frowned. "That's right, sir. . . . Oh, jeez! I get it. The Indonesian navy surplus amphib that's part of the Makara Limited coaster fleet. The one we lost track of!"

Carberry nodded. "Precisely. Given the bulk of the industrial satellite that was pirated, a Landing Ship Medium would be the perfect mode of transport. The satellite would be completely concealed belowdecks and cranes and other such port facilities wouldn't be required. You could beach and off-load in a multitude of places well away from inquiring customs officials."

"By God, Lucas, you're right!" MacIntyre exclaimed. "This would be the logical holding site for the INDASAT. Harconan must be gearing up to move it out of the archipelago. An LSM could shift it anywhere between the Philippines and Aden."

"Very easily, sir," Carberry agreed.

A sudden, startling voice issued from the wardroom's overhead speaker: "Commander Rendino, please contact the joint information center immediately."

Christine keyed the JIC address on her command headset. "Rendino 'by. What's happening, JIC?"

She listened intently to the response. "We've got something going down," she repeated. "The Global Hawk's just detected an encrypted satphone going active on Crab's Claw."

Two hundred and twenty miles overhead, an Iridium II communications satellite intercepted an aimed beam from the coast of southwestern New Guinea. Recognizing the phone of a listed subscriber, it accepted reception, relaying the transmission earthward to a point fifteen hundred miles distant in the central Indonesian archipelago.

At this point another spacecraft became involved, a United States Air Force space maneuver vehicle arcing in a ball-of-yarn orbit above the western Pacific. The robotic mini-shuttle carried a Defense Intelligence Agency "Black Ferret" electronic-intelligence-gathering module in its cargo bay, the spidery antenna arrays deployed through the SMVs open back hatch.

One of a squadron of half a dozen such vehicles, the primary focus of its six-month-long ELINT mission was the monitoring of events in the United Republics of China in the volatile aftermath of that nation's civil war. However, a sliver of the multithousand-channel monitoring capacity of the Ferret Fleet had been retasked in flight for NAVSPEC-FORCE's use and targeted upon the communications flow in and out of Makara Harconan's headquarters complex on Palau Piri Island.

Fortune smiled upon the Sea Fighter Task Force. One of the Black Ferrets was coming above the right horizon at just the right time.

A minute and twenty seven seconds after the initial private satphone call was received on Palau Piri, a cellular link activated, relaying the transmission across to the Makara Limited corporate headquarters at Nusa Dua. From there, the message stream was beamed back into space and to the big Pacificom Starlink satellite in synchronous orbit 24,000 miles above the Philippines, and from there to a destination only four hundred miles away from the message's point of origin.

Obedient to its programming, the SMV-mounted Ferret module sorted this single electronic thread out of the multimillion-message tapestry of transpacific communications and reported the event in real time to its interested masters.

Another voice issued from the wardroom loudspeaker. "Wardroom, this is communications. We have a call coming in on our civil access satphone from a Makara Harconan. He wishes to speak with Admiral MacIntyre. He says it's urgent and that it concerns Captain Garrett."

Glances were exchanged around the wardroom table. Christine Rendino nodded, speaking quietly and urgently to the joint intelligence center through her lip mike. MacIntyre donned and keyed his own headset. "Communications. This is MacIntyre. I'll take the call. Route my voice through my headset, but put Harconan over the wardroom squawk box. And record everything. Understood?"

"Understood, sir. We'll have you set up in a second."

"Keep him talking, Admiral," Christine said softly. "We'll know in a minute if this is a coincidence or not."

"Admiral MacIntyre, are you there?" The questioning voice of Makara Harconan issued from the overhead speaker.

"Right here, Mr. Harconan," MacIntyre replied. "What can we do for you?"

There wasn't a sound from anywhere else in the wardroom.

"I hope I can do something for you, Admiral," Harconan's filtered voice replied, "and for Captain Garrett. I have word of her."

"That's excellent, Mr. Harconan," MacIntyre said, playing the game. "What can you tell us?"

Every officer in the wardroom stared up at the overhead speaker.

"I can confirm to you that she is alive and well. I have good information on this from a source I trust. Unfortunately, I must also confirm she has been taken and is being held hostage by one of the Bugis pirate factions."

"That's what we've been afraid of. Can you tell us where, Mr. Harconan? Do you have any idea of her location?"

"None at all, Admiral," the taipan replied. "She could be anywhere on any one of a thousand islands. You must understand, the situation is very delicate. I have a certain number of contacts within the Indonesian Bugis community. I am trusted to a degree by some of the clan leadership, but only to a degree. They will talk to me, but that doesn't mean they confide in me. At best, I might be able to serve as a go-between for negotiations, but that is all."

"Negotiations?" MacIntyre probed. "For Captain Garrett's release?"

"Maybe eventually, Admiral," the grim reply came back. "Right now, I fear we're negotiating simply to keep her alive. The clans are angry, and please believe me, they are quite ready and willing to take their anger out on Captain Garrett."

Christine scribbled something on her notepad. Ripping the sheet off, she slid it down the wardroom table to MacIntyre.

Get him to say where he is.

MacIntyre glanced at the note and nodded. "I understand the situation, Mr. Harconan. Can you at least tell us how the pirates are contacting you? What is your location?"

"I'm at my home at Palau Piri. The contact is through

one of my Bugis trading agents on one of the outer islands. I hope you'll understand when I say I don't think saying which one would be either wise or productive."

"Why not, Mr. Harconan?"

"Because, as I must repeat, the situation is very delicate, and because I feel somewhat responsible for Captain Garrett in this situation. I know and understand the Bugis. Maybe we can talk her out of this situation, but the slightest precipitous action on anyone's part, your government's or mine, will get her killed—and rather horribly."

Stone Quillain growled deep in his chest like an angered bear. MacIntyre scowled, made a slashing "Cut it!" gesture across his throat.

Down at the far end of the table, Christine tilted her head, listening to her own earphone, then started to scribble furiously on the notepad again.

"Have Captain Garrett's captors given you a list of demands?" MacIntyre inquired.

"Yes, they have, a preliminary one at any rate. Firstly, there are certain amounts of ransom being demanded, in both cash and goods. I'm prepared to deal with that and I'm doing so at this time. Maybe I can buy her a degree of protection, at least in the short term."

Christine passed around her second notepad sheet. *The SOB is lying like a Persian rug. This transmission is originating at Crab's Claw. We have an emission-pattern match through an ELINT satellite. He's relaying his call through Palau Piri to establish an alibi.*

"What else do they want?" MacIntyre inquired, stone-faced.

"The pirates apparently lost some of their people during a recent attack on a Russian freighter south of the Sunda Strait. They want information on their fate, and if any of them are being held by the authorities, they want them released."

"I have no information on that, Mr. Harconan. All we can do is send inquiries to the Indonesian government and the International Piracy Center."

"If that's the case, then please do so. That brings us to

their final demand." Harconan hesitated. "This one I fear could prove more . . . difficult."

"How so, Mr. Harconan?"

"The pirates understand about your capacities, Admiral. They want your Sea Fighter Task Force out of Indonesian waters immediately. In fact, they want all United States naval forces out of the archipelago until further notice."

MacIntyre flipped his lip mike aside, covering the receptor head with a cupped hand. "Damn it, I was expecting this one."

He removed his hand and readjusted the mike. "Mr. Harconan, you have to know that's a call that can only be made by my nation's National Command Authority. There are freedom-of-the-seas issues here that involve U.S. global policy. I can't make any such decision, and I doubt the president would be willing to make such a call even at the cost of a hostage's life."

Harconan's voice was earnest and insistent. "You must try, Admiral. You must convince your authorities to pull back. The Bugis will not yield on this point. If your ships are not headed out of Indonesian waters within twenty-four hours at the most, Amanda Garrett will die, and it will be execution by slow torture. This is not an idle threat. You must make your government understand."

"I can only take this matter up with my superiors, Mr. Harconan. You have my"—a grimace crossed MacIntyre's features—"heartfelt thanks for your assistance in this affair. Can you keep the Bugis talking? Can you get them to speak directly with some of our State Department negotiators?"

"I doubt it, Admiral. As I said, it's a matter of trust. The Bugis will work through me. They aren't interested in direct talks. I will do what I can for Captain Garrett, but I'm afraid there's not all that much that can be done unless you clear Indonesian waters. After that, we can only wait and see."

"I guess so, Mr. Harconan. Will you be available for further contact?"

"I'll be remaining here at Palau Piri until we get some

resolution on this matter. You may contact me at any time, day or night. I am at your disposal."

"I thank you again, sir. We are most . . . grateful." MacIntyre broke the voice link.

The wardroom was dead silent for several seconds, then Stone Quillain spoke.

"Thank you, God, that's real convenient of you. We got the skipper, the sat, and the son of a bitch all at the same location. We can take the whole pot with one hand. Okay, Admiral, when do we go in?"

MacIntyre removed his command headset and tossed it on the wardroom table. "As soon as we can figure out how to do it without getting Captain Garrett killed. Ladies and gentlemen, here are your mission parameters. We have an assault on one of the most perfect natural fortresses I have ever seen. The garrison stands at between three and four hundred combatants with heavy infantry weapons and with all aspects of the terrain and environment on their side. That's not counting the base personnel underground and the crew of the LSM. Our Marine contingent will be outnumbered by better than four to one. As for who we may be fighting, Inspector Tran, do you have any input on that question?"

Tran's face was ominously impassive. "My best estimation would be a mixed force of Bugis pirates and indigenous Morning Star guerrillas in the service of Harconan. You can expect the Morning Stars to be hardened jungle fighters. The Bugis will no doubt be the most trusted and dedicated of Harconan's pirate cadre. With either group, you may expect resistance that will border on the fanatical."

"Hell, that's not all that big of a deal," Cobra Richardson commented from his end of the table. "Like the man said, volume of fire beats superior numbers. Between my Seawolves, the Little Pigs, and the naval gunfire support from the big ships, we can whittle those numbers down real fast."

Stone gave a derisive snort. "I wouldn't know about that. You flyboys and the gundeckers always promise the moon on a silver platter when it comes to gun support, but you generally deliver a horse turd on a paper plate."

MacIntyre lifted a hand to cut off Richardson's heated reply. "Stand easy, Cobra. Stone, that isn't the point. I have no doubt we can effectively scalp that cape with the resources available to us, but it will take time. You know as well as I do that in a hostage op, we have to get a major force in there fast."

The admiral returned his attention to the Seawolf leader. "Cobra, how does it look for an airmobile insertion—say, at the mouths of the landward entry tunnels?"

The lean, mustached aviator frowned and sat back in his chair. "Frankly, not so hot. You got solid double layer rain forest growth over the peninsula and everywhere else along the coast for a good five miles, palms, ironwood, and casuarina. There's nothing even close to a good LZ, and you'd be looking at a wicked rappel or fast-rope environment, a hundred-to-a-hundred-and-twenty-foot minimum from the forest roof. The Marines would be sitting ducks dropping down the lines, and it would be even worse for the helos."

"I got to agree with Cobra on that," Stone added.

"There's only one way we might be able to make airmobile work," the Seawolf leader went on. "We call up the Air Commandos at Curtin and have them lug us in a Daisy Cutter. That would solve a lot of our problems right there."

The mention of Daisy Cutter invoked a soft chorus of whistles and murmurs.

"What is a Daisy Cutter, Christine?" Tran asked, puzzled.

"A bomb," she replied. "A very big bomb. As big as it gets this side of Plutonium."

"Its official nomenclature is the BLU-82," Cobra added. "It's a fifteen-thousand-pound fuel-air explosive too big to be carried by any conventional bomber. You have to roll it out of the tail ramp of a C-130. It doesn't matter what kind of forest you drop it into: when the toothpicks stop raining out of the sky, you've got four or five acres of beautiful landing zone, bare naked and flat as a pancake. What's more, anyone aboveground for a quarter mile in any direction is instantly converted to raspberry jam. But people deep underground in a tunnel complex should survive okay."

"Maybe," MacIntyre replied. "But would this particular tunnel complex survive? The Japanese didn't know about FAE's when they built this place. Would the natural cavern roof be stressed to take that kind of shock wave without caving in?"

Richardson could only shrug. "It would depend on how it was reinforced, sir. We'd have to get inside and look the place over to know for sure."

MacIntyre's dark eyes shifted to Stone Quillain. "That's not a valid option at the moment. Chances for amphibious or landside assault?"

Quillain's usual scowl deepened as he mulled the problem. "Not good. There's nothing in the way of a decent landing beach anywhere on Crab's Claw. The lowest cliff side indicated is ninety feet. The shallowest slope gradient is about seventy degrees. All of it mean black-rock lava. Like the Rangers said at Point du Hoc: 'Three old ladies with brooms could hold us off.'"

The Marine traced a line to the neck of the cape with his fingertip. "We could come in overland and bunker-bust our way up the peninsula. Maybe we could do it with enough gun support. It would be pure hell, though: direct frontal assaults on heavy fixed defenses. It would also be way slow. A day bare minimum to work that half mile to the tunnel entrances, and no sayin' how many men we'd have left alive to go inside."

"That's another nonvalid option," the admiral said flatly. "How about a small-team SOC infiltration?"

"Like underwater through the sea entrance?" Stone shrugged. "Sir, I honestly can't say. The success possibility of any kind of Special Forces operation depends on how much intel you have on the target in a direct ratio. The more you know, the better chance you have of pulling it off. We have no idea what our guys will be facing in those tunnels, and Admiral, telling 'em to just go in and wing it likely won't get the job done."

"Understood, Stone. Steamer, you and the Three Little Pigs are our last chance. A high-speed assault through the sea entrance. Hey diddle diddle and straight up the middle."

"It depends, sir," the ex-surfer replied.

"On what?"

"From what I can see, on dumb-ass luck. Our best bet would be to divvy the assault force up between all of our fast-boat assets, Labelle's RIBs, my Sea Fighters, and the LCAC. As we do the run in, the helos and the big ships put all the fire onto the clifftops overlooking the inlet and the gun emplacements up there, ceasing bombardment at the last second.

"If enough emplacements get taken out, and if the bad guys don't have anything too nasty mounted in the mouth of the sub pen itself, and if nobody gets shot up too bad, well, then we'll be inside fast and kicking butt. If it doesn't break our way, though, we'll be trapped outside in a killing ground with no speed and no room to maneuver. We're pretty much going to be massacred. Roll the dice, sir."

"So it would appear."

"Sir," Christine Rendino said, forcing the words past the dryness in her throat, "there is another factor that must be considered: The task force is being kept under continuous surveillance by an Indonesian warship. In all probability, every move we make is being relayed directly to Harconan. If we move against the pirate base at Crab's Claw, or if we so much as start to close the range with the New Guinea coast, he's going to know about it."

The members of the operations group awaited the call from their commander. Elliot MacIntyre sat with his eyes closed and his forehead resting against his steepled hands. To Christine Rendino, even though the admiral sat in the very midst of his officers, an aura of isolation, of aloneness, surrounded the man.

She found a tremor threatening to ripple through her.

Beneath the shield of the table, Tran's steadying hand rested lightly on her thigh.

MacIntyre looked up. "All right. Here's how it stands. Harconan is probably preparing to deliver the captured IN-DASAT to his buyers, and he wants us out of the way. We have roughly twenty-three hours before we hit the deadline he's given us. After that, if the task force does not withdraw from the Indonesian archipelago, Captain Garrett, in theory, will be killed."

MacIntyre lifted his head. Christine found the bleakness on his expression terrifying. "Ladies and gentlemen, when I discuss these developments with our superiors tonight, I intend to state in the strongest possible terms that this task force must not retreat. There will be no precedent set for the United States Navy to yield one inch, one millimeter, of the free oceans of the world to any criminal or tyrant, for any reason. I believe Amanda Garrett would approve of this policy and sentiment."

MacIntyre came to his feet, his hands braced on the tabletop. "With that policy set, let's investigate ways to get Captain Garrett back—alive. Return to your respective staffs and start working the problem. Work it until you come up with some answers! There will be another O group at oh-six-hundred tomorrow morning. I want an assault plan to crack Crab's Claw. This is a blank-check operation, ladies and gentleman, no holds barred! Feel free to think and fight as dirty as you please. If you come up with something too outrageous, we'll do it UNODUR and tell the bean counters in D.C. about it afterwards!"

Task Force Commander's Quarters, USS *Evans F. Carlson* **0330 Hours, Zone Time: August 24, 2008**

Admiral Elliot MacIntyre paced the length of the office cabin and back, a path he'd repeated a good hundred times or more already that night. He had come to this cabin to think. This had seemed the place for it. As Amanda Garrett was at the center of this conflict, it seemed right to do his own planning here in the space marked with her lingering aura.

A hundred times also he mentally replayed his conversation with Harconan, those carefully guarded words that implied so much but gave away so little.

Harconan had her. There was no question. Just as there was no doubt he had the INDASAT. They knew where. Even in captivity Amanda had managed to point an arrow dead on at the enemy complex. But the fix on Amanda, on the satellite, and on the proof Harconan had stolen them both, was transitory. Within days, if not hours, it would melt away, leaving them nothing once more. If Harconan was to be stopped, it had to be done now.

MacIntyre had the assets in place to do the job. Also, Harconan could have no idea his security had been breached. The raid itself would provide all the evidence needed to justify the attack and to convict the *raja samudra* in the eyes of Indonesia and the world.

There was one problem, a problem that should, by rights, be insignificant if not flatly irrelevant to the equation: the life of a single hostage American naval officer. The life of Amanda Lee Garrett.

Harconan's implication was clear. Take any further action against the Bugis cartel and Amanda's life was forfeit. Oddly enough, the probable intent of his threat wasn't to directly shield himself or his cartel; it was merely to force the Sea Fighter Task Force out of his waters so he could move his INDASAT prize safely. Harconan himself had no idea that it served as a double-edged dagger.

MacIntyre paused in his pacing. Why the hell not simply back off? With the departure point known, it would be easy enough to use satellite and drone recon to track the ship carrying the INDASAT to whatever destination Harconan intended. Try for the takeout later, under more controlled circumstances.

MacIntyre grimaced. *Nice sophistry, Eddie Mac. Let somebody else make the blood call. The only problem is, we have all of the pieces now! We can end it now! We can move in and take incontrovertible evidence while it's aboard one of Harconan's own ships. Let this strike window close, and this tactical setup might never come together again.*

All that was required was for MacIntyre to say Amanda Lee Garrett had to take her chances like any other member of the United States Armed Forces.

And, to his despair, he found that he couldn't.

He imagined Amanda standing before him. He could visualize the stark fury in her eyes at even the suggestion the task force back off for her sake. He could hear the angered scorn in her voice and feel the sting of the enraged slap that, difference in rank or not, would have been delivered.

His fists clenched. *God damn you, Amanda, I'm not holding back for your sake! I'm holding back for mine! Because I'm an old fool who's performed the cardinal sin of falling in love with you and I can't make myself throw your life away!*

MacIntyre stood rigid with the biting self-confession.

He loved Amanda Garrett. He'd loved her for some time now, all without a touch of her hand or a solitary kiss or the slightest hint of reciprocation on her part.

He acknowledged all of the clumsy attempts at self-rationalization, the childish anger he had felt when he had seen Amanda with Harconan. His recall of feelings he'd thought lost forever with the death of his wife . . .

What did the name Amanda mean? Worthy of being loved, wasn't that it? He had never expected to find anyone like that in his world again. He had told himself he was content with his children and his duty and that was all he needed.

He looked around at the picture of the amber-haired little girl and the toy boat on the cabin bulkhead. That little girl had grown up and had shown him he was a liar.

And suddenly, with the confession, there also came clarity of thought, as if a pressure had been released, allowing a subtle distortion to snap out of his worldview.

He loved Amanda Garrett. Live with it. Work with it. Stop mullygutsing over the fact, accept it, and get on with your job.

In his mind, Amanda still stood before him, only now she smiled, that wry, knowing smile MacIntyre had come to know and treasure. *If I'm giving you problems, Elliot, imagine what I'm doing to Harconan, the poor devil.*

MacIntyre's fists unclenched.

Deliberately, MacIntyre recalled the way Harconan had studied Amanda the times he had seen them together. He considered the ways Harconan had used to gather her in— the way he was keeping her near him now. He imagined how any man might feel having lain beside her even for a single night.

His eyes narrowed and he smiled back at Amanda's specter, as understanding came.

Execution, my ass! You aren't a hostage, my dear. You're a prize!

Turning, MacIntyre crossed to the pitcher of ice water on the cabin sideboard and drank two glasses with deliberate relish. Refreshed, he sank into the chair behind the desk. He started to boot up the computer terminal, then impatiently passed on the notion. Rummaging through a drawer, he found an unused notebook and a pen. Flipping the notebook open, he began to jot down the initial parameters of an operations plan.

MacIntyre grinned as he wrote. He wouldn't be throwing Amanda's life away, merely his own career. He found that a trade worth making.

Twenty pages of the notebook had been filled when a light knock sounded on the door. MacIntyre glanced up and found a sunrise flaming in the cabin portholes.

"Enter."

Christine Rendino entered the office space. Her eyes were reddened with crying and shadowed with sleeplessness, but the new wash khakis she wore were pressed and immaculate, as was the parade rest she assumed as she stood before the desk. For one of the few times MacIntyre could remember, she looked every inch the naval officer.

"Sir," she said crisply, "request permission to speak freely with the Admiral."

MacIntyre set his pen aside and nodded. "Granted, Commander."

Christine moistened her lips. "Sir, I'd like to talk to you

about the operations group coming up this morning. There's a factor that might be a little hard to go into in the open planning session."

"What factor is that, Chris?"

"It relates to Captain Garrett's hostage status and how it must not be taken into consideration except as a subject for a rescue operation. I have reason to believe her life may not be as much at risk as Harconan is claiming. However, I also believe that any negotiated release will also be impossible."

Christine's stiff-spine discipline began to weaken with the growing intensity of her words. "Admiral, we have to get her out before Harconan can do a vanishing act with her. Once he gets her off New Guinea and out into the ten thousand hiding places he has in the archipelago, we're never going see her again. For . . . various reasons, he's not going to let her go—ever."

"And that's your professional assessment, Commander?"

Christine took an unsteady breath. "Yes, sir, it is. My assessment is that Harconan does not intend to release Amanda. For Harconan, there are personal factors involved beyond Amanda's hostage value. Her life, as she has known it, is going to end if we don't get her out of there. What happens to her next, whatever you want to call it—captivity, slavery, a forced, bonded relationship, hell, marriage, I don't know—is not going to be in any kind of her best interests."

MacIntyre tilted his chair back, studying the intel. "Chris, I think I understand the grounds for your assessment. It so happens I agree with them fully and I've already taken them into consideration. There's just one final question I need answered before we proceed beyond this point. I need it answered by Amanda's closest friend, and I need to ask it as someone who isn't her commanding officer."

Christine smiled faintly. "Understood, Admiral, sir."

"Think about this one carefully, Chris. What about the possibility that Amanda might want her life, as she and we have known it, to end. Is there any chance she might not want us to get her out?"

Christine looked startled "You mean, like she's turned? That she might actually want to stay with Harconan?"

"As the saying goes, 'Could she have been seduced by the dark side of the Force?' It has to be asked, Chris. And I have to ask it of you."

The intel looked away. MacIntyre said nothing, giving her a chance to work on it. When she turned back, her mouth was set. "Admiral, for as long as I've known Amanda Garrett, the job and her people have always come first and she's put herself second—her wants, her needs, what's best for her, all secondary. The thing is, that's been the way she's wanted it. Makara Harconan could offer her an awful lot. But it would all be for her and to hell with the rest of the world. Amanda doesn't work that way. She never has. She never could."

MacIntyre smiled. "We concur again, Chris. I just wanted to make sure."

"We're going in after her, sir? We're going to get her out?"

"Too damn right we are." MacIntyre tapped his notepad. "We're going to collect Amanda and that damn satellite both. And, as your generation puts it, we are going to kick some serious pirate butt while we're about it."

Christine looked away again, but only for a few seconds. When she looked back, her eyes were wet. "Sir, can I ask you to do something very irregular for a junior officer."

"Why not?" MacIntyre mused. "Compared to what we're going to do, it couldn't be all that strange."

"Then stand up a second, sir."

MacIntyre did, puzzled. Christine circled the desk and slipped her arms around his neck, locking him up in a fierce hug, brushing away a tear on the front of his shirt.

MacIntyre patted her lightly on the back as he would his daughter. "It's all right, Chris. I understand. Go give the mess steward a call and order us a breakfast. A big one."

The meal was delivered and eaten at the desk while the intel and the admiral started walking through yet another tactical assessment.

"Beyond our knowledge of the existence of Crab's Claw, Harconan's infatuation with Amanda is possibly our one greatest advantage," MacIntyre commented, finishing a last piece of toast.

"How's that work, sir?" Christine inquired.

"It means we're guaranteed a window of opportunity. While Harconan may be holding Amanda prisoner, we likely don't have a sword-of-Damocles scenario. She's probably not going to be sitting there wired to five pounds of Semtex. No doubt Harconan will be quite willing to use her as a shield and a bargaining chip for his own survival, but her death is not going to be ordered casually or automatically in the advent of an attack. I'll give him that much. We can exploit this if we can get a large enough force inside his base fast enough."

"Fa' sure, that's going to be the trick, Admiral," Christine said, setting aside her coffee cup. "The Japanese knew what they were doing when they dug in at Crab Claw. I've been networking with the unit tactical groups all night, and so far no one's been able to come up with a valid concept for a fast entry."

"I have." MacIntyre ran a blunt fingertip along the curving reach of water between the blades of the claw. "The frontal assault through the inlet."

"Uh, sir, even Steamer Lane is real iffy on that one, and usually he's sure his Sea Fighters can beat the world. To make that frontal assault work, we'd have to stand off and really rake the place to suppress the defenses. Everyone agrees that would be too slow for a hostage takedown. Amanda would have a kris at her throat by the time we could get in there."

"Not necessarily. I think we can make this thing work. We just have to invoke one of Amanda's pet doctrines. We have to turn our enemy's advantages back against him."

MacIntyre rose from behind the desk and paced out into the office space, his thumbs hooked into the corners of his pants pockets. "For example, the Japanese fortifications. Now, the safe assumption is that Harconan's core personnel, the INDASAT, and Amanda are all underground in the sub pen's tunnel and bunker complex, right?"

Christine considered for a moment. "Yeah, I'd say so. That would give them both maximum concealment and the most livable environment for a non–New Guinea native."

"Thus they're going to be safe under several dozen feet of concrete and lava rock, pretty much permitting us to go crazy topside on the surface of the peninsula. We might have to worry about something on the scale of a Daisy Cutter, but anything the task force can throw shouldn't affect the deep tunnels. Once we get our assault team inside the sub pen, we'll be able to isolate the landward entrances with gun and air power, preventing reinforcement from the surface reaching the complex."

"Yes, sir, that would work, but that still leaves us with the problem of getting inside in the first place. That's the hard part."

"As I said, not necessarily." MacIntyre looked back at the intel, an odd smile on his face. "It just requires a degree of . . . unconventional thinking."

Christine hesitated. "Sir, I've been here before with Amanda, and yeah, you're scaring the hell out of me too. How unconventional are we talking about?"

"Saint-Nazaire, Chris. The *Campbeltown* and Saint-Nazaire."

Christine applied her eidetic memory, flicking back through military history for a match for the names. When she came up with them, her eyes widened. "Oh, shit, sir. Oh, holy shit!"

MacIntyre shrugged. "It should work."

"Yeah, but . . . where are we going to get a spare destroyer from? I mean . . . you weren't going to use the Duke, were you?"

"Oh, no, I never considered that." MacIntyre strolled across to one of the cabin ports and peered astern toward the Indonesian frigate doggedly trudging in the wake of the task force. "I thought that instead we might . . . borrow one."

"Oh, my god . . . !" Christine clapped her hands over her mouth, muffling her exclamation.

MacIntyre's grin had grown, a bold, reckless, and somehow youthful cast coming to it, vastly different than anything Christine Rendino had ever seen before. "That's how we also turn Harconan's Indonesian navy contacts back on him," he continued. "As we move in on Crab's Claw, our erstwhile shadower will be transmitting a series of false position reports that indicate we're buying the hostage package and that the task force is getting the hell out of Dodge. That ought to work. Shouldn't it?"

When Christine lowered her hands, she was grinning as well. "Yes, Admiral, sir, it should work just fine, and afterwards they are gonna throw our asses in Leavenworth for the next three hundred years." She put emphasis on the *our*.

"Very likely, Chris," MacIntyre acknowledged, shoving his hands all the way into his pockets. "But if Amanda's there to testify at our court-martial, won't it be worth it?"

For the second time in his career, Eddie Mac MacIntyre earned himself a fierce hug around the neck from a junior officer.

Flag Plot, USS *Evans F. Carlson*
2253 Hours, Zone Time:
August 24, 2008

MacIntyre leaned forward at the communications console and spoke into the microphone grill at the base of the videophone link. "Admiral Elliot MacIntyre, authenticator Ironfist November zero two one. Ready to receive call."

Truth be told, he wasn't. He wouldn't be for perhaps another twelve hours. But one didn't simply wave away a direct communication from the United States Secretary of State, not even if he was a friend.

The screen before him filled with the Milstar-linked image of Secretary of State Harrison Van Lynden, set against the backdrop of his private office at the State Department.

"Hello, Harry," MacIntyre said levelly.

"Eddie Mac, what the hell's going on out there?"

"A great deal, Mr. Secretary."

"That's readily apparent. What the world and the National Command Authority wants to know is, what? The Indonesians are yelling their heads off about a major firefight in Benoa Harbor. CNN camera crews seem to be backing that up. We have reports of many unidentified Indonesian casualties and rumors of missing U.S. personnel. What we aren't receiving is input from NAVSPECFORCE. You've practically been running EMCON, Eddie Mac. What's going on?"

MacIntyre sat back in his chair, aware of the other figures standing around him in the dimness of the flag plot. "Mr. Secretary, as stated in my preliminary report to the CNO, the task force came under attack by a heavily armed force believed to be an Indonesian pirate raiding party. Our ship's personnel defended themselves and an emergency sortie from Benoa Port was conducted. At this time the task force has withdrawn to the Flores Sea south of the island of Sulawesi and an assessment of the situation is under way."

"That's exactly what I want, Eddie Mac, an assessment of the situation. I'm expected in the Oval Office in forty-five minutes and President Childress wants a nuts-and-bolts update. All I'm getting out of your headquarters are rewritten versions of this initial report. I want the whole story, Admiral, *now,* and do not even begin to bullshit me!"

"Mr. Secretary, what you have is essentially what we have. We've been successful in pushing the Indonesian piracy cartel into a corner, and they've pushed back—hard. The ships are intact and operational, we have taken casualties, two dead and five wounded, also as stated in our incident report." MacIntyre took a deliberate breath. "However, there is an additional factor."

"Do we have a hostage situation, Eddie Mac?"

"Yes, Mr. Secretary, we do. My task force commander, Captain Amanda Garrett, is in the hands of the cartel at this time."

"Ah, Christ!" Van Lynden grimaced. "That is all we need. How in the hell did this happen, Eddie Mac?"

"They had good luck, we had bad, Mr. Secretary."

"Can you confirm if she is alive?"

MacIntyre smiled frostily into the screen. "Yes sir. We can. We can not only confirm that she is alive, Mr. Secretary, but she has given us her location, the location of the hijacked INDASAT, and the location of the primary pirate base."

In spite of the situation, Van Lynden laughed softly. "I should have known, I should have known. All right, Eddie Mac, what do you propose we do about this?"

"Mr. Secretary, we are working the problem at this time."

"I understand that, Admiral, but I want a preliminary briefing I can run past the president, just to get him ready for what you have planned."

"Mr. Secretary," MacIntyre said, emphasizing his double-speak carefully, "we are working the problem at this time. May I have a few additional hours to prepare a full situational update for the National Command Authority? I feel we will be able to present the president with a . . . valid resolution to the situation."

MacIntyre locked eyes with Van Lynden. After a pause, the Secretary of State spoke again: "How long will you require to prepare this briefing, Admiral?"

"Approximately twelve hours, Mr. Secretary. At that time we will be prepared to answer any questions you may have."

"Understood, Eddie Mac. Twelve hours. We'll be standing by."

The Milstar link was broken from the Washington end.

The admiral pushed himself back from the screen and reached for the officer's cap he'd left balanced in the brow of the console. Crumpled soft, salt-stained and oil-spotted, its once polished bill was roughened and green from long exposure to the Persian Gulf sun. It was a relic from another time and another Eddie Mac MacIntyre, the fraying braid denoting a lieutenant commander's rank.

MacIntyre had carried it for years, tucked away in his at-sea luggage. He'd never really known why. Now he did.

Donning the cap, MacIntyre gave it a decisive tug down over his eyes. It still felt pretty good after all these years; maybe it was the most comfortable hat he'd ever worn.

He stood and turned to face the others who shared the

flag plot with him: Captain Carberry, Christine Rendino, Stone Quillain, Nguyen Tran, and Labelle Nichols. The policeman, the Marine, and the special-boat woman loomed as shadows within the shadows, being clad in black utilities.

"Ladies and gentlemen, that's as much authorization as we're going to get."

The phone over the head of Captain Basry's bunk buzzed over the whirr of the air-conditioning. The Indonesian groaned and reached for it once more. "Yes?"

"Captain, this is watch officer Kodi. The Americans have resumed low-grade radar jamming once more."

Basry muffled his second groan. "Any difference from other times today?"

"No, sir. We have received the same notification from the American flagship that they are systems testing."

"Any interference with our station keeping?"

"No, sir. We have a clear visual plot on the running lights of both targets."

"Any alteration of course and speed or any other unusual activity on the part of the Americans?"

"No, sir, nothing noted."

"Then, Lieutenant, advise me when something unusual is noted."

"Yes, sir. My apologies, Captain."

Basry slammed the phone into its cradle and buried his face back into his pillow.

The operative phrase in the watch officer's statement had been *Nothing noted*. The *Sutanto*'s lookouts had been too far away to note the two shadowy shapes that darted away from the flanks of the *Carlson* or the small Cipher reconnaissance drone that lifted off from the LPD's flight deck. Likewise, the degraded Indonesian radar failed to detect the minute radar cross-sections of the three objects.

Half a mile out on either side of the line of advance of the Indonesian vessel, the seaborne shadows went inert, their wakes fading behind them as they powered down. Thermally stealthed as well, neither emitted enough infrared radiation to be discernible through a night-vision system.

The *Sutanto* swept between them, unaware of their presence.

The Cipher drone swung wide around the Indonesian frigate. Dropping in behind the ship, it crept up from astern, a black dot skimming the wave tops.

"Lieutenant Kodi," one of the lookouts called, "something is taking place aboard the American vessels, sir."

The lieutenant swept up his binoculars, aiming them at the distant clusters of running lights that marked the positions of the American ships. The helipad strobe lights on both U.S. vessels had begun their dazzling pulse, and the red flush of night work lights could be made out aboard the LPD as her hangar-bay doors opened. The Americans might be preparing to launch helicopters.

Kodi glanced at the bridge phone and hesitated. The captain had stated he wanted to be notified only if the Americans were up to something out of the ordinary. Would an air operation come under this definition? Perhaps if the Americans actually launched their helicopters ... ?

The watch officer chose to be conservative.

"Lookouts, stay alert," he called to the men on the bridge wings. "Keep an eye on what the Americans are up to."

He meant the American vessels ahead of them. As yet, no one aboard the *Sutanto* was aware of the U.S. craft behind them.

Heavy-duty Velcro parted and the anti-IR shroud split overhead down the length of Raider One. A puff of hot, fetid air was released as the insulated shroud peeled down to either gunwale.

Stone Quillain palmed the sweat from his face, resmearing the thick coat of black camouflage cream he wore.

"Damn, that's better," he muttered. He was one of the dozen people aboard the eleven-meter RIB; half were handpicked SOC Marines, the others Special Boat Squadron hands. "Hey, Labelle. How we doin'?"

Lieutenant Commander Labelle Nichols stood beside the raider's coxswain at the helm station, peering down at the dimly glowing lines on the miniature Cooperative Engagement tactical screen. Even with her naturally dark features, she, too, wore black camou paint to kill the sheen of her skin. "Looking good, Stone. Raider Two is on station and the *Carlson* reports no situational changes aboard the *Sutanto*. It looks like we climbed in their back pocket okay."

"Good enough. Then let's bite 'em in the ass."

"Doing it."

Nichols typed the execute command into her terminal and dispatched it via microburst to Raider Two and the CIC of their mother ship. Then she murmured a command to the coxswain at the helm station.

Engines kicked over with a muffled rumble. With mufflers full on, the diesels were no louder than the hissing hydrojets they drove. Such quieting cost horsepower, but the raiders would still have more than enough speed to pursue and overtake the *Sutanto*.

The Cipher drone popped up astern of the Indonesian frigate. Station-keeping over the *Sutanto*'s wake, the drone's onboard cameras provided an overview of the warship's decks and the events unfolding around it.

Two miles ahead, in the *Carlson*'s Combat Information Center, Christine Rendino stood at the shoulder of the drone's systems operator. Studying the low-light images feeding from the little RPV, she coached the raider force in over a voice communications channel.

"Looking good...the fan tail appears clear...the only lookouts appear to be forward on the bridge wings....No reaction....No reaction...."

The two RIBs appeared at the bottom of the screen, converging on the stern of the Indonesian frigate. Deftly skirting the edge of the larger vessel's prop wash, the raiders merged their own foaming wakes in with that of the larger warship, while keeping their hulls uncontrasted against dark, unbroken water.

Stone Quillain saw the angular stern of the Parchim-class frigate loom out of the darkness. At his station along the inflated starboard gunwale, he lifted the heavy anchor pad off the Fiberglas decking, fumbling a little as the powerful magnets tugged at the metal in his MOLLE harness.

This night, in addition to a wide assortment of gas bombs and flashbangs, he carried a pair of Taser shock pistols at his belt and a SABR slung across his back. The magazine well for the rifle half of the composite weapon was empty, however, while the grenade half had been stoked only with teargas and jellybag stun loads.

The remainder of the boarding party was similarly armed. This night's mission must be totally nonlethal. If this operation was to cling to the rags of legitimacy, no Indonesian sailor could be killed or even seriously harmed.

At the helm station, Labelle Nichols stared fixedly at the side of the ship that towered above them, commanding her coxswain with the slight quick gestures of a hand outlined in the faint glow of the binnacle light.

The RIB slid in closer. Bucking over the frigate's hull wash, it bumped its rubberized Kevlar flank against the steel of the larger ship. Stone socked the rubber-coated magnetic bosses of the anchor against the plating, as did the three other hands along the starboard side. The drag of the magnets alone would not be enough to hold the RIB in place, but they would make station-keeping easier for the coxswain.

The Marines and sailors along the portside swung their preassembled titanium and Fiberglas boarding ladders up to the lip of the frigate's deck, hooking their rubberized ends over the scuppers, the entire docking procedure taking only a matter of seconds.

Stone heard Nichols's voice whisper through his com headset. "Raider One, docking accomplished. Ready to board."

A few seconds later a second voice whispered out of the night: "Raider Two docked. Ready to board."

With that declaration, command of the operation passed to Quillain. "Boarding parties! Board! Board! Board!"

Stone hit one ladder, Labelle Nichols the second, swarming up the thin, quivering yet immensely strong rungs to the frigate's deck. He was just short of the deck lip when Christine Rendino hissed in his ear, "Hold! Hold! Hold! You have activity on deck!"

Stone froze, hanging from the ladder rungs. Three feet away, Nichols did the same, a shadow smeared against the gray hull paint. Overhead they could hear a clattering, a scuffling of feet, and an illegible whining mutter. A faint, foul stench tainted the clean sea air.

Cook's Striker Achmed Singh swore to Shiva under his breath as he struggled to hoist the heavy slops can over the rail. Every night the same. He was always the one anointed to carry out the garbage. He knew that Chief Pangururan had it in for him because he, Singh, was the only Balinese Hindu in the galley gang, but still, every time?

Singh wouldn't have even minded so much if it were daytime, but damnation, it was dark out here on the fantail at night. Singh wasn't enough of a sailor yet to be confident at the rail with the luminous wake boiling furiously at his feet. Even in the face of the humiliating jests aimed at him by the other galley hands, he always donned his life jacket before beginning his nauseating task.

With a final heave he lifted the overflowing can to the top cable of the railing and tilted the garbage over the side, being careful not to spill anything on the deck. No sense in inciting the rage of that snot-nosed deck division ensign.

The can was just emptying out when Singh felt a powerful hand close on his life-jacket collar and a second on his belt.

"Y'all want a hand there, sport?"

Cook's Striker Achmed Singh, garbage can and all, shot over the stern rail to plunge into the frigate's wake, his startled scream temporarily gagged by a mouthful of seawater.

"We have a local in the water astern," Labelle Nichols whispered into her headset. "Drone Control, keep a fix on him. Raider One, drop back and pick him up."

Stone gave the grinning black woman a thumbs-up sign and they headed forward.

The remainder of the sixteen-person boarding party was on deck and ready to deploy. Moving silently on foam boot soles, the black-clad assault force flowed up either side of the *Sutanto*'s deckhouse. Following the ops plan, men peeled off at each hatchway and deck ventilator, grenades coming out of harness pouches.

Half a dozen boarders remained to edge up the ladderways to the bridge wings.

"Lieutenant Kodi, the Americans are launching helicopters."

The watch officer had already seen the lights of the first aircraft lifting from the helipads of the LPD. He also observed that it was swinging back in the direction of the *Sutanto*. This was clearly an event worthy of the Old Man's interest. Reaching for the interphone, Kodi buzzed the captain's sea cabin.

Before he could speak into the handset, however, an odd scuffling thud sounded from the starboard bridge wing, a similar disturbance starting to port an instant later. Night-colored figures rushed the wheelhouse from either side, silhouetted in the back glow from the CRT screens. Grunts, curses, and muffled exclamations followed, along with the smacking of leather-sheathed fists striking blows.

Kodi opened his mouth to yell just as a Taser pistol hissed. He felt the twin metal fangs of the stunner electrodes bite through his shirt, then he lost awareness of the proceedings.

A few feet aft, Captain Basry listened to a peculiar jumble of sounds issuing from the interphone. "Kodi... Kodi...Bridge, what's going on?" he demanded. "Bridge...? Bridge?"

The interphone connection broke with a click.

Swinging his feet to the deck, Basry started for the wheelhouse, not bothering to stuff his feet into his shoes.

Flinging the door of his sea cabin open, he found the door-frame completely filled by a towering nightmare in black battle harness.

"Hello," it said. Then a massive fist engulfed the front of Basry's singlet, and he was yanked into the corridor.

Stone Quillain deposited the comatose Indonesian captain in an out-of-the-way corner of the bridge.

Lieutenant Labelle Nichols stood at the wheel over the body of the helmsman. "Ship is under control and answering," she reported crisply. "Engine control is on the bridge and responding."

"Radio shack and chartrooms secure as well, sir," another Special Boat crewman added. "All systems intact and functional, including the encryption station. The day's codes appear to still be set and valid."

Stone nodded approvingly. "All right. Looking good, ladies and gentlemen. 'Belle, stand by to put her across the wind. Mr. Tran, how are you coming?"

Tran looked up from the interphone deck. "I believe I have this set for what you would call the 1-MC, Captain."

"'Belle, you found the ship's alarm board?"

She pointed to a row of buttons on the overhead. "General quarters, fire, general alarm, and collision. Which one should we use?"

Stone shrugged. "Hell, why not all of 'em." He keyed the command circuit on his Leprechaun transceiver. "Wave Two, Wave Two. This is Wave One. Bridge is secure. All hands in position. Situation is nominal. Ready to execute flush and ready to bring you aboard."

"Understood, Wave One," Admiral MacIntyre's voice sounded over the thudding of helicopter rotors. "Proceed."

"Understood. Proceeding." Stone switched back to Tactical. "All elements mask up! Mask up and stand by!"

As he listened for the acknowledging clicks over the tactical net, he doffed his K-Pot helmet and pulled his antigas hood out of a harness pouch, drawing it on over his head. All of the other boarders did likewise, except for Tran, who would have need of a free and unmuffled voice for a short time longer.

With no further reason to delay and many not to, Stone touched the tactical Transmit key once more. "All boarder elements, execute flush now!"

Up and down the length of the Parchim-class frigate, a storm of hand grenades were hurled through doors, down hatches, and into ventilators as fast as the pins could be pulled, resulting in a veritable barrage of flashbangs, smoke, and riot gas.

The flashbangs had the first effect: A fusillade of explosions reverberated through the length of the frigate's hull, like firecrackers dropped into an oil drum, jarring the watch-standers at their stations and startling awake the sleepers in the bunk rooms. Clouds of choking vapor poured into the interior spaces at almost the same moment.

Stone aimed a finger at Nichols and she reached up and ran a thumb down the row of alarm buttons. A cacophony of jangling bells and shrieking Klaxons joined in the confusion. Unsatisfied with the chaos she had unleashed, the SB woman hauled down on the cord for the ship's air horns, adding its hoarse bellow to the chaos.

Stone aimed his finger at Tran. The Inspector held down the button on the interphone handset and yelled into the receiver in Bahasa Indonesia: *"Fire in the magazines! Fire! Fire! All hands! Abandon ship! I say again, abandon ship! This is not a drill! This is not a drill!"*

With the steel around them ringing with detonations and the air inside the hull solid with eye- and lung-searing smoke, the *Sutanto*'s crew was willing to take the statement at face value.

Topside, the frigate turned across the wind. The gas streaming from her deck hatches served as a windsock for the CH-60 transport helos moving in over her bow and stern. Held steady by the sure hand of Labelle Nichols, the frigate received the fastropes from the hovering Oceanhawks, followed by a double stream of Marine reinforcements.

There was nothing in the way of active resistance. Unarmed, stunned and half blinded, the majority of the Indonesians at first thought the boarders were rescuers rather than invaders. Deftly separating the officers and CPOs from the enlisted personnel, the Americans prolonged the fiction for as long as they could. Corpsmen began washing out eyes and treating the cuts and bruises incurred from the panicked evacuation topside.

In the meantime gas-masked Marines began a systematic compartment-by-compartment search belowdecks for holdouts.

"Ship's arsenal secure, Bridge. Weapons racks and ammo stores are still locked. It appears all arms accounted for."

"Officers' country clear."

"Berthing spaces clear for'rard."

"Main engine rooms secure. Plant appears to be intact and functioning, but we could do with a real black gang down here, along with somebody who can translate the control markings."

"Stand fast, Engine Room. Mr. Tran is on his way down and we have Wave Three coming aboard now. All hands! Open all deck hatches and scuttles! Ventilate the ship!"

The frigate had a small helipad aft, not large enough to handle a full-size Oceanhawk, but adequate for the skids of a Seawolf Super Huey. Again, Admiral MacIntyre acknowledged Amanda Garrett's wisdom in her choice of aircraft.

Ducking low, he and half a dozen volunteer ratings scuttled out from under the turning rotor arc of the UH-1Y. Once they were clear, Marine guards herded the first of the Indonesian navy personnel to the doors of the idling helicopter. The *Sutanto*'s new crew was shuttling aboard while her old one was bound for temporary incarceration aboard the *Carlson*.

Stone Quillain, the camou paint sketchily wiped from his face, awaited the admiral at the aft end of the deckhouse.

"Ship's status, Stone?"

The leatherneck grinned. "We got her, sir. Ship's in one piece and so's the crew. Pretty much, anyway."

"Well done. I'll see you and your men get a commendation." Then MacIntyre added wryly, "In whatever navy we may end up serving in."

The first Seawolf lifted off and the second came in, discharging its passengers. The next cluster of Indonesians was urged forward, numbered among them a wild-eyed man in an officer's khaki pants and a white T-shirt. He noticed the stars on the shoulder boards of MacIntyre's Windcheater.

"I protest," he yelled over the rotor roar. Lunging to stand in front of the admiral, he raged on: "This is my ship! This is illegal seizure! Piracy! This is against all international law!"

"I agree with you, Captain," MacIntyre replied, tilting his cap back. "This is indeed most irregular on our part. I apologize to you and your crew and I am certain further reparations will be made by my government, both to you personally and to the Indonesian navy. However, I regret necessity mandates that we ... acquire your vessel for a time. I also regret we likely will not be able to return it to you in pristine condition. Again, please accept my apology."

Captain Basry lost track of his shipmaster's English in his fury, and his follow-up volley of expletives was lost in the lack of translation. The Marine guard standing behind the Indonesian officer lightly bumped him with the action of his SABR, steering him on toward the waiting Huey.

"Nice try, sir," Stone commented, "but I don't think that gentleman is really goin' to be too good a sport about this."

MacIntyre shrugged. "Well, some people are like that. I'll be on the bridge if you need me."

By 0100 hours, the crew transfer was complete. With American-born engineers at her Korean-made diesels, the *Sutanto* was ready to get under way as a unit of the Sea Fighter Task Force. In addition to her prize crew, the Parchim carried the entire 1st Marine Raider Company crowded below her decks. The last cross-decking payloads had consisted of several pallets of arms and ammunition, the boarding party swapping out their nonlethal weaponry ammunition for their more traditional tools of war.

"Bridge, aye," MacIntyre said, scooping the buzzing interphone out of its cradle.

"This is the radio shack, sir, Chief Haldiman. We have our commo gear installed and operational. We have SINC-

GARS and satphone links established with the rest of the task force."

"Very good, Chief. How are you coming with the Indonesian systems?"

"No sweat, sir. It's all over-the-counter stuff we downloaded manuals for. Lieutenant Selkirk has the encryption gear sorted out and he says the code keys in the system are good for at least the next twenty hours. We've sent out our first phony position report and got a routine acknowledgment from Jakarta Fleet HQ. As far as they're concerned, we're still heading south on course for Darwin."

"Excellent, Chief."

"Captain Carberry and Captain Hiro both report boats, aircraft, and prisoners secure and that they are ready in all aspects to get under way. Drone and radar search indicates we have clear water out to eight miles on all bearings. Awaiting orders, sir."

"Stand by." Eddie Mac glanced at the statuesque black woman who still held sway at the helm station. "How about it, Exec? Ship's status?"

"Ship is secured for sea. Engine room reports ready to answer all bells." Her smile flashed white in the darkness of the wheelhouse. "This old kraut can's a bit creaky in the knees, but she'll get us there."

"Then let's proceed, Lieutenant. We have business on the New Guinea coast. All engines, ahead full. Make your course zero nine four."

"Yes, sir. All engines, ahead full. Making turns for twenty-six knots."

"Chief Haldiman, inform the task group to form up on us. Right echelon at two-thousand-meter intervals"

"Aye, aye, sir. Right echelon at two thousand."

MacIntyre slapped the phone to its cradle. By God, it felt good to be commanding a ship again instead of a political entity. Tugging his ratty commander's cap lower over his eyes, he leaned back against the bulkhead, savoring the growing vibration of the *Sutanto*'s propellers.

"Admiral, can I ask you a question?" Nichols asked from the helm station.

"Of course, Miss Nichols. What about?"

"Our flag, sir. We're running this tub, so she shouldn't be operating under Indonesian colors anymore. But she's not a commissioned vessel of the United States Navy, so we can't officially fly the stars and stripes either. But shouldn't we have some kind of battle flag if we're going into a fight tomorrow?"

"Valid points, I suppose, Lieutenant," MacIntyre replied, wondering where this conversation was heading. "Do you have any suggestions?"

"Uh, yes, sir, the subject did come up within the Special Boat Detachment and we'd like to put forward a proposal. Higbee, show the admiral."

An SB hand dug a mass of dark cloth out of a flag bag and passed it to MacIntyre. The admiral unfolded it, trying to make out the design in the dimness. When he did, his bellow of laughter made the wheelhouse ring.

"Excellent choice, Lieutenant. My compliments to you and to the detachment: It suits our purposes perfectly. Have it run up to the main truck immediately."

Three warships raced on, closing the range with the coast of New Guinea, the light of the Southern Cross and a million more tropic stars caught and reflected in the spray of the bow waves. Aboard the lead vessel, the smallest yet at the moment the most critical of the trio, a bundle of black fabric rose jerkily to the head of the latticework mainmast. A lanyard was yanked and the banner streamed in the trade wind, the stark white skull and crossbones grinning into the night.

0614 Hours, Zone Time:
MV *Harconan Flores*, Crab's Claw Cape   **August 25, 2008**

Amanda Garrett's eyes snapped open and she found herself instantly awake and poised for . . . what? The master's cabin was dark; the dim, silvery glow of the cavern work lights leaked through the slatted blinds of the portholes, sketching shapes, shadows, and outline, including that of the masculine form lying still on the other side of the bed.

Experimentally she held her breath, listening. There was nothing save the purr of the cabin air conditioner and the more distant mumble of the ship's auxiliary power plant. That and the occasional muffled voice and metallic transitory of a crewed ship at a moorage.

Nothing was different. Nothing had changed. Yet, Amanda was totally alert and aware, stimulated by the ringing of some subliminal alarm. She recognized the state as a personal call to battle stations, never to be disregarded.

She closed her eyes against the dark and sought for the central node of the warning.

How long had it been since her kidnapping? Five nights. How long since she had painted her message on the surface of the sea? Three nights. Granted that it had worked, how long might it take to be noticed and deciphered? How long would it take the task force to follow it up and pinpoint this base? How long to plan and position for an attack?

She added the hours up in her mind and opened her eyes once more. Today. They would be coming today—soon.

Amanda brushed aside the single sheet covering her nude form. Flowing to her feet, she silently padded the two steps to the porthole. Peering out, she saw only the shadow-streaked cavern wall and wooden pier side with the gun emplacement at its end. A pair of sentries, one Bugis the other Melanesian, paced listlessly in and out of the work-light pools. All was as it had been for her last two days' imprisonment here.

She was the only one with the warning. When the time came, Amanda knew she must be ready to act. Exactly what she was going to do would depend on circumstances and luck. She had certain ideas, but she would have to see how things broke.

The porthole was located near the foot of Harconan's bed. As she turned away from the port, her eyes fell naturally on him. She paused, then reached back to the blind, silently parting the lattice with her fingertips. A band of illumination fell across Harconan's decisive, angular features, softened slightly in sleep.

He was beautiful, a beautiful, wild, and dangerous animal and a deadly risk to the peaceful flocks she had sworn to protect. Thus, she must destroy him.

Yet, they were alike, as the ancestors of the wolf and sheepdog must have once hunted side by side. Amanda knew it, sensed it in the hunger and recklessness he had inspired in her. So different from any other man she had known. Different from the joyful comradeship she'd shared with her last youthful lover. Different from what she would share with that half-visualized ideal she sought for. Different.

And Makara—had he fallen sway to that impossible dangerous draw as well? He must have. Why else was she here? Why else would he keep her at his side this way unless he genuinely believed that the sheepdog could be called out to run with the pack again?

And it could not be, not in any way or manner, save for maybe one.

Amanda slipped under the sheet beside that powerful, long-muscled form. Covering Makara's body with her own, she brought him fully awake with her mouth on his, her body aching. This time she was the aggressor, urgently demanding her fill, savoring this one last moment of madness.

0721 Hours,
USS *Cunningham*, CLA-79, on Buccaneer Station   Zone Time:
30 Miles West of Crab's Claw Cape   August 25, 2008

"Navicom reports we are on station, sir," the helmsman said, looking up from his station at the central bridge console. "CIC verifies we have matching coordinates for Firing Station Buccaneer as per the action plan."

"Very good, Helm," Commander Ken Hiro replied. "Stop all engines. Initiate active station-keeping. Quartermaster, sound general quarters, bombardment stations!"

Throughout the superstructure and hull, the bawling Klaxons sounded the call to arms. In drill and in reality Hiro had heard them sound many times before aboard the Duke. There was a different tone to them now, though. Before, he had been serving as Amanda Garrett's executive officer. Now he was Captain, under God, and they were sounding the call to battle under his command.

I wonder if your throat was dry that first time in Drake's Passage, ma'am, Hiro thought to a presence not at his side. *It sure didn't sound or look like it.*

It was that way every time, Ken, every time. Trust your ship. Trust your crew. You've got them both ready.

But you're going to be the one under our guns out there, ma'am.

Ken visualized the ironic lift of a pair of brows. *Why do you think I'm glad it's the Duke doing the job? Carry on, Mr. Hiro.*

"Aye, aye, ma'am." He smiled and whispered the acknowledgment aloud. Turning to the racked combat gear on the rear bridge bulkhead, he took down and donned the combination flak vest and lifejacket and the gray Kevlar helmet with the white-stenciled CAPTAIN on its brow.

Down the long open sweep of the *Cunningham*'s foredeck, in the forward-most Vertical Launch System array, half a dozen missile silo hatches swung open, big silo hatches, taking up four of the standard launch cells.

Aft of VLS Array One, in the space taken up by what at one time had been the second of the Duke's three Vertical Launch Systems, another pair of rectangular hatches retracted, revealing a pair of guide tracks set in slots in the deck. A pair of massive gun barrels slid up the tracks, fixed to fire forward at a shallow angle off the bow, they locked into train with only a couple of feet of muzzle protruding.

These were the VGAS (Vertical Gun for Advanced Ships) mounts, 155mm ultrarange cannon designed to take advantage of the revolution in precision-guided munitions.

Why go to all the trouble of aiming the gun when one could simply tell the shell where it was supposed to go?

By taking advantage of a fixed mount braced and set within the hull, the big pieces could be autoloaded from their magazine, giving them a hands-off rate of fire of fifteen rounds per minute per barrel. Likewise, the recoil of a fixed mount could be more readily dealt with, permitting propellant and chamber pressures far in excess of a turreted weapon. Today's mission could be fired with reduced charges and no RAP rocket boosters for the shells. The range was only thirty miles, point-blank for the 110-mile potential reach of the VGAS system.

Directly beneath the *Cunningham*'s bridge, the gun tube of the ax-blade stealth turret whined as it elevated. The forward turret mount was a fleet-standard ERGM (Extended Range Guided Munitions) five-inch 64. A little brother to VGAS, it could only hurl a 120mm round to sixty-three miles.

Ken Hiro wondered at how things ran in cycles. In the Navy he'd enlisted in, the guided missile was king and the cannon only a feeble auxiliary. Now he was partaking in the return of something once thought to be extinct, the big gun cruiser.

"Captain, the ship is at all-stop and is station-keeping."

"Very good, Helm. Stand by to hand off bearing alignment to Fire Control."

"Captain, the ship is at general quarters. All battle boards read green. All battle stations manned and ready."

"Very good, Quartermaster."

"Captain," a third voice sounded in Hiro's command headset, "this is Air One. We have just received a Seawolf departure order from Task Force AIRBOSS. Aircraft are spotted and ready in all respects for launch. Request permission to proceed."

"Carry on, Air One. Launch your aircraft. State the status on our spotter drones."

"Drones Able and Bravo are responding and functional and are holding at Waypoint Jolly Roger. T minus twelve minutes forty-five seconds to advanced deployment by the time line."

"Understood."

As the rotor thunder grew from the helipad aft, Ken crossed to the captain's chair at the corner of the bridge. Faking the appropriate relaxed demeanor for "the Old Man," he lifted himself into the chair and dialed up the MC-1 circuit.

"All hands, this is the captain. We will be commencing

fire shortly. This shoot is going to be for my old boss, and the Duke's old skipper. Let's show the Lady we can do it right."

Lieutenant Commander Michael Torvald, the CO of ASW/Support Squadron 24, still looked uneasy as Cobra Richardson leaned in through the cockpit door of the SH-60 and draped his arm over the pilot's seat.

"I still don't know about this shit, Co," he yelled over the moan of his helo's idling turbines.

"Mike, trust me," Cobra screamed back with the confidence of a used-car dealer explaining away that mysterious squeak. "We got this wired. I got the ballistic charts and manuals downloaded from the Army Aviation Museum at Fort Rucker. The Special Aviation pukes from the 160th have proved the Hydra pod on the Blackhawk airframe and my ordnance guys have set up the igniter harnesses for you. Piece o' cake!"

Torvald inhaled deeply to bellow. "But my outfit's not rated for this kind of thing. We've never done anything like this before! No Navy helo outfit's done this before! Hell, the friggin' Army hasn't even done this since the seventies!"

"Details! Just do the drill, Mike. Follow my guys in to the firing line. Establish a hover on your designated GPU fix. Set your bearing on target, set your aircraft angle by your B charts, and pull the trigger when I give the word! It's going to be fantastic, my man!"

"I hope you know what you're talking about, Cobra!" The SH-60 driver tilted his head, listening to a voice in his helmet earphones. "That's it! We got departure!"

"See you on the firing line. You're going to love it!"

Cobra slammed the Oceanhawk's door shut and hunkered out from under the rotor arc. When clear, he stood erect and watched as the four helicopters of Heloron 24, the two SH-60 Oceanhawk subchasers and the pair of CH-60 Cargohawk utility aircraft, lifted sequentially into the sky.

As an adjunct to the task force's antisurface defenses, Amanda Garrett had insisted that all four of the 24th's Hawk-series helos be equipped to carry and launch both the Penguin and Hellfire air-to-surface missiles. All four had their antishipping snubwings mounted now, but each carried a weapons load different even from what Amanda Garrett had imagined.

Instead of single Hellfire guided missiles on each hardpoint of the multiracks, the Hawks now carried a seven-round pod of unguided 2.75-inch Hydra bombardment rockets. Four pods per multirack, four clusters per aircraft.

When Cobra Richardson had assumed command of the Navy's reactivated Seawolves, he had recognized the squadron's links with the old HAL-3 of the Vietnam era, not merely as a matter of sentiment and tradition, but as a possible source of tactics and doctrine as well. He began an in-depth study of Seawolf operations over the Mekong Delta. This, in turn, had grown into a voracious appetite for the entire history of rotor-winged warfare in the Southeast Asian conflict.

One of the more fascinating discoveries he had made had involved the lost doctrine of aero-artillery.

Modern gunship-warfare doctrine called for helicopters to be used as a precision, direct-fire weapon on specific targets. Aero-artillery called for their use as a fast, mobile platform for area bombardment, a "flying howitzer" versus a "flying tank."

To a man of Cobra's inventive nature, this presented all sorts of interesting possibilities. He'd spent the bulk of his spare time this cruise drawing up an operational outline for the use of aero-artillery within the task force order of battle, and working out the technical problems with his ordnance hands. The chance had come to move from theory to reality faster than he had hoped.

He jogged across the antiskid to where Wolf One awaited him. His crew was aboard, his copilot was already running the preflight, and the pad apes were standing by to roll the Super Huey out of the hangar to its launching spot on the flight deck. The smaller helo carried only two of the quad multirack clusters.

As he harnessed up, his copilot looked up from the checklist to watch the larger aircraft of Heloron 24 form up overhead for their first mission as part of a siege train.

"Co, you sure this rocket artillery shit is going to work?"

"Of course it's going to work—" Richardson paused for a second, running the scenario over in his mind one more time. "I mean . . . it should."

Bridge of the Frigate *Sutanto*   **0721 Hours, Zone Time:**
15 Miles Southeast of Crab's Claw Cape   **August 25, 2008**

MacIntyre looked over as Stone Quillain stepped out onto the starboard bridge wing.

"Got your riggin' inside, sir," the Marine said. "Flak vest, a MOLLE harness with a set of radios, and an M-4 carbine. You got half a dozen magazines in the pouches and one in the well. I could get you a spare SABR if you want one."

MacIntyre shook his head, allowing the binoculars to drop to the end of their neck strap. "No, the carbine will be fine, Stone. I wouldn't know what to do with a SABR if I had one. Too many gadgets."

"Yeah, that's the truth. But they'll sure be the ticket for this show." Quillain dug into his shirt pocket and produced a yellow packet of Beechnut Juicy Fruit. "Stick of gum, Admiral? Good for keeping the thirst down, don't you know."

"Thanks. Why not?"

Quillain took up a lean on the rail beside MacIntyre and the two men stripped the foil from the confection and chewed in silence for a moment. Below them on the forward gun deck, a Marine work detail, bare to the waist in the growing sultriness of the day, labored to strip the shells out of the turret magazine of the frigate's bow autocannon. A bucket brigade of men led to the rail, a steady stream of brassy 57mm rounds going over the side into the sea.

The main magazines had already been emptied. Likewise jettisoned had been the Exocets in the *Sutanto*'s missile cells and the torpedoes in the deck tubes. The bulk of the frigate's fuel supply had been pumped overboard as well, to reduce both her draught and the chance of fire and explosion.

Other preparations were going on inside the wheelhouse. A spalling curtain, a thick multilayer sheet of bullet- and fragmentationproof Kevlar fabric armor, had been crossdecked from the *Carlson*. Now double-folded, it was being bolted into place across the front face of the *Sutanto*'s bridge below the windscreen.

"Shouldn't be too far now, should it, sir?" Stone remarked.

"No, not far at all. We should pick up Crab's Claw visually when we clear this next headland."

MacIntyre pointed ahead along the coastline. The *Sutanto* was steaming at good cruise with the verdant and heat-hazy shore passing some three miles to starboard, the ship striving to look like a routine Indonesian naval patrol.

Christine Rendino had learned that such interdiction operations were commonplace against the Morning Star rebels, a factor that shouldn't arouse excessive concern at the pirate base. At the moment, of all the fleets in the world, Makara Harconan had the least to fear from Indonesia's.

Quillain paused between chews. "Good enough. Admiral, this really isn't a question for a company commander to put to a flag officer, but would you mind if I asked you something?"

"Stand on, Stone. Go ahead."

"Thank you, sir. Then, would you kindly explain to me just what the hell you're doing here? I mean a three-star on a special operation just isn't common, Admiral. In fact, it just doesn't happen unless there's something dang odd going on. If this is the case, as the landing force commander, I'd appreciate knowing about it now before we commit."

That was just the question Elliot MacIntyre had hoped no one would ask, at least until this operation was over.

"It's a matter of command-rated officers, Stone. I can't pull Carberry off the *Carlson*, and Ken Hiro's the new

TACBOSS, now that we've lost Captain Garrett. We need a ship driver out here."

Leaning on the rail, the Marine considered for a deliberate moment before replying. "Yeah, I can see the admiral's point, except that you've got an SB officer at the con in there who could put wheels under this tub and drive it to Atlanta without getting a parking ticket. And at the rush hour at that. And if it wasn't Lieutenant Nichols, you got a dozen other deck officers in the task force who could do this run just as well. If you're running this operation from up front like this, there has got to be a better reason than that."

There was another reason, but as to how much better it was was open to skeptical interpretation, even by MacIntyre himself. But, given who was asking the question, and why, MacIntyre had to answer.

"Request permission to speak off the record, Captain."

Quillain returned the wry grin. "Permission granted, sir."

"You're absolutely right, Stone. It's decidedly not SOP for a flag officer to lead this far forward. By all rights and sound and sensible doctrine, my place is back in the flag plot on the *Carlson,* calling the shots from the rear. That's how I've been doing things for a long time now. I commanded the entire Second Fleet from LANTFLEETCOM in Norfolk and I've commanded NAVSPECFORCE from Pearl Harbor.

"It's the way things are done, Stone, and I'm good at it. But that isn't the only way I've ever done it." MacIntyre removed the battered lieutenant commander's cap he wore. Turning it in his hands, he studied it intently. "Like Steamer Lane and Lieutenant Nichols in there, I got my start in the Special Boat squadrons, Mark IVs in the Persian Gulf, SEAL HSBs in the Adriatic, Cyclones off Colombia for the drug wars. When I first caught duty with Amanda's dad on his destroyer, I thought the old Charley Adams class was the size of a battleship.

"That's where NAVSPECFORCE got its start, in my head anyway. I've done quite a bit of special-operations work in one place or another. Things that nobody heard about at the time. Some I can't even talk about now. The point I'm getting around to is that once I did things like this, from up front—leading—and not just making suggestions from a glorified television studio."

MacIntyre found himself lightly tracing the anchor insignia on the cap badge with his fingertip. "For a variety of reasons, I want to see if I can still do it, from up front."

Eddie Mac donned the cap again and tugged it down over his eyes. "There's the stark truth, Stone. I'm coopting this entire military operation to get me through a goddamn midlife crisis. Why can't I just buy a red Corvette like everybody else?"

A soft rumbling laugh rolled out of Stone Quillain's chest. "You know, sir, back when I was a boot, I could do five hundred sit-ups in an hour?"

"No, Stone, I didn't know that."

"Well, I could. I still can, too, just not as easy and I walk funny for a while longer. The point I'm makin' is that when things start to pile up on me or whatever, I find myself sayin', 'Shit, I can do five hundred sit-ups in an hour; how bad can this be?'"

MacIntyre laughed aloud. "Thanks for the gum, Stone."

"My pleasure, sir. I'm glad you're up here with us. This is going to be a great day, Admiral. We're going to kick ass and take names."

MV *Harconan Flores*   0721 Hours, Zone Time: August 25, 2008

"Professor Sonoo will be breakfasting with us this morning. I trust you won't stress the gentleman too greatly this time."

Harconan sat on the disarranged bunk, already dressed and admiring as Amanda toweled herself dry from her shower. "I had a great deal of difficulty talking the poor man out of his heart palpitations from the last time around."

"How did you manage that?" Amanda inquired, pressing the water from her hair. "We know him and we know his friends. I can guarantee that Interpol will be waiting for them all when they surface."

Harconan chuckled softly. "That is the marvelous thing about the world's judicial systems. They all work on the concept of proof, and proof can be subjective. Between my own organization and Sonoo's employers, we will be able to provide ample evidence to any police agency in the world that the good professor was nowhere near here nor doing anything in the least bit illegal. As for Sonoo and his colleagues personally, their tongues are bound by the fact that if they ever speak up about what they've done, they're finished professionally."

"You're very sure of yourself," Amanda replied softly. She drew open a cabin drawer and removed a pair of cotton panties, drawing them on unself-consciously. The return of underwear was the latest welcome amenity her captor and lover had provided.

"You have to be sure of yourself when you are attempting great things. He who hesitates is lost. You know that as well as I."

Amanda sensed him standing behind her and felt his fingertips resting on her shoulders. "That's why I didn't hesitate with my plans for you. When I saw you stepping down from your royal barge at my headquarters, I knew that here was a great thing to be done, a great challenge to meet."

Amanda felt the brush of his lips along her shoulder blade, and the inescapable frisson he could trigger ran through her once more. She forced a hint of scorn into her voice. "Well, you succeeded in bagging me, I'll give you that. What do I have to look forward to? Are you going to have me stuffed and mounted, or are you content with hanging my head over the fireplace?"

His palms flowed over the curve of her shoulders. "Amanda, I know you are unhappy with this situation. I can't blame you. But in the face of all things, be just with me. You know why I brought you here. You can feel it, as I can. Be honest with yourself as I am being honest with you."

She took a shuddering breath. "Makara Harconan, I am a prisoner here, held against my will. There is no justice and no honesty in that."

His sigh brushed lightly against her bare skin. "Then strive for some honesty within yourself." His fingers closed over her shoulders more firmly. "Are you really any more of a prisoner now than you have been for the past twenty years of your life?"

"What do you mean?" she asked cautiously.

"How many times have I told you that I have studied you, Amanda?" He spun her around to face him, those gray penetrating eyes drilling into hers at point-blank range. "All of your life you have played by the rules made by someone else. You have worn your uniform and the chains that went along with it, at the beck and call of an ungrateful government and populace.

"I know about the United States, Amanda. In your nation, they pay sports figures who play children's games in front of television cameras millions; yet, they begrudge you and the other warriors who defend them the pittance you are paid."

"I was never in it for the money, Makara!"

"Of course you weren't. But what about respect? What about a degree of honor? Even a simple thank-you for risking of your life? They don't openly throw dog excrement at you in the streets anymore or scream 'Baby killer!' into your face quite so often, but still your media and your citizenry look upon you as either a brass-hatted buffoon or a cold-blooded murderer in a uniform. Where is the justice in that? What do you owe them?"

"I never did it for a thank-you, either."

"I know you didn't, Amanda." His hands slid down her arms and his grip firmed. "You were the bright warrior, the guardian. You wanted to right the wrongs, to protect the helpless. But how many times have you been kept from doing just that? How many times have you seen an evil that needed to be destroyed, that was within your power to destroy, and yet your lords and masters held you back? And why? Because of some popularity poll or the fear of what some political pundit would say or because their particular party hacks disapproved."

"Too often," she whispered.

"See?" He released his hold on her and stepped back. "Damn it, Amanda. Don't you see that I'm not trying to hold you prisoner? I'm trying to set you free! I want you to consider alternatives! I'm not in this for self-aggrandizement or for money, either. If I were, I could sit back in the sun at Palau Piri, spending my millions on myself. Instead, I'm willing to risk all that I have on a chance to make things right in these islands: not their way with their politicking and corruption and compromise, but my way with one bright, clean slash of the sword!"

The emotion within him was too great for him to keep still. He paced, but his eyes stayed locked with hers. "Amanda, you felt the fire leap between us the first moment we saw each other. That's why, even as enemies, we can't help but lie in each other's arms and build that flame higher. As allies, there is nothing we couldn't dare, Amanda. As the *raja dan ratu samudra,* leading the Bugis people not as pirates but as a navy, there is an empire we could build here."

Amanda found a very honest tear trickling down her cheek. "The king and queen of the sea. . . . I wish I could say yes. I truly wish I could say yes."

Harconan stopped his pacing. Turning to face her, he peered into Amanda's eyes. "Why can't you? What do I have to change . . . to do?"

"There's nothing you can change, Makara, it's just not the sixteenth century anymore. There are no problems left that can be solved with one bright, clean slash of a sword . . . dammit."

The taipan tilted his head back toward the overhead, looking both very young and hurt and very old and tired at the same time. Then he turned away for the door of their quarters. "Then I will find a way to turn back time. The guard will bring you down to the main cabin when you are ready."

The breakfast party at the cabin table consisted of the *Flores*'s Captain Onderdank, his equally taciturn first officer, Professor Sonoo, Amanda and Harconan. She, the taipan, and the Indian scientist kept to a lighter rice-and-fruit menu while the two Hollanders plowed through their more solid platters of sausage and eggs.

Few words were spoken, save by Sonoo, and his were driven more from nerves than a desire for genuine communication. Amanda kept her own peace and listened to the flow, awaiting developments. They were not long in coming.

"As you have ordered, Mr. Harconan, we have prepared the satellite for transport. This is indicative we will be leaving shortly, to meet with our people?" Sonoo put a hopeful lift in his voice.

"Very soon," Harconan agreed, spearing a slice of jackfruit on the tines of his fork. "In fact, you may commence loading after breakfast." He glanced at Onderdank. "We'll be sailing tonight, after full dark."

"Aye, we will make ready. No problems. Our destination?"

Harconan's eyes cut in Amanda's direction. "We'll speak of that later, after we're under way. Needless to say, Professor, your firm and their cohorts in this project have agreed to pay my price for full access to the INDASAT. They have also agreed on a mutually acceptable facility where you will be permitted to continue your research. We will be taking you and the satellite on to a rendezvous with another ship. That vessel will deliver you to the site."

Sonoo's head bobbed. "Thank you. You will be most efficient in these matters, I'm sure. But the American military . . . There will be no . . . incidents?"

Harconan chewed and swallowed the jackfruit before replying. "None at all. The United States government has agreed to pull their naval forces from this area in return for a guarantee of safety for Captain Garrett. They are withdrawing now. By tonight they will be well clear of our coast. There will be no possibility of their interference."

Amanda froze her features even as her heart leaped in her chest. That simply could not be right. Not under the Childress administration and not on Eddie Mac MacIntyre's watch. Either Harconan was lying or he was operating under erroneous information. Which was the more likely?

"They'll be back just as soon as they realize I haven't been released," she said coolly.

Harconan gave a shrug. "No doubt, Amanda. But they have no way of knowing about this base, and the *Flores* will be on her way. All trace of this operation will have vanished. Even for you, their presence will not matter."

The muscles in Amanda's face ached, suppressing the urge to smile and frown both. *You believe it, don't you, Makara? Somebody was selling a package and you bought it.*

"What about me?" she probed. "Do I sail with the satellite too?"

"For a way," he said, studying his empty plate. "There will be another rendezvous with another ship. You will be taken to another place, an island. You will stay there for a time, until certain events have taken place. You will have every comfort. You will lack for nothing. Anything you wish will be provided. When I can, I will come for you."

"I see."

There is a certain finality to an island prison. Saint Helena, Alcatraz, Devil's Island—all proved the point. Glenda, I think I'm ready to go home to Kansas, Amanda thought feverishly. *Elliot, Chris, Stone, Ken, somebody! Get me the hell out of here!*

With breakfast completed, the cargo handling commenced. Even with nightfall and her departure hours away, the *Harconan Flores* was stirring, coming awake from her dockside slumber. Engine-testing stirred the waters of the ship pen, and work lights blazed on her weather and vehicle decks.

Harconan went forward to the forepeak of the LSM's bow. Accompanied by Sonoo and equipped with a civilian shipmaster's Handie-Talkie, he personally intended to supervise the INDASAT loading operation. He offered no objection and in fact seemed rather pleased when Amanda asked to accompany him. She merely noted that her old friend, the guard from the *pinisi,* was back, a living shadow following at her heels.

On the forecastle she found yet another impressive example of Harconan's forethought waiting for her. The inflatable clean room had been collapsed and withdrawn from around INDASAT 06. The access hatches had all been reclosed in its hull, and the massive space platform had been sealed within multiple layers of plastic, neatly packaged for shipment.

A second trailer had been rolled out of the vehicle deck of the *Flores* and parked directly behind the one that cradled the INDASAT. This trailer, a squat industrial lowboy, carried a huge stainless-steel tank. Slightly larger than the satellite in all dimensions, its end cap was missing. Hazmat warnings in several languages and the international chemical hazard symbol were painted on its silver sides.

As Amanda looked on in grudging admiration, the INDASAT was jackassed slowly back into the empty tank over a set of transfer tracks.

"The consummate smuggler," she said. "I am impressed, Makara. You're leaving nothing to chance."

"Chance is a poor ally, Amanda. I rarely depend on her. Should the *Flores* be intercepted at sea and boarded, the boarders will find her transporting a shipment of toxic waste from a chemical company in the Philippines to an industrial incinerator operation in Malaya. Her captain will have full and legal documentation for the cargo and sworn testimony available at the source and destination to back up the documentation. Should anyone want to open an inspection hatch or a test cock, they will find a rather nasty acid compound that no one in their right mind would want to fool with excessively."

"The old rum in the double-headed vinegar cask ploy."

Harconan chuckled. "For all of the world's technological sophistication, the old ploys still work best." Lifting the Handie-Talkie to his lips, the taipan gave a sharp command in Bahasa.

"I have to ask, Makara: How much?"

"All total?" He scratched the underside of his chin with the Handie-Talkie antenna. "Oh, I'd daresay the gross is about forty-one million U.S. dollars. After expenses, we'll clear about thirty million in profit." He glanced at her. "A share of it, ten per cent, is yours to do with as you will."

"I won't count it yet, Makara. Elliot MacIntyre knows all the old ploys too."

"Ah, but then that's another advantage of transporting toxic waste. This particular compound is very volatile— just the kind of thing that might burst into flames at an inopportune moment, say, as an American man-of-war looms over the horizon. The crew abandons ship, there is a terrific explosion, and the ship sinks, taking its cargo into the deeps with it."

Amanda lifted an eyebrow. "And since the *Flores* was transporting hazmat, you naturally took out extensive insurance on the ship?"

"Naturally."

"But the satellite, Mr. Harconan," Sonoo bleated. "Should this happen, what of the money my company has paid for this technology? We were promised delivery!"

Harconan leaned on the rail, as content as a lolling tiger. "Refer to your contract, Professor, the 'Acts of Man and God' clause. No refunds, so sorry."

Amanda couldn't stop her smile, nor could she stop her hand from lightly touching that broad back. Could there be more than one such corsair left in the world?

"Mr. Harconan!"

There was urgency in the call over the low-powered hand radio. It was Captain Onderdank's voice, and the Dutch officer sounded perturbed.

"What is it, Captain?" Harconan demanded, straightening.

"I am here at the fantail lookout. The surface sentries have reported an Indonesian patrol frigate standing in close to the cape. It looks like a routine coastal sweep, but the latest set of deployment updates from Admiral Lukisan's headquarters indicates that there shouldn't be any major Indonesian fleet units in this area. The closest frigate should be the one shadowing the American task force, and its last position report puts it four hundred miles to the southwest."

Harconan's first instinct was to look toward Amanda. She held her face immobile, suppressing all emotion.

"Captain, get down to the bow and expedite the loading!" Harconan barked into the radio. "Get the satellite aboard the ship now! Sonoo, you stay with me, and you, too, Amanda!"

Harconan hastened aft, snapping out additional commands in Indonesian, both into the radio and in shouts down to the pier side. Sonoo and Amanda were herded along behind him. Amanda wondered if Sonoo had noted that "her" guard had suddenly become "their" guard.

The camouflage curtain across the mouth of the cavern just barely cleared the fantail of the moored LSM. A lookout point had been established there with an observation slit cut through the heavy plasticized nylon. By leaning outboard and releasing the industrial Velcro closing strips, the flap covering the slit could be dropped, permitting a view down the inlet from the ship's deck.

A Parchim-class patrol frigate could indeed be seen emerging from behind the left-hand cliffside, the ship running perhaps a mile off the tip of the cape. Harconan snatched a pair of binoculars out of a rack on the rear bulkhead of the superstructure, leveling them at the passing vessel.

There was a second set of binoculars in the rack. The guard took no action when Amanda lifted them to her own eyes.

There was no doubt that it was an Indonesian Parchim, and yes, those were the hull numbers of her old friend the *Sutanto*. She was riding light, though, very light, with a broad strip of red lead showing along her waterline. There wasn't a soul on deck, either.

Amanda lowered the glasses and dared to wonder.

Bridge of the Frigate *Sutanto*   **0800 Hours, Zone Time:**
1 Mile off Crab's Claw Cape   **August 25, 2008**

Elliot MacIntyre lowered his binoculars as well, his eyes narrowing. Remarkable. He could see right down the gut of the inlet, and there wasn't a sign of anything in the way of an exterior dock gate or passage at its far end. If this all turned out to be some kind of staggering miscalculation, he mused, he was on the verge of earning himself a very unique slot in American naval history.

He lifted a hand to the touchpad of his Leprechaun transceiver. "Lost Prize to Black Beard. We are at Station Privateer. I say again, we are at Station Privateer. Report commitment status on all Freebooter elements."

"Lost Prize, Lost Prize," Ken Hiro's voice replied from over the horizon. "This is Blackbeard. We show green boards. All elements on station. All elements on time line. All elements report ready for mission commit. We show no situational changes on Crab's Claw. Ready to execute on your command."

There was no sense in waiting to see if he'd made a fool of himself. "Understood, Blackbeard. Transmit UNODUR notification and initiate primary Freebooter time line. Commit the attack."

"All elements initiating primary time line," Hiro replied. "Good luck, sir."

"To us all, Commander. To us all."

Washington D.C.   2200 Hours, Zone Time: August 24, 2008

Literally halfway around the world from Crab's Claw Cape, teleprinters in the Pentagon and the State Department began to hiss out priority-flagged hard copy at the same instant.

```
***URGENT***URGENT***URGENT***URGENT***
              URGENT***
      ***TIME CRITICAL MESSAGE FOLLOWS***


***AUTHENTICATOR IRONFIST NOVEMBER
ZERO—TWO—ONE
***FROM: CINCNAVSPECFORCE***
***TO: CNO/SECSTATE***
***HAVE LOCATED HOSTAGE CAPT. A. GARRETT AND
STOLEN INDASAT 06 VEHICLE ON WEST COAST NEW
GUINEA. UNLESS OTHERWISE DIRECTED AM
INITIATING RESCUE AND RECOVERY OPERATION.
DETAILS IN ATTACHMENT FILE***

              MACINTYRE CINCNAVSPECFORCE
```

Somehow, such UNODIR (UNless Otherwise DIRected) notifications never got sent in time to be otherwise directed.

MacIntyre lifted his finger from the communications pad. "Miss Nichols, take us in, please. You have the helm."

Labelle Nichols, still at the helm station she had claimed since the boarding, spun the *Sutanto*'s wheel hard over, starting the frigate's bow on its arc toward the mouth of the inlet.

"Going in, sir." The young woman sounded incredibly cool and collected for her first act of barratry. "Lee helm, all engines ahead emergency."

The enlisted hand at the engine controls rolled his throttles forward to their stops.

MacIntyre strode across the bridge, past the helm stations and past the lounging bulk of Stone Quillain, to the ship interphone. Lifting the handset from its cradle, he rang through to the main engine control.

"Engine Room, this is the bridge. This is it. Lock it all down and get the hell out of there!"

"Engine Room, aye!" the voice answered from the belly of the doomed ship.

"Eddie Mac's taking us in!" the engineering CPO bawled down the narrow passage between the thundering pair of Hyundai marine diesels. "Haul ass, you guys, haul ass!"

The three other members of the skeleton black gang needed no urging. They were the last hands below the frigate's waterline. They raced forward to the ladderway that led up to the comparative safety of mid-decks.

The veteran chief petty officer counted them up the ladder, three in with him, three out ahead of him. Before he followed, instinct made him pause for a last second for a look at the gauge banks on the main engine control boards.

Some needles were already starting their climb into the red zone. Whoever had been running coolant and lubrication maintenance on this plant needed to be taken out and shot after he'd been hung. Oh, well, it wasn't as if it mattered all that much.

He started to climb.

Two levels above, he unlatched the ladder trunk hatch and slammed it shut, kicking the locking dogs solidly into place. All watertight doors and hatches below the frigate's waterline had been tightly closed, just as all doors and hatches above the waterline had been securely wedged open against the risk of their freezing shut from frame distortion.

The central passageway of the main deck, one level below topside, was a rank and crowded place that smelled heavily of both heat and tension sweat. Spalling mats had been run down either side of the passage with the intent that the Kevlar armor combined with the steel ship's hull would keep the space bullet- and fragmentation-free. Or such was the theory. Battle lanterns had also been spaced down the passageway. They were now being switched on in preparation for the loss of the internal lighting.

All hands, Marine and Navy, had their spot staked out. The CPO had left his combat gear parked at his. Hastily he dragged the MOLLE harness and flak vest on over the green utilities he wore. Donning his K-Pot helmet, he sank down with his back to the bulkhead and tried to remember the loading and clearing drill for his twelve-gauge combat shotgun.

From the feel of the hull, they had completed their turn and were reaching flank speed. *Not long before the show starts. Crazy damn way to do things! Hope the admiral knows what he's doing. Hope the main bearings on Number Two hold out. Probably they're red-hot by now. Too late to worry about it. Hell of a way to treat a ship.*

The chief glanced at the three youthful Motor Macs huddled together against the bulkhead across from him. Two guys and a girl, all three of them just out of high school. Good kids and good sailors. They'd all volunteered for this job, practically begging for it, but they were looking scared now. Just about as scared as the CPO felt.

He gave them the slightest nod of his head and a bored smile that indicated that this was just another day leading to twenty and out.

That's part of a chief's job.

Amanda saw the massive gouts of smoke stream back from the frigate's side hull exhausts. It was readily apparent the ship was tacking on more speed. Defining her intent was less easy.

The *Sutanto*'s hull seemed to shorten as she wore around. Reversing course? No. Her helmsman met the turn as she came in line with the tip of the cape. She was standing on straight for the mouth of the inlet, her bow wave building rapidly as the lunatic on her bridge piled on the revs.

"What the hell . . . ?" she heard Harconan's perplexed whisper. "He can't be thinking of entering the inlet. Not at that rate of knots."

What the hell, indeed, Amanda agreed silently. That Indonesian skipper was bringing his ship in like . . .

". . . Like the *Campbeltown*." Amanda said it aloud.

She knew who the "lunatic" was now. Her train of thought jumped across to meet his with admiration and awe. *Boldness countered by boldness. Brilliant, Elliot!*

Amanda lowered the binoculars and looked at Harconan. He had turned to study her in return, seeking for some clue, disbelief and bewilderment warring across his handsome face. He had been found out and he knew who must be responsible.

"You didn't have a chance, Makara," she said with genuine regret, not for what was going to follow, but for its necessity. Also for all of the possibilities that might have been had Harconan been content to be merely a man instead of a king. "There was never a chance."

**USS *Cunningham*, CLA-79,   0803 Hours, Zone Time:
on Buccaneer Station   August 25, 2008**

In the *Cunningham*'s Combat Information Center, the tactical operations officer spoke from the master fire-control console.

"Sir, T minus thirty seconds to ATACMS launch by time line."

"Confirm missile status," Hiro responded. At general quarters, his station was the captain's chair positioned just to the left of fire control. He was getting more accustomed to it now, but the high-backed swiveling seat with its control-studded arms still inspired thoughts of the starship *Enterprise*.

"ATACMS bomblet fusing is set to mission parameters. ATACMS targeting coordinates set to mission parameters. ATACMS flight ready to launch in all aspects," the TACCO replied.

"Very well. Commence firing on the time hack."

"Acknowledged, firing on the hack! Seven...six... five..."

Around the CIC, anyone who could spare the seconds for a look fixed their gaze on one of the foredeck television monitors. To date, they had only fired this new weapon in simulations. That had been impressive enough.

"...three...two...one....Fire one!"

The ordnance-warning air horns blared, a suggestion to anyone still topside that they throw themselves face down on deck *now*!

A geyser of orange flame spewed from the *Cunningham*'s forward Vertical Launch System, jetting to the full height of the main mast array. The projectile used by the Army Tactical Missile System was too large to be popped out of its cell in a cold launch. The raving exhaust gases of the missile booster had to be vented upward and out of the silo, the missile climbing into the sky through them.

The cruiser's frame rattled, and a hint of the screaming shout of power generated by the rocket engine leaked down through the sound insulation. A stumpy yet sleek bulletlike form lifted through the flame on the monitors, guidance fins unfolding at its base. Climbing away swiftly it sucked its inferno up after it.

"...three...two...one....Fire two!"

A second launch geyser erupted...a third...six in all.

Six rounds on the way in thirty seconds. Steering in by a ring laser inertial guidance system, they pitched over toward their target.

Five miles distant, in the USS *Carlson*'s Combat Information Center, an overlapping string of blue missile-position hacks started to crawl between Buccaneer Station and Crab's Claw Cape, tracked by the *Cunningham*'s Aegis radar.

"The Duke confirms six good launches. ATACMS running hot, straight, and normal. Time to target, two minutes twenty-five seconds."

Christine Rendino was not a conventionally religious individual, but now she prayed to her visualization of the universe spirit. *Let her be underground. Please, please, let her be underground!*

<table>
<tr><td>**Fantail of the MV *Harconan Flores***</td><td>0804 Hours, Zone Time:
August 25, 2008</td></tr>
</table>

From beyond the western horizon, a thin straight contrail, like a white pencil line against the tropic azure sky, began a climb toward the zenith.

"It's an attack!" Harconan yelled the one instinctive exclamation in English, then he began shifting between Dutch and Bahasa Indonesia, rapid firing shouted commands into his Handie-Talkie. Somewhere a warning Klaxon began to bleat, its hoarse echoes wavering and distorted within the tunnels.

Amanda's guard began to herd her and Professor Sonoo forward down the starboard deck passageway. Sonoo tried to stammer something to Harconan, extending a beseeching hand, but the guard batted his arm aside with the muzzle of his machine pistol. He followed up with a sharp jab of the muzzle to the Indian's corpulent belly. Makara Harconan had no time for either Sonoo or Amanda.

In the guard's haste to move them off the ship, he failed to note that Amanda still carried her set of binoculars. Cradling them close, she crossed her arms over her stomach, concealing them.

The inlet mouth grew closer, the basaltic jaws on either side of its blue-water gullet gaping wider.

MacIntyre checked his watch against the bombardment time count. "Incoming, ladies and gentlemen. Ninety seconds to impact."

"Yes, sir," Labelle Nichols answered from the helm station. Moistening her lips, she couldn't keep herself from glancing upward. "A short round would be kind of unfortunate, wouldn't it?"

"Wouldn't be good," Stone Quillain agreed, shooting his own look toward the overhead. "What worries me most is that we got those damn things from the Army."

The Army Tactical Missiles engines burned out after a few seconds of furious acceleration, leaving the flight of projectiles to coast up their steep ballistic trajectory. Peaking at more than a hundred thousand feet above the earth's surface, the missiles began their dive to their target, dispersing in a smooth fan pattern down the length of the peninsula far below.

As the missiles plunged back into denser atmosphere, their guidance fins angled, spinning them like rifle bullets as they fell. A laser range finder in each missile's nose bounced a light beam off the earth's surface, and at the moment when the rotation speed reached its peak, a bursting charge fired, peeling back the projectile's outer skin.

Hurled by centrifugal force, M-74 cluster bomblets spewed outward in an expanding cone pattern, nine hundred fifty of them per missile, each with the explosive power of a hand grenade.

Other than the wail of the attack siren, the first warning the Morning Star surface garrison had was the sequential crashes of the empty missile frames slamming into the forest. Then came a soft metallic pattering, like metal rain. Hundreds upon hundreds of small gray cylinders were tumbling out of the sky, filtering down through the tree canopy, bouncing off limbs, thumping into the soft earth, saturating Crab's Claw Cape.

The Morning Star veterans had frequently faced the grenade launchers and mortars of the Indonesian Army. They'd even tasted field artillery more than once, but this was nothing they recognized as a weapon. Some dove for cover, many hesitated, a few even picked up the seemingly inert little cylinders out of curiosity.

Thousands upon thousands of microchip fuse timers all reached zero simultaneously.

Aboard the *Sutanto* they saw something like chain lightning flicker and blaze blue-white beneath the trees on the cape. A billowing gray-brown cloud burst outward from the forest cover in all directions, first lifting, then settling heavily, as if the jungle were somehow reabsorbing it.

The sound came next, like God ripping a continent-size canvas tarp in two.

Stone Quillain nodded approvingly. "That had to hurt. Not bad, Army."

"Indeed," MacIntyre agreed. "Now let's see what Commander Richardson can do."

Inside the cavern, the guard hustled Amanda and Sonoo down the steeply angled gangway from the main deck of the *Flores* to the right-hand cavern pier. Sonoo stumbled in the dim lighting. Wheezing, he clutched at the cable railing of the gangway, begging to be allowed to go slowly.

Amanda found herself sandwiched between her guard and the Indian. For the first time the guard was neglecting to keep his distance.

Impatiently the Bugis snapped something in Indonesian over Amanda's shoulder at Sonoo. Not a reply but a command. The status of the technical representative had apparently dropped suddenly. Amanda could guess why, and was already incorporating the factor into her own plan of action.

The honking *Harconan Flores*'s air horns joined in the clamor of the ship pen Klaxons. Deckhands were hastening topside, dragging the canvas covers off the 37mm mounts, while within the hull, air starters hissed, kicking over the LSM's engines.

Up forward, the work boss of the stevedore gang bawled curses and encouragement to his men as they winched the encapsulated INDASAT up the bow ramp.

Bugis gun crews were mustering at the quad fifty emplacements at each pier end while other guards dashed to internal security posts, some with assault rifles, others with grenade launchers, all responding to a practiced drill.

Just as they reached the foot of the gangway, something exploded outside. To Amanda it sounded like a gigantic chain saw cutting a battleship in two. Her ears popped as pressure waves pressed in from beyond the cavern mouth and down the inland entry tunnels. Scores of tiny starlike holes appeared in the dark inner facing of the camouflage screen; shrapnel hissed and ricocheted within the dock, and the heavy nylon curtain billowed inwardly like a sail in a high wind, the hot acid stink of high explosives flowing with it. Someone got unlucky with a bomblet fragment, his scream rising, then trailing off.

"What is it?" Sonoo squealed to Amanda. "What's happening?"

"As we say in my country, Professor, 'the Iceman cometh.'"

The guard hurried them on toward the tunnel entrances at the rear of the cavern.

Two miles to the southeast of Crab's Claw, a row of eight helicopters went to hover in a parallel line that extended the length of the cape. Sweeping into firing range during the shock of the ATACM's strike, each helo positioned over a precisely precalculated fix on its Global Positioning Unit system. With equal precision, each aircraft aligned on a specific gyrocompass heading and lifted its nose a precise number of degrees by its artificial horizon, flight and navigation systems serving the role of the training and laying gear of a gun battery.

"Guns hot, guns hot, guns hot," Cobra Richardson chanted into his lip mike, his thumb flipping the trigger guard up and off the firing button on his collective lever. "Stand by ... shoot!"

Seven similar trigger buttons depressed.

The helo line was engulfed in smoke and flame and the dinosaur scream of salvoing Hydra rockets. The firing circuits cycled with machine-gun rapidity, alternating between the pods on either side of each aircraft at quarter-second intervals, balancing the weight distribution and reducing the risk of round collision. Each Huey expended its base load of 56 bombardment rockets in fourteen seconds, the larger H-60s requiring twice that time to release their swarm of 112 projectiles.

Six hundred seventy-two rounds delivered on target in less than thirty seconds. This is the advantage of the bombardment rocket over tube artillery: Instead of one round at a time, it all arrives at once.

The Hydras burned out within a second or two of launching. As with the larger ATACMs, their momentum carried them on to target, but each exhausted rocket motor trailed a thin stream of smoke behind it. To Cobra Richardson, peering out through the propellant-smeared windshield of Wolf One, the rocket swarm in flight was like an incredibly swift gray storm front that lifted above, then settled down on, Crab's Claw Cape.

And wherever it touched, the earth exploded.

For a long, agonizing half minute the peninsula looked as it must have looked in its primordial days of creation, when the lava flows boiled down its length into the sea: fire, steam, jagged orange light, and a continuous rumbling roar that could be heard even over the beat of the rotors. And when the last incoming round had detonated, another cloud roiled into the sky, this one dense and black.

"Fuck!" Richardson's copilot whispered.

"Yeah," Richardson agreed. "So that's what it looks like."

Atop Crab's Claw, the torn and stunned survivors of the ATACMS strike were just pulling themselves to their feet when the new holocaust cascaded from the sky. But whereas each ATACMs bomblet had had the approximate explosive force of a hand grenade, the Hydra bombardment rounds each carried a fourteen-pound charge of high explosive.

Few Hydras actually reached the ground. Fused for impact detonation, the thick forest canopy intercepted the bulk of the projectiles. This was no boon to those trapped in the open. Entire trees disintegrated under the rockets' impacts, dagger-sharp wooden splinters and jagged steel shrapnel filling the air. Palm trunks were hurled like cabers, end over end, to crash down and crush, and men were entombed under an avalanche of falling timber.

The Morning Star guerrillas were brave men and good soldiers, dedicated veterans of years of jungle skirmishing, but never had they experienced, known of, or even dreamed of an onslaught such as this. Those on the landward end of the peninsula fled back into the deeper shelter of the mainland jungle, while those inside the shelter of the old Japanese bunkers hung on, screamed, and rode it out. Those trapped out in the heart of the conflagration had no option except to die.

In the ship pen, the rock underfoot shuddered. Rust clouds sifted down ominously from the support girders overhead, and the lighting system flickered.

Amanda, Sonoo, and the guard had just entered the left-hand access tunnel at the rear of the cavern. Here it was as if an enraged thunderstorm were trying to squeeze its way down the passage from the surface, the pressure waves it pushed ahead of itself hammering at the eardrums.

Their guard hesitated, glancing around uneasily. A tunnel carved deep into the earth was not a natural fighting ground for a Bugis sea raider. Cutting a look back over her shoulder, Amanda twisted her fingers into the strap of the binoculars she had so carefully husbanded. For this moment and maybe for a few moments more, this particular length of tunnel was empty save for the three of them.

A rocket slammed into the inlet wall near the pen entry. Its detonation tore loose the supports of the camouflage curtain, sending thousands of square yards of nylon and their guide tracks crashing down into the water at the cavern mouth. An explosion of daylight flooded the cavern.

The unexpected glare at his back startled the already edgy guard. For all his veteran years, the Bugis warrior spun around, taking his eyes off Amanda for the first and last time.

She spun as well, using all of her strength to swing the binoculars like a flail at the end of their strap, aiming for the back of the guard's head. Lenses, barrels, and skull all shattered at the impact.

Before the guard's body had a chance to fall, Amanda lunged at him. Tearing the Sterling out of his flaccid hands, she twisted about once more to bring the machine pistol's muzzle to bear on Sonoo. "The other technical representatives," she snapped. "Take me to them. Move!"

The Indian did so, with alacrity.

Amanda tore the single thirty-four round reload magazine out of the fallen Bugis's belt and followed, praying that in the confusion of the attack no one had noted the turnabout of affairs.

The hammering barrage ceased as abruptly as it had begun, leaving behind the sour puckering scent and taste of picric acid and the charcoal smell of burning wood. Somehow the returning silence was as stunning as the previous crushing concentration of sound. Men tried to shake away the shock, convulsively starting to move. Instinctive leaders sprung into action, hastening the process.

"Get it over the side, heave!" Makara Harconan shouted, adding his shoulder to that of the other deckhands on the fantail of the *Flores*. By brute muscle power they hogged the snagged tangle of tarpaulin and cable off the stern of the ship and into the sea, the mass of heavy fabric tearing a stretch of the aft railing out of its shackles as it fell.

The seaman half of Harconan noted abstractly that clearing the LSM's propellers for departure was going to be pure hell. The more immediate and practical portion of his mind counterpointed with the question of whether the *Flores* was going to sail at all.

Harconan had no idea what was happening atop the cape.

He was only certain that the Indonesians couldn't be behind it, nor were the Australians or any other of the regional navies. None had this brand of firepower at their beck and call. It had to be the Americans. Somehow they had located his base. No, somehow she must have led them here.

For one moment as he stood along side the crumpled railing, Harconan felt a soul-deep explosion of rage and betrayal aimed at Amanda Garrett. That bitch! He had accepted her word, her parole!

And then the taipan laughed. He straightened amid the ruins and he laughed aloud, to the bewilderment of the seamen around him. And what would he have done in her place? How had she gone about it? He was sure he'd covered every eventuality, leaving her nothing. Harconan reached up and wiped a trickle of blood from the corner of his mouth. Someday he would have to ask her about that.

He shook the ringing from his ears, taking stock of this tactical situation. No more fire was incoming. But that Indonesian frigate certainly was. She must be within a half mile of the inlet mouth and coming on like a bat out of hell.

Was she trying to move in fast to put assault boats over the side? Let her try it. The barrage might have taken out most of the clifftop emplacements, but the intact cavern guns could cut any landing party to pieces. He still had time to consider his options. There was always the contingency plan for a fallback to the Morning Star bases in the mountains. But about the satellite . . .

Harconan's thoughts trailed off. There were no landing parties forming up on the deck of that ship. And there was something, an odd flag, flying at the main truck.

Looking around, Harconan found his binoculars lying on the deck at his feet. Snatching them up, he aimed them at the masthead of the charging vessel.

Instead of the red and white of the Indonesian naval ensign, the black and white of the skull and crossbones writhed and winked from the masthead, a message and a signature, both sent with the wry and deadly humor of one certain nation's breed of warrior.

Harconan let the glasses fall, bringing up the Handie-

Talkie. "All gun stations! Open fire! Pour it into her! Turn her back!"

Sparks of orange fire sputtered within the cavern mouth that was revealed at the head of the inlet, and writhing tracer snakes crawled toward the *Sutanto.*

"Here it comes," Stone Quillain yelled, sinking behind the spalling barrier. "Tuck your heads in!"

Labelle Nichols crouched down behind the helm station, chanting the wry prayer of the old days of wooden ships and broadside-to-broadside warfare. "O Lord, for what we are about to receive, may we truly be grateful."

MacIntyre could only recall that spaced between each visible tracer were four rounds that could not be seen.

The bridge windscreen dissolved in a glassy spray under multiple slug impacts, the thick Kevlar padding below it absorbing rounds with a sodden *whock, whock, whock,* like a club swung against a wet rug. More bullets skittered and screamed off the steel superstructure frames.

"That's gotta be coming from some Ma Deuce fifties," Quillain commented in a conversational tone.

"Uh-huh," Labelle agreed absently, "but they got something heavier too. Looks like a Bofors twin mount maybe."

Intermixed with the glittering hornets of the machine-gun tracers were what looked like flaming bowling balls to MacIntyre as he peered over the spalling curtain. As they struck, the ship's structure jolted under each of their impacts, plating tore and caved in, and the spreading stench of fire and high explosives saturated the air.

"That's something like a twin forty, all right," a calm, studied voice stated. MacIntyre was amazed to find that it was his own. "I'll bet they've put the old Russian 37s back on that Frosch-classer."

The *Sutanto* bucked over a last sea swell, then the wave action dropped away as they roared through the cliff mouth and into the calmer waters of the cape inlet.

          ● ● ●

"*Almagtig!* What's that madman doing?" Captain Onderdank screamed over the rhythmic coughing of his ship's guns.

"I don't know," Harconan yelled back. "I don't know!"

The *Flores*'s captain had joined Harconan at the portside of the deckhouse, where the taipan had been driven by the muzzle blast of the aft turret. Fire spewed from the twin bell mouths of the Russian 37mm antiaircraft gun, and a steady stream of shell cases clattered onto the deck from the ejector chutes.

The quad .50-calibers were firing steadily from each cavern pierhead as well, and the aftermost *pinisi* moored alongside the *Flores* had mounted and manned its Russian 14mm machinegun stern chaser, bringing it to bear in the fight as well.

  The fire streams that converged and focused on the onrushing frigate were doing damage. Smoke was beginning to stream from the Parchim's superstructure, but still she plunged on, as unheeding as a charging elephant to a barrage of air-rifle fire.

Still running at flank speed, she was entering the inlet!

"He'll never be able to stop!" Onderdank exclaimed, shouting his bewilderment, "Even if he backs engines full, he won't be able to stop!"

The captain of the *Flores* was right. Without reversible propellers, which the elderly and simply outfitted ex–Warsaw Pact warship lacked, there was no way for the vessel to stop and no room for it to turn in the channel.

And then Harconan was flashing back to his days in the Amsterdam Maritime Academy and a tour he had taken of French Atlantic Port facilities, and the legend of the *Campbeltown*.

During the Second World War, the huge dry dock at the French port of Saint-Nazaire had been the only graving facility on the Bay of Biscay large enough to conduct hull repairs to the German superbattleships *Bismarck* and *Tirpitz*. As such, it was a great convenience to the Kriegsmarine and a deadly complication to the Royal Navy.

The question had been how to eliminate it. Conventional

bombing only chipped the massive concrete structure, and the bristling harbor defenses made it all but impossible for a special-operations force to reach the dry dock with a large enough stock of high explosives to do appreciable damage.

The answer had been to take an elderly American lend-lease destroyer, the *Campbeltown,* camouflage it to look like a German warship, load it with munitions and a team of heroically suicidal Commandos, and crash the whole affair through the dry dock sea gates at flank speed.

As was being done here!

"The bridge!" Harconan screamed into his radio. "Concentrate all fire on the bridge!"

How long to cross half a mile at twenty-five knots? Not long at all, but Elliot MacIntyre had crouched in that disintegrating wheelhouse for eternity, watching the black rock cliff face inch closer with the speed of an advancing glacier. He could feel the deck below him heating from the touch of flame and a trickle of blood down his cheek from a raking metal splinter.

You wanted all this back, damn you! Well, how do you like it?

He lifted a hand slowly as if through chilled honey to stare at it. The callused fingers curved without trembling. *Well, it's no worse than the old days,* he answered himself, bemused. *I guess I'm doing all right.*

Something struck the *Sutanto*'s superstructure with a slam heavier than anything felt before, a whiplash of shock reverberating through the steel.

"Shit, that's heavy stuff!" Quillain yelled.

"And it hit somewhere aft," MacIntyre assessed, twisting to sweep the inlet cliff edges towering above them. "The bombardment must not have taken out all of the shore batteries."

The Marine made his disgust plain. "It never does!"

The frigate was tearing around the shallow curve in the

inlet channel, and gunfire or not, Labelle Nichols was standing half erect behind the wheel, hunting for the critical strip of dark blue water off the bow.

A lurch radiated upward through the hull, and the rev counter on the lee helm console jumped as a prop blade nicked a rock.

MacIntyre caught movement along the forest line above the cliff edge. Amid the wood smoke and barrage-shredded vegetation, a team of Morning Star gunners had brought an artillery piece into the fight, hogging it around and down, angling it toward the ship passing beneath them. The gun and gun crew were damn near on a level with the frigate's bridge, and MacIntyre found himself looking down the stumpy three-inch tube of an ancient American-made 75mm pack howitzer, probably an abandoned weapon from the Second World War.

The piece vomited flame and a shell and the world exploded.

The portside bridge wing caught the round and was torn away, that side of the frigate's wheelhouse caving in. A blow sent MacIntyre's K-Pot helmet spinning, and his vision went from gray to red to black and back again. He found himself on his hands and knees shaking his head like a picadored bull. The helm stations . . .

Lieutenant Nichols was on her side on the deck, making a sound like a badly hurt cat. And the lee helmsman's skull was blown open.

If Vice Admiral Elliot MacIntyre, USN, was going to prove anything to anyone, especially to himself, it had better be now.

He heaved himself to his feet, his hands closing on the blood-slick wheel, stopping its spin, reversing it. *Answer up, you rust-bellied kraut bitch! Get back in the goddamn channel!*

There was a scream and a groan through the frigate's frame as stone ravished steel, and MacIntyre felt a faint vibration that meant seawater was cascading in through sundered hull plates. Still the propellers were turning and she was lining out for the cave entrance.

But that left the Morning Star howitzer. Its crew would have time for one more shot, and it would be aimed squarely at the back of MacIntyre's head.

The sound of autoweapons fire was a steady roar as Amanda herded her charge down the lateral tunnel through the intermittent pools of illumination issuing from the wide-set work lights. So far she had been lucky: The call to battle stations and the following fight had pulled the Bugis garrison into the main ship pen, emptying the side passages.

She took the precaution of shoving Sonoo into a shadowed niche between two stacks of crates before speaking with him again. "All right," she said, grinding the muzzle of the Sterling into the small of the Indian's back. "Where are your quarters?"

Sonoo spoke in a stammering Hindi, then caught himself. "The end of this passage and to the left. A room off the connecting passage in back."

"Will the others be there? The other technical representatives?"

"They should be. We were told to return there should there be trouble."

"Guards?"

"Yes, at the door or escorting us. . . . Please, Captain, we are noncombatants! We have nothing to do with all of this!"

"You are a receiver to stolen property, an industrial spy, and an accomplice to mass murder, Professor," Amanda grated back. "And if you want to come out of this alive and with a chance to turn state's evidence, you will do exactly as I say. Understood?"

"I understand. I will cooperate in every way."

"Good. We will be walking to the end of this passage and turning left. Go to your quarters as if you were just following your emergency drill. I'll be walking behind you with this submachine gun. If I tell you to get down, do it fast. If you don't, you may regret it . . . briefly."

"I understand. . . . I understand."

"Good. Go!"

Here at the end of the laterals, the air was still and dank, and lichen and seepage deposits encrusted the concrete tunnel walls. Heavy steel blast doors, their facings a solid sheet of rust, alternated on either side of the tall-man-high passage.

They made the turn. Perhaps forty yards ahead, past the other three lateral mouths, two armed Bugis stood talking in a light pool at the end of the gallery. Sonoo started toward them, his breathing ragged. Amanda paced close behind him, keeping the Sterling at port arms and concealed behind the Indian's broad back.

As she walked, a thought snagged at Amanda's mind, and she swore in silent fervor.

In his private SOC instruction program, Stone Quillain had been working her through the standard military firearms of the world, but they had yet to put time in on the L2 Sterling. She'd had instructions on how to load and fire weapons of its general class, however, and she knew that there would be a three-notch setting lever on the frame. Her thumb found the Sterling's. One setting would be Safe and one Single Shot mode. The third and the one she wanted would be Autofire.

Which would be which?

They were within twenty yards of the Bugis guards. They were looking up and taking note of Sonoo, and Amanda didn't have time to pause to read her damn gun. She took a deep breath and considered the guard who Harconan had sicced on her during her captivity. He had been good. He would have been one of Makara's best, too smart a soldier to wander about with an automatic weapon not set to safe.

Amanda whispered "God bless our choice" and flicked the mode lever all the way to its opposite stop.

Ten yards. The two-man guard post had been set outside of one of the tunnel side doors, and light could be seen leaking around the corroded frame. The guards, one carrying another Sterling and the other an M-16 with a ducttaped stock, were frowning as they studied the approach of Amanda and Sonoo. Perhaps it was the lack of an accompanying guard or possibly the expression on the Indian's face, but the Bugis with the assault rifle started to bring his weapon up to the ready position.

"Get down!"

Sonoo fell, whether in a swoon or a dive for safety, Amanda couldn't say. She whipped the Sterling's stock to her shoulder with one hand curled around its pistol grip and the other bracing its horizontal magazine.

Stone Quillain spoke to her. *Choppers'll climb as you fire a burst. Aim at their knees and hose 'em down with a zigzag pattern as the muzzle lifts.*

Amanda's call on the mode lever had been as correct as her Marine comrade's training. The Sterling spat, its sharp-edged *briiiiiiiiipp* of firepower reverberating in the tunnel. Enmeshed in the bullet stream, the Bugis door guards twisted, writhed, and fell.

Amanda felt an instant's relief, then an indescribable cacophony of sound... warping and buckling steel, splintering wood, shattering stone—all reverberated through the complex. The entirety of Crab's Claw Cape trembled under an earthquake's shock.

Bridge of the Frigate *Sutanto* 0809 Hours, Zone Time: August 25, 2008

Elliot MacIntyre looked up as something hurtled out of the smoke curtain rising above the head of the inlet: a chunky, sleek gray shadow that seemed to dive head-on for the frigate's ruined bridge. Pulling up at the last second, it flared past, literally at masthead height. Rotor song thundered, counterpointed by the ripping scream of Gatling guns and the hammer of grenade launchers.

The Seawolves were plowing the road.

Cobra Richardson led his four-helo flight in a nose-to-tail daisy chain over the *Sutanto* and down the length of the inlet. With OCSW turrets cranked hard over and door guns flaming, the Super Hueys mercilessly raked the cliff walls in an all-out sterilization pass, doing what the Seawolves did best: being there for the guys on the ground or the water.

The Morning Star howitzer did not fire that last round.

The gunnery from within the cavern mouth had slackened as well. Through the haze filling the inlet from the forest fires along the cliff sides, MacIntyre could see his target. Carberry had called it right. Harconan's LSM was in there, moored to a pier on the right side of the ship pen. But the rest of the available "parking" was filled as well, with a second pier on the left with a couple of good-size *pinisi* tied up to it.

The *pinisi* looked the softest.

MacIntyre set his line with a last half-turn of the wheel and reached up to the overhead, slamming his palm on the collision alarm. Alarm hooters cried belowdecks and the Marines and sailors riding it out in the central passageway interlinked arms and braced their feet against the opposing bulkhead in the old glider infantry crash-landing posture.

Stone Quillain dragged Labelle Nichols into the passageway aft of the wheelhouse, shielding her with his own body from what was to come. A shadow swept across the ruins of the bridge as they plunged beneath the lip of the cavern entrance. MacIntyre dropped to his knees, crossing his arms over his face and bracing himself against the wheel stand.

Crab's Claw Base   0810 Hours, Zone Time: August 25, 2008

The cavern garrison broke and ran, abandoning their gun stations, the crews of the *pinisi* and the *Flores* doing so as well, fleeing down the piers to the rear of the ship pen. Harconan could only join the headlong retreat. There was nothing else that could sanely be done in the face of twelve hundred tons of onrushing metal.

He'd gotten clear of the superstructure, making it as far as the LSM's midships deck when the suicidal frigate roared into the cavern.

The Parchim's sharp stem plowed into the stern of the first schooner moored to the left-hand pier. The smaller wooden vessel disintegrated like an apple crate under an ax blow.

The *Harconan Flores* lurched and tilted outboard as the hard-driven frigate wedged between it and the far-side dock. Pier timbers buckled, four-by-fours tearing loose from their spikes and flipping into the air like tossed jackstraws. Abrading hull steel screamed in torment, sparks and burning molten paint spraying.

The wreckage of the first *pinisi* was driven into the second, both schooners wadding into a mass of splintered timber under the Indonesian warship's bow, the dying shrieks of slow crewmen faint amid the crunch of frames and planking.

Metal howled and tore overhead: The Parchim's lattice masts were too tall for the ceiling of the ship pen. The main truck and antenna arrays sheared off at the cavern lip. Power connections arcing, they twisted as they fell, crashing to wedge between the superstructures of the two ships. The broken stubs of the frigate's masts raked on across the cavern roof, ripping the aged Japanese support girders loose from their anchor bolts. Rusted iron and lava rock rained from overhead.

Harconan had been knocked to the LSM's deck by the initial collision. He sensed a hurtling mass plummeting from above, and he rolled aside an instant before a crumpled length of I beam and a ton of basalt crashed across the *Flores* amidships. One of her Dutch mates was not quick enough, the scarlet pulp spraying.

Looking up, Harconan saw the frigate's battered upper works slide past, riding over the crushed remnants of the *pinisi*. She reached the stone shelf at the back of the cavern, the distorted bow bucking upward as it tried to lift over that as well. But her momentum was exhausted and her last mad ride was over. With a final dying groan, the warship slid back, her keel broken, inert.

The last echo faded and the cavern was suddenly supernaturally quiet.

Harconan knew this silence would last for only seconds, then the real assault would begin. He scrambled to his feet and bolted across the tilted deck for the starboard rail. The INDASAT and his base here were lost. All of Makara Limited was lost. Everything was lost except for the war.

The gangway had been thrown aside with the impact, but the tilting deck of the LSM now leaned over the right-hand pier. The taipan slid under the bottom cable of the rail. He hung from it for a moment, then dropped to the sprung planks, his mind leaping ahead. He must organize the delaying action and the retreat. As per the disaster contingency plan, he must get his people out and away to the Morning Star bases deeper in the jungle.

And he must take Amanda away with him. That was one prize they wouldn't win back.

"Everyone! Follow me!" he yelled, rallying the remaining scattered handful of guards and ship's crewmen on the pier.

0810 Hours,
USS *Cunningham*, CLA-79 on Buccaneer Station   **Zone Time:**
30 Miles West of Crab's Claw Cape   **August 25, 2008**

The *Sutanto* slid out of sight within the cavern. The real-time imaging on the primary large-screen display in the Combat Information Center was beaming back from one of the two Eagle Eye fire control drones the *Cunningham* had hovering over the engagement zone.

"They're in, sir," Hiro's TACCO commented. "So far, so good."

"So far," Hiro replied quietly. "Shift imaging. Bravo drone."

The tactical officer called up the feed from the second RPV. The distant cameras aimed downward on a patch of dense forest growth in the center of the cape. Rents had been torn in the tree canopy by the rocket barrages, and billowing smoke rose in half a dozen locations. Still, there was no visual hint that the landward entrances of the tunnel complex rested below the tree cover. They still existed only as radar traced coordinates in the targeting systems.

Hiro spoke. "Mr. Carstairs, verify gunnery bombardment mission ready to fire."

"All forward mounts ready to fire. Targeting coordinates set and projectile guidance programmed. The mission board reads green."

On the *Cunningham*'s foredeck monitors, the muzzles of the VGAS tubes and the barrel of the bow turret lay trained on the dark smear of land along the blue oceanic horizon.

"Mr. Carstairs, proceed with the mission."

"On the way, sir. Firing the mission." The TACCO's

thumbs flipped a pair of guards up and off from over a pair of glowing green keys. The keys went white as he depressed them.

Whump!... Crack!... Whump!... Crack!... Whump!... Crack!...

Autoloaders and firing circuits cycled sequentially, the two big fixed VGAS tubes fired a round apiece every fifteen seconds, with the lighter five-inch turret mount adding its contribution in between. The black and orange muzzle flashes were small compared to the flame jets of the ATACM launches, but still most impressive.

Like the ATACMs, the 155- and 120-millimeter "smart shells" extended guidance fins as they cleared their gun barrels. In a world of shockproof, solid-state technology, it was easier and more effective to simply tell the projectile to steer where it was supposed to go than it was to try and precisely aim the gun.

Using terminal laser targeting, the average area of probable impact for precision-guided shells such as these could have been reduced to a circle a meter and a half across. For this mission, however, GPU guidance alone with a fifteen-meter area of probable impact had been deemed adequate.

A dozen rounds were in the air before the first struck.

As the CIC crew watched the drone view of the bombardment zone, the fire streams systematically chewed the forest canopy away from around the tunnel entrances, hits alternating between two targets. The hooded fortifications stood momentarily naked amid the splintered tree trunks, then the hammering shell bursts began to gnaw at the heavy concrete.

As a roiling cloud of dust and smoke blanketed the scene, the *Cunningham*'s TACCO spoke quietly. "To paraphrase an album cover I saw once. 'Nobody's getting out of there alive.'"

Crab's Claw Base   0811 Hours, Zone Time: August 25, 2008

In the dusty half-light of the passageway, Stone Quillain rolled off the form he had protected, relieved because he felt movement but concerned because he also felt the hot wetness of blood.

"Belle, you okay?"

"No," the SB officer sobbed, "I'm shot in the butt and I really feel stupid. How's the lee helm? He caught it too."

Quillain glanced onto the bridge, noting that Admiral MacIntyre was dragging himself to his feet. He noted the other unmoving form as well.

"Your guy's dead, Belle," he stated simply. There was no time to fool around.

"Shit! Shit! Shit!"

Quillain hauled himself to his feet as a Marine radioman and a couple of SB hands staggered up from the communications room farther aft in the bridge structure.

"Goldberg, you and one of the other guys get Miss Nichols to a corpsman! You, get on the SINGGARS, get through to the task force, and tell 'em we're operating! Move it!"

"Aye, sir!"

"Yes, sir!"

Stone would have liked to say something more to Labelle—that she was going to be okay—but he didn't have time. Nor could he fool with saying anything to MacIntyre just now.

Unslinging his SABR, Quillain raced for the starboard bridge wing, the port side being gone. Within the hull of the dead ship, boots were hammered on deck plates as his Sea Dragons poured topside. Stone had to seize control of the situation.

This was going to be the tricky part. They'd had no visualization of the tactical setup inside of the ship pen and tunnel complex. Quillain had to get the assault force deployed and advancing, developing his battle plan even as he was executing it.

Hunkering down for cover behind the bullet-riddled spray shield, he allowed himself one good look around, totting up the critical tactical factors.

The light was going to be bad. While daylight streamed in through the entrance, the back of the cavern was still heavily shadowed. The air was heavily smoke-hazed as well. Friggin' twilight, too damn bright for night vision to work well, and too dark for the Mark One eyeball to be fully effective.

The two ships were wedged in solidly between the piers, side by side, the midships rails almost level with each other, the LSM with its ramp still down.

The left-hand pier looked pretty badly broken up. The right-hand one would probably be the same. Slow and careful moving would be required, with no cover. It looked as though there were all kinds of crap back on the stone shelf at the rear of the cavern, though, stacks of crates and such. And weren't those tunnel entrances back there—two of them? That would match up with the surface entrances. There'd be laterals extending out from and maybe a cross connector between those two main shafts deeper in.

Stone could hear the intermittent thud and rumble of artillery fire topside. That was good. The ships were closing the surface entrances. The topside garrison wasn't getting in. There wasn't any shooting in the cavern yet. That was bad. Whoever was pinned down in here with them was holding their fire, staying concealed, conserving ammo, and waiting for targets. The mark of good troops.

Right. Forget the docks. Secure the ship's decks and establish overwatch and suppression fire from the higher positions. Clear the LSM and assault down her ramp to clear the main cavern. Worry about the tunnels later.

It had maybe been twenty seconds since the frigate had crashed the gate and Quillain had his battle plan.

His communications carrier still hissed reassuringly in his earphone, and he slapped the communications pad on his chest harness.

"Dragon Six to Dragon elements. Deployment orders follow...."

Amanda shoved Sonoo into the technicians' quarters ahead of her. Pausing for a moment, she snagged the machine pistol from the dead guard, along with the magazine pouches he had carried slung over his shoulder. Three more sets of reloads plus the ready-use magazine in the second Sterling. She hoped it would be enough.

She backed into the doorway with her back to the frame, positioning to keep an eye on what was happening both inside the room and out in the passageway.

Inside, half a dozen men of four different races stared at her. The room itself had been chiseled and blasted out of solid rock, then lined with concrete. Perhaps forty by twenty feet, its ceiling was curved and low enough so that an average man might hunch to stay below it. The doorway Amanda occupied was the only entry or egress.

Some efforts had been made to improve the habitability. The walls had been scraped and painted white, but the lichen and slime were already creeping through once more. An odorous chemical toilet had been curtained off in one corner, and cots, camp chairs, and lockers had been provided; each claimed patch of floor space testifying by its degree of order and tidiness to the personality of its holder.

Amanda could readily see why Sonoo had wanted to get out of this place so badly.

"Greetings, gentlemen," she said with a degree of grim humor. "I presume most of you speak English. If anyone doesn't, please translate. For those of us who haven't been formally introduced, my name is Captain Amanda Garrett of the United States Navy. And that is the United States Navy attacking this complex, and you are my prisoners."

The technicians took it in varying ways: the Koreans with wary stoicism, the Arabs with fearful disbelief, the Indian with simple fear, and the younger and more fit-looking Russian with anger. Amanda swung the muzzle of the Sterling in his direction.

"It would be advisable for you to want to stay my prisoner as well. Consider it carefully, gentleman. Right now, you six are a huge security risk to both Harconan and your respective corporations. Your testimony about what you have been doing here will destroy them all. At this moment, there is nothing they'd want more than to have you taken out into the jungle somewhere and fed to the crocodiles. Now, get back against that far wall, sit down, and think about how I'm your only way of getting out of here alive."

They did so, obediently, hesitantly, sullenly.

Like a fighter pilot, Amanda kept her head on a swivel, one glance inward toward the technicians, the next out into the passageway. It was dank and almost chilly this deep in the complex, but she felt the sweat accumulate on her palms, slickening her grip on the machine pistol.

Suddenly the crash and clatter of small arms reverberated through the tunnels building rapidly into an echoing roar. The last battle was on.

"Chief Hanrahan," MacIntyre yelled into his lip mike. "What's the ship's status?"

"Flooded to the waterline, sir, but resting stable. One or two small fires under control," the answer hissed back in his headset. MacIntyre had reclaimed his M-4 carbine from the deck but had lost track of his helmet somewhere.

"Right. Stand by to move across and secure the LSM as soon as the Marines get her cleared. Stand fast until you get the word."

"Aye, sir, will do."

The cavern was a chaos of sharp-edged echoes. From the forecastle and upper works of the wrecked frigate, Marine SABR men and SAW gunners were engaging targets on the cavern floor, a score of different weapons types replying from the shadows.

Stone Quillain directed the developing fight from his ad hoc command post on the bridge wing, the Sea Dragon commander issuing a steady flow of orders, some over the tactical radio net, some by sheer leathery lung power.

"Heavy weapons. Hold and secure the frigate! *Corporal, get your fire team dispersed aft along the portside rail. Yeah, to port!* Maintain the suppression firebase. Assault Able, clear the LSM's upper works and put the right side of the dock area under fire! Assault Baker...*Hey you dumb bastard! Keep your head down! You plan on dying young?*...Move into the LSM's superstructure and commence compartment clearing! Watch out for hostages. I say again, watch out for hostages!"

MacIntyre moved in behind the Marine and clapped him on the shoulder. "Keep it up, Stone," he yelled over the gunfire. "I'm going across with Assault Two. Keep me advised. See you later."

Quillain didn't even look around. "Aye, aye, sir. Good luck. Recon Alpha and Bravo, hold in reserve on the main deck. . . ."

It wasn't until after MacIntyre had started down the tilted outside ladderway that Quillain looked after him. "Gillruth, heads up," he said into his lip mike. "Eddie Mac is comin' down to hook up with your platoon. I want him back alive! You hear me, Lieutenant? Alive!"

Assault Platoon Baker made its jump off from the settling stern of the *Sutanto,* crossing to the higher fantail of the *Flores.* This kept the LSM's superstructure between the Marines and the volume of fire from the cave front.

It also mandated a leap up to the LSM higher-deck edge and a five-foot vertical haul to get oneself over the lip. Eddie Mac prided himself on the conditioning he maintained for his age, but as he sprang and straight-armed himself up he heard and felt long-forgotten musculature pop and creak in protest.

Dammit to hell entirely, Eddie Mac, a red Corvette would have been a whole lot easier!

A youthful Marine, carrying three times MacIntyre's burden, effortlessly bounced over the rail at MacIntyre's side. Turning, he reached down, extending a hand to the admiral. He was rewarded with a glare that could have maimed, and he hastily retreated.

Marine fire teams were already at work inside the deckhouse. Flashbangs were plentiful and they were doing a fast and dirty cleanout: a concussion grenade through every door, followed by a charge and a sweep around the space with a ready gun barrel.

Not too ready, however; these were SOC Marines, drilled in hostage-rescue work. Fingers were kept off triggers and held extended out parallel to the weapons' frames, mandating that extra fragment of conscious thought to fire, a deliberate risk taken to avoid a blue-on-blue kill of the hostage they were there to rescue.

"Clear!"
"Clear!"

"Clear!"

The shouted chant from the fire-team leaders resounded through the passageways. No resistance met. The crew of the *Flores* had abandoned rather than fighting it out 'tween decks.

There was no cry of "We got a friendly," either.

MacIntyre attached himself to the squad climbing two levels to the upper deck and to officers' country and the wheelhouse. The things they were looking for would be there if anywhere aboard.

According to the rebuild diagrams MacIntyre had seen of the refurbished Froche LSM, the captain's quarters and those of the three mates were located in a deckhouse just forward of the squat exhaust stack and under the wheelhouse and radio shack.

As he and the Marines worked forward around either side of the funnel, MacIntyre noted a curious sense of oppression and claustrophobia totally alien to what should be felt on the decks of a ship. A man couldn't stand erect atop the LSM's wheelhouse without striking his head on the rock ceiling of the cavern. The admiral jumped as something black flickered past his face, a panic-stricken bat fleeing its sanctuary, preferring even the hated day to the growing chaos.

The fire team rushed the rear entry of the deckhouse, and flashbangs roared again.

"Clear!"
"Clear!"
"Clear!"
"Clear!"

Four for four again. No contacts.

Having gotten the *Sutanto* inside the cavern, MacIntyre hadn't wanted to sit on his thumb aboard the hulk, waiting while somebody else did the dirty work. He'd wanted in on the hunt for both Amanda and Harconan. But he also wasn't a fool. He was quite aware he wasn't an SOC Marine and that many of his Special Boat skills were rusty. He'd been content to be the trailer at the rear of the clearing squad, with no more mission than to look back over his shoulder.

That's what he still was, outside of the exterior hatch with his back to the steel of the bulkhead, when it happened.

Inside the deckhouse he heard the clunk and clatter of something bouncing down a ladderway.

"Grenade! Grenade! Gre—"

There was an explosion—not the sharp crack of a flash-bang, but the crash of the real thing. Two of the SOC Marines who had preceded MacIntyre through the door were hurled back out through it, partially by the force of the bomb and partially by their mad scramble to escape its effect.

He could not consciously recall how he got there, but MacIntyre found himself kneeling in the doorway, his carbine up-angled and firing ready. Only two Marines lay sprawled in the central passage of the deckhouse; the others had either been in one of the four cabins that opened off it or had dove for cover there. The attack had come from overhead, down the ladderway that led to the bridge.

Fortunately the grenade had been an offensive concussion model that didn't spit shrapnel. It had flattened the assault force, however, leaving them open for a follow-up attack.

The carbine in MacIntyre's hands was firing and he didn't know why, ripping off burst after three-round burst at the top of the ladder. Then he caught up with himself and realized he was firing at movement seen through the opening in the overhead.

And what was he yelling at the top of his lungs? *"Hostiles on the bridge! Hostiles on the bridge! Men down! Men down! We need corpsmen!"*

Someone in the wheelhouse screamed and a second hand grenade dropped to the passageway deck. Now totally detached from his own actions, MacIntyre wondered what he was up to now as he dropped the M-4 and lunged forward.

The evil little sphere of the grenade skittered across the linoleum, and frantically MacIntyre groped for it. His time sense was so adrenaline-distorted that he couldn't count the passing seconds. He got his hand on the bomb and twisted to throw it...but where? Semiconscious and wounded Marines sprawled in every adjacent compartment and outside of the only open exterior hatch. The ship's funnel blocked a clean pitch over the stern.

The searing realization of his own mortality seized Elliot MacIntyre by his throat. A crazy, kaleidoscopic jumble of images tumbled behind his eyes. His sons, his late wife on her wedding day, his daughter Judy as he had held her in his arms that first morning in the hospital, Amanda Garrett as she would have looked smiling up at him in that black-lace chemise. He clutched the grenade to his stomach and wrapped himself around it to smother the blast.

A tremendous crash sounded in his ears: the sound of his own next heartbeat. Then he realized that the grenade was wet with someone else's blood and that the safety lever and pin were still in place.

Elliot MacIntyre screamed an oath such as he had never before even attempted. Leaping to his feet, he ripped the pin out of the grenade and hurled it back where it had come from. Why in the name of sweet sleeping Jesus hadn't he thought of that before? The explosion overhead made the plates ring, and he charged up the ladder, clawing his Beretta service pistol out of its holster.

Two Bugis seamen lay sprawled amid the broken glass on the bridge deck. Dead, alive or indifferent, each received a finishing triple tap of a nine-millimeter. There was only one other place to go—the radio shack with its door blown half off its hinges. Forgetting everything he had ever known about sane combat entry, MacIntyre threw himself at it.

The air inside the small communications room was thick with smoke, and fragments of half-burned paper were everywhere. A middle-aged, balding European in a white tropic uniform lay sprawled at the rear of the cabin, a dazed expression on his face, the four gold strips on his shoulder boards marking him as the *Flores*'s captain.

The man's eyes snapped clear as he recognized MacIntyre and grabbed for the Walther P-38 that lay on the deck beside him.

MacIntyre emptied the Beretta. Panting for breath, he went into the automatic-pistol-reload drill, ejecting the empty clip and slapping a fresh one home. As he did so he noted the black and white Bakelite name tag standing out against the spreading scarlet stains on the man's shirt. Onderdank. A funny sort of name.

Gradually, MacIntyre resumed conscious control of his own body, a little amazed at the berserker who had been in possession for a time. It had been rather like that little dustup over that Croatian gunboat. Not too bad, though. His breathing was easy and the old heart was steady. He might be a little out of practice, but he wasn't ready for the breaker's yard yet.

He glanced around at the exceptionally well-appointed communications room, noting the stack of large ringbound notebooks that had been piled on the floor along with the contents of a sturdy-looking document safe. Obviously they had been stacked up and set ablaze in a frantic effort to destroy them, only to have the detonation of the concussion grenade blow the fire out.

As he tramped out a few of the smoldering documents he noted a small red cylinder lying in the corner. MacIntyre recognized it as a thermite bomb, the type used for emergency document destruction. The pull ring had snapped off, but the pin was still frozen in place, a spot of rust showing where the humid sea air had gotten to the device.

And blown into another corner was the flat gray case of a laptop computer, blistered and charred from the fire into which it had been tossed.

But still essentially intact. Collecting it, MacIntyre turned it over in his hands, noting a data card slot but no networking ports. What had Chris Rendino said about those code computers of Harconan's? It would be a standalone, with no physical means of networking it for security's sake.

"Admiral MacIntyre?" A cautious voice called up from below. "You okay, sir?"

For the first time MacIntyre noted that the volume of fire had dropped off again in the cavern. "I'm fine. How's the fire team?"

"The corpsmen are here, sir. I think they're going to be okay." A helmeted head poked up the ladder and looked around. "Holy shit, sir," the leatherneck commented respectfully.

"Yeah, we had a little trouble. We have some critical documentation here. I want a couple of hands to get this compartment secured and get this materiel collected and ready to move. This laptop computer is to be personally hand delivered to Commander Rendino on the *Carlson*. Personally! Got that, Sergeant?"

"Yes, sir!"

"Have we located Captain Garrett yet?"

"No, sir, and we have the ship cleared. The captain isn't aboard anywhere."

Damnation, Amanda, where the hell are you?

The first phase of the operation, the battle for the cavern, had ended in a defeat for the defenders. Crouching behind their barricades of stacked cargo and equipment on the rear shelf of the ship pen, they had found themselves stricken by some inexplicable and frightening force. Not mere bullets: The air itself seemed to explode over their heads, slashing at them with dagger tips of burning steel.

Their barricades provided no shelter, no firing cover, and the pirates and Morning Star mercenaries—those who were still alive, at least—were forced to retreat into the two main access tunnels.

More grim news awaited them there. The surface entrances were blocked, smashed and caved in by the attacker's shell fire. There was no way out.

From the cavern, strange metallic, inhuman voices spoke as loudly as the thunder, demanding in Bahasa that the defenders surrender, promising that none would be hurt. The last few dozen remaining of the garrison were shocked beyond rational thought, however. The flight-or-fight instincts had been triggered, and with flight rendered impossible, they would fight as a trapped animal would fight, to the death.

Crates of ammunition were broken open; they had a mountain of it to resist with. Other packing crates and cases were dragged from the lateral tunnel storerooms, and new barricades were hastily built, walling off the main passages from floor to ceiling with only firing ports left open.

In the haste of the construction, errors, critical ones, were inevitable. No one among the Bugis and Papuan survivors could be blamed for not being able to read the Cyrillic words for MORTAR SHELLS–120 MILLIMETER.

Stone Quillain sprinted across from the bow ramp of the *Harconan Flores,* angling wide to stay out of the line of fire from the tunnel mouths. His path took him behind some of the resistance points used by the cavern garrison, and he had to lengthen his stride to spring over sprawled bodies. Grudgingly he had to admit that the electronic do-jiggers bolted on to the Marine's SABR weapons systems did seem to work as advertised.

The grenade-launcher half of the Selectable Assault Battle Rifle could be used to launch a 25mm "smart grenade." As these rounds were fired, their microchip fuses could be programmed by the SABR's integral laser range finder to air-burst at a specific designated distance from the launcher, such as directly over the head of an enemy concealed behind cover.

Such smart shells were also very handy for shooting around corners. Stone would never have believed it possible, but the foxhole was rapidly becoming obsolete.

Quillain slammed up against the rear wall of the cavern, joining the Marine squad that flanked the right-hand tunnel entrance. "Okay, what have we got?"

The squad leader intently studied the screen of a palm-size low-light television unit while one of his men cautiously extended its optic-fiber scanning head around the tunnel lip on an extendable aluminum rod.

"They're back there just short of the first lateral tunnel, Skipper," the noncom replied. "They got the tunnel blocked off with a whole pile of crap, and they got at least two medium machine guns set up to cover the tunnel mouth. If anybody sticks their head around that corner, they'll saw it right off."

"Damn, how 'bout the other tunnel?"

"Donaldson's squad is covering that side and he says it's pretty much the same setup. What we gonna do, sir?"

Stone scowled. "It looks like we got three choices: blast 'em out, gas 'em out, or wait 'em out. Let's study on this a minute."

The sound of boots slapping on stonework and the creak of equipment on a MOLLE harness sounded in the half-light of the cavern, and Elliot MacIntyre moved up to join the Marines. The admiral was helmetless and his graying brown hair was sweat-slick, but he was holding his M-4 ready at port arms and he was moving easily.

"Situation?" he demanded.

"Checked at a couple of barricades inside the tunnels. We're still up against a valid defense. We've had the loud-speakers goin', yelling at 'em to surrender, but no takers so far."

"Any sign of Amanda?"

Quillain shook his head. "No, sir, not out here. Any sign aboard the ship?"

"Some western woman's clothing in the captain's cabin," MacIntyre replied. "Looked right for Amanda... Captain Garrett's size. There was some indication that the cabin was being used as a prisoner holding site. That's all."

"Hell, then they must have got her into the laterals before we hit. She's inside here."

"If she's here at all," MacIntyre added. "God save us and her, we might have figured this wrong. Have there been any attempts at negotiation by the defenders? Any threats against a hostage?"

"Just bullets so far, but if that's going to come, it's going to come soon." Quillain snapped a command into his lip mike, and the recorded and amplified surrender demand ceased to boom from the crumpled upperworks of the *Sutanto*.

"We have to know if she's in there or not before we can make our next move," Quillain continued, "and if she is in there we need to figure where...."

The Marine hesitated, tilting his helmet slightly to listen, then a rare genuine grin flowed across his blunt-featured face.

"What is it?" MacIntyre demanded.

"A firefight. Listen."

Now that the loudspeakers were silent, the sound of rifle shots and machine-gun fire could be heard echoing from somewhere back in the tunnel labyrinth.

Quillain's grin widened. "Well, bless her heart. We might have known that the skipper wouldn't be one to just sit around, tending to her knittin'."

Amanda hadn't wanted to fool with the sprawled bodies of the guards outside of the technicians' quarters, so she had done the next best thing. She smashed the work light outside of the door with the butt of the Sterling, plunging the end of the tunnel corridor into darkness. She'd done the same with the closer of the two lights inside the room, leaving the remaining one to illuminate her prisoners. From her position in the doorway, she'd be in the shadows while anyone coming at her would be backlit. After adding the last guard's M-16 and ammunition to her arsenal, she crouched down to await events.

Given the multiple explosions and the sound of heavy gunfire, a hellacious fight was going on out in the cavern. Amanda did not doubt her people would win eventually, but she would have to hold out here until they could reach her.

She glanced at her prisoners, who were huddled against the back wall. None of them looked like much of a physical threat, except maybe for the Russian. Still, she wished she could have tied them up somehow. She hadn't wanted to get that close to them or be that diverted from the doorway. Without someone on her side, it couldn't be helped.

"Ah, Captain . . . Captain." It was Sonoo.

"What?"

"You must realize that we, none of us here, have had a part in any of the violence that has been done in this affair."

"Really?"

Sonoo shook his head. "Not at all, nor of any of the decision-making. We are only employees here under the instructions of our firms."

Amanda shifted her vision back down the outside passage. "I see. You were only following orders. Well, Professor, I'm afraid that didn't wash for Nuremberg, and it won't wash here. At least the SS were following an ideology and not just a profit margin."

"But Captain . . . you are a person of great authority in this situation. I am sure that if you could be . . . open enough to assist us in avoiding unpleasantness in this matter, we, our corporations, could be most generous . . . extensively generous."

The breath hissed from between Amanda's teeth, and she swung the stumpy barrel of her submachine gun back into the room to pan across the row of corporates. "I am sick," she snarled, "of people thinking I will sell out for money or sex or anything else! You may take your employer's generosity and shove it up your fat ass, Professor! You and your playmates are going to stand trial for your part in these crimes, and you are going to help convict your lords and masters of the same! Now, sit back, shut up, and pray my people reach us in time, because if they don't, I intend to empty my last magazine into you leeches out of sheer self-indulgence!"

The paralytic silence she desired answered her.

She caught movement in the outside corridor and sank down into a prone firing position, trying not to think about the cooling slickness in which she was lying, using one of the guard's bodies as a barricade and aiming down the passage.

Three Bugis were loping in her direction, their weapons at port arms, obviously in a hurry and obviously with this room as their destination.

Amanda half exhaled and took up the trigger slack.

The Bugis noted the pool of darkness they were running into and hesitated some fifty feet down the passage.

"Aim! Short bursts!" Stone Quillain yelled out of her memory. *"Save your barrel! Save your ammo! Don't hose it!"*

She dropped two of the three men, the third springing aside into a lateral passage so her bullets only chipped concrete. He bounced back an instant later, snapping off a shot from his AK-47. Amanda felt the body in front of her jerk, and she blazed an answer, driving the rifleman back around his corner.

Reaching inside the door, Amanda caught the carrying straps of the second Sterling and the ammunition pouches, dragging them up beside her. *Guns hot, fangs out, and fight's on.*

"Do you really think it's her?" MacIntyre demanded.

"I can't think of who else would be shootin' at these guys." Quillain slammed the touch pad on his harness. "Hey, Donaldson! We're getting fire inside the tunnel complex. You hear it?"

"Roger that, Skipper," the reply from the far side squad leader came back in his earphone. "I can hear it."

"Does it sound like it's coming from your side—you know, from up your primary tunnel?"

"Kinda hard to tell with the echoes, but I don't think so."

"I don't think so, either. Stand by. All Sea Dragon elements, this is Sea Dragon Six. Rally! I say again, rally! Position to the left and right of the primary tunnel entries! Move it!"

Stone tore a smoke grenade from his harness. If the Lady was in a fight at the rear of the tunnel complex, he intended to pull attention to the front. Yanking the pin, he flipped the smoke bomb into the entry. As the white chemical smoke began to billow, the Bugis machine gunners cut loose, their tracer streams snaking wildly out of the tunnel mouth and spraying across the ship pen.

"Admiral, if the Lady's shooting it out in there, we don't know what shape she's in or how long she can hold. We gotta do this fast and dirty."

"I concur fully, Stone. The faster the better!"

"Right! Donaldson, put some smoke into your tunnel entry. Get me some satchel charges up here! We're going in!"

Amanda's lips ached from the tension of the fighting snarl fixed on them. The Bugis recognized that she, as a hostage, might be their only means of escape. Obversely, if they couldn't have her as a hostage, then they wished her dead out of vengeance.

Of the six magazines she'd had for the machine pistols, she'd already burned through five, holding them back. After that, there were only the sixty rounds for the more clumsy assault rifle. The body she had used for a shield had been chopped to hamburger by incoming fire and burned by her own muzzle blast. The scent of charred flesh made her want to vomit.

The shooting had fallen off out toward the ship pen, and she heard, or thought she heard, a noise in the room beyond the ringing in her ears. Convulsively she rolled on her side, whipping the smoking barrel of the Sterling around.

The Russian, Valdechesfsky, had eased to his feet and was lifting a long-shafted screwdriver out of a tool kit.

"Drop it and sit down, you son of a bitch!" she hissed. "Try that again and you're dead!"

Glaring, he obeyed.

From up the corridor someone emptied an Uzi from around a lateral corner. Slugs chopped and whined about her, and a jagged fragment from a ricochet laid the skin of her forearm open. Crying out, she rolled back and fired, spraying the passage side, driving the gunner back at the price of half a precious magazine.

She tried to swallow and wished for just one sip of cool water to clear her powder-parched throat.

Somewhere down the passageway she heard a commanding voice bellow an order in Indonesian, repeating it twice as the speaker apparently met resistance. Amanda thought she recognized it, then she was sure.

"Amanda? Are you all right?"

"Makara, is that you?"

"Just me. I've sent the guards out to reinforce the main tunnels. I don't think it will do much good. We don't have much time." His voice, reverberating up the passage, was amazingly conversational. "We've got to be going, Amanda."

"No one's going anywhere, Makara. You have to surrender. End this without the loss of any more of your people."

"That's simply not a valid option for me," the reply

came back. "Be careful, now, I'm stepping into the passage. I don't want to startle you."

He appeared in the pool of work light fifty feet away. His hands were empty and he wore no weapons at his belt. Disheveled, dust-grimed, yet still standing tall and undefeated. He smiled. "I must say, I am impressed; I'd never have imagined anyone ever finding this place or breaching its security. Your people are good, Amanda, you've trained them superbly, imprinting your flair for the daring and the unexpected onto them. You are everything they said you were."

Amanda rose onto her knees, leveling the Sterling. "Give it up, Makara."

"As I said, that's simply not possible. You would have to hand me over to the Indonesian authorities, and before I could arrange the real thing, I'd be shot trying to escape. I'm too dangerous, and Jakarta knows it now."

He started to saunter slowly forward. "It would be easier to simply end it here. Let me haunt these caverns with the ghosts of the Japanese."

"Don't be a fool, Makara."

He shook his head. "I'm not. It's either leave here or die. And I do not intend to die, because I have too many things left to do. I want you to help me do them, Amanda."

"Stop!"

He hesitated, as she stood with the Sterling still aimed at his chest. "I'll say it, Amanda: I want you as my *ratu samudra,* my queen of the sea, with the golden islands at your feet and a thousand ships at your command."

"That's insane," she whispered.

"No, it isn't!" He held out his arms. "We can do it, you know we can. The two of us, and, with my Bugis, we'd be unstoppable. Five years from now, we'll be sending our ambassadors to the United Nations. All you have to do is let free all the fire and boldness within you. No one can stop us!"

"*I* will, Makara; *I'll* stop you."

She wondered if he'd heard, so faint was the rasping whisper she managed.

He was moving forward again, into the gun barrel.

Somewhere out toward the main cavern, machine guns were firing again.

"Come with me, Amanda. We'll go to that island I had prepared for you. For a week we'll swim and lay in the sun and talk about everything in the world except war and nations and politics. Then you decide. One week."

He was almost within touching range, danger range. She drew up on the Sterling's trigger, feeling the sear ready to drop.

"Stop!" she pleaded.

He smiled gently at her foolishness. "Amanda, I know you can't do it to me, because I couldn't bring myself to do it to you."

The Mark 138 satchel charge is as elementary as a weapon can get. Forty pounds of high explosives in a canvas bag and primed with a nonelectric blasting cap on a length of timed fuse, it is usually delivered by a strong throwing arm.

Simple or not, it's still the weapon of choice for serious bunker-busting.

Thick chemical smoke billowed out of both tunnel entrances, the trapped garrison within firing wildly through it.

"Five seconds, sir," the demolition man said. "You ready?"

Quillain himself had elected to place the charge. "Just about. We'll go on a three count. Hey, Donaldson, you set?"

"Ready, sir," the reply snapped back over the tac radio link.

"Then let's get it done. On my mark, three ... two ... one ... *Mark!*"

Stone's demo man yanked and released the ring of an M-60 fuse igniter, the pop of the shotgun primer and the needle jet of smoke announcing a successful fuse light.

"Fire in the hole!" Quillain roared. Swinging the satchel charge by its strap, he hurled it into the maw of the tunnel. Then all hands fell back fast to evade the results.

In the right-hand tunnel, Stone's placement was perfect, the thrown charge skidding along the tunnel floor to bump against the foot of the barricade fifty feet in, its defenders not even noting its arrival between the smoke and the sound of their own gunfire.

The placement in the left-hand tunnel was almost as good, only the charge came to rest against a crate bearing a certain Cyrillic inscription.

The right-hand charge functioned perfectly as well. Its detonation blew an almost perfect cylinder of white smoke out of the tunnel mouth, the force of the blast being absorbed in the disintegration of the barricade and the fighting men immediately behind it.

In the left hand passage, however . . .

The entrance spewed flame and wreckage like a vomiting dragon, the roar of the blast dwarfing the solid thud of the first charge's detonation, the stone underfoot leaping, taking the assault teams off their feet.

And following the explosion, there came the terrifying grate and rumble of shifting stone.

The world inside the tunnels went black as the power failed. A shock wave hurled Amanda back against the end of the passage. The deeper blackness of unconsciousness almost overtook her. She beat it back, fighting to stay on her feet, screaming at her hands to keep their grip on the machine pistol.

She couldn't see! She couldn't hear! She couldn't breathe! The air was thick with dust and lung-burning fumes.

Then she felt the powerful arms closing around her, hemming her in against the wall. She wanted to scream a denial but she couldn't force the filthy gases out of her lungs. She fought him. She fought madly to maintain possession of the gun, the stumpy weapon caught vertically between their bodies. She felt herself start to lose.

"Makara!" It was a despairing wail inside her mind, but the faintest rusty whimper without. She locked both hands about the Sterling's handgrip, yanking back with the last of her failing strength. She felt the muzzle slip under his chin, and she closed her finger on the trigger.

To her disrupted hearing, the hammer of the automatic

weapon was the patter of a summer rain on a roof. Hot fluid and matter sprayed in her face.

She fell beside him on the stone floor. The Sterling was gone. It didn't matter. She forced herself up onto her hands and knees but could go no farther. She'd lost all orientation. Even if she had had the strength to move, she didn't know where to go. She begged the tunnel atmosphere for oxygen and was spurned.

Harconan whispered his farewell to her: "Amanda..."

"Amanda!" Not a whisper...a shout.

Another voice. Another name. Here?

Hands closed on her, lifting her. Her mind, sputtering along on her last deliberate actions, made her try to writhe free.

"Skipper, hey, Skipper!" Another muffled but recognizable voice exclaimed, "It's okay! It's us! We gotcha!"

Stone?

"Amanda, are you all right?"

Urgent, almost frantic. Elliot?

Someone was forcing a gas mask over her face. She drew in a lungful of filtered air, thin and far from fresh, but infinitely better than what she had been trying to breath. A battle lantern blazed on, and through the murk she saw Stone Quillain and Elliot...Admiral MacIntyre. Both had AI2 vision visors flipped up on their foreheads, but only the Marine wore a gas mask. MacIntyre had pressed his over her face as he supported her in the curve of his arm.

With a flare of strength, she brushed the mask aside. "The corporate representatives, in the room—get them out!"

"We'll handle it, ma'am."

"Harconan."

"We'll handle him too. Admiral, get her the hell out of here! This whole shebang's coming down in about two seconds!"

MacIntyre nodded, holding his breath against the smoke. Amanda found herself being lifted and carried, a pair of strong arms tight and protective about her. They felt good. It was all right now. She could stand down. Consciousness was no longer a thing to cling to.

It was amazing how a premoistened cleansing towelette could be a gift from the gods. Amanda ran its antiseptic coolness over her face, savoring the feel as it lifted the first layers of blood and grime. It wasn't a shower or, dream of dreams, a protracted, steaming soak in a bathtub, but it was a start.

Around her in the ship pen, postassault cleanup operations were in full swing. The Sea Fighters and the LCAC shuttled between the cavern and the task group holding offshore. The wounded, hostile and friendly alike, were being evacuated to the *Carlson*'s commodious and well-equipped sick bay. The dead, hostile and friendly alike, were being laid out in a row of body bags at the rear of the cave. The task force could take grim comfort that the former greatly outnumbered the latter.

Intelligence personnel were hard at the task of documentation and data collection; damage-control and amphibious-operations hands were at work aboard the *Harconan Flores,* keeping her afloat and puzzling how to coax the IN-DASAT and its trailer out of her stern gate for extraction.

Amanda tore open another towelette packet and started work on her arms. "Are you sure you don't want to be evacuated out to the ship?" Elliot MacIntyre inquired, kneeling down beside the blanket on which she sat.

"Oh, no. A corpsman patched me up." She held her arm out, displaying a field dressing. "I'm pretty much all right. I was just short of air for a while."

"The secondary explosions in the far-side tunnel touched off the diesel tanks in the generator room. The fires damn near burned all of the oxygen out of the whole place. It wasn't so good in there even with a gas mask."

"Tell me about it, sir." She wiped down one of her arms. "To tell you the truth, I was pretty sure I'd had it there for a minute. Then you and Stone were picking me up and putting that mask on me." She paused and looked at Eddie Mac quizzically. "Begging your pardon, sir, but just what were you doing in there?"

"God, I don't know." Wincing, he sat down on the stone flooring beside her, putting his back to a convenient oil drum. "Being a damn fool, I guess—at least, that's what every muscle is telling me just now." He let his eyes close, lest he be tempted to look into that bruised, soot-smeared, and infinitely lovely face beside him. "Someone...under my command was in trouble. I didn't like it and I wanted to see her out of it. And just for a change, I didn't want to sit back and delegate and do it by the book. Christ, I am a damned old fool."

"Neither one. Thank you."

MacIntyre felt a cool alcohol bite against his skin as Amanda gently swabbed away the accumulated perspiration from his brow and cheeks. It wasn't a kiss, but for the moment it would do.

The moment broke as a group of Marines in full MOPP anticontamination gear supplemented by damage-control airpacks emerged from the tunnel mouth bearing a tarpaulin-covered stretcher.

Amanda and MacIntyre both stood and crossed to where Stone Quillain was shedding his gear.

"Man, it's really a mess in there," the Marine stated, pulling the MOPP hood from over his head. "We got cooked ordnance scattered all over the place. I'd advise we keep the intels out till things cool down some more."

"There's no rush now," Amanda agreed. She glanced over at the covered body. "He's the last, then."

Stone nodded. "Yes, ma'am. Ain't no one else in there, livin' or dead. We checked all the spaces that weren't caved in altogether."

The deep breath she took wasn't quite steady. "Well, I'd better get it over with." She turned toward the stretcher.

"Uh, Skipper...ma'am," Quillain called after her in awkwardness. "He's pretty bad messed up. Head hits, a lot of 'em."

"I know. But we have to be sure of the identification. I knew him better than anyone else here."

The three crossed to the stretcher and Amanda knelt down beside it, taking another deliberate breath. It was insane to want to weep for an enemy, one you had slain yourself. But there was and always would be one afternoon spent on a perfect beach.

And then she noted the flaccid hand and the khaki shirt-sleeve that had slipped from beneath the tarp.

Harconan had been wearing a denim shirt.

She tore the tarp back, shock nullifying the nausea. Springing to her feet, she spun around, looking to where the captured corporate representatives were receiving first-aid treatment.

The *five* corporate representatives.

"This isn't Harconan! It's Valdechesfsky! The tech rep who was giving me trouble!"

"Are you sure, Amanda?" MacIntyre demanded.

"I'm positive! Stone, were there any other bodies at the end of that corridor?"

"Ma'am, there weren't any other bodies anywhere," the Marine replied emphatically.

Palau Piri Island   **0915 Hours, Zone Time:**
Off the Northwestern Tip of Bali   **August 25, 2008**

Mr. Lan Lo stared at the single line of decoded encryption on the computer terminal and the accompanying unquestionable authenticator. He was Chinese: His features maintained their disciplined stoicism and dignity even in the face of this statement of disaster.

He sat at the primary workstation of the communications center at House Harconan, the white-walled and windowless little room only he, Makara Harconan, and Lo's two meticulously selected administrative assistants had access to. This was, or had been, the heart of Harconan's "Special Consideration" operations.

It must end now.

Lo erased the message on the terminal screen with a tap of a key. Swiveling the silent office chair to face the room's other two workstations, he spoke quietly. "There has been a problem. Execute the Vishnu Program, Variant B, immediately, please."

His assistants, the young Cambridge-educated Hong

Kong expatriate and the female Japanese business executive who had grown tired of battling the sexism within her own nation, lacked Lo's depth of emotional control. An array of trace emotions played across their features: surprise, bewilderment, and a hint of fear. Yet, with the efficiency Lo required of them, they turned back to their terminals. Calling up their Vishnu crisis checklists, they began the liquidation of the Harconan empire.

Lo had other matters to attend to. Dialing up the security chief's desk, he again spoke briefly. "This is Lo. Evacuate the island. Vishnu protocols. This is not an exercise."

A second phone call went through to the seaplane hangar. "Launch immediately. Proceed to Halmahera Island base. Further orders will await you there."

Rising from his workstation, Lo left the communications center for the outer business office. As the steel security door closed behind him, Lo paused for a moment and addressed the lock keypad inset in the doorframe, inputting a code that sealed the door for entrance and exit both.

The four-person outer office staff was hastily making ready for their departure. The air became redolent of burnt plastic and ozone, and thin streams of smoke curled out of computer towers as "drive-killer" security modules incinerated their memory systems.

CDs and data-storage cards went into the degausser unit to the left of the door, hard copy into the shredder on the right. As each office person cleared his desk, a Nung Chinese security guard conducted a swift pat-down, then handed over a sealed manila envelope containing an altered passport and identity papers, transport tickets, and a sizable block of cash, severance pay and getaway money both. Barring the guards who would be rejoining their special force unit, each of the island staff down to the masseuse would be receiving such an envelope.

Except for two.

Lo coded and opened the office safe and transferred the island's liquid assets, some two and a quarter million dollars in various stable currencies and gem-grade diamonds, into a pair of aluminum-sided security briefcases. The imprint of his thumb on the electronic locking plates sealed the briefcases shut, and they were passed to the guard to be placed aboard the waiting helicopter.

Lo had no hesitation in turning this fortune over to the guard. He was Nung.

Lo removed an even greater treasure from the safe, a single CD storage disk in an aluminum security case, tucking it away in his inside coat pocket. This was the sole backup copy of the complete Harconan business files in existence. Even in death it would not leave Lo's body, not if he had the strength to reach the case's integral self-destruct mechanism.

A key from around Lo's neck unlocked a second, smaller door set into the back of the safe. Yet another code was entered here, with a T-minus-twenty time designation.

The only thing remaining in the safe was a tiny Seecamps .32-caliber automatic pistol. Lo checked its clip, then slipped it in the side pocket of his coat.

He moved back through the now desolate and abandoned office to the door of the communications center.

Within, he found that his assistants had done well in the limited time they'd had. Hundreds of prerecorded E-mail warning notifications had been flashed around the world to key Harconan personnel, instructing them to secure their positions against outside inquiry and to conduct other specific designated duties. Bank accounts had emptied, the funds starting through an automatic series of laundering transfers and cutouts that would render their tracking all but impossible. Brokerages had been instructed to execute an immediate mass sell-off of stocks, bonds, and futures at undercut prices, the liquidated assets also to vanish into numbered offshore accounts.

When the inevitable move was made to seize Mr. Harconan's monetary assets, there would be none left identifiable to seize.

Lo stood beside the door, waiting as the last few crisis programs were initiated and the last points on the checklists were cleared. When they were, Lo's assistants looked up, awaiting his further orders.

He had none to give. "Thank you," he said simply. "Your

performance has been admirable. I regret the current circumstances." Then he drew the automatic from his pocket and killed them both. The man fell facedown on his terminal keyboard, a single bullet through the side of his head; the woman had the time to rise from her chair and scream before Lo walked a three-round burst across her chest, the blood spraying on her white blouse.

Lo returned the pistol to his pocket. Indeed regrettable. This last phase of the evacuation plan was Lo's concept, undertaken on his personal authority. Mr. Harconan would likely disapprove of the act when he learned of it. He was a man of sentiment where his servitors and employees were involved. Unlike the other members of the island's staff, these two individuals had known far too much about Mr. Harconan's plans to permit them a departure. The risk of their falling into the hands of the authorities was too great. Such unpleasant details were Lo's responsibility within House Harconan.

Lo made a last circuit around the communications center, tripping the drive killers and verifying that all removable memory media had been eliminated. In all probability this was a redundancy, but Lo was meticulous.

He even closed and locked the security door behind him as he made his departure.

Outside, the moan of aircraft engines broke the island's peace. Out in the strait, the Canadair amphibian was lifting off. Turning to the east as it climbed, it sped away toward its distant rendezvous.

The Eurocopter sat on the helipad, its rotors turning, the pilot and the security chief waiting for Lo. In moments they, too, would begin their own evasive multistaged journey to the rallying point.

Lo paused to take a final look around the groomed estate grounds and the low, elegant buildings dozing in the palm shade. It was a sadness to be leaving this place of tranquillity and beauty. Lo had known that this day must come, as had Mr. Harconan. It had been hoped that it could have taken place under more controlled conditions so that an evacuation of the artwork and Harconan family memorabilia would have been possible. Fate had decreed otherwise.

"Regrettable," Lo murmured.

The drone of the helicopter's rotors had faded almost to silence when the first sequence of thermite incendiary charges exploded. Smoke climbed into the azure sky, thickening swiftly.

Royal Australian Navy Fleet Base   **1325 Hours, Zone Time:**
Darwin, Australia   **August 27, 2008**

The boxy LCAC backed carefully out of the *Carlson*'s well deck. Bearing a great plastic-wrapped lozenge shape in its open cargo bay, the hovercraft translated away from the pier with a lateral snort of its thrusters. The moan of its turbines reverberated off the shoreside warehouses and machine shops as it trundled across the oil-rainbowed waters of the fleet base to a shore access apron. There, a small army of INDASAT Industries trucks, cranes, and manpower eagerly awaited it. Battered, bullet-scarred, and sea-stained, INDASAT 06 was at last going home.

So were the other unwilling passengers of the Sea Fighter Task Force.

A bus convoy with a heavy military police escort rumbled through the shipyard en route to the Royal Australian Air Force Base at Darwin. Aboard it were the Melanesian and Bugis survivors of both the Crab's Claw garrison and the *Piskov* raid, including a silent, disillusioned man called Mangkurat. They rode in nylon handcuffs, staring out at the strange, white-faced world beyond the steel mesh bolted over the bus windows. Indonesian air force transports awaited them at the air base, tasked with flying them back to Java. There they would face prison and possibly, eventually, a trial for high-seas piracy and treason.

Another group of Indonesians was being bused to Darwin's civil airport and to a chartered Garuda Airlines 757. Although they wore no shackles, nor were there metal grids over their transport's windows, the former crew of the frigate *Sutanto* were subdued, especially her captain.

None were looking forward to the very official reception that would be awaiting them.

The third party was small enough to be transported in a Darwin city police van. Their destination was closer as well: the Darwin civil detention center. There, Professor Sonoo and the other surviving techno mercenaries would be held while assorted lawyers, diplomats, and police agencies wrangled over charges ranging from industrial espionage and criminal conspiracy to accessory to multiple murder.

As for the respective corporate entities Sonoo and the others had served, their responses when challenged had been essentially identical: "We're sorry, but we aren't acquainted with the gentlemen."

Amid this outbound traffic, another motorcade had been inbound to the naval base. A pair of Navy-gray Ford Crown Victoria sedans, one of which bore four white stars on its front bumper, and a black Lincoln town car with U.S. Embassy plates.

Cleared through Darwin base security with alacrity, it proceeded to the main base pier where the USS *Carlson* and *Cunningham* lay moored. Drawing up alongside the LPD, they found the amphib's crew manning the rail in dress whites, a Marine honor guard and a full suite of side boys at the gangway.

The *Carlson*'s bell chimed repeatedly, and her MC-1 sounded the sequence of calls.

"Secretary of State . . . arriving."

"Chief of Naval Operations . . . arriving."

"CNO staff . . . arriving."

Once aboard, the protocols rapidly broke down. There was simply nothing "in the book" for this particular situation.

"Jesus H. Christ, Eddie Mac! I know you and Captain Garrett both operate outside of the box sometimes, but this is so far beyond—"

Admiral Jason Harwell let his string of words sputter out. White-haired and baked gaunt from decades of sea service, he aimed an icy, blue-eyed glare across the wardroom table at MacIntyre "Damm it, man! The only reason

I haven't initiated a formal investigation into your actions in this affair is because I can't believe the reports I've been reading. That's why I'm here personally, to get a handle on this mess before every officer in this room, including me, gets hit with a general court! If we're lucky, maybe we can limit it to just you!"

The small group of prime players had gathered in the *Carlson's* wardroom, off the record and with no subordinates present, for a preliminary meeting. Harwell, MacIntyre, a somber and thoughtful Harrison Van Lynden, Christine Rendino, and Amanda Garrett.

"Jace, I've already stated I accept full responsibility for all aspects of our antipiracy operation down here," MacIntyre replied stolidly. "I've put it in writing and it's on your desk."

"I know it is, and I want to know why it was necessary! When did one of my best flag officers go foaming-at-the-mouth crazy on me, Eddie Mac?"

"It was known from the beginning that this job was going to be unconventional, Jace. That's why you gave it to NAVSPECFORCE and not the Seventh Fleet. I made both the State Department and the National Command Authority aware of that fact as we began to work the problem."

MacIntyre nodded toward Van Lynden at the head of the table. "You can check with the Secretary of State himself on that. They were informed that we would not get results going by the book, and it was acknowledged that they understood the situation."

"That's true, Admiral Harwell," Van Lynden said mildly. "I do remember the conversation."

Harwell turned to address Van Lynden. "I'm sure that's true, Mr. Secretary, but you surely couldn't have imagined that extending to the hijacking of a naval vessel of a sovereign nation on good terms with the United States. That's not unconventional, sir, that's insane!"

Van Lynden steepled his hands before him on the polished wood. "Actually, Admiral Harwell, it's irrelevant."

The CNO did a double take. "What's that, Mr. Secretary?"

"Jakarta doesn't give a tinker's damn about the loss of their ship or how it came about. In fact, today the Indonesian government will be issuing a press statement about the frigate *Sutanto* and how it was lost in an operational accident: She struck a reef and sank while assisting the Sea Fighter Task Force in the recovery of the INDASAT space vehicle."

Van Lynden nodded to the officers grouped at the table, a slight, ironic smile on his face. "In fact, the Indonesian government extends its thanks to the U.S. Navy for their successful rescue of the *Sutanto*'s entire crew. Just as we are extending our thanks to the Indonesian government for uncovering the plot by a group of New Guinea separatists to steal the INDASAT and hold it for ransom."

Van Lynden met the eyes of each seated individual. "And, by order of the National Command Authority and until further notice, that is all that has taken place on this cruise. There was no *Piskov* boarding. There was no attack on the pirate base at Adat Tanjung, and the incident at Benoa Port was a clash between two smuggling gangs, with no direct involvement with the United States Navy. There will be no court-martials. There will be no investigations. This affair, or at least this aspect of it, is now closed."

Van Lynden sat back in his chair, watching the exchange of startled looks flow around the table. "That's why all the Sea Fighter personnel were ordered held aboard ship until my arrival," the Secretary of State continued, rather enjoying the joke of it. "And why the press blackout has been invoked. We had to have the chance to tell you what you've been doing lately."

"Begging your pardon, Mr. Secretary," Admiral Harwell said, "but just what the hell is going on here?"

"Sorry I couldn't fill you in beforehand, Admiral, but I flew in from Jakarta just an hour ago. I've spent the last two days in emergency consultation with the Indonesian Foreign Ministry and with President Kediri. Needless to say, what you are about to hear does not leave this room under any circumstances."

The murmur traveled around the table: "Understood, Mr. Secretary."

"All right; here, as you would say in the fleet, is the dope.

The Indonesians are terrified and they have every right to be. We have a potential 'government killer' scenario developing for the fourth largest government on the planet.

"Makara Harconan was a major player in Indonesia, a major power, and a stabilizing influence in the archipelago economy. Should word get out that he's actually a world-class criminal and that his holdings have collapsed, it is going be a body blow to the rupiah on the world money markets and decisively damaging to overseas investment.

"Furthermore, the Indonesian people are sick and tired of corruption by their officials. Corruption charges almost brought down the Walid government back in 2001, and this scandal will make the Walid crisis pall in comparison.

"From the communications traffic seized aboard the Harconan transport, we know at least one Indonesian navy flag officer had sold out to Harconan. The gentleman in question has since disappeared, apparently warned that the show is over. Six other senior government and military officials have also dropped out of sight in much the same way. A seventh committed suicide during an arrest attempt, and two more have been found assassinated within the last forty-eight hours."

The Secretary of State continued to tick off his points. "When the world's maritime powers gain the proof of what they have long suspected—that Indonesian officials have been allowing their shipping to be victimized—they're going to start screaming reparation. A lot of Indonesians have suffered at the hands of the archipelago pirates as well. The word that the Bugis clans have been actively involved in a major criminal conspiracy against the other island groups is not going to be taken easily. Some damn fool is going to start shoving Bugis around, and the Bugis are going to shove back, so we can add a race war to the brew."

"What do the Indonesians intend to do about the situation?" MacIntyre inquired.

"Stonewall. Overtly say and do nothing about the situation."

"That won't wash, Mr. Secretary," Christine Rendino protested. "This thing is too big, with too many factors involved. Indonesia doesn't exactly maintain what you could call a free press, but no way are they going to be able to bury this, even if we help."

Van Lynden peered over his glasses. "They're very aware of that, Commander Rendino. President Kediri knows he's sitting on a keg of dynamite with a lit fuse. The best he can hope for is to try to limit the explosion when the truth does come out. He literally begged me to help him buy some time."

"For what?" MacIntyre asked. "What are their intentions?"

"To locate Makara Harconan and to ascertain his intentions."

"If, in fact, this Harconan even survived the attack on his base in New Guinea," Harwell said. "From what you say in your after-action reports, I can't see how he got out of that place alive."

"But he did, sir," Christine Rendino stated. "His body was never located anywhere within the tunnel complex or on Crab's Claw Cape. We know now that Harconan had a whole escape-and-evasion operation preprogrammed and ready to go. He knew that sooner or later he was going to have to bail out of his international businessman persona. This E-and-E program was initiated after we hit Crab's Claw. Harconan must have been the one to order its execution."

"What-all did this bail out program entail?" Harwell asked skeptically.

"When the Indonesian authorities moved in on Makara Limited, anything left was an empty shell. All bank accounts and stock portfolios had been emptied. The vaults of Makara Limited's banking division were even emptied of cash assets. Harconan's personal residence on Palau Piri Island and his corporate headquarters on Bali both self-destructed, burning to the ground and leaving nothing for the investigators. The disappearances and assassinations mentioned by the Secretary of State indicate that Harconan is also pulling his trusted lieutenants under cover with him while eliminating his not-so-trusted ones. He's gone to ground somewhere within the Indonesian archipelago with a war chest we estimate to be in excess of three hundred million dollars."

The intel leaned forward, meeting Harwell's gaze. "Sir, Harconan and his whole organization has just executed a crash dive like a submarine. He's still out there, running on course and continuing with his mission. We just can't see him anymore."

"The question then is, what is his mission?" Van Lynden asked.

"The destruction of the Indonesian government," Amanda Garrett said, speaking for the first time. Her voice was level and controlled, her eyes distant, as if she were looking into the future. "Mr. Secretary, you were quite right with your assessment of this situation as being a government-killer scenario. That's always been Harconan's intention. But he doesn't want to just bring down the Kediri government; he wants to destroy the state of Indonesia as a whole, blowing the entire national structure as we currently recognize it apart."

"I see," Van Lynden said quietly. "I presume you gained some insight into this while you were his prisoner."

"Enough to make some suppositions, sir, if you'd care to hear them."

Van Lynden nodded. "Very much so, Captain. How does he intend to do this and why? What's his justification?"

"A deep discontent with the way things presently are in Indonesia. This is an attempt by one man to restructure his world into what he visualizes as a better place."

"A common-enough phenomenon. What's his plan?"

Amanda turned to Christine Rendino. "Chris, how many major separatist and revolutionary movements are there in Indonesia, both in active hot-war mode or as a dangerous potential?"

"Jeez, ask me a simple one," the intel replied. "Currently you've got two fair-sized shooting wars going on either end of the archipelago, New Guinea with the Morning Star separatists and the Islamic extremist separatists in the Aceh district of Sumatra. You've got another big batch of cranky hard-core Islamics, the leftovers of the Walid movement, in eastern Java, making the Balinese Hindus nervous.

"You've got a UN peacekeeping force still trying to keep that septic mess on Timor under control. You've got the Dayak tribesmen going after the Javanese *transmigrasi* in Borneo. You still have a bunch of Moluccans who haven't really been happy since the Dutch left. You have all kinds of coup-grade factionalism within the Indonesian army and navy cadres.... I could go on all afternoon, Boss Ma'am."

"That's adequate to prove the point, Chris. Mr. Secretary, this is how Makara Harconan intends to bring about the downfall of Indonesia."

"You mean, by somehow uniting all of these factions against the Jakarta government?" Van Lynden adjusted his glasses, puzzled. "I've put some time in on the Indonesia question of late, and I can assure you that's all but impossible. Many of these groups are in diametric opposition to each other."

"Unity is not what Harconan wants, Mr. Secretary. He's promoting chaos, anarchy, and factionalism, a total breakdown of the Indonesian national order. He wants to return Indonesia to a scattering of independent island kingdoms, each with its own cultural group, religion, and leadership."

"And what does he get out of this?" Admiral Harwell demanded.

"All of these diverse island groups will have only one thing in common," Amanda replied. "They will, in fact, be islands dependent upon the sea for their communications and trade, and the *raja samudra* and his Bugis followers will control the sea. His will be the true power in the archipelago. Anyone who wants passage rights through his waters will have to pay him tribute. And that will include us."

"Christ," Harwell murmured, "do you have any idea how he intends to do it, Captain?"

"His plan is simplicity itself, sir," Amanda replied. "Indonesia is a hotbed of rebellion. Harconan intends to throw a bucket of gasoline on the coals.

"As Commander Rendino has pointed out, there are any number of rebellious factions within Indonesia. Many of them haven't been a major threat to Jakarta so far because of one simple factor: It takes money to run a good war.

"Back before the old USSR and Red China went under, they were always ready to supply some eager young group of insurgents. In recent years, however, things have gotten a little lean in the revolution business. Arms and support have been hard to come by. But then Harconan turns up. Chris, explain what we've been learning about Harconan's arms trade."

Rendino took over the flow. "Over the past few years, Makara Harconan has been a major arms purchaser. Nothing big at any one time, but all kinds of small-lot purchases using false front companies. Nothing fancy either: Third World and used First World armaments and ammunition, whatever could be picked up cheap without attracting a lot of attention. Your basic rifle, machine-gun, hand-grenade kind of thing."

"What's he done with it?"

"We think he's been dispersing it out in hundreds of small, heavily camouflaged arms dumps located in isolated areas throughout the archipelago," the intel replied. "We've uncovered a couple of them already. Crab's Claw was apparently being used as a major disbursement point for the operation."

"And his intention for these weapons?"

"That's the gasoline I mentioned, sir," Amanda resumed the briefing. "Wherever there is a Bugis colony, Harconan has agents provocateurs. It would be very easy for him to provoke incidents to increase national tension: religious violations, race riots, any number of things. His own corruption scandal could lay the groundwork for it. When popular disaffection reaches its peak, and the Jakarta government is strained to the breaking point, Harconan releases a location list of the arms caches to the leaders of the different rebel factions throughout the archipelago."

"Kaboom!" Christine Rendino vividly put the punctuation to the thought.

"God," Van Lynden whispered. "And Indonesians thought they were in trouble before. Half a million people were killed in the 1965 anti-Communist purges. This would trigger a bloodbath that would dwarf that. How can we stop this thing?"

Amanda's jaw tightened. "Find and kill Makara Harconan," she said tonelessly. "Fast. That's the only way. He's the linchpin to the entire operation. Pull it, and things might decouple, at least to a controllable level."

"I'll pass your recommendation on to the Indonesian government," Van Lynden replied. "How much time do you think they have?"

"Not long, Mr. Secretary. Not long at all. Harconan won't wait. We've broken the piracy cartel he was using to finance his operation, and we've knocked out his legitimate business holdings. The Indonesians have been tipped about his plan, and he knows he's not going to get any stronger. He has to go with what he has now ... and he will."

Following her part in the conference, Amanda Garrett spent the rest of the afternoon caught up in a whirlwind of work. Rations and fuel were pouring aboard both the LPD and the Duke, along with whatever replacement parts and munitions could be matched out of Australian military stocks.

The task force's more exotic and specialized needs were on the way as well, being flown in from the U.S. Fleet bases in Hawaii, Singapore, and Guam. So were the living spare parts for the Table of Organization, new Navy and Marine personnel to replace those lost in the recent campaign.

Within the task force hulls, crews labored, watch on watch, swearing at Eddie Mac and the Lady. Australia was known within the Fleet as the greatest shore leave in the world. There would be none, however, until all battle damage had been repaired, all onboard maintenance and servicing programs had been brought up to date, and the Sea Fighters were ready in all aspects for an immediate combat sortie.

Amanda had stoically issued those orders, along with a knife-edged command for all elements to expedite their readiness preparations. She knew that their next order for sailing would be for a war cruise.

The disintegration of Indonesia would simply be too big an event for the United States to ignore, nor could half a dozen other sea powers around the Pacific Rim. All would be involved in one way or for one reason or another.

Repeatedly, when she was topside, Amanda found her gaze drawn northwestward across the shimmering waters of Port Darwin and the Beagle Gulf beyond, her mind's eye extending her vision across the Timor Sea to the Indonesian archipelago. The *raja samudra* was there, safe among his seaborne subjects and his thousand-island strongholds, moving his plans toward fruition.

She would find him again. Somehow she would find him. She sensed that she and Makara Harconan were locked in some strange, fated ritual like the Balinese dance they had watched together. The music had not yet ended and they each had steps left to perform.

So be it. She was a dancer and she would dance this one "right to the ground," as her Celtic ancestors would phrase it. And if the gods were choreographing this, let it be that the last movement would leave her eye to eye with Harconan one more time.

Amanda crossed back and forth between the *Carlson* and *Cunningham* half a dozen times that afternoon, consulting with her officers and making it plain to all hands that there would be no stand down for her, either, until the Sea Fighters were ready to fight again. The stars glittered in an otherwise lightless sky when she crossed the pier tarmac to the LPD's gangway for the last time, a cooling wind from the sea drying her perspiration-damp shirt.

She found herself suddenly looking forward to a shower, a long hot pier-side one. And after that, midrats and a peanut butter and jelly sandwich before turning in.

No, cancel that. Captain's privileges: She'd have the steward run her up a steak sandwich... and french fries. She was suddenly ravenous.

"Hey, Boss Ma'am. Hold up!"

Clad in shoreside whites, the little intel ran breathlessly to Amanda. "Begging the Captain's pardon, but may this lowly one, pretty please, ask a flagrant personal favor of the TACBOSS?"

"Anything's possible, Chris," she said, smiling at the thought of how they were back to comparatively normal. "What is it?"

"Relating to your no-shore-leave order, would it be possible for a little bitty exception to be made? Inspector Tran's leaving with Secretary Van Lynden's party, and I'd like to see him off at the airport."

Glancing over Christine's shoulder, she noted the dark, hawkish policeman leaning back against the fender of a staff car parked under a pier light. He nodded in silent acknowledgment, awaiting the decision.

"The inspector is going with Van Lynden? What's up, Chris?"

"It seems that Singapore has given Tran an indefinite leave of absence so he can serve as a regional adviser to State on the Indonesian and piracy problems. I gather that Tran's been made a kind of 'company' temp, if you get my meaning."

"Hmm, interesting. I'm glad we're going to have him on board." Amanda's brows suddenly knit. "But wait a minute: the Secretary of State's party isn't leaving until tomorrow morning."

Christine endeavored to look innocent and failed miserably. "Well, I was kinda going to help him buy some toothpaste and a good book for the trip . . . and stuff."

Amanda rolled her eyes and smiled. "Permission granted . . . for stuff."

"Thanks, Boss Ma'am. Much appreciated."

"Are you two . . . ?"

The little blonde shrugged and grinned. "We're running together for a little while. We're the same breed of cat. You understand?"

"I do. Very well."

Christine studied Amanda's face. "How are you doing?" she asked, lowering her voice.

"I'm fine, Chris. I can't really explain what happened to me back there. I guess I met the same breed of cat, too. But he was on the other side of the fence."

"You told me once about your teenage fantasy of meeting a bold, swashbuckling buccaneer and running away to the South Seas with him. Sorry it kind of got all screwed up."

"It's all right." Amanda glanced away toward the northwest

again. "Maybe, once upon a time, when all of the world's ills could be solved with one bright, clean slash of a sword, it would have been fun to run away to play pirate but not now."

"Understood. 'Night, Boss Ma'am."

"Have fun, Chris. Say so long to the inspector for me."

Climbing the *Carlson*'s gangway, Amanda honored the flag aft, and after exchanging a few words with the OOD, she made the climb to her quarters. Maybe, when the task force was ready to sail again, she'd hit the beach for a day or two. She'd check into an ultra-plush hotel room and spend an entire afternoon soaking in a steaming bath. Then she'd just sleep for hours and hours in a huge, soft king-size bed. She was still mentally luxuriating when she nodded to the sentry outside of her cabin door and entered her office.

Elliot MacIntyre startled her for a moment as he stood up at her entry. "Sorry about intruding like this, Amanda," he said diffidently, "but I had to pick up some hard copy I left in your desk." He nodded toward the briefcase leaning against the desk leg.

MacIntyre was wearing a black Navy Windcheater over his khakis, and an officer's cap sat upside down and ready to hand on the desktop. "I'm flying back to Hawaii tonight, and before I hauled out, I also wanted to tell you it's been a damn interesting ride-along. It's quite obvious you've accomplished everything I've asked you to do with the task force. Well done, Captain. Exceedingly well done."

"I'll pass that along to my people, sir. Thank you."

There was a silence in the little room then, encompassing them both and extending for a long time. Yet, strangely, Amanda didn't find it uncomfortable and she sensed that Elliot didn't find it so, either. It was merely a mutual acknowledgment of many words that could not be said.

"There was one other thing as well," MacIntyre said finally, reaching for a book on the desk. "I never did get a chance to finish this. Would you mind if I borrowed it for the flight?"

Amanda looked and saw that it was her battered old copy of *Count Luckner, the Sea Devil*.

"Keep it," she said, smiling into MacIntyre's face. "I'm done with it."

Author's Note

Dedicated followers of the Amanda Garrett series will likely note the change in designation for the USS *Cunningham,* from DDG (Destroyer Guided-Missile) to CLA (Cruiser Littoral Attack)-79. There were a couple of reasons for this.

For one, the Duke in her original destroyer incarnation had become hopelessly obsolete. Back in the early nineties, when I set out to write *Choosers of the Slain,* I was endeavoring to project what the U.S. Navy's next major class of surface combatant would look and operate like. In a few ways I got fairly close. In many others I was totally off the mark, a frequent problem with prognosticators of the future.

By all indications, the actual DD-21–class stealth destroyers the U.S. Navy will soon be building will actually be far more advanced, sophisticated, and capable vessels than I ever dreamed of. I wish I could go back and start over.

This is a curse the technothriller author is living under currently. Possibly the greatest revolution in military affairs since the introduction of gunpowder is under way. Technologies and doctrine are changing almost on a daily basis, and the military author, like the military professional, is caught in a perpetual round of catch-up to stay on top of the game. Portions of this book had to be rewritten half a dozen times because seemingly solid assumptions were proven wrong.

The future looks to be an interesting and challenging place.

As for my second reason for changing the Duke's DDG-79 designation: There is now a real DDG-79 in commission with the United States Navy, the Block II Arleigh Burke–class destroyer USS *Oscar Austin*.

I would not wish to claim any credit for the honors this fine new ship and crew will no doubt rapidly accumulate. May she always have fair seas and good hunting.

Glossary

Boghammer. Generic name for a light, high-speed motor gunboat. Generally an open 30-to-40 foot fiberglass hull propelled by powerful outboard motors and armed with an assortment of machine guns and shoulder-fired rocket launchers. The name originates from the Swedish boat-building firm that manufactured a large number of the craft used by the Iranian Revolutionary Guard during the Persian Gulf tanker war of the late 1980s.

Cipher UAV (Unmanned Aerial Vehicle). Another of the rapidly growing family of Remotely Piloted Vehicles proposed for use by the United States Armed Forces. A small vertical-takeoff and -landing drone aircraft, the Cipher uses a set of ducted fans for lift and flight power. Literally a "flying saucer," the Cipher offers great potential as a very compact, very stealthy reconnaissance and special-missions platform.

Eagle Eye UAV (Unmanned Aerial Vehicle). Built by Boeing Textron, the Eagle Eye reconnaissance drone uses the same Tilt Rotor technology developed by Boeing for the V-22 Osprey Vertical Takeoff and Landing transport aircraft, permitting it either to maneuver as a conventional aircraft or hover like a helicopter. With a 300-mile radius of operation, the Eagle Eye's dual-mode flight capacity has rendered it of great interest to the Navy, permitting comparatively small surface warships to have an aerial search and surveillance capacity.

ELINT (Electronic Intelligence). The collection of battle-field intelligence (target location, systems type, nationality, force strength, etc.) via the analysis of emissions produced by radars and other electronic systems.

GPU (Global Positioning Unit). A mobile navigation system that utilizes radio impulses beamed down from an orbital network of satellites. Simple, compact, and extremely accurate, this technology is finding hundreds of uses in both the civil and military arena—so much so that serious consideration was once given to building a GPU into the stock of every rifle issued by the US Armed Forces.

Hellfire. U.S.-designed heavy antitank missile. A powerful and accurate surface- and air-launched weapon, utilizing either laser or radar guidance. The Hellfire is rapidly finding a second mission with the United States Navy as an anti–small-craft missile.

Hydra 70. A 2.75-inch folding-fin war rocket. Originally designed as an aircraft-launched air-to-surface weapon, it is also carried as a weapons option by the *Queen of the West*–class Sea Fighter. An unguided projectile, the Hydra is usually fired in salvos from a cluster of launching tubes. Effective and simple, it can be modified in the field to carry any one of a number of different warheads: antipersonnel, antiarmor, incendiary, and high explosive.

LPD (Landing Platform Dock). A large amphibious-warfare vessel with a floodable "well deck" in its stern, permitting it to load, launch, and recover conventional displacement landing craft, hovercraft, and amphibious armored vehicles.

LPDs also have a large helipad flight deck and servicing facilities, permitting them to act as seaborne bases for a large number of Marine and Navy helicopter types.

Current U.S. amphibious-warfare doctrine calls for its amphibious forces to stand well offshore, shuttling their

Marines, equipment, and supplies to the beach via landing craft and helicopter, improving the amphibious group's survivability against modern weapons.

LSM (Landings Ship Medium). A small, lightly-armed amphibious warfare vessel used to deliver motorized transport and armored fighting vehicles to an invasion beachhead. Carrying the bulk of its payload in a large vehicle deck within its hull, the LSM's hull is designed to permit the ship to run its bow up onto a beach without doing damage to itself. Once beached, a pair of watertight doors open in the bow and a ramp is extended, permitting the vehicles stowed on the vehicle deck to be driven ashore.

Still found in many Second and Third World navies, LSM- and the larger LST (Landings Ship Tank)-type vessels are now obsolete within current U.S. Navy amphibious warfare doctrine.

M-4 Modular Weapons System. The new firearm of choice for the U.S. military special-warfare units. Essentially a short-barreled carbine version of the 5.56mm M-16A2 assault rifle, it comes equipped with a telescoping shoulder stock and the Picatinny Arsenal's "Grab-Tight" rail-mounting system.

This latter permits the weapon to be modified to suit the mission requirements and personal preferences of the user. Various handgrips and carrying handles can be installed, and either a 12-gauge riot gun or an M-203 40mm grenade launcher can be mounted beneath the barrel in an over-and-under configuration to augment firepower. It can be equipped with a variety of targeting systems ranging from simple iron and telescopic sights to laser, nite-brite optics, and thermographic imaging.

Marine SOC (Special Operations Capable). A U.S. Marine combat element that has undergone a rigorous enhanced-training program, giving it the capacity to function both as a commando-style Special Forces unit and as a conventional infantry assault force.

Since the Korean conflict, the United States military has fielded a growing number of small elite units to deal with the problems of counterinsurgency, counterterrorism, and Special Warfare. The Army has its Green Berets, its Delta Force, and its Ranger regiment. The Navy has its SEAL (Sea-Air-Land) teams, and even the Air Force has its Air Commando squadrons. To date, the United States Marines have bucked this trend, flatly stating that, since the entire Marine Corps is an elite formation, such specialized units are redundant.

MOLLE (Modular Lightweight Load-carriage Equipment). New-gen combination backpack and load-bearing harness issued to U.S. ground forces.

NAVSPECFORCE (United States Naval Special Forces). Existent in the year 2006, NAVSPECFORCE is an evolved Fleet-level follow-on to the current-day Naval Special Warfare Command (SPECWARCOM).

A component of the U.S. Military's Joint Special Operations Command (SOCOM), NAVSPECFORCE places all USN special operations and "silver bullet" assets and their supporting elements under a single, independent headquarters, similar in concept to the United States Army's Special Forces Command.

Included in its table of organization are the Navy's SEAL teams, Patrol Craft and Special Boat and Submersible Squadrons, SOC (Special Operations Capable) aviation and submarine elements, and the Sea Fighter Task Force. Selected United States Marine Corps Force Recon and SOC Raider elements are also "chopped" to NAVSPECFORCE.

NAVSPECFORCE coordinates all U.S. Navy special operations worldwide from its headquarters complex at the Pearl Harbor Fleet Base, Hawaii.

SigInt (Signal Intelligence). The collection of battlefield intelligence via the interception and decryption of enemy radio and land-line communications.

SINCGARS (Single Channel Ground and Airborne Radio System). Developed by the U.S. Army and also coming into service with the other American Armed Forces, SINCGARS is an integrated family of man- and vehicle-carried radio systems for tactical battlefield communications. SINCGARS is an "anti-SigInt" technology, encrypting voice- and data-link transmissions via digital scrambling and using "frequency hopping" to render them difficult to jam or locate via the use of radio direction finding.

UH-1Y. The latest incarnation of one of the world's truly legendary aircraft, the Bell UH-1 Iroquois Assault helicopter. Introduced in the early 1960s, the "Huey" was the mainstay of American airmobile operations during the Vietnam conflict. Four decades later, it continues to operate in military and civil service around the world.

The UH-1Y "Super Huey" will be a rebuilt variant of the twin-turbined UH-1N currently in Marine service, incorporating improved avionics, uprated engines, and a common rotor and drive system with the Marine AH-1W "Whiskey Cobra" gunship, greatly increasing its range and lift capacity.

So modified, the Huey is projected to soldier on for another twenty years, and likely beyond.

The author of *Target Lock* may be reached at DDG79@AOL.COM. All criticism and commentary are gratefully accepted.